HONOR OR DEATH . . .

"You were gone for four hours, Dr. Weber," Strosnider said carefully. "You could reach Bearpaw, but you don't go there. You could've short-cut to Cotton's place, only you don't go there either. Or you could've made them hard-scrabble outfits under the Bench. Which was it?"

"Let's call it the people under the Bench."

Willis smiled slowly. "You rode south, Doc. That's north."

"So I lied," he said to them both.

"I never liked you," said Strosnider quietly. "None of us do. You walk a little too proud for a man to buy you a drink, and you love them farmers a little too much. It wasn't McFie that lost that money. It was insured with me. You show us where he is. We'll find the money."

"Maybe you better find him, too, then," Doc murmured.

Strosnider hit him in the face. He staggered back against Willis, and then was sent to his knees by a blow behind the ear from Willis. He caught Strosnider's kick by rolling his shoulder, and then a rap across his skull sent him into a warm, wet, aching sleep . . .

MORE OF THE HOTTEST WESTERNS!

LUKE SHORT'S

* BEST OF *
THE WEST

Introduction by H. N. Swanson

ZEBRA BOOKS
KENSINGTON PUBLISHING CORP.

ZEBRA BOOKS

are published by

Kensington Publishing Corp.
475 Park Avenue South
New York, N.Y. 10016

Printed in the United States of America

These stories originally appeared in Argosy, The Blue-book Magazine, Colliers, The Saturday Evening Post, Street and Smith's Cowboy Stories and Street and Smith's Western Story Magazine.

CONTENTS

INTRODUCTION

Meeting Luke Short (the writing name for Frederick Dilley Glidden) you would have thought him to be a very mild-mannered man, possibly an accountant or schoolteacher, certainly not a writer who thrilled readers with his Western adventures which occasionally reached a crescendo of violence. Fred did not wear cowboy boots, a half-gallon Stetson nor fringed leather jackets. He had warm brown eyes and a smile that stayed on. Fred liked people and people liked Fred a lot because he was a good listener. The characters he saw and the dialogue he heard went into his memory bank for good use in the future.

He was born and during his adolescence lived in a small Illinois town named Kewanee. He used to kid about saying that since the town was an Indian name, it might have influenced his thinking about cowboys and Indians. My own mother lived in Galva, an adjoining town. She and Fred's mother visited each other occasionally. She said the Gliddens were "a fine family."

Fred was an outstanding scholar in high school, played basketball and was captain of the football team. He attended the University of Illinois at Urbana and later, in 1930, was graduated from the School of Journalism of the University of Missouri.

Young and bewildered by the Great Depression into which he was suddenly dumped, Fred scrambled hard for any kind of employment. He succeeded in getting five brief jobs as a reporter on five different Midwestern newspapers. When his luck ran out he went to Canada, where he became a fur trapper in Northern Alberta. This was survival time; he lived in a log cabin the first winter when the temperatures were often thirty degrees below zero. He wrote to his mother back home admitting that he was lonesome and occasionally on the ragged edge, but he would not give up. In one letter he said, "I feel very much as if I'm addressing a stone wall, since it was more than a month ago that I got any news from you. Of course I went for over a month during the summer between letters but snow somehow seems to add to isolation. I've watched every weekend pass on the calendar and have mentally pictured you at football games. . .As for myself I have the same rounds: one day in three shut up in the cabin cooking and the rest of the time tramping the country."

Summer was not much better, as he described in another letter: "all travel back into the bush is done by trails, very much on the order, I suppose, of travel in the tropics. The insects, of course, are beyond description. Once off the trail in this man's country and you're done for. On the trail the 'bulldogs,' or horseflies, flying ants, nits and mosquitoes follow you in a cloud, but only the mosquitoes and nits are bothersome. With the exception of the low drone of the bulldogs, the irritable whine of the mosquitoes and the hushed clump of your own feet there is not a sound to be heard; yet all the time there is that pervading sense of something hidden and watching that puts me, who am not used to it, on a fine edge all the time."

Although those first months were very difficult, he

became an experienced fur trapper and fell in love with the environment, as indicated by this excerpt from another of his letters to his mother: "all the glamor of dog teams, hunting, snow and snow shoes, living with a rifle, etc., turns out to be hard punishing work. But there is a joy and complete satisfaction in doing hard manual labor until you are so tired at night that you could drop; when every smoke tastes so good you'd like to eat it; when every meal no matter how bad it is tastes better than the previous one; and when you get that sense of completely fitting into the scheme of things. All that supplants the glamor and romance, but it's better. If you spent a year living that way, you'd never, never be content to go back to an apartment in a city and live through the thousand daily irritations of living by clock, talking when you'd rather be silent, shaving when you'd like to look like a bum, taking exercise as a medicine (not as a pleasure), haggling over money and all the rest of it. If you had the courage of your convictions after such a year, you'd note mentally, 'To hell with it!' and come back here for good."

Nineteen thirty-three found Fred looking for ranch work in Wyoming. He had traveled the West, moving from state to state, searching out ghost towns, listening to toothless old Indians chiefs tell about their past exploits, crossing rivers and deserts. He wrote back home to his mother saying that what he saw overwhelmed him. The whole golden horizon seemed to fill with brave frontier men and women with their stories to be written about. He was worried that he might not fully capture the look of the Old West, its sounds, colors and excitement. What hit him the hardest was the realization that this was a place and a time in America that would never come again. He wanted to get down on paper as quickly as he could the magic of those starlit nights, glowing campfires, the soft sounds of the horses moving in the dark.

In 1934 at Greeley, Colorado, while on his way to a ranch where he thought he might find work, he met at a sorority dance Florence Elder of Grand Junction. Romance blossomed and soon after they were married and went to live in Santa Fe, New Mexico, in a house they rented for ten dollars a month.

He decided to try his hand at writing. He studied the pulp magazines filled with action stories and decided to write about his experiences as a fur trapper. His stories went to almost every magazine he could find an address for and they all promptly came back. He realized he needed a literary agent and was fortunate enough to get Marguerite E. Harper in New York City. She represented a large number of authors who specialized in Western tales. Publishers respected her judgment on stories, found it to be sound and often followed her recommendations on newcomers. Fred also decided around this time to take a pen name which might sound more probable than his own, and either he or Marguerite Harper came up with Luke Short. Luke Short, according to Robert Gale, a professor at the University of Indiana who is a keen student of Glidden's work, was in fact a real person. He lived from 1854-1893 and, according to Gale, was "a dapper little gambler, saloon keeper and gunfighter in the environs of Dodge City, Kansas, well known for his fearless exploits and also such hairtrigger cronies as Bat Masterson, Doc Holliday and Wyatt Earp, among others."

Discouraged by the rejection slips his stories continued to receive, Fred told his agent that he was on the point of abandoning his idea of becoming a writer, and she told him there was nothing wrong with him except his choice of locale—the frozen North was not too attractive to readers. She told him to forget about the frozen North and to write about the Old West, realizing he had researched it and was entranced by it. In 1935 she sold his first story for one hundred thirty dollars to Street and Smith, a large producer of several pulp magazines. Fred smelled blood and tore into his new job at top speed. In his first year of writing for the pulps he averaged a very considerable—for those days—eight hundred dollars a month.

The Street and Smith magazines, which became his best customer, featured violence and fast-moving stories in which characterization was usually forgotten. Soon he decided to write a full length novel the way *he* wanted to write it. Miss Harper came to me knowing that our company, H.N. Swanson, Inc., was a literary agency in Los Angeles experienced in selling stories to film studios, and from that time on we represented him, dividing our commission with her. The first sale we made for him was a short story, "Hurry, Charlie, Hurry, There are Indians in the Parlor." RKO Studios bought this story and made it as a forgettable short comedy film starring Leon Errol.

Fred persisted in his determination that he would do novels as far away from pulp formula writing as he could get. The result was *Blood on the Moon*, which was serialized in the Saturday Evening Post. It was a top bestseller and RKO produced the film starring Robert Mitchum.

In the years that followed, every major studio and several leading independent producers bought at least one Luke Short story, and the resulting films had great acceptance with the public. Metro bought "Cabin in Manhattan," "Ambush," "Vengeance Valley" and "Coroner Creek." Republic bought "Silver Rock" and "Ride the Man Down." "Stage Station" went to Warner. RKO brought "Mission in Mufti," "Finish the Fable" and "Blood on the Moon." Nat Holt made "High Vermillion." Harry Sherman took "Ramrod," and Fred worked in Hollywood on the script of it after the studio developed one screenplay that was unsuccessful. Fox bought "Sunset Graze."

The top male actors were anxious to star in Fred Glidden stories. Very often they would call up a studio head and say they had just read his latest book and wanted the studio to buy it. Some of the top casting on pictures released were: Burt Lancaster starring in "Vengeance Valley," Joel McCrea in "Ramrod," Randolph Scott in "Coroner Creek," Dick Powell in "Station West," George Montgomery in "Ride the Man Down" and Robert Taylor in "The Hangman."

In the music business "Stardust" is an example of what is called a "standard," a piece of music which is played over and over through the years. A Luke Short story or novel is a standard in the publishing world. He wrote fifty-one novels, all of them highly profitable, with sales continuing through the years at a steady pace. By 1972 over thirty-five million copies of his hard- and softcover books had been sold; obviously many more have sold since that time. Not all his books are historical Westerns; some are modern, others have a political or mining background.

He had and has fans all over the world, including Presidents Dwight D. Eisenhower and Harry S. Truman. The Wild West Club in London declared him to be its favorite author. He has been translated into twenty languages and published in hard- and softcover all over the world.

Fred also became the highest paid magazine writer of Western stories. Saturday Evening Post and Colliers competed with each other to serialize him. An unusual situation developed when Colliers stopped publication, having run two parts of a three-part serial entitled "Doom Cliff." The Saturday Evening Post, which had been a spirited rival for this author's work, bought the third installment from Colliers and ran it with a long synopsis of the first two installments. When Fred asked the Post editors why they did such an unusual thing, they said it was a move to get Colliers readers, and besides, they indicated they would buy almost anything he submitted to them.

Fred's work habits were steady. He dictated to a secretary because he had very serious eye trouble most of his life. One year he had three eye operations for cataracts and detached retinas. He actually did his writing in three different homes—in Colorado Springs, in Wickenberg, Arizona, and in Aspen, Colorado. He probably did most of his writing in Aspen, where he had a large corner office on the third floor of the Elks Building. While working he liked to look out of the big windows and noted "an increasing number of pregnant girls." He was a civic-minded person, was on the city council and had much influence in the affairs of Aspen. On one occasion the city council unanimously opposed the last wishes of a friend of Fred who, when he died, wanted his ashes scattered over the city. Fred took the problem into his own hands, hired a private plane and had the matter taken care of properly. He was disenchanted with Aspen during the winter season and with its growth of condominiums he said it was now Aspen, Hong Kong. In one letter he wrote me: "I read that more people are moving out of California than are coming in. I know where they are moving to—Aspen and the rest of Colorado. The traffic in this town of two thousand five hundred was so heavy this summer that we are having to install four traffic lights on our main street. I'm glad I won't be here for the winter pile-up!"

His writing productivity was steady even though he and his wife spent six months in the Virgin Isles and also on a working vacation in Scandinavia. In an average month he was able to produce fifty thousand words

15

in spite of the severe eye trouble. And in spite of the "winter pile-up" he liked Aspen; it had everything valuable to him—hunting, fishing, skiing and skating. And it was close to Denver, where the public library had excellent files on the early West.

Fred was a close watcher of television and thought some of the series of Westerns on the tube were so bad, so filled with clichés that he felt they were self-destructive. He thought the public could get along without those greedy cattle barons, the heavily mustachioed villains and dancehall girls with sleepy eyes and hearts of gold. Nevertheless he occasionally wrote for television, and "Zane Grey Theater" produced three of his teleplays. He was partnered briefly in a television production company with Lucille Ball and Desi Arnaz, but after a few months this project was abandoned.

Fred felt writing for television or feature films a waste of time and preferred his own work. He did want, though, to do a continuing story on television about a small pioneer town which he called Primrose. In this he wanted to tell stories of ordinary people there at a time when the railroad had gone through and Indian raids were forgotten. He saw it in the pattern and tradition of *Our Town*, by Thornton Wilder, and wanted to include a church, a school, livery stable, half a dozen saloons and a tiny jail where the rowdies had to calm down. He knew there was love and warmth as well as excitement here, and thought that viewers would accept it over the kind of shows they were getting, shows about outlaws thundering down the dusty main street with guns blazing. Fred never went forward with this because the networks discouraged him on this project, claiming that Westerns were not prime merchandise at the moment.

This prodigious, creative chronicler of Western Americana died in 1975 of throat cancer, leaving a daughter Kate and a son Dan. Florence, his good wife of many years, died in 1981, and he had previously lost a son, John, who was drowned in an accident at Princeton in 1960.

This man and his work are a genuine, lasting part of Americana. He really was tall in the saddle. I was very proud to represent him as a literary client, and so happy to have known him as a true friend.

—H.N. Swanson
Los Angeles, California

PULL YOUR FREIGHT!

It was close to the supper hour when Johnny Bishop wheeled his six teams and heavily loaded lumber wagon through the wagonyard gate of the Primrose Freighting Company. At the moment the yard had a leisurely end-of-the-day tempo, with a half dozen returned wagons and teams filling its dusty expanse. Johnny pulled in his teams, tossed the reins down to the stocktender and then climbed down from the high stack of pale, raw lumber.

Drawing off his gloves, he started for the office, calling over his shoulder to the hunchbacked stocktender, "That goes to Jessup's tomorrow, Humpy."

Johnny Bishop was a tall young man, perhaps in his middle twenties. Fine dust powdered his long jaw and clean shaven face, blurring its sharp planes. His pale gray eyes were red-rimmed from the dust. He halted before the door of the office for a moment, beating his dusty clothes with his gloves, then went inside.

He tramped up to the railing that separated the reception area from a pair of paper-littered desks. At the closest desk Herb Loftus, older than Johnny, sober-faced and harried, his Stetson shoved back from his forehead, was scowling down at a bill of lading before him.

Johnny took his battered Stetson from his head, reached inside the crown, extracted a bill of lading and laid it before Herb.

Herb looked up and his scowl disappeared. "Howdy, Johnny! Didn't think you'd make it before dark."

"It's downhill all the way, Herb," he said grinning, "too downhill in some places."

Herb smiled and picked up the bill of lading but did not look at it. Johnny started to turn away, waving a parting salute, when Herb said, "Got a minute, Johnny?"

Johnny halted, turned, and then looked carefully at Herb. "Sure." He came back to the desk.

"How long you been working for us, Johnny?" Herb asked idly. "About a year?"

"Closer to a year and a half," Johnny said. "Any kicks?"

Herb shook his head and smiled slightly, then picked up a pencil, held it between his two thumbs, leaned back in his swivel chair, and regarded Johnny. "Nary a kick," he said slowly. He hesitated. "I had a caller this morning, Johnny—a fellow by the name of Bill Minifee. You know him?"

Johnny shook his head in negation. "Should I?"

Herb shrugged. "He's a special agent for Wells Fargo. Seems he's tracking down the tag end of a big holdup job that happened a couple of years ago down in Wyoming." Herb studied his pencil thoughtfully. "He didn't say who sent him to Primrose, and he didn't say why he came to me, except he was interested in our teamsters."

"Any particular teamster?" Johnny asked slowly.

Herb pitched the pencil on the desk. "Well, I wouldn't blame him for being curious about Big

20

Murph or Harry Tatum. If they thought of it, they'd likely try to hold up an Army payroll that was guarded by two companies of infantry."

Johnny smiled faintly and Herb continued, "He was looking for somebody younger." Now he looked at Johnny. "He described him as a little over six feet tall, maybe twenty-five, blond hair, gray eyes, handy with stock, and with a tattoo on his left upper arm. His name," Herb added, "was Jim Byers."

There was a long moment of silence.

"I don't recall any Jim Byers who worked here, do you?" Johnny asked. He and Herb were regarding each other levelly.

"Yes," Herb said. "I remember him very well. He quit us about a year ago. Don't you remember?"

Puzzled, Johnny shook his head.

"Think, man, think," Herb said softly. "He quit us about a year ago. Jim Byers."

The light dawned on Johnny. "You told him that?"

Herb nodded. "He didn't believe me either, but that's the story. Jim Byers quit us a year ago. You got it?"

Johnny smiled wryly. "I've got it, Herb."

Johnny turned toward the yard door, tramped across the room, and when his hand was on the knob he halted, then slowly turned and regarded Herb. "Was this Byers married, did he say?"

"Single," Herb said.

Johnny nodded. "Good night, Herb."

"See you in the morning, Johnny." Herb looked up. "Or will I?"

"You will," Johnny said quietly.

He stepped out into the busy wagon yard, his lean face grave and reflective. Herb knew, of course. This was Herb's way of warning a friend, of protecting him and of rewarding him for a year's faithful work.

For brief, bitter seconds Johnny weighed the situation. This Minifee hadn't believed Herb. That meant trouble. A year ago he would have cut through the alley to Jessup's Livery, rented a horse and under cover of darkness left the country. At one time, for months on end, that had worked, but it was a way that was closed to him now.

Out in the dusty yard the stocktenders were unhooking the teams and manhandling the big freight wagons under the openfaced shed. Across the way Al Cruse, another teamster and Johnny's best friend, was examining the front shoe of one of his mules.

Johnny cut across the yard to his lumber-loaded wagon, and drew out his battered round lunch bucket from the tool chest ironed to its side. At the same time, he heard the voice of Big Murph raised in sudden anger.

Looking over his shoulder, he saw the big teamster in heated argument with the crippled stocktender they all called Humpy. Humpy was a middle-aged, cheerful man, whose deformed and twisted back prevented him from doing a working man's heavy labor. His way with animals, however, had won and kept him a job here, where he was a favorite among the rough teamsters.

Johnny could hear nothing of the argument, but he saw Big Murph suddenly belt Humpy across the face with the back of his hand. Humpy staggered back and fell in the slime at the base of the water trough.

Instantly, Johnny was in motion but Al Cruse was even quicker. So was Ed Ganton. The three of them, from different parts of the yard, converged on Big Murph. When Big Murph wheeled to face Ganton, Cruse took a flying leap and landed astride Murph's back. Brushing off Murph's hat, Cruse sank a hand in his coarse hair and steadying himself with this grip proceeded to drive his fist into Big Murph's face.

Big Murph was a mountain of a man, bull-strong and pig-dirty. He paid no attention to Al Cruse on his back, but concentrated on trying to grab Ganton, who was slashing at his arms with a lunch bucket.

Johnny, his left shoulder forward, dove solidly at Big Murph's knees. The impact drove the breath from Johnny, but he felt Murph's thick legs fold. Murph crashed to the ground with all three of them, Johnny, Ganton, and Al Cruse, piled atop him and slugging savagely at his broad bearded face.

When Big Murph's body relaxed, Johnny put a hand on Al's shoulder and said, "That's enough, Al."

Al Cruse rose. He was a lean, slight man in his thirties, with a tough, likable face. He was dressed in the dusty, ragged calico shirt and corduroy pants that were almost the teamsters' uniform. He looked briefly at Johnny, his eyes still hot, then he said, "You see him hit Humpy?"

Johnny nodded.

"He must be looking for something real safe," Al said bitterly.

Now Al glanced from Big Murph to the watering trough, and anger drained from his face. "Come on, Johnny," he said softly. "Let's wake him up real good." He gestured with his thumb toward the trough.

The three of them lifted Big Murph by the arms and legs, stumbled with him over to the watering trough, and pitched him in.

As Big Murph came up sputtering, Al Cruse shoved his head under the water again, then backed off. "You lard-legged jackass," Al said. "I thought we told you to leave Humpy alone."

"This's the third day he sawed off that crippled roan jack on my wagon!"

"If you can't skin mules, why don't you quit?" Johnny said derisively.

With a growl Big Murph lunged for the side of the tank. Johnny, who had been watching for this, took a step backward, reached out and picked up a pitchfork. Bringing it up, he moved slowly toward Big Murph until the tines gently nudged Big Murph's belly. One leg over the side of the tank, Big Murph halted. He looked down at the pitchfork, then at Johnny.

"Better change your mind, Murph," Johnny said softly. "None of us are hunchbacks."

Al Cruse reached out. "Give me that, Johnny. I'll let some of the air out of this big wind."

Big Murph backed up and then straightened, eyeing the three of them. He was beaten, and his expression showed it.

"Next time you beat up on a cripple," Al said softly, "you'll get throwed back in there with an anvil tied around your neck. Now get out."

Dripping rivers of water, Big Murph stepped over the side of the tank, swearing bitterly. Then he picked up his hat and tramped out the alley entrance of the yard.

Cruse, watching him, observed, "That's the first bath he's had since the last rain." He eyed Johnny soberly. "He'll remember this, Johnny. He's an Injun. Better carry a rock in your pocket."

He'll forget it," Johnny said carelessly.

Laughing, the three of them broke up. Johnny picked up his lunch bucket where he had dropped it and then headed for the street gate, the old depression again upon him.

As he passed through the gate, he glanced idly at a tall, middleaged man leaning against the gatepost, a toothpick in his mouth. The man wore cattlemen's boots, and a worn shell belt and holster sagged below his open buttonless vest.

Johnny was already in the street when he heard him

24

call, "Jimmy?"

For the briefest instant alarm came to Johnny Bishop, but he did not break step and did not falter.

"You, out there! Bishop!" the voice called sharply.

Now Johnny halted and slowly turned to regard the man. This was Minifee, of course, and Johnny felt a cold hatred for the man that he was careful to keep out of his eyes.

Minifee walked slowly out into the road and hauled up before Johnny, regarding him carefully. "Your name Bishop?" he demanded.

"That's right. Johnny Bishop," Johnny said with a forced mildness.

"You work for this outfit?" Minifee asked, nodding toward the freight yard.

Johnny nodded.

"Know a young fellow named Jimmy Byers—about your height, twenty-five maybe, looks something like you?"

"A teamster?" Johnny asked. At Minifee's nod, Johnny, remembering Herb's admonition, lied glibly. "Sure. He worked here awhile. Quit about a year ago."

"Sure about that?"

"Why shouldn't I be?"

"Funny that you and Herb Loftus are the only two who remember Jimmy Byers."

Johnny shrugged. "Why should anybody remember him especially? I just happened to. Maybe Herb did too."

Minifee smiled faintly. "Where'd you come from?" he asked.

Johnny's eyes grew cold. "Would that be any of your business?"

Minifee only smiled. "Just curiosity," he murmured.

25

"Get curious somewhere else," Johnny said. He turned then and headed for the far sidewalk. He could almost feel Minifee's glance boring into his back.

Johnny turned left at the corner where the plankwalk ended into a street of small stores, plain frame buildings, and an occasional modest frame house, unpainted and weathering. He turned in alongside a log cabin, traversed the narrow passageway between it and the next building, and came out into a small yard back against the alley shacks. The front portion of the cabin was occupied by old man Pritchard, who owned the harness shop. The two rear rooms were home for Johnny and Lillie Bishop.

Hand on the door latch, Johnny halted, composing his face. What was he going to tell Lillie? *The truth, of course,* he thought grimly. Then he opened the door.

The room he stepped into was a plain one, the combination kitchen and living room of a working man. There were gay curtains at the two small windows; and the small iron range, cracked but shining, threw a pleasant warmth into the room. A curtain divided this room from the one next, their sleeping quarters.

As Johnny closed the door, the curtain parted and Lillie came into the room. She was small, not quite pretty, with dark thick hair pinned atop her head. There was a measuring tape around her shoulders and her dress front held a cluster of pins. Crossing the room, she threw her arms around Johnny and kissed him.

"You're early, Johnny. I haven't even started supper yet."

"I got an early start from the mill," Johnny said cheerfully. He gave her an affectionate hug, then set his lunch bucket on the table and stripped off his shirt. Crossing the room to the washstand, he poured out a basin of water and began to soap his arms and upper body.

Lillie, meanwhile, was chatting about the dress she was making as she stirred the fire and put a kettle of water on the stove.

Johnny, drying himself, listened idly, looking into the mirror. Suddenly, his hands halted and he stared at his own somber face.

Lillie, watching him, ceased her chatter. "What's the matter, Johnny?" she asked, and started across the room to him.

Slowly Johnny balled up the towel in his fist, a kind of suppressed anger in his movements, and dropped it gently on the washstand. Then he turned to her.

"I told you once, Lillie, I'd never hide anything from you." He paused. "Well, they're after me again."

Lillie halted momentarily and then came into his arms. He held her awhile in silence and then, pressing her to him and speaking over her head, he said, "Herb warned me tonight. A Wells Fargo special agent, name of Minifee, stopped by the yard today. He had my description, even down to my tattoo." He paused. "I saw him. He tried to trip me up by calling me Jimmy."

Lillie looked up at him. "Did you give yourself away?"

"Not any," Johnny said. "He knows though."

"But he can't prove it!" Lillie said passionately. She stroked his upper arm, running her fingers over a rough triangular scar. "You've got no tattoo, Johnny. Anybody can have a scar there."

"Sure, sure," Johnny said softly, almost absently.

Lillie looked up at him, tears beginning to come into her eyes. "Oh, why can't they let us alone? Do you keep paying all your life for just one mistake?"

"All my life," Johnny echoed, bitterly. "All yours too."

Now Lillie seized him by both arms and shook him. "Johnny, we've got to clear you of this! Couldn't you go with this man? Couldn't you tell the judge all you did was bring four fresh horses to a certain spot and take four tired horses back? What's the crime in that?"

"I helped in a big express robbery," Johnny said tonelessly. "That's all the law wants to know."

"But you didn't even know what the horses would be used for!" Lillie protested.

Johnny looked down at her. "I knew," he said. "Nobody would have paid me what they did if they hadn't been breaking the law."

"But you didn't have a gun," Lillie protested. "You can tell them you were just out of the Army—sick, broke, and a stranger. You did it to live."

"Other people live and don't break the law," Johnny said grimly. "That's what the judge will say. That's what he'll tell me when he sentences me."

Lillie put her cheek against Johnny's shoulder, holding him tight. "What are we going to do, Johnny?" she asked softly.

"Bluff it out," Johnny said grimly. "They can't prove anything. I don't have to answer his questions."

"If he goes to the sheriff you will." Lillie looked up at him. "Won't you?"

Johnny sighed. "I reckon so."

Bill Minifee watched Johnny Bishop until he turned the corner, then glanced back into the wagon yard. The big man whom Johnny Bishop and the other two had ducked in the trough was gone, but Minifee guessed he would not be hard to find. During the few hours he had been in Primrose, Minifee had quietly reconnoitered the town. There were two saloons, one at the Primrose House and one next to the livery stable. The teamster was unlikely to patronize the quiet and orderly hotel bar. Chances were, then, that now or later he would be at the other saloon.

28

Minifee turned and headed up the plankwalk toward Main Street, his pace unhurried. He knew, in spite of Loftus's attempt to cover up, that Johnny Bishop was Jim Byers. Trouble was he lacked final proof of the identifying tattoo. But he thought he knew now how to get it.

Minifee mounted the steps of the Bella Union and shouldered through the head-high batwing doors. The babble of voices filled the big high-ceilinged saloon, and the bar on the left was packed with customers. The gambling tables on the right were also filled down to the very last chair and onlookers circulated among the tables idly watching the games.

Minifee cruised down the bar and presently spotted his man. Big Murph had changed from his filthy wet clothes into equally filthy dry ones. He was engaged in desultory conversation with the man on his right while he drank great gulps of whiskey from a water glass.

Minifee edged up to the bar alongside him, and Big Murph turned now to see who his neighbor was.

Minifee sized him up immediately as a born bully-boy, uneducated, simple-minded, surly, and truculent.

Minifee gestured with his thumb to the glass of whiskey. "A little of that stuff in the water tank would have helped," he observed amiably.

Big Murph gave him a surly glance, and then regarded his glass of whiskey.

"That was an Injun trick," Minifee observed. "It took three of them to do it though."

"It'll take six next time," Murph growled. "If they hadn't got me down, I'd of taken 'em."

"Know who threw you?"

Murph scowled. "Cruse, wasn't it?"

"Bishop," Minifee said, and added, "Why don't he stand up and fight like a man?"

Big Murph grinned. "He ain't one, that's why." He

29

took another swig from his glass of whiskey. "Just you wait, I'll get him."

"How?" Minifee challenged.

Big Murph looked at him, a kind of surprise in his broad face. "There's lots of ways," he said slyly. "Suppose I lock wheels with him next time we pass on the mill road? I'll dump him off a couple hundred feet into the canyon."

"That sounds kind of trifling," Minifee observed. "Still, he's a hard case to tangle with."

Big Murph looked scornfully at him. "If I could catch him alone, I'd stomp him flat. Trouble is, Cruse or somebody always buys into the fight."

"Then catch him alone."

Big Murph shook his head. "We won't even come out after dark. His woman won't let him."

"What's the matter with daylight?"

Big Murph looked sharply at him. "What do you care, Mister?"

Minifee shrugged. "I don't. I just watched that pile-up, and I wondered why a big man like you would take it. Especially," he added softly, "if you can make a double eagle by not taking it."

Big Murph gently set his glass down on the bar and turned his head to regard Minifee. "Say that again."

"A double eagle." He reached in his pocket, put a coin on the bar, and covered it with his hand. "There's ten—and ten more when you lay him out." Then he added softly, "And I mean laid out."

Big Murph scowled. "Why laid out?"

Minifee smiled as if to himself. "I want a close, careful look at him when his eyes are shut."

"When?"

"Tomorrow morning, say?"

Big Murph looked first at Minifee, then at Minifee's hand covering the coin. Slowly Minifee withdrew his

30

hand, and now Murphy regarded the coin with a kind of crafty disbelief.

Suddenly Big Murphy held up his right hand, fisted it, and laughed. He brought his hand crashing down on the bar alongside the coin. The impact sent the coin six inches in the air. Big Murph opened his palms under it when it dropped. He pocketed the coin, nodded to Minifee, and winked.

On week days the Primrose Freighting Company was astir before daylight. The big wagons heading for the railroad sixty miles away, for the sawmill, and for distant mines were on the road at earliest light. From the gate Minifee watched the stocktenders, who were working by lantern light, maneuver the teams into place and harness them almost by touch. There was a steady background chorus of profanity.

Teamsters passed him on their way to the office to receive orders, and Minifee, standing in the shadows, observed that Johnny Bishop was among them. Big Murph, noisy and cheerful, arrived at last and stepped into the office to pick up his orders.

Minifee, watching him, began to doubt the wisdom of his investment. Certainly Big Murphy didn't appear to be a man who was carrying a grudge.

Already the first wagon had pulled out past Minifee, its empty box rumbling, its wheels jolting against the axles and the driver cursing his somnolent mules. As the wagon rolled into the street, Minifee heard a shout, and he moved a few tentative steps deeper into the dark yard. He saw teamsters and stocktenders looking toward the open-faced wagon shed.

Then Johnny Bishop came into his line of vision. Backing slowly, Johnny was slugging viciously at Big Murph. The big teamster's shoulders were hunched, his beard buried in his neck, and he was making little effort to parry Johnny's blows.

Then, with an astonishing agility Murph lunged forward, and a big hand fell on either of Johnny Bishop's shoulders. The big man lowered his head and, yanking Johnny toward him, butted him savagely in the face. Minifee could hear the thud from where he stood, and he winced.

For a second Johnny stood motionless, and then his knees buckled and he fell. Instantly the yard boiled with activity. From all directions teamsters and stocktenders dropped their work and headed for Big Murph. Minifee saw the office door open and Herb Loftus, shouting angrily, jumped down the steps and headed for the fight.

Minifee was already in motion. He ran directly to where Johnny Bishop lay in the cool dust. The fight now centered at the rear of the wagon shed where Big Murph, his back to the wall, was taking on all comers.

Kneeling, Minifee took Johnny's left arm and, holding it out, grasped Johnny's shirt. With a savage yank he ripped the cloth and exposed Johnny's upper arm. Quickly Minifee examined the scar where Johnny's tattoo had been, and a faint elation touched him.

Then he moved down to Johnny's feet, lifted Johnny's left leg, and grasped his boot in both hands. With a tremendous tug he yanked at the boot and it slipped from Johnny's foot. Quickly Minifee pushed up the leg of Johnny's trousers until his lower leg was exposed. There on the shin was a long, deep scar.

Minifee was aware now that the shouting had subsided and he glanced over to the shed. Big Murph lay in the dirt against the shed wall, and now Herb Loftus's angry voice could be heard.

"—back to work or I'll fire the whole lot of you! This is a business place, not a saloon!"

The group broke up now, laughing, apparently unconcerned at Loftus's threats. Loftus, seeing Minifee kneeling beside Johnny, tramped over to him. Al Cruse, nursing a bloody nose, saw Minifee at the same time. Both he and Loftus arrived together.

Al, seeing that this stranger had removed Johnny's boot, asked Loftus, "What's he doing here?"

Minifee rose now, ignoring Al. He looked at Herb, nodded toward Johnny, and said, "That's my man, Loftus. You knew it all the time too."

Loftus knelt, lifted the cloth on Johnny's sleeve, and saw the scar. Glancing up at Minifee, he said, "That's no tattoo."

"That's where a tattoo used to be," Minifee said dryly. "If you don't mind a little pain, it's easy enough to cut out the tattooed skin. It all depends on whether you figure it's worth it."

"You figure that'll hold up in court?" Herb asked skeptically.

"Together with the other it will."

Herb scowled. "What other?"

"Look at his left shin. I didn't tell you about that." Minifee smiled faintly. "An old ax scar went along with the tattoo as identification marks."

Herb pushed Johnny's trouser leg up until he saw the scar.

Al Cruse, who had been watching this in silence, said, "Who are you?"

"Wells Fargo special agent," Minifee said.

"What's Johnny done?"

"Helped in a big holdup a couple of years ago."

"I don't believe it," Al said flatly.

"I don't care if you believe it or not. You aren't the jury, friend."

Herb Loftus rose. Other teamsters had drifted up to them and were listening in silence. Herb said, "You're dead sure this is your man?"

"Dead sure. So are you."

"There's nothing we can do about it?"

"You can go get the sheriff," Minifee said.

"Get him yourself," Cruse cut in angrily. He looked around at his fellow teamsters. "I feel like another workout," Al observed. "How about you, boys?"

"Quit it, Al," Herb cut in. He looked around at the assembled teamsters and stocktenders. "That's the way the cards fall, boys." He looked now at Minifee. "He's married, you know. Got a pretty young wife."

"He won't be the first married man ever to go to jail," Minifee said dryly.

"He's a good man, the best. Steady, sober, and a hard worker. I don't suppose that means anything to you."

"Not a thing," Minifee agreed.

Al Cruse said softly, "Just give the word, Herb." He was looking at Minifee with pure hatred.

Herb glanced over at Al and then at the other teamsters. He took a deep breath then and sighed, "No, Al, I can't do it. I did all I could, but I can't stop him now. It's up to a jury to decide about Johnny." He inclined his head toward Minifee. "After all, this man's paid to do a job. He's only doing it."

Al Cruse took a step forward. "Herb," he said softly, "don't it strike you that this fight between Murph and Johnny come in awful handy for this gent?"

Herb scowled. "How's that?"

"He couldn't go up to Johnny and say, 'Listen, friend, I'd like to see if you got a scar on your leg. I'd like to see if you got a tattoo on your arm.' " Al looked at Minifee now, and then returned his glance to Herb. "Johnny wouldn't have showed him and he ain't man enough to take a look himself. I figure he put Murph up to it."

"You're exactly right," Minifee said calmly. "I did."

"Just give the word, Herb," Al said.

"I never like to put a gun on a man if I can help it," Minifee said slowly, suggestively. "But that doesn't mean I can't."

Al looked at him a long moment. "You ain't out of town yet."

"Quit it, Al!" Herb said sharply. "Now break it up. Let's get to work."

Al gave Minifee a lingering look that held something of promise in it before he turned away.

It fell to Al Cruse to tell Johnny's wife, and it took him the best part of an hour to steel himself for the job. First, he had to let his anger settle a little and then he had to dredge among the bitter facts for some consoling word with which to comfort Lillie. The trouble was there was nothing he could tell her that would offer any consolation. Wells Fargo, he knew, were implacable; they never quit and when they nailed the man they usually made the charge stick.

Al had taken down deliveries that morning and after his first load, he drove his team around to Pritchard's house and swung down. He was thinking then of how Johnny Bishop, a little less than a year ago had pulled him, drunk and sick, out of the barrooms, of how Lillie had fed him, and of how Johnny had talked Herb Loftus into giving him a probationary job. Everything he was today—*Which isn't very damn much,* he thought—he owed to Johnny Bishop. A lot of other people in Primrose—humble, insignificant people like himself—were in debt to Johnny, too. Why, even Herb Loftus, with his crew of tough, irascible teamsters, was in debt to Johnny; somehow, with persuasion, logic, and sometimes fists, Johnny kept harmony and brought a sense of order to Herb's outfit.

At the Bishops' door, Al took a deep breath and knocked. Lillie appeared immediately and when she saw Al she smiled warmly. Slowly then, as she caught Al's mood reflected in his face, her smile faded.

"I got bad news, Lillie," Al began.

"They got him?" Lillie demanded swiftly.

Al nodded miserably.

Lillie sank into the nearest chair, folded her hands in her lap, and stared at the floor. "How did it happen?" she asked presently.

Al told her of Minifee's ruse. He finished by saying, "Weston's got him locked up for Minifee."

It was as if someone had kicked her, Al thought, and his anger returned. *Damn any law that could do this to a person,* Al thought, and then he knew that was wrong, but he still thought it.

Lillie took a deep, shuddering breath and rose. There was a kind of determination in her small face as she said, "They can't do this, Al. I'm going to see Weston."

Sheriff Burt Weston was seated at his desk, writing, when Lillie and Al stepped into his office. When Weston saw them he rose slowly and indicated the barrel chair against the wall beside his desk.

"I don't reckon I have to guess why you're here," he said wearily. He was an old man, white-haired, with heavy roan mustaches bisecting his lean face.

Lillie crossed the room to the chair and sat down, and Al took up his station beside her. "Why have you arrested Johnny?" Lillie asked quietly.

Sheriff Weston slacked into his swivel chair and eyed her patiently. "There's a warrant out for him down in Wyoming. He's charged with being an accessory in the murder of a stage driver and a Wells Fargo shotgun messenger. His real name," Weston added wearily, "is Jim Byers."

"Who said that?" Lillie demanded.

"Minifee. He's a Wells Fargo special agent. He's identified him."

"I grew up with Johnny Bishop," Lillie said flatly. "If he's named Jim Byers, why was his father's name Jim Bishop?"

"Quit it, Lillie," Weston said gently. "You grew up on a ranch in Kern County. There's not a Bishop in Kern County."

Lillie's face flushed, but she held the sheriff's gaze. "Have you checked all the gravestones in Kern County, too?" she asked bitterly.

"I don't have to." Weston's voice was gentle and held a quiet despair, and Al knew that the sheriff was hating this too.

"Why is this Minifee so certain Johnny's guilty?"

Weston made a wry face and said, "A tattoo and a scar that Minifee got from his army record identified him."

"He's not got a tattoo," Lillie said hotly.

"He's got a spot where one was."

"How can you prove that?"

"It's no use, Lillie," Weston said gently. "Johnny is Jim Byers. He's been identified by an old army man who was in Johnny's regiment."

"I don't believe it. Who?"

Lillie was fighting every inch of the way, Al knew, and he ached to help her.

"It's just plain bad luck, Lillie," Weston explained. "Johnny had just served out a cavalry enlistment. His regiment had been chasing Sioux all summer on half rations. He was sick and he couldn't work. His pay was gone. He figured to make a quick stake and get out of the country. That's what he did, just in case he never told you."

"I asked who identified him, not for a fairy story from Minifee."

"I'm coming to that," Weston said patiently. "This Minifee is a stubborn man. He's paid to be stubborn. As soon as he found out Johnny was in the holdup he went down to Fort Union where Johnny's regiment was stationed and asked around about Johnny. Sure as you're born, he ran into a trooper who talked. Remember that government survey party that was through here last summer?"

Lillie nodded.

"Well, they cut across the Raft Range with their cavalry escort. They just happened to take the logging road as far as the mill, and who do you guess they met bringing down a load of lumber?"

Lillie was motionless, waiting.

"It was Johnny," Weston said glumly. "This trooper that recognized Johnny had transferred out of Johnny's old regiment to a new one. The escort was picked out of that regiment." Weston spread his hands. "That's how things happen, Lillie."

"That's no proof," Lillie said stubbornly.

Weston looked at her a long moment. "Lillie, give up. Minifee will take him away. He'll be identified. There's nothing you can do to stop it."

Al Cruse said bluntly, "There's something you can do, Burt."

"What's that, Al?"

"You could forget to lock the cell, for one thing."

Weston only shook his head. "You know better than that."

"What's this Wells Fargo man to you?" Al demanded hotly.

"Nothing. I'll never see him again."

"Then just leave the key in the cell door. If Mr. Wells Fargo gets tough, let us know. We'll run his luck

38

out and mighty sudden."

Weston shook his head. "I took an oath, Al. Sometimes I wonder why, but I did. That oath was to uphold the law against lawbreakers. Johnny's a lawbreaker." He spread his hands. "It's that simple, Lillie. You might as well face it."

"Can I see him?" Lillie asked.

"Of course." Weston pointed to the door on the alley side of the office, and Lillie rose, crossed the room, and entered the cell block.

Al was silent for a long bitter minute, his mind refusing to accept this. He looked at Weston then and said, "Why don't you quit?"

"I'd like to, Al," Weston answered.

"You know what kind of a man Johnny is. How can you do it?"

"How can I not do it?"

"But, damn it, you don't understand!" Al said hotly. "Johnny's going to be something. He's not like the rest of us. He's going somewhere. He's going somewhere big and he ain't going to step on nobody's neck getting there."

"I know that, Al," Weston said gently. "He's a fine boy. I wish he was my son, but even if he was, I'd have to do this."

Al was licked and he knew it. "What happens now?" he asked glumly.

"Minifee takes him out tomorrow morning as soon as the papers are in order."

Lillie stepped out of the cell block then and Al pushed away from the wall. "Take you home, Lillie?"

"I'd rather walk, Al, thanks." At the door she halted and turned to regard Weston. "I'd hate to have this on my conscience, Sheriff," she said quietly.

Weston dipped his head. "I do hate it."

She left, and Al said, "Can I see him?"

39

"Sure. You got a gun on you?"

Al shook his head and Weston said, "Go ahead then."

Al tramped across the room and opened the door to the cell block. There were two cells, and in the one on the right Johnny was sitting on the cot, his back against the wall, looking out the barred window. When he heard Al enter, he swiveled his head. There was a bruise on his chin where Big Murph had butted him.

Al came up to the cell, grasped the bars and he and Johnny looked at each other in sober silence. "Is that Wells Fargo story true, Johnny?" Al finally asked.

Johnny nodded.

"What can I do?" Al asked.

Slowly Johnny rose from the cot. He came over to face Al. "Lillie's going to have a baby, Al."

"Fine, fine," Al said bitterly.

Johnny smiled crookedly. "Old man Pritchard was in here this morning. He offered to forget about the rent."

"Don't you worry about grub and clothes," Al said. "As long as I eat, she does."

"Somebody'll have to take care of her. She's got no family and neither have I. After the baby comes, she can work."

"Don't worry about that," Al said. "How long will you be gone?"

Johnny shrugged. "Minifee says Wells Fargo'll ask for ten years."

"That's real fine," Al said bitterly. "What's ten years? Nothing! Why, by that time your kid'll only be punching cattle on the horse he earned the money to buy."

Johnny said nothing.

Al said slowly, "You ever thought of Canada, Johnny?"

40

"Canada? For what?"

"You can start over up there and the law will let you alone. They tell me it's not much different than here."

Johnny smiled crookedly. "When I get out of jail, the law won't be interested in me any more, Al."

"I mean now."

Johnny and Al looked at each other in silence. "If you're thinking what I'm thinking," Johnny said slowly, "don't do it."

"I'm old enough to vote," Al said dryly. "Just tell me how Canada sounds to you. As soon as you're settled, we can send Lillie up."

Johnny shook his head. "Don't do it, Al. Somebody'll get hurt. Even if they don't, who takes the blame?"

"There won't be any blame. Take my word for it. Now answer me about Canada."

"I won't even talk about it."

Al grinned. "You think real hard about it. There'll be a horse and grub tied behind the jail. Remember that, just in case it rains tonight and washes a hole in the roof."

Next morning before daybreak Al Cruse got his orders to pick up a load of concentrates at the Ajax Mine in the Raft Mountains. It meant a day each way on the road.

Al helped the stocktender load two days' rations for his teams, mounted to the seat and drove out of the yard, cheerfully cursing his mules. He swung left, crossed Main Street, headed north for the Raft Range.

When he had passed the county offices, however, he suddenly cut left into the alley and pulled through it as far as the corral behind Jessup's Stable. Here he swung down from the high wagon, walked into the livery and past the hostler who was sleeping in the hay. From a dozen saddles hanging on the wall in back of the office,

41

he took one and went back with it to the corral. A score of horses, mostly rental mounts, were standing patiently in the quiet morning as he stepped inside the corral. It took him only a few minutes to catch and saddle a horse.

Al rode through the livery centerway, across Main Street, and turned in at the alley alongside the jail. Behind the sheriff's office Al dismounted and tied his pony to a ring at Packard's loading platform. It was full daylight now, and the town was beginning to come awake. Al left the alley, crossed the street, mounted the veranda of the Primrose House, selected a chair and slacked into it. *This beats freighting,* he thought wryly. *This is the life.*

He had smoked down five cigarettes and shifted to another chair before it happened. Soon after the breakfast bell rang in the Primrose House, Al saw Minifee, mounted and leading a second horse, turn off Main Street and rein in before the sheriff's office. The extra horse, Al knew was for Johnny. Minifee dismounted and went into the sheriff's office.

Al rose. The time was here. Descending the veranda steps, he sauntered idly across to the two horses and stroked the nose of Minifee's mount, meanwhile looking first up the street and then down it. Al slipped his sheath knife out and quickly slashed the cinch of Minifee's saddle, leaving only the thinnest thread uncut so that the cinch would not fall and betray his act. Casually, unhurriedly, he did the same with the cinch on the saddle of the second horse.

Whistling, he headed back for the livery, tramped through it, mounted his high wagon and drove his teams through to Main Street. Turning left, he drove down a block, turned right, and was at the wagon yard.

He paid it no attention, however; he checked his leaders when they tried to turn in the wagon yard and held them straight until they were abreast the alley that ran behind the wagon yard, behind Packard's, and alongside the jail, where he reined in his teams and set the brake.

Still whistling cheerfully, Al dropped down in the bed of the wagon. Here was coiled a heavy length of logging chain which was used to lash loads. One end of the chain in his hand, Al swung up the steep side of the wagon box, which put his head level with the high barred window of the jail.

Putting one foot against the jail to brace himself, Al slipped the chain in back of the five iron bars of the window, then fitted the hook firmly into a link. He dropped to the ground, still whistling, and slowly pulled out the length of chain.

Taking the other end of the chain, he knelt and secured it around the rear axle and stringer beam of the wagonframe. Coming erect, he glanced over at Packard's loading platform. The pony he had left earlier was standing hipshot in the warm morning sunlight.

Al swung up on the wagon seat and uncoiled his whip, secured the brake even more firmly, and then started to swear at his lead mules. They danced back and forth, lunging into their collars as Al's whip cracked out and his curses poured forth. The other teams now caught the panic, lunging into their collars and inching the braked wagon forward.

With a fine sense of timing, Al knew when his teams were all pulling. Then with a tug of the brake strap, he let the brake off. At the same moment he vaulted from his high seat to the ground.

The wagon shot into the street, the lead team turning left at a dead run.

Hunkered against the wall of the jail, Al saw the chain play out, then rise horizontally into the air, taut as a fiddle-string. There was a rending crash, and the rear wheels of the big freight wagon rose two feet in the air, but the mules never halted, and the hitch did not break. The wagon careened into the middle of the street, turning on its two outside wheels, and then Al, watching it, smiled. Trailing at the end of the logging chain were the five jail window bars still set in the heavy oak window frame.

Al set his shoulders against the wall waiting, listening. He heard a sound in the alley as if a weight had fallen. Then he heard the pounding of footsteps, followed by the sound of a horse working into a dead gallop.

The noise on his right swiveled Al's head. The door of the sheriff's office crashed open and Minifee came out at a dead run. His horse, ground-haltered close to the jail steps, turned his head. Minifee didn't bother to mount. He simple vaulted into the saddle.

When his heavy body hit the saddle, the cinch broke. Minifee kept going. The saddle slipped, and with Minifee's legs locked to it, it tore off, and Minifee crashed into the street on the far side of his horse.

Al knew now it was time to act. He ran out into the street, his whip trailing him, in apparent pursuit of his runaway team. He could see them a block down the street, still running.

Al was sure that Minifee had seen him, and he halted and turned. He was just in time to see Minifee swing into the saddle of the second horse. The horse, excited by all the commotion, reared, and Minifee began to saw the reins. Suddenly the cut cinch gave way entirely and Minifee, still in the saddle, slid down his mount's back and sat heavily on the ground.

By this time Sheriff Weston was on the steps of his office. Al, panting heavily as if he had run a great distance, came up to the sheriff and halted. He looked

44

closely at Weston. The sheriff was regarding him with a quiet benevolence which Al could not exactly read.

Minifee, swearing bitterly, was kicking his legs free of the saddle stirrups when Al spoke: "Them jacks spooked there in the alley, Burt. When the wagon hit the jail it throwed me a country mile."

"You boys keep taking that alleyway too fast," Weston said in gentle reproof.

Elation touched Al Cruse then. The sheriff was playing along. They both looked at Minifee. The Wells Fargo agent was bent over the saddle. He looked briefly at the cinch, then straightened. "Cut," he announced. He looked balefully at Al. "You wouldn't know who did that, would you?"

"How could I?" Al said in a tone of surprise and injury. "I was trying to hold in twelve jacks!"

Minifee looked angrily at the sheriff. "You believe that, Sheriff?"

"Shouldn't I?"

"You believe that wagon rammed the jail so it tore out the window?" Minifee demanded.

Weston looked at him in amazement. "Now what else could hit it so it would tear out the window?"

"Your prisoner is gone," Minifee said angrily. "What do you aim to do about that?"

"He's your prisoner," Weston said flatly. "I just finished signing him over to you."

Minifee looked at the two men with quiet hatred, then pointed to his saddle and said, "You aim to find out who did that?"

"If a man rides a horse," Weston observed mildly, "he ought to learn how to saddle him."

This was too much for Minifee. He stalked over to the sheriff and said, "Sheriff, I demand you call up a posse."

"Sure thing," Weston said amiably. "There'll be a

dozen or so men at the freight yard around noon. Good men, too. I'll deputize them all."

Despairingly Minifee looked from Weston to Al.

Al said quietly, "You better get going. Johnny's got a head start on you."

For a bitter moment Minifee looked at Al, and Al wondered if the man would pull his gun. Then Minifee's glance shuttled to Weston.

"You going to let it ride this way, Sheriff?" he demanded.

"Why, man," Sheriff Weston said sharply, and there was an edge of anger in his voice, "he's your prisoner. You want him. If you want help, I've offered to help you. All you got to do is speak up. What is it you want me to do?"

Minifee looked at him a long moment, and then he said bitterly, "Just fall down dead."

Under the curiously serene gazes of Al and Sheriff Weston, Minifee picked up both saddles, turned, and tramped down the street toward Jessup's.

Sheriff Weston settled his glance on Al, who was grinning. They looked at each other in silence.

"One thing you forgot," Weston said slowly. "Johnny will be picked up for stealing a horse, sure as shooting."

Al shook his head, grinning. "It was my horse, Burt. My bill of sale to Johnny is in his saddlebag."

GUNSLICK GOLD

I
THE NEW SHERIFF

On election day San Tolar County voted according to its conscience and was not surprised when it found that another Storr had been elected sheriff. It had been voting Storrs into that office since time immemorial and it saw no reason to regret it.

This time it was Dan Storr, just turned twenty-two and the youngest of the long line of Storr sheriffs. Old Zack Storr, whose name was hallowed in history as the "fightin'est, git-down, cold-steel lawman west of the Ruidoso," had established a campaign custom that all his successors followed. Three days before election he loaded a buckboard with the finest whiskey money could buy and drove through the county.

Dan had done the same. The only difference between Zack and Dan was that Zack had drunk only a reasonable share of the whiskey, while Dan managed to stay roaring drunk for three days.

"He'll git over it and sober down into a steady sort," was the seasoned opinion of the voters who shared the whiskey.

But Doc Whalen, his spare frame bellied up to the bar of the Ocotillo the night the election returns were counted in Seven Troughs, wasn't so sure. He had known three Storrs, but none of them were like Dan. Usually, they were lean, dark men like Dan, but they were slow-spoken, tolerant, men who lived in a saddle and bowed to no man, and who never wore a star.

To a man, they had treated the sheriff's office as something incidental to ranching, and Doc always thought that their easy going indifference to writs, complaints, errand-running and county attorneys was what made them so successful.

The Ocotillo was full now, and Doc could hear Dan's loud voice, drunken and maudlin, raised above the clamor. Dan was ridiculing the aims of the opposition party; his talk was a confounded nuisance, Doc thought.

"What about this runnin' vice and gamblin' out of Seven Troughs?" an inquisitor asked of Dan. There was a crowd around him now, and already the star of office reposed on his vest.

"To hell with that," Dan announced loudly. "A pity if a man can't sit down to a quiet game of poker without havin' preachers and old women tellin' him it's sinful."

The crowd gathered around him applauded, and Doc saw they were saloon bums and riff-raff. His gaze shuttled to Mike Roarty, the Ocotillo's owner, behind the bar. Mike was a huge, red-faced Irishman and possessed a thick mane of black hair which he parted in the middle and tried to slick down.

In keeping with the revelry of this night, Mike had shed his checked coat, donned a bartender's apron, and was dispensing free rounds of drinks with an abandon that Doc Whalen could not help but suspect.

When Dan made this announcement that there

48

would be no cleanup, Mike looked over the heads of the crowd at the bar to a small, still-faced man dressed in black, who was dealing a desultory game of poker to three other men. This man was Two-Deal Hardwick, and Doc saw the broad wink that was exchanged between them. Doc turned away from the bar.

"Stick around, Doc," Mike called to him. "Have a round on the house, boys."

"I got all I can carry, thanks," Doc shook his head.

"Why hell, Doc," immediately, Mike bridled. "It don't hurt to take on a load now and then, and this is now and then. We don't elect a sheriff every day."

Doc wanted to say that it didn't look as if they'd elected a sheriff—an honest to goodness sheriff—this time, but he refrained. Again he shook his head, his old seamed face lighting up with wry amusement.

"I'm gittin' old, Mike. I'll leave it to you young bucks."

Doc looked at Dan as he went out. Dan Storr had the build and the looks of all the Storrs, but instead of their quiet ways and dress, he was a man who rode high, wide and handsome. Over his red shirt, he wore a buckskin vest; his boots were tooled leather with red insets; his guns were pearl-handled, the shellbelts and holsters studded with silver. Right now, he grinned at Doc and waved his hand in mock salute.

"So long, Sawbones. Don't fergit the milk 'fore yuh go to bed," Dan called, and got a laugh.

Outside, Doc fought down his anger, and tried to be reasonable. Dan Storr was just a kid, alive with all the hellery and spirit of his years, but still—Doc didn't know. He turned gloomily down the street and in front of the general store, he ran across Sue English.

"What's up, Doc?" she asked pleasantly.

Doc saw that there were lines of worry on her tanned

49

oval face, and that her usually bright blue eyes were clouded, as if she were tired. Her smile lacked something, and Doc could guess what it was.

"I've just been watchin' that monkey yuh've promised to marry," Doc said wryly.

"Still blotting it up?"

"Uh-huh. And announcin' to the world that Seven Troughs will stay wide open as long as he's sheriff—which won't be long, I'm thinkin'."

"Oh, Doc, what's the matter with him?" Sue asked huskily.

Doc looked at her strangely, at the mass of copper hair which framed her proud fine face in a halo of smoldering fire, and again he decided to hold his tongue. He grunted.

"Turned politician, looks like."

"But you know he isn't that way!" Sue said.

"Sue," Doc said gravely, "tell me. Is he a reasonable kid? Does he know right from wrong? Would he rather have folks live in decency, or is he out to raise all the hell a kid kin raise while he's got the chance, and be-damned-to-everybody?"

"But you know him, Doc, as well as you do me," Sue sighed.

"I thought I did until this week."

"Yes, he's reasonable," Sue said staunchly. "He always was before."

Doc looked off down the street. A couple of drunks down by the stable let their guns go off in the air, but the few people on the streets were so used to it, they did not even turn to look.

"All right," Doc said slowly. "We'll see."

"How?"

"I dunno," Doc said. "I will tomorrow mornin', though."

He said good night, but instead of crossing the street

to his combination office and living quarters above the land office, he continued on down the street toward Ben Holt's feed stable.

Holt, older than Doc, untidy, smelling of horses and liniment and dust, was in the office up front. A feed catalogue lay open before him, and he did not look up immediately after Doc entered. Doc took a chair, tilted it back against the wall and lit his pipe.

"Yuh sick of him, too, huh?" Holt said, turning a page.

"Plenty," Doc said. "Ben," he announced slowly, after puffing on his pipe a moment, "yuh remember those two jaspers I was tellin' yuh about the other day—the two I met over in McGaffey?"

"Yuh was called over to dig a slug out of Hank Beaufort and he died. His gunnies was goin' to cut yuh to doll rags when these two gents stepped in? Shore, I remember," Holt nodded.

"Could yuh send a man over there tonight with word for them to drift thisaway and see me?"

"What for?" Holt asked bluntly.

"I dunno all of it," Doc shrugged. "I got a hunch they kin help me—yuh, Sue English, the whole town and county—and Dan Storr, too."

"How?"

"I don't know jest how. By provin' that Mike Roarty is runnin' crooked games, and by wakin' young Dan Storr up."

"Shore, I'll send someone."

Doc rose and began to knock out his pipe.

"Yuh do—"

Crash!

Doc Whalen spun around on his heel, facing the open door, caught himself, stumbled a step and then staggered into Ben Holt's arms.

Holt laid him down gently, and ran to the door with

51

drawn gun. The street was empty. Then he called back into the stables for two men, and together, they carried Doc across the street to a floor room in the Overland House. In quicker time than Ben Holt could ask for them, three women were tending Doc. Ben Holt waited until they had Doc's coat off, and saw the bullet wound in his chest, and then he left. In the hall, he called one of the men to him and gave him orders to ride to Mc-Gaffey hell for leather for the doctor there.

"And after that," Holt said, "I want yuh to hunt up two men." He described them as Doc Whalen had described them to him. "Tell them to drift in here singly and look me up. Now hightail it—and if yuh've ever rode, son, ride now."

II
A POKER GAME

Dan Storr took a last look at himself in the mirror and shook his head.

"Eyes look like burnt holes in a blanket," he decided, and wondered if it was time to come down off this bender. His head was rimmed with iron. He'd been pretty drunk last night, and right in the midst of it some fool had shot old Doc Whalen.

He remembered having a look at Doc and asking a lot of questions of old Ben Holt, but Ben had been pretty surly. He remembered Holt's words.

"Yuh come back when yuh're sober, young feller. As a sheriff yuh ain't much good, but as a drunken sheriff, yuh're just plain poison. Now git out!"

That rankled. He'd see Holt today and tell him to keep a civil tongue in his head. But before that, he'd have a drink—just one.

His quarters were behind the sheriff's office which

52

was joined to the thick 'dobie jail. He let himself out to the street whistling softly.

He turned onto the sidewalk and almost bumped into Sue English. She caught herself, stepped back.

"Hello, honey," Storr greeted her, an amiable grin on his face.

"Have you seen Doc this morning?" Sue asked coldly.

"Huh-uh. I jest got up."

"Ten o'clock," Sue said dryly.

"Yeah, I had a night of it," Storr admitted. "I saw the elephant and heard the owl-hoot, won eighty dollars in a poker game, got my insides all torn up with barbwire drippin's and got to bed at five this mornin'. Not bad, huh?"

"Doc Whalen is down here barely alive," Sue said coldly, "and you have the nerve to talk to me about what kind of time you had last night. Dan, what's the matter with you?"

For a moment Storr looked at her, but his glance fell before her level stare. Then Sue began to talk. She told him what a fool he'd been, how she hated the way he'd been acting, how *everybody* hated the way he'd been acting, how disappointed Doc Whalen was with him, and a good many more things. Under the lash of her scorn, Storr winced and tried to get a word in edgewise, but he could not. He could only listen and nod.

Suddenly, however, he interrupted her harangue and laid a hand on her arm.

"Lady," he said softly, "would yuh look at that man on a hoss!"

Sue looked over at the street. There, coming down the middle of the road, on a chunky roan, was a cowpuncher hunched over in his saddle. Even sitting down, he was the tallest person either of them had ever seen—a great, lean scarecrow of a man with a hawk nose and gray eyes. His clothes were dusty, puncher's clothes, but he was whistling softly, eyeing the town with frank curiosity.

But Sue was in no mood for this interruption. She whirled on Storr.

"Did you hear a word I said?"

"Every word," Storr said, but he was watching the puncher. He wanted to go over and ask the man to dismount, so he could see how tall he really was. When he turned again to talk to Sue, she was gone down the walk. He stared after her for a mournful moment, then went up the street.

Quake Aspen, the scarecrow on the roan, saw this little scene and smiled to himself.

"Was that a star I seen on that jasper's vest, or is he jest a catalogue model of what a western sheriff ought to look like?" he wondered. He approved of the girl, whoever she was, and he approved more of the way she left her flashily dressed friend.

At the feed stable, Aspen turned in, dismounted and handed his roan over to the stable boy.

"Where'll I find the boss here, son?"

"He's up front."

Aspen made his way back to the office and entered, stooping so as to be able to manage the door.

Ben Holt looked up as he entered, and without saying a word, he motioned Aspen into a chair.

"Doc Whalen may not live," Holt announced quietly.

"That's too bad," Aspen said. "He was a mighty nice old boy."

"He liked yuh—you and yore partner."

"We liked him," Aspen said. He rolled a cigarette while Ben Holt regarded him with curious eyes.

"It was really Doc that sent for yuh—'fore he got shot, that is," Holt said suddenly.

Aspen paused in lighting his cigarette, his eyes questioning.

"He seemed to think yuh two could give us a lift here." And without further preliminaries, Holt launched into the story of the election of Dan Storr. He told of Storr's refusal to clean up the gambling dives in the town, and he also told a little of Storr's history.

"Like Doc said," Holt finished. "Somethin's got into that kid. The Storrs have all got level heads, and they're good lawmen. But the kid's gone loco—too big for his hat. Doc thought it might help if yuh two would come in here and kind of straighten things out—make the kid see what's right in front of his eyes."

Aspen nodded.

"Will yuh do it?"

Again Aspen nodded.

"I never aimed to hunt trouble," he drawled softly. "But on the other hand, I like to do a good man a favor. Doc Whalen was a good man."

"And he may die," Ben Holt said gloomily.

"I'll do it," Aspen said. "I may be talkin' through my hat, but I reckon whoever it was shot Doc, overheard him layin' plans to clean up the town. Is that right?"

"I reckon."

Aspen stood and hitched up his pants.

"When Stubby comes in, yuh send him on up to the Ocotillo. That's Roarty's place, ain't it?"

"I will. But how will I know him?"

"Yuh couldn't miss," Aspen said, and stepped out.

Sauntering into the Ocotillo, Aspen looked around him on his way to the bar. His one casual glance had picked up the fact that the flashily dressed sheriff, another man, and a professional gambler were chatting idly at a table.

He ordered a beer from the bartender, and passed the time of day.

"If yuh don't mind my sayin' it, Mister, yuh're about the longest thing I ever seen upright," said the bartender, after Aspen had bought him a cigar.

"That's a fact," Quake agreed. "I got that from gamblin'."

"Gamblin'?" the bartender echoed.

"Uh-huh. I was raised by a crooked gambler. He set me down dealin' poker for him when I was ten. We had a bunch of under-the-table kick-in-the-leg signals. We got in a big game one night with two five thousand dollar pots. The only trouble is, we was playin' at a long table and he was at the other end of it. I wanted that money so bad, I stretched out my leg until it reached him. That's why I'm so tall."

"That was only one leg, though," the bartender said gravely. "Yuh got two legs."

"I got that from the second five thousand dollar pot a minute later."

The bartender guffawed. Hardwick, who had been listening along with Storr and another man, laughed too. They all came up to the bar and in a moment Aspen was yarning away as if he had known them all his life.

Hardwick seemed the most interested in what Aspen said.

"Yuh said a gambler raised yuh. Is that the truth?"

"Huh-uh," Aspen said, grinning. "I have to make up some story about how I got to be so tall, and I just happened to settle on that one."

"Here I thought I'd get up a poker game this mornin' with a professional," Hardwick sighed. "It's only about once every three weeks I kin get in more than a dollar-limit game, and I like it when it's fast and chancy.'' He shook his small, neat head and smiled crookedly. ''I wish all these gamblin' punchers would stick to faro. They kin get all that agony of losin' thirteen dollars out of their system without it takin' up a whole evenin'.''

Aspen laughed easily. He knew an invitation when he heard one, and he decided to bite as innocently as he could.

''That's right, I like a fast game too, with no pikers. But yuh don't get 'em often.''

''Looks like we want the same thing, don't it?'' Hardwick said.

''Don't it?'' Aspen echoed.

''Like a game, then?''

''That's what I was tryin' to say.''

Hardwick approached Storr and the other man, Frank Scott, a sharp-faced, soft-handed man in puncher's clothes whose pallor and white hands gave away the fact that he never got far from a saloon or a card table.

Storr begged off, but Scott agreed to play. Scott offered to dig up a fourth man and left, returning in a moment with a lean, sly looking man dressed in a black suit—Jay Burnett, by name—whom Aspen judged to be a storekeeper.

In another five minutes the game was under way. Aspen had only thirty dollars in his pocket and he knew that if he were to stick in this game at all he would have to build his roll in a hurry, before they began to understand each other's game. He did. In ten minutes it was two hundred and fifty, and he had taken one hundred-dollar pot by betting himself blind on three kings. He was lucky, but he had counted on the game's being square for the first half hour anyway; and it was.

Then they settled down into tight, shrewd poker and

Aspen drew in his horns. He knew now that Burnett, Scott and Hardwick were staying out of each other's pots, and that Hardwick was cold-decking him, but he ignored it. The time wasn't ripe yet.

In mid-afternoon, the trade at the bar livened up, but the players paid little attention to it. Aspen looked up on one deal and saw that Stubby was at the bar. In another ten minutes Stubby had ambled over to the poker table and was watching the game. His broad, innocent face gave no hint that he recognized Aspen, and not once did his china blue eyes meet his partner's.

First he placed himself behind Hardwick's chair and grunted approval when Hardwick took a big pot. Then he moved around to watch Burnett, but soon moved away. By this time the others were aware of his presence, and Hardwick scowled at him, but Stubby blithely played on. He looked like any ordinary not-too-bright puncher who thought he knew how to play other people's hands of poker.

Now he moved around to Aspen, and stood behind him. Aspen drew a poor hand, and blew up the pot. Finally he was called, and showed nothing but a pair of nines and a pair of threes. Hardwick took the pot.

Stubby, from behind Aspen, sniggered. Aspen turned around.

"What's so funny, Mister?" he drawled.

"Nothin'." Stubby grinned. "Only it takes better poker than yuh're playin' to make a sandy like that stick."

"Are you playin' this hand, or am I?" Aspen glared at him.

"Neither of us," Stubby said cheerfully.

Aspen looked at Hardwick.

"There's manners to watchin' a poker game, stranger. One rule is, a watcher never talks," Hardwick said to Stubby.

"Why hell, his card was up. Why not say he don't know how to play poker?" Stubby shrugged.

"Maybe yuh ought to show us how," Aspen drawled.

"It'd be like trimmin' a kid for candy," Stubby said smugly.

"Yuh want to play?" Hardwick's eyes narrowed.

"I never said I did, did I?" Stubby yawned.

This time Aspen sneered openly.

"The quickest way to shut up one of these flap-mouths is to call his bluff, Hardwick."

Hardwick nodded. Stubby flushed; he glared at Aspen.

"If I couldn't have the pants off yuh in an hour, I'd never look at a deck of cards again," he said.

"There's one way to prove that, stranger," Burnett said.

Stubby whirled a chair away from the wall and planked it down next to Aspen. His jaw was outthrust.

"By God I will." He pulled a roll of bills from his pocket and peeled off a hundred dollars in fives. "Gimme chips."

Stubby's play was ludicrous. He bet a stack of blues on the first hand and Aspen, the only one who wasn't cautious with this beginner, called him. Stubby turned up a busted flush, and Aspen sneered taking the pot with a pair of deuces.

"Nice poker," he said gravely, and smiled.

As the game progressed Stubby kept losing, and as he lost he got madder. When the deal came around to Aspen, he shuffled and dealt. Stubby watched him suspiciously. When they had discarded and called for more cards, he dealt them and was just picking up his hand when Stubby stood up in his chair. It was so sudden his chair tipped over backwards with a crash.

"I got Hardwick's discard!" Stubby said flatly, leaning over toward Aspen.

"If yuh say that, Mister, yuh lie in yore teeth!" Aspen laid down his cards.

Stubby's hand dropped to his gun, and in the same motion Aspen turned the table over on top of him. Stubby went down, his gun already out and shooting, just as Aspen dived over the table and slammed down on top of him. It took only a few moments for him to grab Stubby's gun hand and pin it to the floor, and then he clipped him smartly on the shelf of his jaw. Stubby went limp, and slowly Aspen stood up.

"Mister, yuh got guts," Hardwick whistled softly. "Why that fat little jasper was already shootin' when yuh jumped the table."

"He made me mad," Aspen drawled.

The loose circle of watchers around the table broke to let Dan Storr through. He looked at Stubby.

"What's the fuss here?" he said officiously.

"That jasper was losin' and he accused this gent of dealin' discards, Dan. He never did it, 'cause I was watchin'. Then that fat jasper pulled a gun on him and then this gent just smothered him, that's all," Hardwick said.

"Who is this other ranny? Ever see him?" Dan looked up at Aspen.

Aspen shook his head.

"He got to playin' my hand for me from behind my chair, so we asked him to sit in. He was losin' and he got proddy."

Storr signaled to a man in the crowd.

"Bring him along, Henry. We'll see if he'll cool off in the lockup."

While they were hauling Stubby out, Aspen motioned Hardwick off to one side.

"I'm much obliged for that lie," Aspen said when they were by themselves.

"What lie?" Hardwick blankly asked.

"About my not dealin' discards."

Hardwick stared at him a long moment, then—

"Did yuh?"

"Sure. I dealt him my own discard." Aspen grinned.

"Now don't yuh go turnin' pious," he said as Hardwick's eyes went cold.

"Yuh've been cold-deckin' me about every fifth hand the whole day." He said it so frankly, and so without anger, that Hardwick's jaw sagged a little.

"Yuh see," Aspen explained mildly, "when yuh did it, I'd jest drop out that hand. Hadn't yuh noticed?"

"Shore," Hardwick said huskily. Suddenly, he smiled. "Mister, yuh been around, haven't yuh?"

"I really was raised by a gambler," Aspen nodded. "No hard feelin's, is there?"

Hardwick shook his head. He laid a hand on Aspen's arm.

"Say, yuh oughtn't to leave this place. Yuh'll find a lot of work around here."

"Like what?"

Hardwick thought a moment, and all the time he was watching Aspen with a searching, speculative gaze.

"Kin yuh take orders, keep yore mouth shut, and fergit yuh have a conscience?" he finally said.

"I kin. I've never discovered this conscience yet, either," Aspen grinned.

"Come along," Hardwick said. He crossed the room and knocked on a door which was set in the wall at the rear of the bar. When his knock was answered, he motioned Aspen through the door, which led into a small office containing a big desk, a safe, and a couple of chairs. Mike Roarty was seated at the desk.

"Did yuh see that, Mike!" Hardwick asked as he shut the door and leaned against it.

"I jest got in on the tail end of it," Roarty nodded.

61

He looked at Aspen. "That took nerve, Mister."

"The funny thing was, Mike, this gent really did cold-deck that fat fella'," Hardwick said as he walked over to Roarty.

"That's all right," Hardwick said when Mike scowled. "He caught me cold-deckin' and kept his mouth shut." He jerked his head toward Aspen. "Don't that give yuh any ideas. Mike?"

Roarty regarded Aspen blankly.

"Go on," he said to Hardwick.

"Why, dont' yuh see?" Hardwick said. "This jasper staged once of the nerviest plays I ever saw pulled in the face of a gun. Dan Storr was pretty impressed. This long gent has got a head on him, too. Why not go down to Dan Storr and suggest this jasper be made a deputy sheriff? He's made a name for himself here already. He could work with us, and still he'd be makin' Dan a good deputy. What about it?"

For a long while Mike Roarty stared at the tip of his cigar.

"Yuh ain't very particular how yuh pick up money, are yuh?" he asked Aspen.

"Jest so it ain't honestly." Aspen shook his head.

"Good." Roarty laughed now. "I'll see what I kin do for yuh. Yuh hang around town and drop down here in an hour or so. Don't hang around this place, or it'll look funny."

III
THE RED MINE SHIPMENT

Aspen spent an hour in a bar down the street, then returned to Ocotillo.

"Roarty's lookin' for yuh in the back office. Better go back," the bartender told him.

Aspen knocked on the rear door and was bid to enter. Dan Storr sat in one of the chairs, Hardwick sat on the desk, and Roarty in his own chair.

"Yuh sent for me?" Aspen asked.

"Yeah. Sit down, Mr.—"

"Aspen."

Roarty introduced him to Storr, and Aspen took a chair.

"Roarty's been tellin' me how yuh handled that fat ranny this afternoon," Storr began.

Aspen scowled a moment, as if at a loss.

"Oh, the poker player. Yeah. He was a nuisance."

"Considerable," Hardwick said. "He'd of been more than that if yuh hadn't put a saddle on him."

Aspen waved a hand deprecatingly.

"Look here, Aspen," Storr said. "What are yuh doin' here?"

"Jest driftin' through," Aspen said. "Nice little town."

"Ever do any deputy work?"

"Lots," Aspen said. "South of here."

"Well, here's the proposition," Storr continued. "I was elected sheriff yesterday. There's been one shootin' so far. I want a man that kin handle himself and knows his way 'round. From all appearances, yuh look like the man I want. Would yuh consider bein' my deputy?"

Aspen did not want to appear too eager, so he only scowled.

"Mike and Hardwick here say they never seen anythin' like the way yuh tromped on that tin-horn hard-case. Seein' as yuh're a stranger here and wouldn't take sides easy, they said you ought to make a good deputy."

"How much is in it?" Aspen asked.

"Ninety a month and board. That enough?"

"Why not? I'd as soon be here as anywhere else,"

Aspen shrugged.

"Good work, Dan," Roarty growled. "Yuh got a sensible man in there. He'll be able to handle anythin' that comes up and still he won't let these reformers run over him." To Aspen, he said, "We'll be seein' a lot of yuh, Aspen. I think we're lucky in gettin' yuh."

Aspen nodded and thanked him.

"Come on down now and I'll swear yuh in," said Storr.

Aspen left with Storr and went down the street to the office. The courthouse, a white frame building, was apart from the sheriff's office up the street.

The office itself contained only a desk, the usual chairs, a cot and wall gunrack. The door in the rear wall led on to the 'dobie jail, the door in the side wall into Storr's quarters.

The oath was administered, and Aspen received his badge, after which he took a chair and talked with Storr, who was more than willing to unburden himself.

"Yuh see, a bunch of these old women in men's pants around here want to shut down the gamblin' in this town. They claim it's crooked. What kind of a town would it be if we did that?"

"Not much," Aspen agreed.

"Now this Doc Whalen shootin'. I can't figure that out. Doc's a fine old boy, kinda' crotchety, but he's all right. The way I figure it, some crank that'd heard Doc squawkin' about the crooked gamblin' here, got a bellyful of whiskey and decided to get even with Doc. Some puncher, mebbe, that didn't want gamblin' took away. Anythin' kin happen on an election night."

"That's a fact," Aspen said.

"Well, I'll be runnin' out." Storr rose. "Nothin' on this afternoon, less yuh talk with Ben Holt and find out what he knows about that shootin'."

"I'll do that."

Storr went out. As soon as he was gone, Aspen opened the door to the jail and went in. Stubby was asleep on the cot in the end cell. When Aspen entered, he wakened and then sat up.

"Well?" he growled.

For answer Aspen brushed off the badge which hung on his shirt pocket and Stubby, seeing it, whistled.

"Long jasper, that was quick work. A deputy! How in hell did you do it?"

Aspen told him everything, but especially that Roarty considered him working for him, and that Dan Storr, apparently, was a cocky fresh kid who was being run by Roarty and didn't know it.

"How'd my act go?" Stubby asked as he rubbed his jaw reflectively.

"Perfect. That's what got me the job. I'm a hero."

"Yuh didn't have to slug me so hard gittin' there," Stubby growled. "That was almost so good it was too good." But all the time he was growling, Aspen could see he was thinking.

"I begin to savvy a little of this, now," Stubby said, presently. "Roarty, Hardwick and that crew are the jaspers Doc Whalen knew were runnin' crooked games here. That Dan boy is jest a kid too big for his pants, and he's playin' right into their hands. What Doc wanted of us before he was shot, was to come in here, pull this kid sheriff away from the fire and clean up Roarty's crowd. Yuh're in the crowd, now, huh?"

Aspen nodded.

"All right. But it'll be a long time 'fore they know they kin trust yuh. They'll give yuh a bunch of piddlin' jobs runnin' squawkers that lost in their games out of the county. That's about the way it goes, ain't it?"

Again Aspen nodded. Stubby was having one of his thinking-out-loud spells, and more often than not they led to something.

"Now," Stubby said slowly, "unless yuh aim to stay here for a couple of months, we got to bust this wide open, don't we?"

"How?"

Stubby leaned back against the wall and rolled a smoke, lighted it, and smoked it down before he answered.

"Here's one time I beat yuh to it, pardner," he grinned.

"Let's have it."

"All right. There's mines in this county, ain't there?"

"A lot of 'em west of McGaffey." Aspen nodded.

"All right," Stubby said. "Supposin' my name was Saunders. Supposin' that I was sent out here by an insurance company."

"What insurance company?"

"A company that insures gold shipments."

Aspen stared at him a full moment, then rose.

"Catch on?" Stubby asked.

Aspen was already heading for the door.

"Wait a minute!" Stubby called.

"I already know what yuh're goin' to say," Aspen called over his shoulder. "Get yore story fixed up. I'm bringin' back the sheriff."

Two minutes later, Aspen was talking to Ben Holt.

"That's how it lays," he finished. "I'm in with them. They'll swallow it all. Now what I want yuh to do is this. Do yuh know a mine owner here in the county?"

"Curt Hand," Holt nodded. "He owns the Red Head high up in the San Tolars. Good friend of mine."

"Then ride up there tonight," Aspen said. "Get that all fixed up so a fake gold shipment will be ready in two days. Kin yuh do it?"

Holt nodded immediately and for the first time since Doc Whalen was shot, he smiled.

"I think yuh got it, Aspen. I hope yuh have."

"I know I have," Aspen said, rising. "How's Doc today?"

"Still unconscious. When he does come out of it, though, he won't be able to tell yuh any more than I will about who shot him."

"I got a hunch that will work out with this, too," Aspen said, as he stepped outside.

He found Storr in the Ocotillo. He was standing behind a faro table, watching the play, when Aspen touched his elbow and motioned him away.

"Yuh better come down and cork that fat jasper. He's yellin' his head off," Aspen said, when they were out of earshot of the curious crowd.

"What about?"

"Wants the sheriff. I asked him if I'd do and his mouth jest flopped open. He says he's got to talk to yuh."

"But what about?"

"He's shore makin' a noise." Aspen shrugged.

"I'll go down with yuh," Storr said.

They found Stubby yelling through the bars.

When Storr and Aspen came in together, he subsided.

"What do yuh want?" Storr asked brusquely.

"Plenty," Stubby growled. He indicated Aspen. "Is that jasper really a deputy?"

Storr nodded.

"What does he do? Take his badge off when he wants to cheat in card games?"

"Mebbe he better cool off a little more," Aspen said to Storr.

"Wait a minute, now Sheriff. Take it easy," Stubby

yelled when Storr turned to go out.

"Git it over," Storr growled.

"I got to git out of here," Stubby said. "I *got* to, I tell yuh."

"Yuh should have thought of that before yuh called a man a cold-decker."

"Gee, Sheriff. Listen to me a minute, will yuh?" When Storr nodded, Stubby said, "Tell that big jasper to git out of here."

"If he goes, I go with him," Storr said.

"All right, then," Stubby sighed. "Now look here. My name's Saunders. I work for an insurance company, see? This company insures gold shipments against robbery, flood, fire, tornadoes and acts of God in general, see?"

Storr nodded, his eyes curious.

"Well, I was sent by my company to guard a shipment of gold from a mine, clean through on the stage to Phoenix."

"What mine?" Storr asked. "In this county?"

"Yeah."

"What mine?"

Stubby looked pleasingly at Aspen who cautiously pointed to his red neckerchief, then to his head.

"The Neck and Head mine," Stubby grinned.

Storr stared at him blankly. Aspen, behind Storr, shook his head and pointed again to his red neckerchief, then to his hair. He took a strand of his hair between his fingers. Just then Storr turned around and Aspen smoothed his hair.

"He sounds daffy to me," Aspen said soberly.

"No, that ain't it!" Stubby said. "I forgot. It's the Red Head mine."

"Who owns it? Who sent for yuh to come?" Storr was still suspicious.

* * *

Aspen held up a hand behind Storr's head.

"Hand was his name," Stubby said.

"What's his first name?" Storr demanded.

"How in hell should I know," Stubby said curtly. "I didn't read the letter. I was told."

"All right," Storr said. "What about it?"

"Well, this here shipment is comin' down tomorrow night. I drifted in town today aimin' to ask yuh for a loan of a deputy to help me." He indicated Aspen. "Then I run into him."

"Look here, Sheriff," Stubby pled, when Storr's face showed no sympathy, "I admit I was a sorehead. But it ain't no reason for keepin' me in here until I lose my job. Come on. Be a good fella."

He looked so heartbroken and downcast that he seemed ready to cry. Storr shrugged, and indicated Aspen.

"This is the jasper that'll prefer charges against yuh. He's the one yuh shot at."

"I take it all back, Mister. Lemme out, will yuh?" Stubby looked pleadingly at Aspen.

"I dunno," Aspen said thoughtfully. To Storr he said, "What do yuh think?"

"Why, it'll be all right with me, Aspen." Storr suddenly grinned. "Only, yuh're the only deputy we got here and I'm damned if I'll ride up there jest to ride back on a buckboard with a shotgun across my knee. If yuh want to go, drop the charges and I'll let him out."

"I think I'll prefer charges." Aspen shook his head.

Stubby almost wept. His pleading was eloquent, designed to wring tears from stone. At last, Aspen got sick of hearing it.

"Oh, all right, I'll drop 'em. But not before yuh take back what yuh said about my cheatin' at cards."

"I do!" Stubby said fervently. "I never meant it!"

Storr grinned and went back for the key. In a moment he returned and let Stubby out.

"I'll hightail it up there now. Yuh drift up some time Monday and we'll bring the stuff down that night," Stubby said to Aspen.

"To where?" Aspen asked.

"McGaffey. I'll pick up the early mornin' stage there."

Aspen nodded and the three of them went out. Stubby thanked them both fervently, then stepped out in the street to get his horse.

Storr, watching him, laughed.

"That's mighty white of yuh, Aspen. If yuh wanted to be mean, he'd be out of his job."

"Everybody deserves a chance," Aspen said, "although he'll git fired some day for bein' too dumb to keep out of trouble. I jest put it off."

They separated, and this time Aspen headed for the Ocotillo. The bartender said Roarty was in, and Aspen knocked on the office door. Roarty greeted him with a grin.

"Worked swell, didn't it?"

"Yuh'll think it's a little too good to be true when you hear this." Aspen nodded.

"What?"

Aspen told him the fat poker player was an insurance field agent named Saunders and that he had called Storr in to beg for his release. Slowly, skillfully, Aspen told the story, making it appear as if Storr had heard it all, which he had.

"Then I got to thinkin'," Aspen said, smiling a little. "If jest me and him was guardin' that gold shipment and we was jumped by a dozen rennihans, there's nothin' much we could do, is there?"

Roarty slowly rose out of his chair, whistling an exclamation.

"Man! Yuh hit the biggest thing that's ever come our way!" He walked over to Aspen and wrung his hand. There was a broad and grateful smile on his red face. "This has earned yuh a fifth cut out of it, Aspen."

"Well, I'm new," Aspen said. "I didn't exactly know whether yuh had men enough to swing it or not, but I thought it'd be a good chance."

"I have the men," Roarty said eagerly. "And I'll swing it."

It took only a few minutes to settle the details of where Roarty's men would wait for the shipment on the mine road down to McGaffey.

"Yuh don't know the road, of course, but yuh'll recognize that lightnin' blasted pine by the rim rock on the way up. It'll be there we'll do it." He grinned delightedly and rubbed his hands together. "How much gold is comin' out? Did he say?"

"Didn't mention it. Enough to have an insurance company send a guard, though."

"We'll find that out right here after the stuff is brought in," Roarty chuckled. "After all the runnin' around is over and the sheriff can't find a trace, yuh come back here. I'll have the stuff brought in here and yore share will be waiting."

After being thanked again, Aspen started to leave when Roarty called him back.

"Another thing I almost forgot," he said. "Yuh ain't seen a couple of strangers ride into town from the north today, have yuh?"

"I wouldn't know a stranger from anybody else," Aspen said, as he shook his head.

"That's right," Roarty said. "Well, if yuh see any suspicious characters, ask somebody who they are. If they're strangers, come let me know, will yuh?"

"Be glad to," Aspen said.

Outside, he cursed softly. Roarty then was the man

71

who had had Doc Whalen shot. How else would he know that Doc had sent to McGaffey for a couple of strangers? That score would be evened up when the others were, Aspen vowed.

Things were shaping up. He decided to drop in and see how Doc Whalen was doing.

IV
THE HOLDUP

The next night Curt Hand, Stubby and Ben Holt were waiting at the neat company shack when Aspen pulled into the clearing that held the shaft and buildings of the Red Head mine.

Hand was a big man, dressed in faded khaki breeches and shirt, and he smoked a pipe which seemed to have grown into his wide and pleasant mouth. He shook hands with Aspen and asked if he had eaten. Upon learning that he hadn't, he took him into the shack and rustled up a meal which had been waiting on the stove.

"What'd Roarty say?" Stubby asked while Aspen was eating. He was so eager for news he couldn't wait until Aspen was finished.

"Swallowed it. He'll have his men waitin'."

"Where'll he take the stuff?" Holt asked.

"Back to the office. I'm to call for my share there."

Afterwards, while Holt was hitching up the buckboard, Hand showed Aspen the thick chest which was to hold the gold. It was double padlocked, stuffed with several canvas sacks of gravel, so that its weight would not be questioned.

"The chances are," Hand said, "they'll take the buckboard away from yuh when they find there's so much, and that they can't carry or open the chest. They'll want to leave a horse for yuh to ride in on, but they won't dare do it because Stubby will suspect yuh. Yuh'll be afoot, then. Ben and I will ride down a half hour after yuh with two extra horses. Think of anything else?''

Aspen couldn't. He smoked, and then they went outside, Stubby and Hand carrying the chest, which was placed between two two-by-fours nailed to the floor of the buckboard to brace it.

It was dark when they pulled out of the clearing, Stubby with a shotgun across his knees, Aspen at the reins.

"How's Doc?" Stubby said.

"Better. I saw him this morning when I left. He recognized me but he couldn't talk."

"If this goes through he ought to talk," Stubby said. "Yuh know, I think he really likes this Storr kid."

"Dan's all right," Aspen conceded. "He jest needs a little salt on his tail."

They were perhaps an hour from the mine, when the road started to wind around the side of a butte. Aspen waited until he was sure.

"Pretty soon, now," he said.

"I'd like to shoot at those whippoorwills," Stubby said grimly.

"Don't yuh do it, or they'll cut us to doll-rags. When they yell, yuh give up."

But they didn't yell. As Aspen swung around the bend and saw the stark and jagged limbs of the lightning-struck pine gauntly silhouetted against the sky, there came a shot that whistled over their heads and on the heel of it, a thunder of horses' hooves which seemed to surround them.

"What's goin' on here?" Stubby yelled.

"A stick-up," someone shouted, and shot. Stubby groaned as he slid out of the seat, and Aspen cursed the

73

horses as he fought them. He managed to get a gun out and shoot into the air before it was knocked out of his hand by a downsweeping rifle barrel.

"One more break like that, buddy, and yuh'll git it in the guts," somebody said from the ground beside him. "Git down out of there. Yore horses are held."

Aspen cursed helplessly, but none the less fervently. He wondered bleakly if they had killed Stubby, but to ask them to see would give the whole thing away.

Once on the ground he was disarmed and a gun jabbed in his back. Someone struck a light, and by its flare he could see Stubby sprawled backward over the chest. They hauled him off.

"Shoulder. It's bleedin' a little. He's out cold," was the announcement.

Then they examined the box and found it padlocked. One of the men, whom Aspen could not see, came up to him.

"The damn thing's padlocked," he swore.

"Take the buckboard," Aspen whispered. "I'll stick out here till mornin' and flag the mail on the way to the mine."

"I oughta' leave yuh a horse."

"Hell, no!" Aspen said. "It'll put off discovery that much longer. Besides, if Saunders comes to, he'd think it was funny."

"Tough luck, Aspen." The man laughed.

"Tough, hell," Aspen growled. "It's worth it."

After a lot more cursing, two of the men climbed into the seat of the buckboard and drove off, leaving Aspen standing in the night. He ran over to Stubby and knelt by him.

"That was plenty clumsy," Stubby drawled quietly. "Yuh'd think they never done it before."

"How bad yuh hurt?" Aspen asked.

"Nicked in the shoulder. I thought I'd faint and hear

it all.''

"Let's look at it.'' Aspen bandaged it as best he could, first pouring dust over it so the blood would clot. Then they sat by the roadside to wait for Holt and Hand. It seemed an eternity till they came, but when they did it was to bring horses, guns, shellbelts and even bandages, which Hand had thought of at the last minute.

Stubby was bandaged and they set out, this time in no particular hurry, since they wanted to give the buckboard time enough to reach Seven Troughs.

It was close to three when the four of them pulled into the alley behind the jail.

"I'm goin' to look, first,'' Aspen said as they dismounted.

He crept down the alley until he could see the buckboard still waiting behind the Ocotillo. The saloon was dark, except for a light in the office window. Aspen went down between the two buildings, climbed a rain barrel and from this vantage point he saw several heads through the office window. It was enough.

He returned to the other.

"This time it may take a while. Yuh better wait at the back door to see none of 'em get away,'' he said.

Then he went around and let himself in the office. He did not light a light, but walked straight to the door that let into Storr's room.

"Another step and I'll shoot,'' he heard Storr say as he swung it open.

"It's me,'' Aspen said quietly. "Don't light a light.''

"What's up?'' Storr asked.

Aspen walked over and sat on the bed. He did not know how to begin this, but he plunged.

"Dan, how well do you know Roarty?''

"Pretty well,'' Storr said. He was sitting up now, his

75

voice almost excited.

"Trust him?"

"Shore. He'll do to ride the river with."

"Yuh don't think he'd steal, then?"

"I know he wouldn't."

"I know he would, did, has," Aspen said. And before Storr could answer, he launched into the story, telling it from the time he and Stubby had helped Doc Whalen out of a jam in McGaffey. He gave Storr facts, and drove them home with a blunt, homely speech that neither criticized nor blamed.

"So yuh see yore friend Mike Roarty is a crook, and a pretty cheap one. A crook, a robber and a killer, for it was his men that gunned Doc, remember."

"Where is he now?"

"In his office with that crowd of gunnies countin' out the Red Head gold."

Storr climbed out of bed and silently got into his clothes. He only spoke once, and then it was humbly, grimly.

"I've been a fool, haven't I, Aspen."

"A damned fool," Aspen corrected gently. "No sign yuh have to be one all yore life."

"I hope not," Storr said.

"Have yuh thought how we're goin' to get in?" Storr asked when he was dressed.

"Back door. They were likely too excited to lock it."

Outside, the others were called together and a plan discussed.

"Plan, hell! We'll walk right in and shoot," Storr broke in.

And carrying out his words, he walked up to the back door, opened it and stepped inside before anyone could stop him.

"What's got into him?" Stubby said.

"Conscience," Aspen said. "Come on. There'll be

plenty of smoke.''

As they stepped in, they heard the mumble of voices from the office which served to cover up the little noise they made as they tiptoed down the length of the room to the bar.

Storr paused here in front of the door, and whispered.

''Ready?''

Without waiting for a reply, he palmed the knob softly, then flung the door open, leaping into the room.

There were eight men crowded into the room. The chest was on the floor, and Roarty and Hardwick were working on it with hammers, screwdrivers, and files.

As the door swung open, they looked up into the twin barrels of Storr's guns.

''Hello, Danny,'' Roarty said very weakly. ''We got—''

''The gold from the Red Head,'' Storr said grimly. ''This is yore last play, Roarty. Fight or surrender.''

Roarty, for all his crookedness, had guts. He reached out, yanked Hardwick in front of him, and streaked for his guns, just as Storr's gun blasted out.

Aspen jumped in beside him, his guns already spouting orange, their rocketing crash drowning curses and yells. Storr's first shot caught Hardwick in the head as he was pulled in front of Roarty, but it was Aspen's slugs that nailed Roarty in the chest as Hardwick fell. Roarty's guns were clear of leather, but he never got them raised.

He was driven back against the wall under a hail of lead. Then Aspen was driven into the room by Stubby, who wandered in, and the place turned into a six-by-eight shambles. Men picked up chairs because their guns were useless in these quarters, and a fog of gunsmoke strangled them. But they would not give up.

One man leaped at Aspen, and Aspen, his guns empty, went down with him. In the stamping, tromping mass of maniac fighting, Aspen got his hands around the man's throat and was slowly strangling him until another man piled down on top of him.

Holt and Hand were in the room now, shooting, slugging and clubbing. The table holding the light crashed over and the place was in darkness. Aspen leaped for the door, arriving the same time another man did. They tangled and went down, and Aspen, now that his arms were free, clubbed the man into insensibility.

When he was through, he realized that the shooting had stopped and that a man was standing in front of him.

"I've got a loaded gun here," the voice announced, and it was Storr's. "Anyone tries to git out, they shoot me. How about it?"

He got only groans for an answer. Then he struck a match. By the flare of it, they could see the heaped bodies on the floor. One man, his hands high above his head, sat against the wall, terror in his eyes. Stubby was lying with a dead man on top of him. Holt, erect and bloody, was in one corner, his guns trained on the room; Hand lay on his face, twisting around trying to rise. His leg was covered with blood, but he was smiling.

"You watch that man, Ben," Storr said to Holt, as he turned and went out. Stubby crawled out from under his burden and picked up Hand, while Aspen lighted the lamp again. Only the chimney had broken.

"We'll take Hand over to the Doc, Ben. We'll send someone over."

Aspen and Stubby each took one of Hand's arms and between them carried him out, and headed down the street to the Overland. They met people running toward the saloon, and Aspen told them to go in and help Holt.

In the lobby of the Overland they laid Hand in a chair. Down the corridor they could see a door open and light issuing from it.

Aspen went down and entered. It was Doc Whalen's room. He was lying propped up in bed, a smile on his pale face. Doc Layton, the visitng doc, was standing beside him. On the other side of the bed, Sue English was standing proudly and Storr's bloody arm was around her.

"Customer out here, Doc," Aspen announced and Layton went out to Hand. Aspen walked over slowly to Doc Whalen and Doc extended a hand. Aspen took it and grinned.

"Yore sheriff cleaned things up after all, Doc," Aspen said quietly.

"I did not," Storr announced flatly, and to Doc Whalen he said, "Here's the man who did it, Doc—him and his partner and Ben Holt and Curt Hand. I was a blind damn fool who jest got tolled in on the tail end of this ruckus."

"Hell, yuh'll make a sheriff, son," Doc Whalen said softly.

Sue came across to Aspen and held out her hand.

"You'll never know how much you've done for me, Mr. Aspen. I—"

"Forget it," Aspen said.

"We never will," Storr put in. "It's taken all this to show what a damn fool a Storr can be."

"And a fighter, too," Aspen added. He turned wearily, smiled at them all and went out in the hall. Stubby was waiting for him.

"How's Hand?"

"Jest nicked."

They stepped out into the night.

"Did yuh git that shoulder fixed?" Aspen asked sternly.

"That ain't what's hurtin'," Stubby said. He looked at Aspen. "I got the saddle itch."

"So've I, pardner," Aspen said quietly. "We'll cure that tomorrow."

"We always have," Stubby said quietly and began to whistle softly, "Over the River and Far Away."

LEAD WON'T LIE

I
TROUBLE BETWEEN PARTNERS

The Friday night crowd had thinned considerably on Sabinal's main street, and the store lamps were being extinguished one by one. Will Kehoe's Gem Saloon on the four corners, however, was contriving to make up in noise and light for the rest of the town, so that Otey Davis, who was waiting for Fred Farnum to lock his store and join him in their usual nightcap, observed, "Better stop in at my place for your drink, Fred. Sounds like the Bench cowboys have took on the job of raising the Gem roof a good three feet."

As if in contradiction to his statement, the noise in the Gem dribbled off into silence. Seconds later, Jim Hutchins shouldered through the doors of the saloon, and with scarcely a pause in his stride, ducked under the tie-rail and headed across the dusty street.

He was a young man, thick and well built in the shoulders. Around the narrow waist of his frayed and faded Levis there was no belt or gun.

Hutchins was just past the middle of the street when a man stepped through the still swinging doors of the

Gem and shouted at him, "Come back here, you yellow-bellied crook, and hear the rest of it!"

Jim Hutchins didn't even pause in his determined stride.

The man in the door laughed nastily. "The feudin' man from the mountains," he taunted. "Won't fight without a gun, and won't carry a gun."

Jim Hutchins stopped abruptly in midstride and turned in time to catch the laughter of the men who jammed the doorway behind his tormentor.

Slowly, Jim retraced his steps as far as the tie-rail, on which he leaned both elbows. He thumb-prodded his Stetson back off his forehead and regarded the young man on the steps with thoughtful intentness.

"You drunk, Jeff?" he asked in a voice whose mildness surprised the listening men.

"No. You think I got to be drunk to name you?"

"I always reckoned you did," Jim drawled. "I been partners with you three months, and I learned one thing about you. Without a bellyful of whiskey, you ain't got the guts to ask for a second cup of coffee."

Jeff Warnow swore under his breath and stalked over to the tie-rail, his hands fisted at his side. He was a tall young man, lean, with a thin face that had turned gray with anger.

"I'm warnin' you," Jim Hutchins said, without even raising his voice, "don't climb aboard unless you aim to stay the whole trip."

Jeff lashed out at him. Jim ducked, reached out and grabbed Jeff's shirt and hauled the man toward him. Then he hit him, and the sound rose above the shuffling of the men who were spilling out of the Gem. Jeff tripped on the boardwalk and sprawled on his back. He was up in a second. Jim Hutchins slowly backed out into the road. Jeff ducked under the tie-rail on the run, and then they met.

There was no skill, no patience, no cunning in their fighting. The two men set to it gladly, in silent fury, as if it were something for which they had been waiting a long time. Jeff was the more eager, and, arms flailing, he took anything Jim gave as long as he stayed erect to return it.

But Jim Hutchins fought with a kind of savage, indomitable hotheadedness. He crowded Jeff, aiming at his body, pulling him off balance and then pouring solid smashing blows under Jeff's guard. It was not so much clever fighting as it was the fighting of a man raised to it, who had raging inside himself.

As Jeff took a wild swing, Jim ducked down, and when he came uncoiled his fist slogged into Jeff's chest just above the heart. Jeff folded at the hips, took a step backward and fell into the crowd. Two men caught him, stood him on his feet and, without hesitating he lunged in again.

This time one of Jeff's wild blows ripped through Jim's guard and set him back on his heels. A second unexpected blow put Jim down in the dust on his back. Jeff rushed in, but Jim rolled aside and came up with a lacing uppercut that every man in that silent crowd heard connect with Jeff's skin.

Jeff straightened up almost mechanically, and then he started to weave on his feet. Jim came in then in a fury of vicious wicked hooks, and in the midst of the barrage, Jeff's knees buckled and he folded up like an empty sack.

Jim stood over him a second, breathing deeply, and then he looked up at the spectators who were watching with tense interest. There was not a man there whose eyes held any friendliness toward him.

Two punchers stepped forward and knelt by Jeff Warnow. Then one of them looked up at Jim.

"If you're smart, mister," he said bleakly, "you'll light a rag before these Staircase riders hear about this. Jeff Warnow might have been disowned by his old man, but the Staircase riders will still stick up for the kid."

"That'll be a pretty sorry pastime for anybody that tries it," Jim said dryly. He turned on his heel, picked up his Stetson, and walked across the street to the opposite boardwalk.

He strode through the archway at the feed stable, down the drive and out to the horse corral, where a big watering trough stood. A lantern hung from a nail on an upright close by so that the late revelers could see to get their horses.

Jim stripped off his shirt and soused his burning face and knuckles in the water. He was not a particularly big man, but the thick muscles that lay in flat ropes over his shoulders and chest told of work. There was a set to his jaw, too, that suggested that this work had not been easy. But a man could see none of that in the deep-set gray eyes. They neither protested nor defied; they were the eyes of a man well tempered by trouble.

When he came up spluttering the last time and reached for his shirt to dry himself, Jim saw a motionless figure seated on the top pole of the corral. That man had not been there when he came. Once the water was wiped out of his eyes, Jim recognized Sheriff George Neil. The lawman's gaunt and bony frame was hunched over, elbows on knees, and he sucked at a straw that projected at a sharp angle from under his straggling gray mustache. He and Jim looked at each other for some seconds.

"You picked up a nice shiner," Sheriff Neil remarked at last.

"Sure," Jim said, and ran his fingers through his thick chestnut hair.

"You can fight," Neil declared.

"I could have told Jeff that before we started."

The sheriff murmured assent, watching Jim put on his torn shirt.

"What was it all about?" Neil asked suddenly.

"You see it?"

"Sure. Heard it, too. What did he say that graveled you so?"

Jim looked up swiftly, but the sheriff's face was guileless. "Were you in the saloon?" Jim asked levelly.

"Nope."

Buttoning his shirt, Jim made his explanation in a matter-of—fact voice. "I come into this country three months ago with a hundred and fifty cows. I was lookin' for grass, because it was close to calvin' time. Jeff Warnow had this piece of land his old man gave him when he kicked him out, but he didn't have any stock. Jeff and me made a deal." He regarded the sheriff closely now. "Jeff was to supply the range, and I was to give him half the calf crop. But as soon as the calves were born, Jeff claimed half of them and then tried to kick me off the range. I wouldn't go." He added to that firmly and suddenly. "I won't go, either. That's what I told him in the saloon."

Sheriff Neil shifted the straw to the other side of his mouth. "You were right," he said. "About the calves, I mean. But not about goin'."

Jim Hutchins became immobile. He stared at the sheriff from eyes that looked smoky in the light of the lantern. "You kickin' me off?"

"Can't," Neil declared. "Don't want to, neither. Only I reckon it would be wise if you took your herd and vamoosed."

"I don't get it," Jim said mildly.

Sheriff Neil seemed reluctant to speak. He cleared

his throat twice, and then spoke in a persuasive tone. "Hutchins, I know what you're buckin'. You see, I know where you come from, an' so does everybody else around here. You come from over in Weyboldt County. They say you're the only survivor of a feud over there that killed nine men."

Jim didn't say anything, and the sheriff took his silence for assent.

"You can't help it, but you're a marked man. Folks are afraid of you, and when a man is afraid, he's unfriendly. And then you had to get in this fight."

" 'Had to,' is just about correct, sheriff," Jim pointed out.

"I know, I know, but look," Sheriff Neil said earnestly. "Jeff Warnow is so no good his old man even gave him up. But he's growed up in this county. He's goin' to marry Nancy Whitehill, about the nicest girl any of us ever knew. And you—well, you're just a hard-case stranger that beat up Jeff Warnow. Don't you see what you're buckin'?"

"I see," Jim said slowly. "What do you want me to do?"

"Pick up your herd and drift on and forget about us."

Jim was silent a long moment, staring at the lawman. Then he shook his head. "I don't do things that way, sheriff. I think I'll stick."

Sheriff Neil climbed down off the corral fence. Upright, he was a tall man, stooped at the shoulders, and there was something about his slow movements and his mild voice that was friendly and wise.

"I didn't think you would," he said. "Good night, son."

"Good night."

Neil started to walk away, and then paused and turned to regard Jim. "Do somethin' for me, will you, son?''

"Anything short of runnin'," Jim answered.

"Don't go out to your place tonight. A couple of Laurel Leaf riders took Jeff out. Give him time to cool off before you go back.''

"All right," said Jim, and his squarish face set in a frown, watched the sheriff go out through the stable drive to the street. A man who had seen tonight's happenings, had heard tonight's conversation between Sheriff Neil and Jim Hutchins was pondering the sheriff's advice, or something equally grave.

But he wasn't. He was only wondering, as poor men will, where he was going to get the money to pay for a hotel room this night. And like a sensible man, he decided not to try. He had his soogans on his saddle. He'd sleep out in the brush at the edge of town.

II
GAMBLER'S ADVICE

Next morning, in Fred Farnum's Emporium, the clerk did not make any comment on the fact that the man he was waiting on had a black eye that was turning into a purplish green. Nor did he comment on the fact that the man's shirt was hanging on only by ribbons. He gave him a sack of flour, received the money, thanked him civilly, and Jim Hutchins walked out to his horse at the tie-rail in front of the store.

Throwing the sack of flour over the saddle, Jim paused long enough to pull out a sack of tobacco and make a cigarette. He heard a team and buckboard pull in to one side of him, but since there was scarcely a soul in this town he knew well enough to speak to, he did not turn.

He was surprised then, to hear a woman's voice say

pleasantly, "Good morning, Jim."

Sweeping off his hat, Jim turned. Nancy Whitehill was perched on the seat of the buckboard, and her grave face was quizzical as she regarded him. She was a slim girl, narrow-hipped even in Levis, and the flat broad-brimmed hat she was wearing hid a mass of corn-colored hair that was done in a loose knot at the nape of her neck.

If there was anyone Jim did not want to see on this morning, it was Nancy Whitehill. But when he looked at her eyes, the warm friendly blue of them reassured him a little.

"Mornin', Miss Whitehill."

"Nancy, Jim, for the tenth time." She smiled, and surprisingly enough, Jim smiled back. She jumped lightly to the ground, spurning his offer of help. Facing him, she was some inches shorter than he, so that she had to look up when she carefully regarded his bruised eye.

"I heard about it," she said.

Jim fumbled with his hat. "From Jeff?"

"No, Larry was there and saw it." Larry was Nancy's brother and Jeff Warnow's best friend. Jim wondered what was coming next.

"I'm glad you did it, Jim," Nancy said suddenly. "He had it coming to him."

Jim's face showed his surprise, and Nancy said swiftly, with an undercurrent of irritation in her voice, "Did you expect me to stick up for him?"

"No, I don't reckon . . . only, well, seein' as you and Jeff are . . . well—"

"Well, what?" Nancy asked coolly.

Jim cleared his throat. "You know what I mean," he said stubbornly.

"I think I do. You think because there's some talk about my marrying Jeff that I ought to side in with him." Her eyes were suddenly sharp, and her voice took on a firmer tone. "There's just two things wrong with that, Jim. In the first place, I don't think I'm going to marry Jeff. I don't want to marry any man who cheats his partner. And in the second place, even if I was, I don't think that would stop me from telling the truth."

Jim said nothing to that. "It's going to be bad for you, isn't it, Jim?" Nancy continued.

"It'll work out," said Jim.

Nancy impulsively put a hand on his arm. "It's got to, Jim. You see, I have an interest in this quarrel, too. Because if Jeff doesn't admit he's wrong, then I don't want to see him again."

She flushed a little at her words, murmured good-by, and slipped under the tie-rail. On the walk, she paused and turned back to Jim, who was still watching her.

"Will you do me a favor, Jim?"

"Anything," Jim said, and he meant it.

"Will you tell Will Kehoe something for me? I can't very well go into the Gem and tell him myself."

"Sure."

"Tell him that Larry says he'll have it for him to-morrow. Just that. And thanks."

She went on into the store and Jim headed toward the saloon. The girl's friendliness had thawed out his gloom, and he had a warm feeling for her that he tried to explain to himself. He knew what it was, all right. It was the bare fact that save for Sheriff Neil, Nancy Whitehill was the one person in Sabinal who, in all these three months, had had a friendly and kind word for him.

Somehow, Nancy understood that his brusque talk, his quick temper and his stubborn ways were a defense that only time would melt. And with a woman's under-standing, she had chosen to overlook them and be friendly to a stranger. Jeff Warnow, Jim thought somberly, was getting a girl he could neither understand nor appreciate.

The Gem was deserted at this hour of the morning, save for the half dozen men who seemed to be in Will Kehoe's employ, but never appeared to do any work. They were a hard-faced bunch, and they regarded Jim with quiet hostility as he passed them. He was used to that look from this town.

Beyond the bar were a dozen gaming tables, and beyond that the dance floor. Against one side wall, stairs rose to a balcony on which the rooms of the percentage girls opened, and a swamper was sweeping the balcony now. At one of the poker tables Will Kehoe was going over his accounts while a second swamper cleaned out his office at the end of the bar.

Kehoe was a big man and had undoubtedly been an active man once, but the soft flesh of easy living had overtaken him. Looking at him, Jim was reminded of a mushroom that could not stand the light of the sun.

At Jim's approach Kehoe looked up, revealing a face that was at once handsome and webbed by deep lines of dissipation. The dead-black frock coat and black string tie that he always wore only emphasized the doughy color of his face. His black eyes were veiled as Jim came to a stop in front of him.

"Larry Whitehill says he'll have it for you tomorrow," Jim reported.

Will Kehoe stared at him a long moment. "What are you talkin' about?" he drawled.

"I dunno," Jim said. "His sister told me to tell you that."

Kehoe frowned, as if trying to remember something, but his hard eyes continued to regard Jim craftily.

"Oh," he said suddenly, smiling.

"The spurs. Sure. Larry had a pair of old Spanish ones that he thought I might like to buy. Thanks."

Jim nodded, and was about to turn when Kehoe said, "In a hurry, Hutchins?"

"No." Jim paused, looking down at the gambler, who tilted back in his chair and rammed his thumbs in the lower pockets of his vest.

"I saw your fight last night," said Kehoe.

Jim didn't comment.

"You're a tough customer with your fists. I wondered how good you were with a gun."

"I never wear one," Jim said coolly.

"So I noticed. I just wondered why."

Jim looked at him intently. "What's that to you, Kohoe?"

The gambler shrugged, and regarded Jim levelly. "Nothin'. I'm just givin' you some friendly advice, and it don't matter a damn to me whether you take it or leave it."

"I haven't heard it yet."

"Wear a gun," Kehoe said bluntly. "I keep my ears open, Hutchins. I hear things around here that an ordinary man don't hear, and I heard somethin' last night. This town never liked you much, and after your scrap with Jeff, they don't like you at all. From now on, they'll start crowdin' you."

"Thanks," Jim said dryly. "Only I don't think much of the advice."

Kehoe's face was enigmatic. "No?"

"No. The safest man in any country is an unarmed man. Strap on a gun and you'll be crowded into usin' it. Don't wear one, and all you'll get is talk." Jim smiled faintly. "I can take talk. It's never killed me yet." He nodded to the saloon owner and walked out, aware that by his usual blunt manner he had added to the host of men here who already disliked him.

Mounted, Jim rode south out of town, with the sack of flour across his saddle. It was a fine desert morning, with the sky an empty bowl of deep-purple blue and the sun not yet hot enough to make riding uncomfortable. This valley of the Sabinal was poor range, as the White-hills with their Seven Cross outfit at the foot of the bench, were finding out. Its dry sage flats kept a steer gaunted from rustling for feed. But beyond, rising like the sharp rim of a pan, was the Sabinal bench, and there it was different. The big outfits like the Laurel Leaf, the Staircase and the Bar 88 all shared the bench, coming down to the desert only to ship cattle at Sabinal where the railroad turned north to get out of the valley.

Ahead, Jim could see the bold outlines of Ten Rock, almost black in the morning sun. At the base of the big butte was the stone shack he shared with Jeff Warnow. Their graze wasn't particularly good, but once up on the butte the land broke away in a long grassy slope to the south and the badlands, and it was that land over which he and Jeff were quarreling.

Riding closer, Jim looked off across the flats and saw a horse approaching the shack along the base of the butte. At first he thought it might be Jeff, but as both he and the rider converged on the shack, Jim recognized Larry Whitehill's gaudy pinto horse. Jim almost breathed a sigh of relief. With an audience of one, Jeff would be a little calmer, and there was less chance of trouble, even though Larry Whitehill was Jeff's friend.

Jim reached the yard of the shack some hundred yards ahead of Larry. He waved lazily before he dismounted and saw Larry's answering wave. Then he hefted the sack of flour to his shoulder and headed for the house.

The door was open, as if Jeff were home. Jim gave a call from the yard, walked inside—and stopped short.

There, on the dirt floor of the shack, lay Jeff Warnow. He had a bullet hole in his back, and the slow blood seep from the shot had channeled down the trough of his spine. Only the blood wasn't red now; it was brown.

Jeff Warnow was hours dead!

III
BLACKMAIL!

Jim was kneeling by Jeff, and had started to turn him over when he heard Larry Whitehill in the doorway.

"Well, well," the young rider said softly.

Jim looked up. Larry Whitehill had drawn his gun and had it leveled at Jim. For a brief moment they looked at each other, Jim wondering if Larry had as cool and sane a head as his sister. For the way young Larry Whitehill looked at that moment, it didn't seem as if he would have. He was a slim young man, quick, lean and high-strung, and at the moment his thin, aware face held a strange look of gloating. His blue eyes burned with a feverish fire, and his mouth was twisted into a sneer.

"Got him after all, didn't you, Hutchins?" Larry snarled.

Jim came to his feet. "That's a damn lie, Larry," he said quietly.

Larry laughed and stepped inside the shack. He stood with his back to the wall, and looked from Jim to Jeff's body and then back again.

"Well, that's one way to settle a quarrel, but it's a bushwhacker's way," he observed dryly.

"I wasn't even here last night," Jim said.

"Where were you?"

"I . . . well, I slept outside of town in the brush. I didn't come home."

93

"Anybody see you?"

"No."

Larry grinned and cocked his head. "Didn't I see a rifle out in your scabbard?"

Jim nodded.

"And Jeff was shot in the back with a rifle. Look how he's layin'."

Jim didn't need to look. There was an overturned water bucket at Jeff's head, and a dark spot on the floor where the water had soaked in. It was plain as sight that Jeff had gone to the spring house for water. The bushwhacker had waited out in the brush in the yard until Jeff returned with the full bucket. Framed in the doorway, the light behind him, Jeff was a perfect target.

"You had the motive," Larry said calmly. "You had the rifle and you don't have an alibi. That's goin' to be hard to explain to Sheriff Neil. And even if you can explain it to him, mister, you can't explain it to a jury."

They looked at each other a long moment, Larry with a kind of callow triumph in his expression. Jim found himself unaccountably sweating. With a half dozen questions, Larry had revealed Jim's position, with all its implications. It was true that he was the only man known to have quarreled with Jeff, and in public. And he didn't have an alibi. And what was worse, the town was willing to believe anything of him, an unfriendly man known to be the only survivor of a bloody feud.

Jim cleared his throat, and when he spoke he tried to keep the desperation out of his voice.

"If you'd let me talk, I could prove he killed himself," Jim said quietly.

Larry's face was suddenly attentive. "How?"

"By turnin' him over. He's lyin' on a gun, and there's a hole in his chest."

"Turn him over," Larry said skeptically.

This was what Jim had angled for. He straddled Jeff's body, so that he himself was between Larry and Jeff. Then with much more effort than Jeff Warnow's weight warranted, Jim turned him over. His head was lowered and out of the corner of his eye, he watched Larry's boots.

As Jim rolled Jeff over, Larry took a step to one side and approached closer to look. And in that moment Jim acted. He came uncoiled from his kneeling position and dived for Larry's waist. The gun went off with a bellow above him, as he hit Larry. They crashed into the stove, and then both went down, Jim on top.

Jim found the wrist of Larry's gun hand, pinned it to the floor and straddled him. The lighter man fought with a fury that was proving more futile each second. Finally, Jim said harshly, "I'm tryin' to keep from sluggin' you in the face, damn it! Lie still!"

Larry did. Jim pinned the young man's arms with his knees, then reached over and pried the gun from Larry's hand. In Larry's eyes there was a look of stark fear.

Jim came erect and palmed up the gun and Larry struggled to his feet. He glared at Jim, his face flushed with exertion. "All right, shoot me," he said bitterly. "I didn't mean to shoot at you, though."

"Don't talk like a fool," said Jim. "I don't aim to shoot you. We've got to talk, and I don't talk good lookin' down the wrong end of a gun barrel."

Jim indicated the bench, but Larry wouldn't sit down. In some way, Jim thought, he had to make this wild-faced kid see what had happened.

Suddenly, Larry Whitehill blurted out, "I don't think you killed him, Jim. I never did. Still, nothin' short of shootin' me will keep me from doin' what I'm goin' to. And I don't need to back it up with a gun."

"You mean you're goin' to Neil with the story of how you found Jeff?" Jim asked.

Larry nodded. "Unless you make a deal."

"Like what?"

"Money. If I get money, I won't go to Neil."

Jim stared at him intently. "What do you mean, you won't go to Neil? We've both got to go to Neil and tell him Jeff was murdered. All I want you to do is tell Neil we found Jeff out in the brush, and that I stayed at your place last night."

"We're not goin' to Neil," Larry said grimly. "We're buryin' Jeff."

"They'll miss him and make a search, you fool!"

"That's a chance we've got to take."

"Why?" Jim demanded hotly. "Why?"

"I'll tell you why!" Larry said, desperation in his voice. "You're goin' to give me money, Jim! Have you got any money?"

"No."

"Then instead, you're goin' to give me a bill of sale for your cattle and help me round 'em up. It'll take at least three days to round 'em up. Now, if we go to Neil with Jeff's body and I give you an alibi for the murder, we'd have to do it today. All right, once I've given you your alibi, what's to stop you from refusin' to give me the cattle?"

"A bill of sale."

"You could take that away at the point of a gun!"

"My word, then."

Larry shook his head stubbornly. "Nothin' doin', Jim. I can't take a chance. Once I've given Neil your alibi, you could double-cross me. If we bury Jeff, then I'll always have that body to make sure I get the cattle. Don't you see that?"

"But, you fool, they'll miss him, I tell you! We can't

96

hide him!''

''That's a chance you and me are goin' to take,'' Larry said stubbornly. ''We're playin' this my way—or else I'm ridin' in to Neil now with the straight story. Or you can shoot me. Take your choice.''

Jim stared at him a long moment, debating the thing. Then he tossed the gun on the table. A gun wouldn't do any good. Nothing would, short of shutting up Larry Whitehill forever, and he wouldn't do that. ''Take your choice,'' Larry had said. What choice had he? The straight of the story would get him hanged and Larry refused to provide him with a reasonable alibi. Nothing was left but to let himself be blackmailed out of all his cattle, and take the chance that nobody would ever find Jeff's body.

Yes, there was one more choice. Jim looked out the door at the tawny shimmering sage flats. He could slug this young fool over the head, mount his horse and ride away. But that was running, and Jim knew if he ever mounted that horse to run, he would never feel peace again.

''Well, what'll it be?'' Larry asked in a tight, tense voice.

''You know what it'll have to be. There's a shovel in the wagon shed and a dirt-floored *rincon* in the butte, about a mile west,'' Jim said wearily. ''Go ahead and dig. I'll build the coffin.''

The sun had heeled far over behind the distant blue sawtooths of the Santa Cruz Mountains when Jim and Larry Whitehill returned to the shack. Jeff Warnow was buried under six feet of dry dirt and a great heap of rock, slid down from the face of the butte, served as a headstone that only two men could read.

As Jim hunted for pen and paper, under Larry's wary gaze, he knew he was taking a step that was irrev-

97

ocable. He was putting his life in the hands of this fresh-faced, wild-eyed kid, and he didn't like it.

Seating himself at the table, he put the paper before him. Then he looked up at Larry. "There's just a couple of things you're goin' to answer, kid, before I do this."

"What?"

"How do I know you didn't kill Jeff? You were on the spot at just the right time to frame me."

Larry grinned cockily. "I had a date to meet Jeff this mornin'. Ask Sis. I told her. And I was home last night; Sis can prove it."

Jim nodded slowly. "What do you want the money for?" he asked quietly.

Larry's face hardened. "None of your damned business," he said harshly.

Jim didn't write. He kept staring at Larry until the latter's glance shifted.

"Get goin'!" Larry snarled. "It's too late to back out of this now!"

Jim looked down at the blank paper. Yes, it was too late to back out. Jeff's body was like a man with a gun standing at his elbow, forcing him to write. He wrote out a bill of sale and handed it to Larry.

"You and me will start the roundup tomorrow," Larry said, touching his hat brim in mock salute. "And much obliged."

Jim didn't say anything. But as he watched Larry mount and head for town, several things began to run through his mind. He was remembering the message Nancy had asked him to take to Will Kehoe that morning. Was this bill of sale the "it" that Larry was going to have for Kehoe tomorrow morning? And did Larry really have an alibi for Jeff's murder, as he so glibly stated? A slow anger was burning inside Jim as he watched Larry disappear over a ground swell out of the flats. He hated to be played for a sucker, especially by a smart-aleck kid. And even more than that, he hated the idea of burying a man like a dog, and then hiding the thing. Something was shaping up for trouble here, and at least he could try to find out what it was.

By the time Larry had vanished from sight, Jim's mind was made up. He ran for the corral, saddled his horse, then went along the face of the butte until he found the deep arroyo running north. He put his horse into it and lifted him into a long lope, a pace that was intended to beat Larry Whitehill to Sabinal.

Jim rode into town, left his horse in one of the alleys that backed the dusty main street, and took up his vigil in the darkness of a store front across from the Gem. Within twenty minutes he was rewarded by the sight of Larry pulling in to the tie-rail in front of the saloon.

Jim waited until the kid had shouldered through the swing doors. Then he crossed the street and, on tiptoe so as to see over the painted lower half of the Gem front window, watched the interior of the saloon.

Larry walked back to a poker game, spoke to Kehoe and together they disappeared in the saloon owner's office at the far end of the bar.

Certain that it was Kehoe who would receive the money from the cattle sale, Jim went down street to a lunchroom, wolfed down a meal, and, by the time he was finished, knew what he would have to do.

IV
AN OFFER FOR THE SEVEN CROSS

Once he had his horse again, he took the east road from town, heading for the Whitehill's place, the Seven Cross. The evening was still young when he rode through the break in the low foothills into the long val-

99

ley that sprawled deep into the bench. Here, in this valley, lay the Seven Cross buildings. Eli Whitehill had come late into this country, and so had had to content himself with the desert range of the valley flats. But as if to compensate for this, he had homesteaded this tight little valley behind the first rank of foothills, and there built his house. He had Sabinal Creek at his front door, timber at his back door, and a kind of paradise on all sides of him.

Lamps were lighted in two rooms of the Whitehills' adobe ranchhouse as Jim crossed the plank bridge over Sabinal Creek. As he rode into the yard he saw Nancy come out onto the long porch that ran the length of the house.

"Hurry up, Larry. Supper's cold," Nancy called into the darkness.

"It's me, Jim," was her answer, spoken in Jim's grave voice.

"Oh." Nancy sounded mildly startled. "Anything wrong, Jim?"

"Just callin' on neighbors," he replied more lightly. He tied his horse to the ring in the great cottonwood that shaded the house, and came up to the porch.

Nancy met him with a smile. "I thought maybe Larry was in trouble or something."

"Maybe he is," Jim said. "That's what I come out to talk about."

"Why, Jim, what's—"

"It's nothin'," he said slowly. "Just sit down and listen."

Nancy sat down on the top step and Jim sat beside her. He turned over in his mind what he was about to say, and he didn't like it. But he didn't see any way out of it.

"I just got to thinkin' about somethin' after I saw Kehoe this mornin'," he began, fumbling idly with his

100

hat. "You told me to tell him that Larry would have it for him tomorrow, didn't you?"

"Yes," Nancy said reluctantly.

"Kehoe thought I knew somethin' I didn't," Jim lied. He let it go at that, waiting.

"Oh, Jim, did he tell you about Larry's gambling?" Nancy cried.

"Not exactly," Jim said, "but I guessed it."

"I'm so ashamed," the girl said miserably. "And Kehoe promised not to tell anybody, too!"

"Is Larry in pretty steep?"

"Hopelessly steep, Jim," Nancy answered in a dull voice. "You wouldn't believe the sum if I told you. We may have to sell the Seven Cross."

"Because Kehoe's calling for his money?"

"Part of it. Just the tiniest bit, a payment. Oh, Jim, I don't know what's going to happen! If someone hadn't helped this time, I don't know what we'd have done. That's what I meant when I said that Larry would have it tomorrow. You see, Jeff promised to lend him the money."

In spite of himself, Jim made a movement of surprise. There was Larry's alibi, all right. He had ridden over to Jeff to borrow the money for a gambling debt. And this news, too, automatically let out Kehoe as a suspect in Jeff's murder, for he would certainly not destroy the source of Larry's money. Jim reflected bitterly that all his hunches were killed now before they were fully born.

Nancy was speaking again, and Jim roused himself. "Did he get the money from Jeff, I said," she repeated.

"He got the money, all right," Jim said, his mouth dry.

"What did Jeff say?"

"Well," Jim faltered, "he didn't say much. It was like—"

Nancy laid a hand on Jim's arm. "Listen," she said. "Someone's coming."

Jim came to his feet quickly. "I don't want Larry to know I'm here," he said.

Before Nancy had a chance to say anything, Jim faded back into the deep darkness of the porch. Then, not one rider, but three pulled up alongside Jim's horse at the cottonwood and dismounted. They came up the gravel walk, silent. Jim heard Nancy say, "good evening."

The men stopped. "Ah, good evening," their spokesman said—"Miss Whitehill?"

"Yes."

This man walked forward. In the thinned lamp glow, Jim could vaguely make him out to be a thick, burly man dressed in expensive broadcloth. His companions were dressed neatly, but not as showily as he.

"My name is Major Thornton, ma'am," He doffed his hat and bowed. "I have a little piece of business to talk over that might interest you."

Nancy came to her feet, smiling. "I doubt that, but come inside."

Jim felt his curiosity stirring. This strange trio of visitors interested him. Slowly, and feeling a little guilty, he tiptoed down the porch to the window of the living room, which was open, and looked through the curtains.

Nancy was seated in the chair by the lamp. Major Thornton stood with his back to the fireplace, one of his men on either side of him.

Jim passed up the major as a bland-faced, middle-aged man whose appearance told him nothing, and concentrated on his men, hoping for a clue there. The one on the left was a hawk-faced, pale-eyed Texan with an impassive, secretive face. Nothing there. And then Jim considered the other man, and in one second he knew that he had seen this man before.

While his mind fumbled back to the time and the place, he noted the man's hair, red almost to black, his flat nose which had evidently once been broken, and his pale freckled face that no sun could tan. And then Jim had it. This was Cas Ruffing, a border outlaw from Arizona. When the law in Weyboldt County had turned passive in the face of its long feud, Cas Ruffing had taken advantage of the fact to use it as a hide-out. When the feud ended and the law came back, Cas had had to run, but not before he had used the feud to cover half a dozen brutal killings.

The major, his cigar lighted, was talking. "I'm out here from the East for my health, Miss Whitehill. I passed this place this morning."

"Did you? I didn't see you," Nancy said.

"Oh, we stuck to the ridges. That's how I happened to get such a fine look at your little valley here." He shifted his feet and smiled amiably. "Not so long ago, I hated the thought of being condemned to the West for the rest of my life. In fact, I thought so until I saw this valley today. I'm completely won over." He paused. "Have you guessed what I've come for?"

"Why—no," Nancy admitted.

"I have my heart set on this place," the major said. Before Nancy could speak, he raised his hand. "Wait. I know what you folks out here think of Easterners who come West to buy up the land and the work that has gone into it. I have no apologies. All I can say is that the price I am willing to pay is the price you yourself set on it."

"But it's hardly for sale, Major Thornton."

"Exactly, exactly. I understand how you feel. But consider this." He came over and seated himself by Nancy, and went on talking in his persuasive, mellow voice. His two companions remained standing, their

103

faces impassive.

Jim backed away, climbed the rail and dropped to the soft dirt of the yard. He had heard enough, and it interested him. For one thing, this Major Thornton was a poor imitation of an Easterner. He looked like some spellbinding judge from an Arizona county. He had undoubtedly adopted this front merely as a pretext to try to buy Seven Cross.

Jim led his horse out of hearing distance, and then mounted. It seemed a little queer that this phony Easterner should come to Nancy Whitehill with his proposition just when Larry was so deep in debt that the sale of the Seven Cross might save him. Things were too well-timed, too neatly worked out.

And then there was Cas Ruffing. What was he doing here, with this major? Jim made a sudden and stubborn resolve to understand this business before it went any further, and, with this in mind, headed for town.

He rode into Sabinal, and dismounted in front of the Desert House, the town's one hotel. It was late and the streets were deserted, but the gang at the saloon was carrying on its usual noisy revelry.

Jim went into the lobby of the hotel and crossed to the desk, where the night clerk was reading the newspaper.

"I'm lookin' for a Major Thornton," Jim said. "He drifted in today?"

"Oh, yes. He's here. I mean he ain't here now, though."

Jim nodded and leaned on the desk, regarding the oldster. Lazily then, he pulled out his tabacco and rolled a cigarette, as if he had nothing better to do, for the register which would have told him what he wanted to know was not on the desk top.

"Sure he ain't in?" he asked finally. "I thought I

saw him come in about fifteen minutes ago."

"I tell you he ain't in," the clerk said.

Jim straightened up and put his cigarette in his mouth. "What's his room number. I'll go look."

"Seventeen and eighteen, them two big rooms at the back. Only you're wastin' your time. He left about seven thirty."

Jim shrugged. "Well, if you're sure, I won't bother. Thanks." He went outside. Walking down the street, he turned the corner, reached the alley, came up in back of the hotel and regarded it thoughtfully. The window that marked the end of the second floor corridor was open, and the lamp that was in the wall bracket beside it was guttering in the draft.

In the thick darkness, Jim began looking around for a way to get up to the window. He had taken two steps when he bumped his head sharply against an object that he could not see. Swearing softly, he put out his hand and touched a ladder that was leaning against the back of the hotel. For a moment he was puzzled and then he connected the open window with the ladder. Somebody else had also wanted to get into the hotel without being seen. Jim pondered this a moment, and made nothing of it.

Softly, then, he crawled up the ladder, climbed through the window and stood there listening. There was no sound. Then was a precautionary measure, he reached out and lifted the ladder to the left as far as he could reach.

Once that was done, he had his choice of Room 17 or Room 18, and he chose Room 17, because it was farthest from the window. At the door he softly tried the knob, and found the door locked. But the wide crack between the door and its jamb gave him some encouragement.

He fumbled in his pockets, found a nail that was left

105

over from the coffin-building that morning, and, using it as a pry, pushed the latch back and heard the door give. Silently and quickly, then, he stepped into the room and closed the door behind him.

He listened a moment, then satisfied, he struck a match whose flare revealed a bedroom. It revealed something else, too, for the connecting door into Room 18 was just swinging back into place.

Jim let the match die, his heart pounding. Had someone in Room 18 just closed the door, or had the draft from the corridor door swung it into place?

He walked softly to the connecting door and listened. Not a sound inside. Stepping to one side, Jim turned the knob and pushed the door open, flattening himself against the wall. Nothing moved, not a sound came out of the room.

He had been alarmed by a mere draft. Still moving quietly, however, he walked through the doorway. A soft swish gave him a warning, but no time in which to act.

Jim leaped to one side, off balance, just as something crashed into his body. He went down. As he struck the rug, he rolled as fast as he could, came to a stop, feeling a throb of pain in his shoulder. His hand was against a chair-leg. He came to his feet, picking up the chair, and waited.

Across the room there was a soft sound of footfalls on the rug. Jim hurled the chair and stepped aside. He heard its crash against a man's body, a muffled oath, and then the whole night exploded with the roar of a gun.

In its glare Jim knew he was seen, and he dropped to his knees just as the second shot bellowed out, and the slug slapped into the wall above him.

He rolled out into the room, groaning, and the other

man, apparently deceived by the groan, ran for the corridor door. As he swung it open, Jim could see only a figure of huge bulk. He allowed ten seconds to pass without moving, then he came to his feet and ran softly for the door. Peeking out, he saw that his assailant had been trapped by the moving of the ladder. He had swung out the window, hoping to catch the ladder by feeling for it with his feet, only to find it gone. Two pair of knuckles grasping the sill were the only parts of him visible.

Jim leaned out the window and struck a match on the sill, and in its flare he saw the strained face of Will Kehoe peering up at him.

"Help me!" Kehoe groaned. "The ladder's gone!"

"I'll help you," Jim said grimly. "Hold tight."

The steps of the clerk were sounding in the corridor now, and down the hall somebody had opened a door. Jim knew he had to get away quickly. Suddenly he swung out the window on top of Kehoe. It was too much for the gambler. He bellowed, "Help! Help! Get off, damn you!"

Spreading his legs, Jim let go and holding onto Kehoe's shoulders and then his coat—where he clung long enough to get the gambler's gun—and then his pants and his boots, he finally dropped the six feet to the ground. Kehoe, still bellowing, hung from the sill above.

"You want to talk, Kehoe?" Jim called.

"Get me off here!" moaned the gambler. "I can't hold on any longer! I'll do anything!"

Racing against the sound of footfalls that were pounding in the corridor, Jim found the fallen ladder and swung it under Kehoe. Shaking visibly, the gambler found the top rung. He half fell, half rolled down the ladder, and Jim caught him and yanked him back into the shadows of the woodshed just as the night clerk,

107

leaning out the window, a sputtering match in one hand and a gun in the other, peered down.

Jim rammed the gun into Kehoe's belly and together they waited until the clerk vanished inside.

Then Jim spoke savagely. "Talk yourself out of this, you whippoorwill!"

Kehoe, still breathing hard, brushed off his suit. "You come darn near givin' me two broken legs, you fool!" he said sullenly.

"That's all right with me," Jim said. "You're goin' to get a broken head if you don't start talkin'."

"About what?"

"Why were you in that room?"

"Why were you?" Kehoe countered.

Jim rammed the gun in deeper. "Come on, you and me are goin' to pay a visit to Neil. And don't think I haven't got an alibi. I was comin' down the alley and saw the ladder and the open window. I went up to investigate, and you shot at me." He yanked Kehoe's collar. "Come on."

"I'll talk! I'll talk!" Kehoe cried softly. Jim let go. "Come on over to the saloon where we can be private."

Jim nodded. "I got your gun. Just remember that."

V
POISONED CATTLE

When they were in Kehoe's office, a small room, containing only a big desk, two extra chairs and a stout iron safe in the corner, the gambler seated himself, trembling. He was still unnerved, and he wiped his pasty face with a handkerchief, glaring at Jim. Then he pulled out a bottle and two glasses from the lower drawer of the desk, and under Jim's wary gaze poured out two drinks, indicated one, and drank the other. Jim didn't take the drink.

When Kehoe had finished, Jim said, "All right. I'm still waitin'."

"Sit down," Kehoe invited. His old affable manner was returning.

"I'll stand. You talk."

"Know whose room that was?" Kehoe asked shortly.

"Major Thornton's."

Kehoe looked abashed. "How'd you know?"

"Never mind."

The gambler twisted in his chair. "Well, if you know Major Thornton, you know why he's here?" He looked searchingly at Jim, whose face was half shadowed from the lamplight.

"You tell me," Jim drawled softly.

He and Kehoe stared at each other, and Jim stared the longest.

"Thornton ain't a major, he's a tinhorn swindler," Kehoe said finally. "I know."

"What's that got to do with you?"

"Well"—Kehoe looked uncomfortable—"he's tryin' to swindle a friend of mine. I figured I'd get the goods on him and expose him."

"Larry Whitehill?" Jim asked softly.

Larry's name hit the mark. Even Kehoe's impassive face betrayed a little flicker of surprise. "You got pretty big ears, Hutchins," he said softly. "All right, you guessed it. He's tryin' to swindle Larry."

"Out of the ranch," Jim drawled. "And you don't want him to, because you figure you'll get the Seven Cross in payment for gamblin' debts."

Kehoe put both arms on the desk, and he was smiling, seemingly undisturbed. "Hutchins, I'd hate to be as suspicious as you. Sure Larry owes me gamblin' debts. I want my money, too. But I stick at some things, and one of those things is seein' a nice kid and his sister gypped out of their place." He pointed his finger at Jim. "Look, if I wanted my money and didn't care how I got it, why wouldn't I tell Larry to sell to this Thornton to get the money to pay me back?"

Jim considered this a minute. "You would. Then you must want the place."

Kehoe shook his head slowly. "I'm a gambler, Hutchins, not a rancher. I don't believe in owning property. I don't even own this building. If I wanted the Seven Cross, I could have had it. Instead, I'm lettin' Larry Whitehill pay me his gamblin' debts in little spots of hard cash."

"Cattle?" Jim suggested.

"No cattle. I said cash."

"And Larry's doin' it?"

"He's payin' me back a part of it this week in hard cash from the sale of cattle that he got from your partner, Jeff Warnow."

Jim's eyes were veiled, watchful. But Kehoe went on talking in the same tone of voice. Jim was dead certain he didn't know of Jeff Warnow's death.

"That way suits me," Kehoe continued. "I want the kid to keep the Seven Cross. I always have. We'll fix up our debts without those two Whitehills havin' to sell that ranch." He leaned back in his chair and spread his hands. "There you are. That's why I was up in Thornton's room. I don't give a damn what you think, either."

"You don't give a damn, now, but you will, I reckon, Kehoe," Jim continued. "I don't like your story. I don't believe it. And especially I don't like gettin' shot at in dark rooms."

"Then keep out of 'em," Kehoe advised dryly.

"I won't promise that," drawled Jim, "but I'll promise somethin' else. The next time you and me meet in a dark room, there'll be two of us shootin' instead of one."

He threw Kehoe's gun on the desk and turned to the door, just as someone knocked.

"Yeah?" Kehoe called, and the door opened to reveal one of the bartenders.

"Young Whitehill's passed out again in the back room," the bartender said, "what do you want me to do with him?"

Kehoe flushed. "Take him over to the hotel and pay for his room," he said curtly. Then he looked at Jim, his expression one of surly embarrassment.

"You're a great friend of the Whitehill's," Jim drawled. "Strap the kid at gamblin' games, and then liquor him up until he don't know what he's doin'." He smiled tightly. "I'm glad you and me are just acquaintances, Kehoe. I'd hate like hell to be a friend of yours."

He went to the bar then, and waited until a couple of the swampers carried Larry Whitehill across the street to the now quiet hotel. Jim went up with them to the room, and when Larry had been put on the bed, told them that he'd take charge.

When the swampers were gone, Jim stood over Larry Whitehill and looked down at him, his face thoughtful. Somewhere, somehow, this kid who was pulling his sister down with him, was connected with all this. He held Nancy's fate, and Jim's own fate in the palm of his soft hand. And Will Kehoe was Larry's master, playing a game whose cards Jim couldn't read.

It was all wrong, he thought gloomily, and the fact that he was cadging a night's sleep on a drunken kid who had him bluffed, did not help lift his spirits. He took off his boots, put out the lights and lay down in the bed.

Next morning Jim was as brutal as he ever got. Larry was sick from Kehoe's rotgut, but by ten o'clock Jim had bullied him awake. Once he had the kid dressed, he stubbornly forced him to the barber shop and made him take a cold bath. By the time Jim had some food crammed down him, it was early afternoon. The day was wasted, but Jim made Larry send out a note to his sister, telling her that he was rounding up cattle. Then, sick as Larry was, Jim made him ride out with him to the shack.

Next morning, Larry was feeling all right, but sullenly angry at Jim's harshness. They set out on the roundup then. The whole south face of the butte, from the rim to the distant badlands, had to be ridden, and they parted soon after breakfast, agreeing to meet at the holding corral by the windmill that was in almost the exact center of the long slope.

But by midmorning, after riding the country around two small seeps where the cattle came to water, Jim had found exactly one cow. That wouldn't have bothered him much if he hadn't seen so many horse tracks, and fresh ones.

By noon, his suspicions were beginning to harden. At the holding corral about midday, Larry was waiting for him—with two cattle.

"Where's all your beef?" Larry asked when Jim pulled alongside him.

"Must have drifted down the slope," Jim answered.

"They've *been* drifted."

"So you saw tracks, too?" Jim queried.

Larry nodded, eyeing Jim suspiciously. They turned the three cows into the holding corral and split up again. All that afternoon, Jim saw horse tracks and cow

112

tracks, but no cattle. In late afternoon, he broke out of the scrub cedar and piñon that dotted the slope and entered the chalk-streaked dun waste of the badlands. By following the tracks of the cattle, he found the place where they had entered the badlands, all in one big bunch. There was no doubt of it now; his cattle had been driven off, and not long since.

Without waiting for Larry, Jim rode on into the badlands. Whoever had taken the cattle didn't have much of a start, and it shouldn't take long to catch up with their slow pace.

He had been riding in the fawn-colored hills for two hours, his horse kicking up a fine dust in the powder-dry trail, when he heard Larry's hail behind him.

When he rode up, Larry's face was tense with excitement. "They've been rustled!" he cried.

Jim nodded grimly. "Got a gun?" When Larry nodded, he went on, "They haven't got many hours start on us. We'll get them."

They lifted their horses into a steady trot, and Jim kept watching the country ahead for the telltale banner of dust that the cattle would be sure to raise.

Then, rounding a twist in the trail, they came upon something that pulled them up short. In the dusk they could see a shallow bowl dotted with the dark carcasses of the cattle. For one brief moment, Jim regarded it, and then raised his glance beyond the cattle. He knew what had happened.

Off there, the alkali around it a dirty yellow, lay Poison Springs, and his cattle had drunk out of it after the long thirsty drive.

Jim and Larry rode up to the springs in silence. Many years ago, ever since there had been cattle in this country, men had tried to destroy this poison water. Hundreds of pounds of powder and dynamite had been

113

used in trying to bury it, but after each attempt it would seep up to the surface again. Finally, in desperation, they had fenced it with the stoutest wire on all sides and marked it with a sign.

That fence, Jim saw, had been pulled down, and lay in a tangle of wire up the slope. And all around the spring, as they had drifted away after slacking their thirst, lay the cattle where the poison had struck them down. Off against a cutbank, one cow was struggling to get to her feet, feebly fighting the death that would soon take her. All the rest were down, dying or dead.

Larry looked wildly at Jim's bleak face.

"You did it!" Larry accused him. "You killed 'em rather than let me have 'em!"

Jim looked at him with cold contempt. "Sure," he said dryly. "I rode five horses at once, rounding 'em up."

"You hired it done!"

"With all my friends? With all my money?" Jim asked. "Someone," he said slowly, "knew about me givin' you these cattle to pay a debt. Who else knew besides Kehoe?"

Larry looked at him, and Jim went on harshly, "I know all about it, so save yourself the trouble of denyin' it. Who else did you tell besides Kehoe?"

"I dunno."

"You were drunk that night. You shot off your mouth, didn't you?"

Larry was silent, but the rising flush on his face was proof enough.

"Well," Jim went on dryly, "that leaves every saloon bum in the Gem that would like to see you get in a jam, includin' Kehoe."

"Will didn't do it!" Larry said hotly. "Why would he wipe out his chance of bein' paid?"

Jim shrugged, watching Larry, whose hands were

114

trembling so that he could scarcely hold the reins. Larry looked obliquely at Jim, and then away. Suddenly, he pulled his horse around to face the older man.

"My deal still holds," he announced abruptly.

"What deal?"

"I want five hundred dollars from you, Jim, or I go to Neil!"

Jim stared at him, then said patiently, "Why, you damn fool, I haven't got a thing to my name now but a gun and some grub! My cattle are dead! Can't you see that!"

"Then get some money!" Larry said.

Jim scowled. "I don't get it. You don't talk sense."

"Sense or not," Larry cried wildly, "I got to have that money! And you got to get it for me. I'll give you three days to get it, Jim. If you haven't got it then, I'm goin' to Neil!"

He pulled his horse around, and galloped off into the darkness. In a sudden fury, Jim pulled his horse around to follow; then he reined up, all the anger draining out of him. Even if he caught Larry, what could he do to stop him? Jim sat there, the dusk settling around him, and knew the bitter flavor of defeat.

But in the quiet peacefulness of the ride home, Jim did a lot of thinking about this day's happenings. All he could be certain of was that Will Kehoe, the man he felt sure was capable of driving the cattle to their death, wouldn't have done it. For as Larry said, why would Kehoe wipe out his own chance of getting a gambling debt paid? And this Major Thornton must be counted out, too, for he wanted the Seven Cross and would want Larry's debt paid in any way but through the possible loss of the ranch to Kehoe.

When he pulled into the home corral and offsaddled, Jim was fairly sure of those two things. And being sure of them, he could afford to forget them until he had this matter of Larry's debt settled. And he thought he had a way out of that.

The horses fed and the pasture gate open, he went into the shack and lighted the lamp. From the rafters he got down his warbag and dumped the contents on the bed. There, among a dozen things that a man is apt to treasure and not throw away, was a pair of worn guns and a shell belt wrapped in an oily cloth. Jim slowly reached down and took one of the guns. He looked curiously at it, his face dark with thoughts he did not like.

And then, before he went to bed, he oiled one gun.

VI
DEAD MAN'S BOUNTY

When Sheriff Neil came to his office the next morning, he found Jim Hutchins packed on the doorstep. The first thing he noticed was that Jim, for the first time since he had come to Sabinal, was wearing a gun.

"Mornin', Jim," he said. "What can I do for you?"

"Do you keep all the reward dodgers that get sent to you?" Jim asked.

"Sure I do. Why?"

"Other states, too?"

"Certainly." Neil gestured to a rickety file case against the side wall. "I keep 'em all."

"Are they private?"

Sheriff Neil shook his head slowly, curiosity edging him. "Help yourself."

Jim thanked him. He went over to the file case and began looking through it. Jim was just well into his search when Sheriff Neil, who had been opening his mail, cleared his throat.

"Jim."

Jim looked over his shoulder. Sheriff Neil extended a single piece of note paper. Jim took it and his eyes fastened on the four words printed on it: *Where Is Jeff Warnow?*

That was all, for it was unsigned. Jim felt his face go stiff, and he knew that he would have to play this carefully. He looked up at the sheriff, a quizzical frown on his browned face.

"What does it mean?"

Sheriff Neil was observing him with an expression that might have reflected some inner doubts. "I dunno," he said slowly. "Ain't he around?"

"I haven't seen him since the fight," Jim replied. "But I figured he had a bellyful of me, and had either come into town or gone back to the Staircase."

"You mean you ain't seen him since the fight?"

Jim shook his head. "Have you?"

"Come to think of it, I ain't," Neil said. "I didn't think nothin' of it, until this."

Jim acted on the theory that the best defense is a strong offense. "That note ain't any ordinary question, though sheriff," he said in a puzzled voice. "If Jeff had just drifted out of town or somethin', nobody'd write a thing like that."

"That's what I figured." The sheriff crossed his thin legs and brushed his untidy mustache with the flat of his hand. "Sounds like somethin's happened to Jeff."

"It sure does," Jim agreed cautiously.

Neil finally shrugged and picked up another letter. "Well, I'll ask around and try and locate Jeff. If he ain't here, then's the time to worry."

Sweating in spite of himself, Jim forced himself to return to the business in hand. When he had found what he wanted, he rose, and waited until Sheriff Neil's attention shifted from a new saddle catalogue to himself.

"Somethin' else, Jim?" Neil asked.

Jim nodded, searching for the words to frame his question. "Is it true," he asked slowly, "that these counties always pay the reward they name on the dodgers?"

Sheriff Neil contemplated the young man before him. His glance lifted from the gun on Jim's hip to the clear gray eyes.

"Depends on the county," he answered casually. "What county were you thinkin' of?"

But Jim was wary now, too. He smiled faintly. "It's a good strong county," he replied. "Not Weyboldt, if that's what you're thinkin'. But will it pay the reward without a kick?"

"Likely."

"How soon?"

"I dunno." Now the sheriff's interest was sharp.

"Suppose," Jim went on, "it's a dead or alive reward. They'll pay if the man is dead and take the sheriff's word for it that it's the same man?"

"They might have to send a man over to identify him. Why?"

Jim ignored this, and continued. "If a man had to wait for the reward money, and he needed money bad right now, and he'd satisfied the sheriff that the man he killed was the right one, do you reckon the bank would let him have a loan until the reward was paid?"

Sheriff Neil laid down the catalogue and straightened up, his old eyes keen. "What are you drivin' at, Jim?"

"You didn't answer my question," Jim said gently.

Their glances were locked for a full ten seconds before the sheriff said reluctantly, "I can't answer that, either. Maybe it could be done, if the sheriff went on the man's note."

"And if the sheriff was satisfied, would he go on the note?" Jim persisted.

Neil settled back in his chair, his eyes at once shrewd

118

and curious. "He might. But he wouldn't think a hell of a lot of a man who shot a wanted man when he could have took him alive."

"Thanks," Jim said. He nodded to the sheriff and stepped out on the street. The voice of panic told him that things were closing in on him now, that he'd better run while he could. And then that voice died, and Jim knew that he was going to gamble. If the writer of that letter would keep his mouth shut, there was a way out of this, a way of getting Larry Whitehill his money and shutting him up.

Up the boardwalk ahead of him, Jim saw Nancy and Larry approaching. The gravity of Nancy's face was only lightened by her smile.

"Jim, I got a letter this morning."

His face inscrutable, Jim smiled wryly. "So did Sheriff Neil," he said.

"About Jeff?"

He nodded, not trusting himself to look at Larry. "What did yours say?"

" 'Where is Jeff Warnow?' And where is he, Jim? I haven't wondered at not seeing him because I thought you told him about my not wanting to see him if he couldn't be honest." Suddenly, she turned to her brother. "Have you seen him, Larry?"

Larry's face colored a little. "I told you I haven't seen him, sis."

Nancy's troubled face looked as if she didn't believe him, and Jim silently cursed Larry for his giveaway expression.

"Well, we're going down to see Sheriff Neil," she said finally.

Jim put his hand on Larry's arm. "Larry, you and me have a game of pool to play today."

"I'm goin'—" Larry began, when Jim interrupted,

119

"Fine, let's get goin'."

He tipped his hat to Nancy, and Larry, amazement on his face, said uncertainly, "see you later, then, sis."

Nancy looked puzzled, but she started down the street without demur. Jim shifted his glance to Larry, and he couldn't keep the contempt and anger out of his voice.

"Stay away from Neil," he said grimly. "The way you looked when Nancy accused you of knowing something about Jeff was a dead giveaway. Neil would tear you to ribbons if he saw that look on your face. You stay away from him, you hear?"

He turned away before Larry had a chance to answer. A cold anger was raging inside him at the thought that he was at the mercy of this callow fool kid who might give him away without even knowing he'd done it.

Jim crossed the street and shouldered through the doors of the Desert House. The same old clerk was behind the desk.

"Major Thornton in?" Jim asked.

"Ain't you found him yet?" the clerk asked. "No, he ain't in. I think I seen him go over to the Gem."

"His friends with him?"

"That's right."

Jim stepped out the door and headed for the saloon. He was halfway across the street when he heard his name being called. "Jim! Jim!"

He paused. It was Nancy, and she was running along the sidewalk toward him. Slowly, Jim walked over to her. Breathless, her eyes bright with excitement, she came to a stop in front of him.

"Sheriff Neil told me!" she burst out.

Jim felt his jaw go cold. "Told you what?" he asked tonelessly.

"That you're heading for a gunfight! Oh, Jim, don't

do it! I know all about it!''

Jim's eyes widened: ''All about what?''

''About Larry and that gambling debt! Oh, Jim, you're trying to make good on the money for Larry! And now you're going to collect a reward on a criminal—by killing him, Jim!''

''Supposin' I am?'' Jim said grimly. ''If there's a dead or alive reward on him, it means he deserves killin'.''

''But not in cold blood, Jim!'' Nancy cried. ''Not for money!''

Jim looked into her eyes, and suddenly felt sick. Last night he had thought this over for a long time, fighting the revulsion that kept rising in him at the thought of killing a man for reward money. And last night, goaded by desperation, he thought he had conquered this revulsion. But now he knew that he hadn't, and that the small tinder of his conscience had been lighted by the glow of this girl.

''I . . . got to,'' he said softly, miserably.

''Oh, Jim, you don't! You'd hate yourself, and I'd hate you! It isn't that important, Jim! It just isn't!'' She put a pleading hand on his arm. ''Don't do it, Jim! Everything is against you, even yourself. When I went in to see Sheriff Neil, he was telling three men that you were out to collect head money on somebody. The whole town knows it already, in just ten minutes. One man went to the saloon, another to the stables, another to the barber shop. Don't you see, you'll just get shot in the back.''

''I—'' Jim began miserably, and then looked beyond Nancy to the Gem, his attention attracted by the noise of a man running. The saloon doors broke open and Cas Ruffing hurried out. The gunman half ran down the steps, ducked under the tie-rail and ripped loose the reins of a saddle horse tied there. He put a foot in the stirrup, looked wildly about him, and then his eyes settled on Jim. He stopped, stone-still. The gossip had reached him, Jim knew.

"Get away from me, Nancy!" Jim said quietly. *"Quick!"*

Nancy, her face pale with fright, backed down the walk.

Jim took two steps, dodged under the tie-rail, and came erect.

"Better give up, Cas," he called. "It's dead or alive, you know."

For answer, Cas Ruffing bolted into the saddle and pulled his horse in a rearing turn. His gun came up and bellowed once, and a geyser of dust shot up in front of Jim. His hands still at his side, Jim called, "Get off that horse, Cas, or I'll shoot him out from under you!"

But Ruffing's horse was stretched out in a run now. The gunman took another wild shot, and the store window behind Jim jangled down onto the boardwalk.

Jim's gun streaked up. It was only hip-high when it exploded. Cas Ruffing's horse lunged, then its knees buckled under and it went down. Cas left the saddle, sailing over the animal's head and landing in a wild skid of dust in the street.

"Put down the gun, Cas," Jim called. "I'm givin' you a chance!"

Out of the moil of dust Cas Ruffing came to his knees, his gun in his hand. When he got to his feet, he had a second gun in his other hand now, and both exploded at the same time.

Jim felt the sharp whisper of a slug as it flicked past him, and he knew that within the smallest fraction of a second, Ruffing would be set and his aim perfect.

Jim's gun swung up in a swift arc and then it bellowed. Ruffing's heels came out of the dust as his back

122

bent and his arms fell. He shot twice more, into the dust at his feet, and then he pitched on his face, his boots beating a jerky tattoo on the dusty street.

"The Gem, Jim!" Nancy called.

Jim wheeled and saw the pale-eyed Texan and Major Thornton come to a stop on the sidewalk.

The Texan's hand streaked to his gun, but just then the major laid a swift hand on his wrist. The Texan struggled, and then gave up.

"Cut loose your dogs, mister," Jim drawled. "I got three slugs left."

The Texan's hand left his gun butt, reluctantly.

Sheriff Neil's voice lifted in the silence as he walked out to Ruffing. "The next hombre that draws a gun is goin' to have two men to fight!"

VII
ROBBED!

Pandemonium broke loose then as the townspeople swarmed out of the stores into the street. Jim gave his gun to Sheriff Neil and went over to the latter's office to wait. It was a miserable ten minutes for him, sitting there listening to the crowd talk, remembering Nancy's pleading voice.

Presently the sheriff came back to the office. He was alone and his grim look was a warning. Jim came to his feet.

"Well, you done it," Neil said crisply. "But you better make your story good."

Jim went to the file case and pulled out the reward dodger for Caswell Ruffing, alias Red Mike Pardee, alias Con Rentlow. It contained a smudged picture which Sheriff Neil studied for a long time.

"Yes, that's the man," he admitted.

"I gave him a chance to surrender," Jim said. "I've got witnesses to that."

"I heard you."

"About that reward, sheriff," Jim said stubbornly. "You reckon I can claim it now?"

"You want that money in an almighty hurry, don't you, Jim?"

"That's the idea," Jim answered.

Sheriff Neil scrubbed his face with his rough hand, regarding the younger man with probing eyes.

"I don't savvy what's behind all this, Jim," he said finally. "You ain't a killer, but still you'll strap on a gun and walk into somethin' like that." He shook his head. "All right, I'll go on your note."

Ten minutes later when they parted at the bank step, Jim had five hundred dollars in his pocket. His first move was to go to the Gem in search of Larry White-hill, but the bartender informed him that Larry left, saying he was going home with his sister.

Jim ate a quick meal at the café, and then sought the street, heading for his horse which he had left in front of the hotel. He crossed the street and had his hands on the reins to untie them from the hitch-rack when he looked up and saw the pale-eyed Texan lounging in the hotel door watching him.

"I'd take it a lot better, mister," Jim said politely, "if you'd drag it into the hotel lobby before I turn my back to you."

The Texan dropped his cigarette and strolled out to the tie-rail. Jim straightened up, but the Texan made no movement to go for his gun. He said insolently, "The boss wants to see you."

The Texan nodded his head toward the hotel. "He's up in his room."

Jim went over to the lobby door. There he paused and looked at the Texan who had followed him. "You said he wanted to see *me*, didn't you?''

The Texan looked carefully at him, raised his eyebrows, shrugged, turned and walked down the street.

At Room 18, the corner room, Jim knocked on the door and was told to enter. Major Thornton was seated at the desk writing, and doubtless thinking it was his guard entering, he did not even look up.

"Want to see me?" Jim asked, leaning his back on the door.

Major Thornton jumped up at the sound of his voice, and made an instinctive gesture toward the gun at his hip. But he checked himself and looked at Jim. He was too good an actor to smile in welcome at the man who had killed one of his gunmen.

"Sit down," he said noncommittally.

"I'll stand," Jim drawled. He wanted to make the major's job as hard as possible.

The major leaned back and lighted his cigar. "You must've been around some in your day, mister, to spot my man," he observed. "The sheriff tells me he was a notorious Arizona outlaw."

Jim nodded.

The major poked at his papers, puffed on his cigar and then cleared his throat. "His job is open," he said finally.

Jim raised his eyebrows. "What was his job?"

"I'm out here for my health," the major explained. "Ruffing was recommended to me in Santa Fe by an army surgeon. So was Doug, my other man. Ruffing was my secretary, and Doug is my male nurse. I have attacks of asthma that leave me weak as a kitten for days."

Jim smiled cynically, and the major's eyes narrowed. "You're a skeptical cuss," the major said amicably, and grinned a little himself. The ice was broken now,

125

and the major relaxed. Ruffing was forgotten.

"Know many people around here?" he asked pleasantly.

"Some."

"The Whitehills, brother and sister?"

Jim nodded.

"I'm tryin' to buy their place," the major confided, watching his visitor closely.

Jim didn't say anything and the major seemed satisfied. He cleared his throat. "The night I got in here, my bags were rifled, my room searched and some valuable documents taken," he announced.

So Will Kehoe's search had been successful, after all!

"What kind of documents?" Jim asked idly.

"Never mind," Major Thornton said quickly. "All that matters is that they were in a brown envelope and that they're valuable to me. I want them back. I've got to have them."

"You got a job findin' them," Jim drawled. "Any idea who took them?"

The major pulled out a drawer in the writing table and handed a crumpled paper to Jim. It was the receipt for one sack of flour, bought from Farnum's store on Saturday morning last! Fortunately, the space for the customer's name was left blank.

"Where'd that come from?" Jim said in a steady voice.

"After that shooting ruckus that took place in this room the other night, the clerk found that slip of paper at the bottom of the ladder."

"Have you tried checkin' with Farnum?" Jim asked in the same steady voice.

"I have. And he says that for the life of him he can't remember who the sale was made to."

For once in his life, Jim was glad that he always paid for his purchases with cash, for cash sales weren't recorded in Farnum's books.

"What do you want me to do?" he asked.

"You're a local man," the major pointed out. "You can ask questions without gettin' people suspicious, where Doug or I couldn't. There's the clue. If you find out who was in this room, there's five hundred dollars in it for you. If you get back the papers, there's another five hundred due you." He reached in his pocket and brought out a wallet. "And just to show you I'm serious, here's a hundred to start with." He counted out a hundred dollars in gold eagles, and laid them on the desk.

Jim shook his head. "I'll take the job, but not the money, Thornton. I don't take pay when I can't deliver."

Major Thornton smiled. "Good man. I know you're honest. And you'll take the job?"

"Sure. I'll try it."

The major shook hands and told Jim to keep in touch with him. Walking down the corridor, Jim could feel sweat beads on his forehead. That dropped receipt that he had automatically tucked in his shirt pocket last Saturday morning had almost earned him a shot in the back.

Doug, the Texan "nurse," was lounging in the lobby. He looked at Jim indolently, then looked away. Jim knew that there was a truce between them only as long as Major Thornton employed him. After that, Doug would revenge himself on his friend's murderer.

It was close to six o'clock when Jim rode across the plank bridge that led on to the big yard of the Seven Cross. Nobody was in sight except a couple of Seven Cross hands out by the corral, but smoke issued from the lean-to at the west end of the house.

He tied his horse to the cottonwood and was coming

up the walk when Nancy stepped out the door, the usual smile of welcome absent from her face. Larry, his face sullen and flushed from drinking, came out after her.

Jim took off his hat, then reached in his pocket and brought out the reward money.

"There's your five hundred dollars, Larry," Jim said. He purposely did not look at Nancy, for he did not want to face the censure that was sure to be in her eyes.

Larry took the money silently.

"Jim," Nancy said hesitantly.

He looked at her, and saw tears starting in her eyes. "You gave Ruffing his chance, Jim. I knew you wouldn't shoot him on sight, like a killer gunman! He was guilty, or he wouldn't have run. And you tried to take him alive!"

Sudden relief flowed through Jim. "Then you don't . . . you aren't—" he stammered.

"I know how you hated it, Jim," Nancy said more calmly. "I could see it. Even if you did shoot him, it was self-defense. And . . . and we're very grateful for the money." She smiled shakily. "You're going to stay for supper, Jim. I'll have it on the table in a moment." She turned back into the house, leaving them.

Left alone with Larry, Jim turned determinedly. "Take that money in to Kehoe tonight, kid. And if you go near a gambling table before you pay him, I'll knock your teeth down your throat!"

"Don't worry," Larry said sullenly. "He'll get it. And not over a gamblin' table, either. I'm cured."

"What's the matter, kid?" Jim asked. "Losing your nerve?"

"Who wouldn't?" Larry cried. "She's been pickin' at me all day, askin' about Jeff! She won't let me alone!"

"Quiet," Jim murmured. A second later Nancy

128

called them to come to supper, which was laid on the big table in the corner of the kitchen.

The meal was scarcely under way when Nancy looked at her brother. "Are you going to tell me, Larry?"

"Let me alone!" Larry cried.

Nancy turned to Jim. "Larry knows something about Jeff, Jim. He won't tell me."

"That so?" Jim asked.

Nancy eyes him carefully. "So do you, Jim."

Larry slammed down his fork. "Do you have to pick on your guests, too!"

Nancy leaned back in her chair. "Now I know it," she said. "Jim, will you tell me?"

He looked at Larry, who was watching him fearfully. "We might's well do it, Larry. This is the time," Jim said, putting his fork down.

"I wish to hell you would!" Larry said bitterly. "Then maybe I'll get a little peace."

Nancy was watching Jim with breathless expectancy. While Jim was fumbling for the words to begin, she spoke quietly. "I know. He's dead, isn't he?"

Jim nodded. "How did you know?"

"I've known ever since this morning, when Larry was so afraid of my questions. How did it happen?"

Jim told her. As Nancy listened, her face grew tense and white. Then she started asking questions, the questions Jim knew she would ask. Why did they bury Jeff under the butte, instead of providing an alibi between them and going to Neil? And then it came out, fact upon fact, how Larry had forced Jim to do his bidding.

When the whole thing was thrashed out, Nancy turned on her brother with a still-faced fury. "And you've blackmailed Jim out of his cattle! And into killing that gunman! Oh, Larry, how could you?"

Larry came to his feet, his chair tipping over behind him. "I'm through! I've taken enough raw-hidin' to last me for ten years! Sure, I blackmailed him! I had to have money, didn't I? And I couldn't get it, and he could! Believe me, sis, when your neck's in the balance, you aren't very careful about what you do!" He turned his hot gaze upon Jim. "And you might as well realize that I've just started. This five hundred dollars is just the beginnin'! You're goin' to get me more money, Jim! How do you like that?"

Nancy came to her feet, her firsts clenched at her sides. "If you ask for one more cent, Larry, I'll give Jim an alibi for that day and I'll see you hanged for Jeff's murder!"

The very violence of her speech appalled Larry. And as soon as she had spoken, Nancy was sorry. She put a hand to her mouth, and then fled from the room, sobbing.

Jim was watching Larry who looked sullenly ashamed of himself.

"You're a pretty sorry man, kid; if your own sister can speak that way to you," Jim said quietly.

"I . . . I didn't mean that, Jim," Larry said miserably, his eyes fastened on the door through which Nancy had disappeared.

"Get out," Jim said wearily. "Get along to town. Pay off Kehoe and lay off the liquor and try stayin' home nights. We'll pull out of this some way."

Larry looked at Jim, and his eyes were glimmering with hope. "Do you think we can, Jim?"

"How much do you owe Kehoe?"

"Fifteen thousand."

"How old are you?"

"Twenty-two."

"You're of age, all right. Still, nobody makes you pay a gamblin' debt, you know."

"I'll pay it," Larry said miserably. "I want to. I hate Kehoe's guts, and I think he'd kill me if I didn't pay. But outside of that, I want to. It's . . . it's only honest."

This was the real Larry Whitehill, Jim thought. With all his weaknesses, the kid was honest at bottom. He was only bewildered with the bearing of a burden that had broken many an older man.

"Are Kehoe's games straight, kid?" Jim asked.

"If I thought they weren't I'd kill him," Larry said simply.

Jim shook his head and squeezed Larry's elbow. "Go on into town and pay him his money. We'll figure out a way."

Larry went out the back door into the settling dusk and Jim sank into his chair. In the distant bedroom, he could hear Nancy sobbing. Pity made Jim want to comfort her, but wisdom told him that he could not, that he must let her find her own consolation.

And as darkness came and the lamp out in the bunkhouse was lighted, Jim sat there in the peace of the kitchen, trying to see a way out for them.

A knock on the front door roused him from his reverie. He rose, meaning to answer the door, but when he heard Nancy's heel taps in the living room, he settled back into his chair.

He recognized Major Thornton's voice saying:

"Why, good evening, Miss Whitehill."

Nancy invited him in and lighted the lamp.

"I was only riding by," the major said. "I can't stay but a minute. I wondered if you'd thought over my proposition."

"No, I hadn't," Nancy replied.

"And your brother? We passed him on the way out from town, I believe, but we didn't talk."

"He doesn't know," Nancy said. "I didn't think it

worth while to tell him. You see, we haven't any intention of selling.''

"A pity," the major said, and sighed. "A hundred thousand dollars isn't a mere trifle, you know."

Jim came to his feet, suddenly alert. A hundred thousand dollars! Nancy expressed it for him when she said, "Goodness, isn't that a lot of money for this place?"

The major chuckled. "I thought that would surprise you. A lot of money? Well, for me, it isn't. My parents made a fortune in steel, Miss Whitehill. It allows me to indulge my tastes. And if I may say so, this place is very much to my taste."

"You must want it badly."

"I love it," the major said simply.

Jim wanted to shout with laughter. The major, fishy-eyed and as calculating as an octopus, loving anything was a little too much to swallow.

Evidently sensing that he was on the verge of over-playing his hand, the major said, "Well, I won't trouble you any longer. But I'll be around Sabinal, Miss Whitehill, in case you change your mind. I haven't given up hope, you see. Good night."

"Good night."

Presently Nancy, carrying a lamp, came into the kitchen. She started with surprise at sight of Jim, but when he reached hurriedly for his hat on the chair, Nancy said, "Don't go, Jim. I'm glad you stayed. Did you hear Major Thornton's offer?"

"I couldn't help hearing it."

Nancy looked searchingly at him. "You know, Jim," she said in a low voice, "that's a lot of money. And we need money."

"Funny, how he always comes out at night, isn't it?" Jim said obliquely. "Like maybe he was afraid somebody would see him."

132

Nancy frowned. "What do you mean, Jim?"

"Nothin'," Jim said, "only there's somethin' queer here. Thornton isn't any more a major than I am, Nancy, he's not from the East. He's got hired gunnies workin' for him, and he's willin' to pay five times what this place is worth. What do you think?"

"I think this place is valuable to him. I don't know why. Gold?"

Jim shook his head. "It's been prospected with a fine-tooth comb, I've heard. No. It's somethin' else, and I don't savvy it. I—"

He broke off, his head cocked.

"Somebody rode in," Nancy said.

They listened a moment longer, and there was no sound of anyone dismounting in the yard. Jim picked up the lamp and, with Nancy behind him, went out to the front porch. Holding the lamp high, he looked out into the night.

"That's Larry's horse!" Nancy said, brushing past him.

As they approached the horse, they could see Larry's inert figure slumped over the saddle. He was completely relaxed, and his feet were tied under his horse's belly. Jim gave Nancy the lamp, and in dread silence, he unroped Larry and lifted him down. Larry's head was bleeding from a great cut, but Jim felt his pulse and found it strong.

"He's been rapped over the head," he told Nancy. "Get a bed ready."

He carried Larry into the kid's own room and put him on the bed. Then he forced a drink of whiskey down his throat while Nancy bathed his face and head.

The whiskey brought Larry around. Coughing, he opened his eyes and looked around him, and then his glance settled on Jim. As memory slowly came back, Larry's face took on a hopeless expression.

"Jim . . . I've . . . I've been robbed," he whispered. "They asked for my money, and when I wouldn't give it to 'em, they . . . they slugged me."

VIII
A HUNDRED-THOUSAND-DOLLAR DEAL

Jim only learned one more thing from Larry that night while a Seven Cross hand was riding for the doctor. Larry was sure that Thornton and Doug—the two strangers he had passed—were not the ones who held him up and robbed him. And since Kehoe was provided with the same alibi as in the rustling, Jim was more at sea than ever. Yet it seemed that someone, of whom they had no clue, was making it impossible for Larry to pay Kehoe.

The doctor arrived and took several stitches in Larry's scalp, and afterward, at Nancy's request, Jim bedded down in the living room for the night. Next morning, while Larry was still sleeping, Jim got an early breakfast from Nancy and, with the promise that he would return that afternoon, left for his cabin.

He had done all he could, and had failed miserably. Kehoe did not have his money, and whether or not Larry, driven to rashness by last night's robbery, was going to make good his threat to go to Neil, depended on Nancy's ability to argue him out of it. But beyond that, the notes Nancy and Sheriff Neil had received were troubling Jim, too. To prove a murder you had to have a body. Did the letter writer know where Jeff's body was, and could he produce it?

Jim spent all that morning and part of the afternoon examining the *rincon* where Jeff's body was buried. He reconstructed every move he and Larry had made, accounting for their tracks. Then he looked for others. By early afternoon, he was certain there were none, and he breathed a shade easier. Providing Larry did not talk, he was safe so far, and with that small consolation to comfort him, he returned to the Seven Cross. When he arrived, Larry was gone.

Nancy, calling the news from the porch before Jim could dismount, was almost hysterical.

"Jim, he shouldn't have done it! In this heat, and with his head the way it is, I'm afraid he'll faint!"

Jim's heart almost stopped beating. "Why'd he go in, Nancy?" he asked. She was standing beside his horse now, looking worn and close to the breaking point.

"He's going to Thornton, Jim! And he's sick!"

Jim looked closely at her. "Is he going to Neil, too, with the story?"

Nancy shook her head. "No, he won't do that, Jim! He knows you're his friend now—our friend."

"You told him about Thornton's offer?"

Nancy nodded. "When I mentioned the price Thornton offered, Larry insisted on getting up and dressing."

"What did he say?"

"Something about this being the way out, and that I was a fool for not telling him before."

"Nancy," Jim said quickly, "did your dad leave this place to Larry?"

"To both of us."

"Then no deed is legal unless you've both signed it?"

"That's right."

"Are you going to sign, Nancy?"

Nancy's voice was weary. "I hate to, Jim. But I don't see any other way out."

"Larry wants you to."

She nodded. "It'll end all our troubles, Jim. Larry can pay his debt to Kehoe and we'll have money

135

enough to start some place else.''

Jim slipped out of the saddle and faced her, his eyes burning with determination. ''Don't do it, Nancy! Don't do it!''

''Why, Jim?''

''Because that's what somebody wants you to do! Either this place isn't worth anywhere near a hundred thousand, or it's worth five times that much!''

''But Larry's debt?''

''All that's part of it,'' Jim said savagely. ''Don't ask me how. I don't know. Larry's over a barrel, desperate for money! Somebody's got him that way on purpose, or else they're takin' advantage of it! And I'm goin' to find out who it is, and why!''

''But how, Jim?''

''I dunno,'' he said grimly. ''But I want a promise from you, a promise that's got to be kept.''

''What?''

''Promise you won't sign any kind of a paper at all, for three days. Will you?''

He knew he was trading on the favors he had done Larry and her, and he was ashamed of it, but Nancy seemed not to think of that.

''If you say so, Jim,'' she agreed readily, ''I'll promise.''

Jim mounted his tied horse.

''Please send Larry home to bed,'' Nancy begged.

''I'll watch out for him,'' Jim promised. He smiled down at her. ''Just hold on tight, Nancy. It's time to bust this thing wide open, and I aim to do it and see what makes it tick.''

Larry had evidently arrived in town safely, for he was not on the road. Jim rode into Sabinal, his horse breathing hard, and dismounted in front of the Desert House. Doug, like a wise and waiting vulture, was leaning against the front of the hotel.

"Where's the chief?" Jim demanded.

"At the Gem. Got any news?"

"Yeah. He alone?" Jim asked casually.

"No. Young Whitehill's with him."

Jim raised his eyebrows. "That so? Don't tell me he got the place."

Doug shrugged. "Looks like it. If he can get the girl to sign."

Jim shrugged. "Well, news'll keep. I'll see him later." He turned downstreet, unable to shake off a feeling of hopelessness. He had been too late to stop Larry from signing the deed. Could Nancy hold out as she had promised until he turned something up? Even if she could, where was he to start? He felt wild urgency pushing him, but he was helpless to do anything about it.

He was as far as the barber shop when he heard his name called, and turned. Sheriff Neil was just emerging from Farnum's. For one wild second, Jim wondered if Larry had told Neil about Jeff.

"Been lookin' for you," Sheriff Neil said. He reached in his pocket and pulled out a soiled envelope. "Read that."

With sinking heart, Jim read the inclosure. *Ask Jim Hutchins About Jeff Warnow.*

Jim studied the letter until he was sure he had his face under control. Then he handed the letter back to Neil with a grin.

"Looks like somebody don't like me," he drawled.

"Why do you say that?" Neil asked shrewdly. "You know somethin' about Jeff?"

Jim shook his head. "Nothin'. Only this feller is tryin' to make you think I do."

"He seems pretty sure of hisself."

"Don't he, though?" Jim murmured.

"Funny thing, Jim," Sheriff Neil said slowly. "Jeff ain't around. I rode out to the Staircase yesterday afternoon. His dad ain't seen him. Nobody around town's seen him." His eyes almost bored through Jim. "I even stopped at your place."

"Was he back?"

"From where?" Sheriff Neil asked quickly.

Jim only grinned, trying to display a confidence he didn't feel. "Don't jump down my throat, sheriff. If he ain't here, he must be somewhere else. I mean, was he back from somewhere else?"

"He ain't even left," Sheriff Neil retorted. "His horse, his saddle and all his stuff is there at the shack."

"I could have told you that."

"Why didn't you?"

Jim frowned. "What are you aimin' at, sheriff?"

"I dunno," Neil said slowly. "Somethin' funny is goin' on, though. When a man don't show up for three, four days, and his horse and his gear is right where he left it, there's only one thing to think."

"What's that?"

"When you've figured it out, come and see me," Sheriff Neil said dryly. He nodded and walked back down the boardwalk. No warning had ever been framed in plainer language, and Jim felt that slow implacable feeling of doom build within him. At all costs now, he had to keep Larry away from Neil. He took up his position in front of the saddle shop where he could watch the front of the Gem.

Presently Jim saw what he wanted. Larry, his head swathed in a white bandage, came out of the Gem with Major Thornton. They shook hands, and then the major crossed to the hotel while Larry, after teetering on his heels for a moment, went back into the Gem.

* * *

Jim drifted across the street and shouldered into the cool, lamplit depths of the saloon. The place was slightly crowded, for it was the evening drink hour. Jim saw Larry in conversation with Will Kehoe at the far end of the bar.

He approached them, and when Larry saw him he waved and beckoned him over.

"Well, Jim, it's all over," he announced. His face, pale but animated, told the story better than words. "I've sold the place!"

"That so?" Jim said, his face reflecting mild pleasure. "I don't believe it. Who to?"

"Feller named Major Thornton." Larry glanced at Kehoe, whose bland loose face wore a look just between indifference and polite interest. "I can square things with Will, now."

Jim turned to regard Kehoe. "That ought to make you happy," he remarked.

Kehoe looked at Larry and shook his head. "It does, in a way. In another, it doesn't. I hate to see Larry sell his place for next to nothin' just because he's pinched."

"Next to nothin'!" Larry cried. "Do you call a hundred thousand dollars nothin'?"

Jim was watching Kehoe. The gambler's face took on a look of surprise that seemed genuine enough, as far as Jim could tell. "A hundred thousand! And it's a sure thing?"

"Practically. Soon's Nancy signs the deed it'll be finished. We're goin' out tonight to get her signature."

"Well, that's fine," Kehoe said heartily. "Fine for both of you. Glad to hear it." He mentioned something about business and walked back to his office.

Larry beckoned for a drink. "Better ease off, kid," Jim warned. "You're pretty weak."

Surprisingly enough, Larry laughed. "All right. Only I feel like celebratin'."

"Let's go eat."

At the café, Jim told Larry of Sheriff Neil's stopping him and producing the second letter. Larry's face sobered.

"I'll stick with you till the end, Jim," he declared. "I'll back you and we'll make 'em believe it." Jim wondered somberly if he'd still feel that way when Nancy refused to sign the deed.

After supper Larry left Jim, saying that he and Thornton, as soon as the major arranged credit by telegraph, were going out to get Nancy's signature and clinch the deal.

IX
KILLER'S CAT'S-PAW

Jim stepped out into the dark, a plan half forming in his mind. He went up the street and took up his station against the back of the railroad depot, just beyond the half circle of light cast by the lamp in the telegrapher's window. Soon Major Thornton, alone this time, appeared at the end of the street and cut across the cinder stretch to the telegrapher's office.

Jim waited for a couple of minutes, then walked into the waiting room.

Thornton was writing at the wicket, while the telegrapher inside waited for the message. The major looked up at Jim's entrance.

"Howdy, Jim," he said heartily.

Jim nodded and came up to him. "Just heard the good news," he said, smiling. "Glad you got it."

"Thanks. Wait'll I finish this."

Jim exchanged a few casual words with the telegrapher, so the man would be sure to recognize him. After the major finished, they went out together. Jim fabricated a story of tracking down the clue of the flour receipt. He had the field narrowed down to five, he reported, as they walked back to the hotel.

"After tonight, you can give it up," the major broke in. "I'll pay you, of course, only I won't need to know the identity of the man."

They parted at the hotel, and Jim turned back to the depot. Entering, he hurried across to the telegrapher's cage.

"Sent Major Thornton's telegram yet?" he asked.

"Wire ain't open yet," the man answered.

"Good. He wasn't sure he had the address right. Read it back to me, will you?"

"Which one?"

So there were two! "The first one, I guess."

The telegrapher read: "Congressman J. Harley Griswold, House Office Bldg., Washington, D.C."

Jim shook his head. "No, the last one is the one he meant, I reckon."

"First Arizona Bank, Tucson, Arizona," the telegrapher read out.

"That's right," Jim said. "That's what he thought he'd written. Much obliged."

Out in the night, Jim paused. Two telegrams, one to a congressman, the other to a bank. The one to the bank was probably for credit. The one to the congressman could be about only one thing, the purchase of the Seven Cross. Jim turned that over in his mind, considering the hundred thousand dollars, the Seven Cross and a Washington congressman. How did they all tie up? Try as he would to make sense out of it, he could not. But it was one more fact to work on. And Major Thornton's stolen papers were another. They might hold the clue to the whole thing.

Jim drifted down the alley that ran behind the Gem. He had decided what he was going to do, and he knew

141

the risk he was going to take. But now was no time for caution. Will Kehoe had stolen Major Thornton's papers. Where would a man keep papers he had stolen? In a bank? Not if he had a safe in his own office, and Will Kehoe did have a safe, Jim remembered. Those papers, he was sure, were in Kehoe's safe.

Jim stopped in the alley behind the Gem. The barroom of the saloon ran the whole width of the lot, but at the part where the gaming tables and the dance hall started, the building narrowed, so that the rear part was twenty feet narrower than the front. It was in the angle at the end of the bar, where the building narrowed, that was where Will Kehoe's office was located. One office door to it opened from the saloon and another opened onto the passageway that ran between the saloon and its neighboring building. The window in that office was lighted.

Jim moved down the passageway and approached the window. Its panes looked as though they hadn't been washed in years, and a sleazy curtain hung limply. Standing on tiptoe and looking in, Jim could see Kehoe's desk, and beyond that the safe in the corner. The room was empty. Gingerly, Jim tried the door, finding it locked as he had expected. Will Kehoe wasn't the kind to leave his office unlocked.

While Jim was watching, Kehoe came into the office with one of his house men, and Jim backed away from the window so that he would not be seen. The walls of the office, flimsy as they were, effectively shut out the murmur of conversation. Kehoe sat down, his back to the window, and the house man twirled the dial on the safe and opened it. Then he brought out some coins, counted them in front of Kehoe, and then went out.

Kehoe glanced at his watch, rose and unlocked the passageway door, and then sat down again.

Here was the chance, Jim thought, as ready-made as Providence could devise. Should he cast caution to the winds and stick up Kehoe at the point of a gun and demand the papers? Slowly, his doubt hardening into certainty, he drew his gun and moved toward the door.

His hand was almost on the knob when he heard someone swing out of the alley into the passageway. He dropped to the ground, crawling under the window so that he would not be in the light when the door opened. Then he waited, his gun pointed toward the sound of the footsteps.

A man came confidently up to the door, knocked three times, then stepped back. The door opened, and in the light that fanned out, Jim saw the lean, hungry shape of the gunman, Doug.

"Decided to come, eh?" Kehoe said. "Step inside."

"Sure you're alone?" Doug asked suspiciously.

"Draw your gun and walk in," Kehoe invited. "You can shoot anybody you find in this office besides me."

Doug drew his gun. He stepped in cautiously, and Kehoe closed and locked the door behind him.

Jim came out of the darkness to his feet and looked in the window. Doug and Kehoe! Something was queer here, damned queer.

The two men were talking, and Jim cursed silently. He could see Doug's thin lips moving, but he couldn't hear a sound. Suddenly, Kehoe got up, went over to the safe, drew out a brown envelope, held it up, smiled, and put it back in the safe and twirled the dial. Thornton's documents! Then Kehoe talked some more.

Doug listened carefully, looked as if he was trying to arrive at a hard decision, and finally nodded his head. Immediately, Kehoe knelt at the safe, opened it, drew out a sack, emptied its contents on the desk, and then counted out fifteen hundred-dollar bills. Doug pocketed them.

When the deal was concluded and Doug moved slowly to the door, talking with Kehoe, Jim knew he'd better get going. Once on the street, he tried to guess the meaning of what he had seen. That he had just witnessed a double cross, he had no doubt. Yet how would it come? Jim resolved to warn Larry first, so that the kid might be on guard. A twenty-minute search of the town did not reveal Larry, however, so Jim took up his position in front of the Gem. Larry would start from the hotel; he could have a few words with him there.

He was rolling a cigarette, teetering on his heels, when he heard a voice beside him say, "I been lookin' for you."

It was Doug.

"I been around," Jim drawled.

"The boss wants to see you. Got your horse saddled?"

Jim nodded. "What for?"

"I think we're both ridin' out to the Seven Cross."

Jim glanced obliquely at him, but could not read that secretive, insolent face.

"O.K.," he said.

"Come along."

They crossed over the Desert House and climbed the stairs together. When they arrived at the door to Room 18, Doug knocked. Although there was a pencil of light showing under the door, there was no answer.

"Must be still asleep," Doug said, and opened the door. When it was halfway open, he stopped abruptly, and gave a low whistle of exclamation. He stepped aside. "Look at that!" he said quietly.

Jim shoved past him. He just had time to see the figure of Major Thornton sprawled out on his face on the floor, a gun in his right hand, when he felt his own gun being lifted out of its holster. He wheeled, to see Doug raise his foot. Doug shoved him in the side, knocking him into the desk and then, strangely, shot once into the floor with Jim's gun, threw it across the room, then dodged out the door. Jim leaped for his gun, but halfway across the room he had to dodge a shot that came through the door and he knew Doug had him. As he hesitated, the key turned in the lock. A second later the key was thrown through the transom. It landed at Jim's feet.

Jim bent and picked up the key, knowing what had happened. It was a slick, air-tight frame-up, with himself as Major Thornton's murderer! But there might still be time. He found his gun, and ran to the connecting door of Room 18. He yanked at the knob, and for answer there was a shot through the top of the door. He could hear Doug yelling now, the pounding of many feet in the corridor.

Jim ran to the window and looked out into the night. There was a thirty-foot drop there, too far unless he wanted to invite a broken leg.

Swiftly, then, he yanked the covers off the bed, tied the two sheets and two blankets together, shoved the bed up against the window and slung his rope into the night. He had one leg over the sill when a shotgun out in the back alley crashed, and the shot slapped into the clapboard just underneath Jim's leg.

He ducked inside, just as the second charge ripped all the glass out of the window and spattered into the ceiling.

Someone was kicking on the door now, and there was a great shouting in the corridor. Desperately, Jim rushed for the connecting door again. Even as he did, someone sent a shot ripping through it.

Then the noise suddenly quieted and Sheriff Neil's voice rose in the silence. "Jim, we got men in the alley, men in the next room and men in the corridor. You can't break out. Will you give up?''

Jim looked bleakly at the door, and then at the gun in his hand. He could fight it out, killing innocent people before he died like a rat in a trap, or he could surrender. And cold reason told him that he had no choice. He walked to the door, inserted the key and turned it.

"All right, come in, sheriff," he said quietly.

X
A CONFERENCE BEHIND BARS

The door was kicked open and Sheriff Neil entered with a shotgun in his hand, Doug and several other men right behind him. Neil hauled up to look at Major Thornton's body on the floor, while Doug looked at Jim.

Jim smiled meagerly. "Nice work, mister. Only we ain't done yet."

Doug stepped over and hit him in the face, knocking him onto the bed. Sheriff Neil shoved the gunman back into the crowd.

"None of that!" he said sharply. "This is my prisoner. He's goin' over to the jail right now—and I'll kill the man that lays a hand on him!"

He took Jim's gun, put the shotgun in his back, and told him to march. With men in front of and behind him, Jim walked down the steps and across the street to the sheriff's office. Once there, Neil directed two men to get a cell ready, then dismissed all the others except a half dozen prominent townsmen and Doug. Jim was shoved in a chair, and Neil looked at Doug.

"What happened?" Neil demanded. "You started yellin' first."

Doug, his eyes shaded with malicious satisfaction,

looked at Jim.

"The major told me to get Hutchins here and get ready to ride out to the Seven Cross," he explained glibly. "I got Hutchins and went up to the second floor. My room's seventeen, the major's eighteen. I'd run out of tobacco"—here he reached in his shirt pocket and drew out a deflated sack of tobacco—"so I stopped in at my room to get a fresh sack from my warbag. I heard Hutchins knock and heard the major come to the door to let him in. A few words was spoken and then there was a shot. I run for the corridor door, thinkin' maybe somebody would break out there. When I got there, I heard the door bein' locked. Then I run for the connectin' door. Hutchins beat me to that, too. So I started to yell, and sent the clerk out in the alley with a shotgun."

"How do you know Jim killed Thornton?" Sheriff Neil said.

"I don't. He's got a gun. See if it's been shot."

Sheriff Neil smelled of the barrel of Jim's gun, nodded his head, then turned to Jim. "What's your story?"

"Just a frame-up, that's all!" Jim said thickly. "Ask him if Kehoe didn't pay him to gulch Thornton! Search him and see if he's got fifteen hundred dollars in his pockets!"

Doug looked shrewdly at Jim, then raised his hands. "Go ahead and search me," he invited.

Neil did. Outside of some change and a few odds and ends, Doug had nothing in his pocket. Jim knew then, if he hadn't known it before, that Doug wasn't green at this game. He had a finesse in crookedness and the gall to face it out. He didn't overplay his hand, either, as he drawled, "Might's well call in Kehoe, sheriff. See if I know him."

Kehoe was brought in. He heard Neil's story and

then looked at Doug.

"You know him, Will?" Sheriff Neil asked.

Kehoe nodded. "Naturally. He's brought drinks at the Gem."

"Give him any money tonight?"

"Money?" Kehoe said blankly. "What for?"

Despair settled on Jim. These two were too slick, too slippery, and their act was thoroughly convincing.

Neil turned to Jim, his eyes glinting coldly. "I'll give you a chance to tell your story, Jim. It don't look like much." He looked at Doug again. "Got any idea why Jim would want to kill Thornton?"

"I can make a guess. But it's only a guess, understand," Doug said.

"Go ahead."

"The major hired Jim Hutchins to find out who broke into his room the other night and stole some papers. Them papers had to do with the major's business of buyin' the Seven Cross. Today Larry Whitehill accepted the major's offer, and the major told Jim he wouldn't need him any longer and wouldn't pay. My guess is that they quarreled about the money Jim thought the major owed him, sheriff."

Sheriff Neil's glance settled on Jim. "You've wanted money bad enough in the last couple of days to kill two men for it, haven't you, Jim?"

A red fury seemed to cloud Jim's eyes. Every word he said, every word Doug said, pulled the hang noose a little tighter. And now, Neil was lending a hand.

With a maddened growl, Jim lunged out of his chair for Doug's throat. But Sheriff Neil was expecting that, too. He rapped Jim across the head with his own gun, and Jim melted to the floor.

"Take him to his cell," the sheriff growled.

* * *

148

The Sabinal county jail was a three-cell affair, strung out behind the sheriff's office and connected with it by a door to the right of the sheriff's desk. It was an inadequate affair, small and dark and hot, with a narrow corridor along the north side, that held a barred and screened window in its end.

Jim was dumped onto the cot in the first cell, and then the sheriff herded the angry townsmen out. He came back with a lantern and a cup of water. Setting the lantern on the floor, he reached through the bars and dumped the water on Jim's face. When Jim came to and sat up shakily on the cot, it was to see Sheriff Neil leaning against the bars regarding him without any pity.

"Well, Jim," Neil said in a toneless voice, "looks like you're at the end of your string."

Jim nodded mutely.

"I had a notion if I gave you enough rope you'd hang yourself," Neil continued.

Jim looked at him, puzzled. "Enough rope?"

For answer, Neil pulled out a soiled envelope which Jim recognized. "When I talked to you this afternoon, I already had this note, besides the one I showed you. I found this on my desk when I come back to the office this afternoon." *Jim Hutchins killed Jeff Warnow and he's hid his body.*

Jim handed back the letter and looked straight into Sheriff Neil's eyes. "You can't hang me for killin' a man until you prove the man's dead, can you, sheriff?"

"That's the law."

"Then you fog out of here and let me alone," Jim said harshly. "When you find Jeff Warnow's body, then you can start to crow."

Sheriff Neil straightened up. "I'll crow, all right," he murmured, and went out.

And Jim, too confused and weary to even think

149

about what had happened to him, lay back on his cot and went to sleep while he was rolling a cigarette.

Sheriff Neil brought him late breakfast next morning and stated that Jim had a right to hire a lawyer, adding, "We're goin' to make this hangin' legal, Jim. So you better put up a fight to make it look good."

Jim didn't answer. He ate his breakfast and was smoking when the corridor door opened and Larry and Nancy Whitehill came in. Sheriff Neil opened the cell door for them, after searching Larry, then locked it behind them and went out.

As soon as Neil was gone, Larry blurted out, "I hope you're satisfied, Jim. Your damn temper has lost us a hunderd thousand dollars!"

"Larry!" Nancy said sternly.

"Don't 'Larry' me!" he cried hotly, beside himself with rage. He turned to the door and shouted, "Sheriff! Sheriff!" When Neil appeared Larry cried, "Get me out of here before I kick his head off!"

"Larry, you promised you'd be reasonable and—" Nancy began.

"Reasonable?" Larry said bitterly. "You be reasonable. I'm goin' to get drunk!"

When the corridor door closed behind him Nancy, biting her lower lip, came over and sat beside Jim. She was wearing Levis and shirt, and they made her seem slimmer and smaller than ever.

"Well, go ahead," Jim said glumly. "You think it, I reckon, but you figure you can't say it."

"Don't say that, Jim!" Nancy said in a low, unhappy voice. "I don't believe you killed Thornton! I've come to help you, if I can!"

Jim smiled slowly, and then all at once the smile died. "Thanks," he said. "Only it's no use, Nancy. If Larry believed in me, it wouldn't be so bad. But if I get out of this, Larry'll help hang Jeff's murder on me."

150

"I'll make a liar of him!" Nancy declared. "You wait. Oh, Jim, you're not licked! You can do it. Tell me how it happened, so I can help you!"

Jim laid all his cards on the table then, talking in a hopeless voice. He told what he knew about Thornton and about Will Kehoe. He told of seeing the frame-up being built by Kehoe and Doug, and not having the sense to understand it. As closely as he could figure it, Doug, on leaving Kehoe, had gone over to the hotel and killed Thornton, then arranged things for Jim's entry. He had walked into the trap with full knowledge that Doug was forked. Bitterly, Jim accused himself of this, but Nancy only put her hand in his and said nothing. When Jim was finished, the girl's face held a look of quiet excitement.

"Jim, let's cut away all the lumber and see what we have. Kehoe had the major killed because he didn't want the major to buy the Seven Cross. Furthermore, from the papers he stole, he knew why the major wanted it. But you say Kehoe doesn't want the Seven Cross. How do you know?"

"He told me."

"Can't we offer it to him and see?"

Jim's eyes narrowed. "Has Larry ever offered it to him?"

"No. He's been scared to on my account. But now Larry can offer it to him. He'll have to. His money was stolen, and now the major's offer is no good. Larry hasn't any money, and the debt still stands. What if he offers it to Kehoe, with my permission?"

"He can try," Jim said.

"And if Kehoe accepts," Nancy said excitedly, "it would prove—" She stopped, her enthusiasm fading. "What would it prove, Jim? That he wanted it. But why?"

151

Jim hammered his fist into his palm with exasperation. "I don't know, Nancy! There's Thornton, a big bank in Tucson and a Washington congressman! What can we make out of that?"

"Those papers!" Nancy cried. "They'd tell!"

"Sure they'd tell!" Jim cried. "Only they're in Kehoe's safe! Neil won't ask for them, and even if he would, Kehoe would deny he had them. Larry won't get them! You can't get them! And I can't get them!"

"You could if you were out of here, couldn't you, Jim?" Nancy said in a low voice.

Jim looked closely at her. "Don't talk nonsense," he growled.

"But if you were out, couldn't you?"

"Of course, I could!" Jim said bitterly. "But when I walk out of this jail, it'll be to a courtroom and then to the gallows."

Nancy didn't even seem frightened by his blunt despair. There was a faint, enigmatic smile on her face as she stood up. "I'm leaving, Jim, I'm going to have Larry offer Kehoe the Seven Cross. If he accepts, then we can go on from there. I'll be back this afternoon."

XI
JAILBIRD'S FLIGHT

It was close to three o'clock when Sheriff Neil let Nancy into Jim's cell again. Her face told him nothing as long as Sheriff Neil was there, but when the door closed, excitement mounted in her eyes.

"What is it, Nancy?" Jim asked.

"I'll tell it the way it happened," Nancy said swiftly, "and you judge, Jim. I got Larry and told him that we were beaten, and we might as well sell the place. He seemed to agree. We brought Will Kehoe over to the

Desert House lobby, and I told Kehoe we didn't have any money, didn't have any prospect of getting any now, and that we'd have to give him the Seven Cross for Larry's debt. At first he just scowled, but then he said all right, but that he didn't like the idea much." Nancy's voice was excited now as she continued.

"I pretended to be angry and took back the offer. He tried to soothe me, and then, to cap the climax, he said he'd give us five hundred dollars, just out of friendship, to get started on somewhere else. I still pretended I was angry. I did it for a long time. And then guess what, Jim?"

Jim didn't answer.

"He offered me fifteen thousand dollars and the cancellation of all Larry's debts for the Seven Cross!"

They looked at each other, and finally Jim said softly, "Then he wanted it all the time. That's why he had Thornton killed, to keep Thornton from buying the ranch!"

"I'm sure of it, Jim."

Jim's jaw slowly sagged, and he sat down on the cot. "Nancy, I think I—" he paused.

"What, Jim?"

Jim came to his feet abruptly. "I've got to get out of here, Nancy! I've got to! If I can nail Kehoe, I've got it—all of it! Except why he wanted the Seven Cross. And the papers will show that!"

"What is it, Jim?"

Jim shook his head, and looked for the ten thousandth time at the steel bars that kept him here.

"You *can* get out, Jim," Nancy said in a low voice.

Jim's gaze shifted to her. "How?"

Nancy looked at the door, then came over to the cot. Jim sat down beside her. She talked in a low voice. "I remember when this jail was built, Jim. The whole building used to be the sheriff's office. But when they changed it into a jail, they put the office up front and made the cells back here."

"What about it?"

"I remembered that today. I remembered something else, too. I borrowed a pair of field glasses from Mr. Farnum and then went over to the Desert House and up into the second floor corridor that looks out over the store roof."

"Go on," Jim said impatiently.

"The last cell is where the sheriff's desk used to be. And in that corner was a stove, with a pipe up through the roof." She paused. "Jim, there's tar paper over that hole now, and probably a board. If you could get into the third cell tonight, I could pull up that tar paper and board after it's dark and get a gun to you down through the chimney hole."

"Are you sure?"

"Positive. If you could only get to that cell, Jim!"

"I will," Jim said. "I dunno how, but I will. You be up there at nine o'clock, Nancy. Can you make it?"

"Of course. But Jim, you've got to be there!"

"Don't worry," he said, confidently.

He called Sheriff Neil then, and Nancy left, the shining excitement in her face once more dissolved into a look of despairing helplessness.

Jim waited ten minutes, then peeled off his shirt. His body was glistening with sweat, but up to now he had accepted the heat as the least of many annoyances. He called out, and when the sheriff came to the cell, Jim held out his cup.

"Can't you give me some water?" he demanded. "Bring me a pitcher of it?"

Sheriff Neil did. As soon as he was alone, Jim drank the water, then, after waiting a few more minutes, called Neil again.

When the sheriff came in this time, his patience was wearing thin. "Water," Jim said. "Hell, do you have to fry a man before you hang him?"

"I dunno why not," Neil said, but he got more water.

This time, Jim poured the water over his skin and onto his Levis to make it look like sweat. Twenty minutes later, he called again. This time, the sheriff came in with an angry glint in his eye.

"I'm meltin' in here," Jim complained. "Look at me. You wouldn't keep a dog in this heat, sheriff."

"But I'll keep you," Neil said. "And furthermore, I'm gittin' you this pitcher of water and no more, understand?"

When he returned with the water, Jim made him a proposition. "Look, sheriff," he said. "This whole cell block is empty. But you got me as far away from the air as you could put me. What's the matter with me changin' cells. Put me in the end one where I'll get a little air from the window."

The sheriff considered this, and then, probably because he was sick of carrying water into the cell block, agreed. Under gun point, Jim took his shirt and his pitcher of water into the end cell, and Sheriff Neil left him.

Immediately, Jim pulled his cot over to examine the ceiling in the corner. Nancy was right. There used to be a chimney hole through the roof, but boards had been sawed to fit the hole and nailed in place. It would be impossible for a prisoner to pry them out. From the roof, it might be different. All he could do was wait and see if Nancy had the strength to rip up the boards.

Nine o'clock dragged around, and Jim waited. Presently, he heard a soft noise up on the roof that continued steadily. Soon dust began to sift down through the crack in the boards. The noise was louder now, and to

155

cover it Jim began to sing. A few minutes later he heard a stealthy knock on the boards of the chimney plug.

He raised his voice a little louder, and then there was a ripping of wood, and the plug dropped to the floor. Nancy's hand, holding a gun, followed immediately. Jim grabbed the gun, just as he heard the corridor door open. He whipped it into the waistband of his Levis in the small of his back and kicked the board plug under the cot. He was still singing as the door swung open.

He stopped singing at sight of Neil. "Didn't I hear a noise in here?" the sheriff said.

"I was singin'," Jim said. "How about some more water, sheriff?"

Neil, a look of resignation on his face, came forward. Jim waited for him to reach through the bars for the empty pitcher, then he seized the man's right arm, hauled him toward him, and at the same time whipped out his gun and rammed it in his belly. For one brief second they looked into each other's eyes.

"Go ahead and yell! I been waitin' to kill you!" Jim whispered.

Sheriff Neil's gaping mouth snapped shut. "Either I get out of here or we're both dead!" Jim said. "Make up your mind!"

"My keys are in the office," Neil argued desperately. "Don't shoot, son!"

And there was something in his voice that told Jim he was telling the truth. With the keys in the office, he was sunk. In that one black moment, Jim knew utter defeat. He was whipped, beaten by a stupid oversight.

And then, uncertain what to do, knowing only that he couldn't shoot Neil and knowing, too, that no man would keep his word to come back under this sort of threat, Jim heard footsteps. Before he had time to turn his head, Nancy burst into the corridor, and Jim heard

156

the welcome jangle of keys.

She had remembered!

It was the work of a few scant minutes to bind and gag Sheriff Neil and lock him in the cell. Then Nancy went out into the office, extinguished the lamp, and went out onto the boardwalk. At a signal from her, Jim slipped out the door, and dodged back between the buildings into the alley. Nancy followed, and came up to him in the dark alley.

"Now what, Jim?" she asked in a whisper.

"Where's Larry?"

"He drank a lot this afternoon. I made him go sleep at the Desert House."

"Do one thing more for me, Nancy, and we'll have it."

"Anything," Nancy said.

"Go over to the Desert House and write out a note. Write: 'I'm in trouble and have got to see you. When you get this, let me in the back door of the office.' Sign it 'Larry.' "

"Who will I send it to?"

"Don't address it. Pay somebody you know to go to the Gem. If Kehoe is there, the man is to give it to him. If he isn't, then he's to give it to the head house man. Understand?"

She nodded. "You'll be careful, won't you, Jim?" she said softly.

"Not very," Jim replied grimly, and he disappeared into the night.

XII
"TALK OR DIE!"

When he arrived at the rear of the Gem, he looked down the passageway and saw that there was no light in

Kehoe's office. That meant the house man would get the note. Was he a good enough friend of Larry's to heed a call for help?

Jim leaned up against the Gem, listening to the night sounds. Presently a match was struck in the office. Through the window Jim could see the house man enter, walk over to Kehoe's desk under the window and light the lamp on the desk. Then Jim stepped to the door. He heard the lock turn, the door swung open and Jim stepped across the sill, his gun leveled.

"Quiet!" he commanded.

The house man licked his lips. "I . . . I don't know the combination."

Jim smiled wolfishly. "I might believe that, mister, if I hadn't stood outside this window the other night and seen you open the safe in front of Kehoe. Do you want to open it, or do you want a slug in your belly?"

The man looked at the gun. "I'll open it," he said weakly.

Jim stepped over, took a gun from the man's shoulder holster. Then pointing both guns, he said, "Now's the time to begin. And hurry it!"

Jim stood over him while the house man knelt and fiddled with the dial. In a moment the safe door swung open, and there, on the second shelf, was what Jim wanted.

"Hand up that brown envelope," he said swiftly.

The house man complied. Jim holstered one gun to accept it. He folded it, and was ramming it in his waistband when he heard the knob turn on the door from the saloon.

Jim wheeled, lunged behind the door, and flattened himself against the wall as the door swung open.

It stopped there, suddenly, and Will Kehoe strode into the room. He looked at his house man, saw the fear on his face, and his hand dropped to his gun, just as Jim

158

stepped out, gun leveled.

"Freeze!" Jim said. Kehoe didn't move. Jim kicked the door shut and he and Kehoe looked at each other. The gambler's lower lip was trembling, and there was nothing but pure fright in his eyes. Jim walked over, took Kehoe's gun, rammed it in his waistband beside the envelope.

"Well, well, you whippoorwill," he drawled. "I got a lot of questions to ask before they hang you."

"Listen, Jim," Kehoe said desperately. "I can explain everything!"

"Sure you can," Jim agreed. "That's just what you're goin' to do."

As Jim walked forward, Kehoe backed up, until he was against the wall, his hands raised high over his head.

"Sit down!" Jim commanded. "This is goin' to be a long session, mister, and a happy one."

And then a cool wicked voice spoke from the saloon doorway. "That's right. Only you better drop that gun, first!"

It was Doug's voice. He had softly opened the door. Without having to look, Jim knew a gun was leveled at his back. Kehoe's sly expression told him so. Kehoe lowered his hands.

"Come in, Doug," he said. "We got a visitor."

Jim acted blindly then, by instinct fortified with desperation. He moved his gun in a tight arc toward the lamp and before Kehoe could even yell he shot at the light. The next moment he had dropped on his side.

Three things happened then, one after the other. The lamp crashed out and he fell, Doug shot, and Kehoe screamed. The shot that was intended for Jim's back had taken the gambler full in the chest. Even as he was falling, Jim rolled away into the dark. In that one

159

second, he knew that Kehoe was shot, and that if the story was ever to be fully known, it would be Doug who would tell it. He could not kill Doug, neither could he let Doug kill him.

Outside of the beam of light that came in the open door, Jim was safe for seconds. And Doug was framed in the doorway. Jim raised his gun, took aim, and pulled the trigger. Doug's gun flew out of his hand and he was yanked half around.

Then Doug turned and ran. Jim lunged to his feet, swinging wildly at the house man who dived for him. His gun rapped across the man's skull, and the house man fell in front of Jim, tripping him. Jim fought to his feet, and lunged out the door. The whole barroom was emptying as fast as possible at the noise of the shots. Jim saw Doug streaking for the stairs that led to the balcony, fighting his way through the panicked customers.

Jim lunged into the crowd, clearing his path with his gun. A percentage girl screamed, and men began to shout and curse. With a savage fury, Jim fought his way clear. Doug was on the steps now, taking them two at a time.

As Doug reached the landing, Jim was a dozen steps behind. He lunged, his hands out, and touched Doug's boots. That small touch was enough to trip Doug; he sprawled and crashed against the wall at the top of the landing.

He was just coming to his feet when Jim reached the landing and dived. As they went down, he heard a stentorian voice raised above the noise of the crowd.

"Get Jim Hutchins! He broke jail!"

It was the sheriff's voice that Jim heard dimly as he crashed into Doug. He fought with an extra fury then, as Doug went down, kicking furiously. Jim managed to straddle him, then reached down in his waistband, brought out his second gun and rapped the gunman

160

across the head. Doug's eyes glassed over and he went limp, and then Sheriff Neil's first shot boomed through the barroom and the slug slapped into the wall beyond Jim's head.

Jim flattened himself, gathered Doug's shirt front in his fist, and then came to his feet, hauling Doug up in front of him. Sheriff Neil was halfway up the stairs, a gun in each hand, and a mob of townsmen behind him. At sight of a man's back turned toward him, Sheriff Neil stopped and spread his arms to check those behind him. The saloon rippled to a strange quiet.

"You're cornered, Jim," Neil said grimly. "We'll cut you to doll rags. Throw down that gun!"

"Like hell I will!" Jim rapped out. "One shot and you'll kill a man. Go ahead and shoot!"

Sheriff Neil didn't move. He wasn't a killer, and there was a shield of living flesh between him and Jim.

Jim seized his advantage. "I'm givin' up, Neil. But not before you take that mob out of here. Listen to me, will you?"

"Go ahead and talk."

"I've got evidence here that'll clear me! This man is part of it. Tell that mob to back down the stairs. I'm carryin' this man to Kehoe's office. You be there to meet me, sheriff. Here I come."

He half slung Doug over his shoulder, but Doug's broad back still faced the crowd.

There was a moment of indecision, and then Sheriff Neil bellowed, "Give him way!"

The crowd backed down the stairs, and Neil followed them, keeping his gun trained on Jim. He backed across the room and toward Kehoe's office. By a faro table, he paused long enough to pick a lamp out of a wall bracket, then backed into the office and set the lamp on the desk. In utter silence, Jim walked by the staring faces of the crowd.

As he was passing the end of the bar, he heard a commotion and then Nancy called, "Wait for me, Jim!"

He paused long enough to watch Larry and Nancy break through the crowd of townspeople who had swarmed into the saloon. They went ahead, and Jim followed. Once inside the room, he felt Sheriff Neil's gun rammed in his back, and heard the door close. He threw Doug to the floor, and turned to face the sheriff, his hands above his head.

"Take that envelope out of my pants and give it to Nancy to read," he ordered, "it's the papers Kehoe stole from Thornton."

Sheriff Neil, his face deadly grim, obeyed.

Then while Nancy was ripping open the envelope, Jim knelt by Doug and slapped his face. The man groaned and flinched, but his eyes remained shut.

Jim looked up at Nancy. "What is it?"

Nancy was reading swiftly under Neil's watchful gaze.

"This is it, Jim!" she cried. "This is a letter from Congressman Griswold to Major Thornton. It says that as soon as Griswold gets a telegram from Thornton saying that the Seven Cross has been purchased, he'll introduce his bill for the Sabinal Conservancy Dam."

"Dam?" Neil asked. "What dam?"

"Don't you see?" Jim cried. "The Seven Cross valley is the place for a reservoir, sheriff! That's it! The Sabinal Creek flows through it, and the break in the foothills is the place for the dam!"

"Wait, Jim, there's more!" Nancy cried.

They listened as she read: " 'After the purchase, you assume sole ownership, as per our agreement. However, in the Land and Irrigation Company subsequently formed to market the Seven Cross range, I expect seventy-five per cent of the stock to be issued in

162

shared to the five people I have already named. Any hitch in this, and I will turn the whole affair over to the authorities for investigation.' " She ceased reading, and looked at Sheriff Neil. "So our desert range was to be his Irrigation Company land, sheriff. Does that make sense?"

Sheriff Neil nodded in bewilderment. "But that's only the reason for this fight. There's Jeff Warnow dead, Thornton dead, and Kehoe dead. You still got to talk, Jim."

"Hand me that pitcher of water, Nancy. Sheriff, you give me an unloaded gun and watch Doug here."

Reluctantly Sheriff Neil handed over the gun. The din in the barroom was rising now. Jim took the water pitcher and he doused it in Doug's face. The gunman's eyes opened, and he groaned.

Jim grabbed Doug's shirt front with one hand, and with the other stuck the gun in his face.

"Hear that mob out there?" he asked softly. "I've told them about your killin' Thornton, Doug. There's just one way you can get a jury trial in this town. You talk, or Neil hands you over to the mob."

Doug's face was ashen. He looked at the sheriff, and Neil, for once in his life, kept silent. There was only the yelling of the crowd behind the door to listen to, and Doug could not know that it was Jim Hutchins for whom they were howling.

"I'll talk!" Doug cried feverishly. "I'll talk, if you'll keep me from 'em!"

"What part did Kehoe have in this irrigation scheme?" Jim shot at him.

"The congressman's secretary double-crossed him in Washington," Doug said quickly. "The secretary and Kehoe were all set to get the Seven Cross and then put the squeeze on the congressman for title to the

163

ranch.''

"That's why Thornton was killed?''

Doug nodded. "Because Kehoe and the secretary couldn't match Thornton's price,'' he explained.

"Ah,'' Jim said softly, looking at Nancy. "Remember what I wouldn't tell you this afternoon, Nancy? I guessed it, but I wasn't sure. Now I can tell it.'' He looked down at Doug. "Kehoe wanted the ranch, but he didn't have the money to buy it outright. He figured if he could strap Larry and keep him from payin' his debt, that sooner or later Larry would have to turn the ranch over to him, didn't he?''

Doug nodded.

"So Kehoe killed Jeff Warnow,'' Jim went on swiftly, "because Jeff was goin' to give Larry money to pay the debt. Is that right?''

Again Doug nodded.

"And he stole my cattle and drove 'em to poisoned water, so I couldn't give Larry the money. He sent those letters to the sheriff, too, didn't he?''

"That's right.''

"How do you know this?''

Doug looked from Jim to the sheriff and licked his lips. Jim rammed the gun closer and Doug shrank away.

"Because Kehoe and me were partners on the deal and he told me!'' he cried.

Jim dropped the gun and rose. "There you are, sheriff. Kehoe and his saloon riffraff killed Jeff Warnow, and Doug here killed Thornton. All you got against me is that I hid Jeff Warnow's body, and I'm ready to face that.''

Sheriff Neil's bleak face didn't change. But he did something that was far more eloquent than words. He handed Jim a loaded gun. "There's a heap of people I got to set straight out there,'' he said mildly. "Watch

164

that coyote.''

Later, with Doug locked safely in the jail, Jim elbowed his way through the townsmen who crowded the sheriff's office, smiling at the awkward apologies of these men who had wronged him. Just before he reached the door, Larry took his arm and led him out to the sidewalk.

"Jim," Larry began, and stopped, at a loss for words.

"Don't say it, kid," Jim said, smiling. "Anybody can make a wrong guess, and you aren't the only one in this man's town that did.''

He put out his hand, and Larry took it, saying huskily:

"You can tell Nancy one thing for me, Jim. She's got a new brother that learned his lesson the hard way.''

"I'll tell her when I see her," Jim agreed.

Larry caught hold of his arm. *"When* you do?" He grinned. "I put the buckboard in front of Farnum's. It's dark there, Jim, and she's waitin' for you.''

"How do you know she is?" Jim asked suspiciously.

"Because she told me to put the team there herself.'' Larry let go his hold. "Ask her quick, Jim. And good luck!''

And Jim headed for Farnum's at a dead run.

THE WARNING

The stage road had not yet cleared the piñons at the tip of the mesa when it took the first of three slanting hairpin turns on its way to the flat below. From the middle turn a passenger could look straight down onto the flat and weed-grown roof of the sprawling adobe stage station. It whipped by and then a few seconds later the stage was in a wide grinding skid down on the flats by the stone corrals. When it had come fully out of its skid it was alongside the station.

Three people waited for it today—heavy Ben Davis, who leased out the station, his daughter and a gangly kid whose right leg was thick with bandages of flour sacking and who used an old long-barreled musket as a crutch. He was slim, almost tall, towheaded.

The driver kicked on the brake and simultaneously tossed the ribbons down to Ben, saying, "Don't bring them fresh teams back till we get a package unloaded, Ben." He dismounted and called back to the three alighting passengers, "Fifteen minutes is all you get, folks."

Ben said abruptly to his daughter, "You heard, Mary."

Mary nodded and laid a hand on the burly driver's

arm. "Can't you make room this time, George?"

George's face looked harried under the dusty beard stubble. He didn't answer at once but looked past Mary at the kid on the crutch. He didn't talk to Mary either; he talked to the kid, whose drawn face was still not full-formed.

"Listen," he said. "I said no last time. I meant it. No pay, no ride."

Ben led the two teams away from the stage and walked them back to the corrals. Two stockmen and an Army lieutenant walked over and went into the stage station. George went back to the rear boot and started unlacing the ropes. Mary glanced briefly at the kid. He grinned and it was a wry grin, too old for that young face.

"I'll make out," he said. "You go on in." He watched her go into the station and regarded the door thoughtfully. The Army man came out, took off his coat and gave himself a wash at the basin and bucket on the bench by the door. Slowly, then, the kid turned and hobbled back to George. He watched while George tugged at the leather apron of the boot, and then his curiosity sharpened immediately.

"What's that?" he asked. There was a tarp-wrapped bundle atop the luggage that stretched clear across the boot.

"A dead man," George said.

Ben came up then. He'd heard George and asked, "Who is it?"

"Some whiskey drummer they took on at Yuma."

"What happened?"

George's head turned and he gestured with his outthrust chin to the stage. "Didn't you see that inside? Them two men?"

The kid looked up swiftly, wariness shaping his face.

168

On the inside seat facing backward two men were sitting. One was asleep in the corner, his head sunk down on his chest. Across his lap and gripped in both big hands was a rifle, its muzzle against the other man. This man was grinning faintly around a cigarette.

Ben Davis walked warily up to the stage under the amused gaze of the smoker. Through the open door, Ben and the kid took it in at a glance. Pinned on the shirt of the sleeper was the small gold shield of a deputy U.S. marshal. The smoker was wearing leg irons and he was handcuffed so that his hands were folded peacefully between his knees. The smoke from his cigarette curled across the side of his face and he squinted one eye. His face was weather-burned, young, but a stubble of blond beard seemed to soften its tough, faintly insolent cast.

He said, "If you wake him up, take that gun out of my side first, will you?" His speech was a soft, amused drawl.

Ben turned and said to George, "He do it?"

"Hell, no," George said bitterly. "That marshal is takin' him back to Texas. I guess this fella has got some friends. Anyway, for three nights straight now riders have been shootin' at this stage. Last night three of 'em tried it all the way down Four Mile Canyon. They got the drummer last night. Here, give me a lift."

"Hadn't we better wake this marshal up first?" Ben asked.

"All right."

George climbed into the stage and removed the gun from the smoker's middle. Then he shook the marshal, who did not move. He punched him and still no response. Then he slapped him.

"Harder," the smoker said.

George glared at him and turned to Ben. "Bring me a basin of water, Ben."

Ben returned with the water and George threw it in the marshal's face. He came awake then, but barely, and George yanked him to a sitting position and shook him. The marshal, sitting erect now, looked like a sick man. The whites of his eyes were almost the color of blood and his middle-aged face was slack with dead weariness. He turned to look at his prisoner and even as he did his head settled gently on his chest.

"Get out," he mumbled to the prisoner. The smoker climbed out. His movements were necessarily awkward, but even when he moved with the short, mincing steps his leg irons allowed him, he had a kind of careless grace.

George helped the marshal down. Once erect, he had to lean on the driver. He made a vague motion toward the wash bench and George led him over to it. Once there, he took off his dusty hat and shoved his head in the pail of water. It helped him. When he had dried off with the flour sacking towel, he walked back to his prisoner. He had a six gun rammed in his left hip pocket.

"Want a walk, Pete?" he asked.

George said, "If you want to eat, you better hurry," and went around the end of the stage where Ben was waiting to help him with the drummer. The kid stood there leaning on his crutch.

"Ain't you afraid Kirk will ride up?" Pete drawled.

The marshal's face, not so slack now, didn't change. "Suit yourself, but let me worry about Kirk," he said.

"I'd like a walk," Pete said.

"Lie down then and hold your feet up here."

Still grinning, Pete got down on his back and held his feet up. The leg irons were unlocked. Pete got up and started off down the road which headed straight and undeviating across the sunbleached flats. The marshal followed a few paces behind him, rifle cradled in his elbow. The kid began to notice the sun's heat now. He hobbled over to the shade of the adobe and leaned against the wall, watching the marshal and his prisoner. So this was what it meant when the government got after you, he thought. This was what it meant to kill a man. Unconsciously, his bony hand lifted up to the butt of the gun in his waistband. He looked up to see the Army lieutenant regarding him from the doorway.

The lieutenant took the cigar from his mouth. "You're pretty young to tote a gun, son," he said quietly.

The kid's face settled into sullen defiance and he quit looking at the lieutenant. What did that fool in Army blue think he was going to do: shoot the marshal and free this man Pete? Bitterness rose up in him. Why was everybody so suspicious, so hard? Why did they always want to jump down your neck? Ben Davis had grudged him shelter for these last two nights. Both the upstage and downstage drivers had refused to give him a lift, the downstage driver twice. Only Mary, who had seen his horse pitch him and who had nursed him through that first night of almost unbearable pain, had shown any sympathy. Didn't any of them understand that he *had* to get out of here, that he wasn't just any tough kid trying to bum a ride?

Despair was in his eyes as he turned his head and saw Ben leading one team out of the corral. George followed with the other. He waited patiently until George had his team hooked up.

"I got to get out of here," he then said simply.

George wheeled slowly and when he spoke his voice was patient. "Kid, try to see my side of it. If I give you a ride and I get caught at it, it's my job."

"Loan me the money, then."

"I ain't got it."

The kid stared stubbornly at him. He wasn't defeated, wasn't cowed; he had simply run out of argu-

171

ments.

"How did you get here?" George asked.

"I was ridin' through. I stopped here to eat. When I went to ride off, somethin' spooked my horse and he pitched me. I reckon I broke my ankle. Anyway, David took my horse for board and medicine. I couldn't ride even if he hadn't. I got to get out of here."

George shook his head. "Try borrowin' from that outlaw, kid. He oughta have a lot of money."

The kid turned away and went back to the shade of the station. The other passengers were all outside. Pete and the marshal headed toward them across the hard-packed yard. The two of them talked with George and the kid saw that the marshal was weaving on his feet. Presently, the marshal and Pete went inside the station and the stage rolled out. The kid saw Ben Davis leave the wagon shed with a shovel and a pick-ax. He turned and went inside.

The station consisted of one long room which held a huge dining table and benches facing it. Another room opened off the dining room. It was a windowless, airless hole with a dozen rickety bunks from floor to ceiling lining the wall. When a traveler or the stage itself had to lay over, or when the Indians to the north were riding, the bunks were filled. Other times, its dusty stillness was undisturbed.

Mary was laying four new places at the table. Ben came in, looked around and stood in the doorway.

"I'm layin' over," the marshal told him thickly. "I'd rather get shot here than on a stage."

"Plenty of room," Ben said, and went out.

Mary came in with two tin plates of biscuits. The marshal motioned to the table and Pete went over and sat down.

"Not there," the marshal said. "Take a corner seat

172

down at the far end." Grinning, Pete complied. When he was seated, the marshal snapped the leg irons around the heavy leg of the plank table, then unlocked Pete's handcuffs. He came back and took a place at the table. The kid hobbled over and sat down beside him, and Mary, seeing them seated and their plates turned up, brought the rest of the food.

The marshal drank two cups of coffee and picked up his fork. A big fly yawed noisily over the table and flew out the door into the sunlight. Mary, her face still and breathless and watchful, was in the door. Presently, the marshal put down his fork, shook his head and began to nod. The kid watched him, fascinated, as he fought against sleep.

Pete said quietly, "You better take that plate away, kid, before he falls in it."

The kid did so and gently the marshal slumped forward on the table, asleep. Pete grinned and went on eating. The kid looked at Mary and then rose and went down the table close to Pete.

"I got to get out of here," the kid said stubbornly. He told his story. Could Pete loan him the money?

Pete listened, his mild gray eyes on the kid's face.

"I'll make you a trade, kid," he said.

"What?"

"Stage fare if you'll snake them keys out of that marshal's pocket."

The kid looked up beyond Pete to Mary, who was watching him with serene face. "I guess not," the kid said. He picked up his musket crutch and looked up to see Pete smiling.

"You're all right, kid. If I had the money I'd give it to you. Only, I ain't got it. They cleaned me out before I started. I'd sure like to get away from him before somebody gets hurt."

The kid went back to his plate, but food had lost its savor. His ankle was hurting him. He left the table and the sleeping marshal and went into the hot, dark room and lay down on the bunk. This way, his leg felt better.

Ben came in and ate. The kid heard Pete try to talk Ben into freeing him, but Ben refused.

"You better wake the law up then and let him have a bunk," Pete said at last. The kid heard Ben go out and get the water and wake the marshal up. Presently, the marshal and Pete were framed in the doorway.

"Take a bunk across the way," the marshal told Pete. Pete took one of the lower bunks and in that dim light the kid saw that the marshal was chaining his legs to the bunk upright. Ben, after watching this, went out.

The the marshal turned and spoke from the door and Mary ceased the clatter of dishes.

"Is that your father?" the marshal asked her.

"Ben? Yes."

"All right. Now don't take offense, Miss, but I never saw your father before in my life, understand?"

"No."

"Look. I'm dead for sleep. I got to sleep. All I want you to do is watch. If you see a man ride into this place, you grab a bucket of water and come in and souse me with it. You understand that?"

"Why—yes."

"I got nothin' against your father, understand," the marshal persisted. "Only I know you're honest."

"So is he."

"Sure. Only so are you. Will you do it?"

"Certainly."

The marshal came back and tumbled into a lower bunk beyond Pete and was snoring in three seconds.

Presently Pete said in a low drawl, "What's the hurry, kid? In trouble?"

The kid didn't answer for a moment and then he said

174

in a low voice, "I reckon."

"What kind of trouble?"

Again the kid was silent. He hadn't told anybody about this, not even Mary. It was no good to drag her into it. Maybe she wouldn't understand. But this Pete, he was different, he'd understand.

The kid said, "I was ridin' down the wrong trail one night and I seen somethin' I shouldn't've. That's all. He's been followin' me for a week. I throwed him off my trail up in the Mimbres, I think, but he ain't the kind that quits."

A pause. "That's tough. I wish I could help you."

"Thanks," the kid said.

Suddenly, through a drowsy half awareness, he heard someone running and it yanked him awake. Then he heard the close slosh of water followed by a mumbling.

"Please, please!" It was Mary's voice. "Someone's here!"

"All right," the marshal answered.

Mary ran back through the door and then the kid saw her stop abruptly.

A heavy voice said, "What's the matter, Miss. He expectin' me?"

The kid's heart almost stopped. Here it was, then. Here was Sime, the kind of man who didn't quit. His hands trembling, the kid pulled at the gun in his belt.

He heard Sime say roughly, "Get out of the way." Mary disappeared and there, framed in the doorway, was the huge bulk of Sime Gilbert. The kid's gun came free and he swung it up and then pure terror seized him. He was about to shoot at a man.

And then Pete's drawling voice said clearly, "Watch out, Kirk!"

Behind the kid the marshal's gun, needing only that name, blasted loose in three hammering explosions.

175

The gun Sime was holding in his hand went off, stirring the dust of the floor at his feet. He made one wild grab for the doorjamb as he fell backward and missed it and pitched his length on his back. The kid heard Mary scream and then he looked over at Pete in the darkness, but he couldn't see him. The marshal lunged past and out into the other room, where he paused, gun still in hand, looking down at the man.

The marshal turned his head and said slowly, "Your friend Kirk isn't a cautious man, is he?"

"It don't look like it," Pete drawled.

The kid got up and hobbled over to the door. Yes, it was Sime Gilbert. Slowly, the kid turned to look into the darkness at Pete. Pete's trick had saved him. He opened his mouth to speak when he heard Pete say softly, "Now throw away that gun, kid. Throw it a long ways away and come back here and sleep."

BOUNTY HUNTER

The rincon was well chosen. One side abutted the mountain; the other was blanketed with dry brush. The way into it was narrow and tortuous; the way out a rocky, secret defile.

Curt Lessing, still mounted on a weary black, powdered gray with alkali dust, looked it over by the light of the small fire Riggs had built.

"Good," he said briefly. "Safe as a church, Rig. Couldn't even see the smoke fifty yards off." He dismounted wearily.

"Go back and get the rest of the boys. Tell Darling he's lookout till chuck's ready; then we'll spell him."

Curt studied the place, and his glance settled at the base of a black, granite outcrop near the west wall. He took two long strides of his saddle-stiff legs, then turned to Rig.

"Why, damn me, it's water, Rig."

Rig, a slow, quiet man whose face under his beard stubble was really kind and mild, chuckled softly. "I thought that danged Blackie of yours would give it away."

Curt gave a little whistle of pleasure, and his somber, almost gaunt face creased into a smile. "Plenty of grub,

Rig," he murmured. "I'd almost forgotten what the stuff tastes like."

Double gun belts were looped around the waist of his worn levis, and cedar-handled guns sagged them for readiness. He stretched lazily, removed his hat, and walked over to the spring.

Blackie whinnied a little and followed him, his thirst making him ignore the trailing reins. Rig loafed over to him casually.

"Curt," Rig said quietly.

Curt looked up, questioning.

"I'd have the boys drink their horses plenty tonight, and peg 'em close."

Curt raised on one knee. His black, sweat-wet hair reflected the fire. "So you saw him, too?"

Rig nodded. "He's alone, though."

"That's what I figured," Curt drawled absently. He indicated the rincon. "The lookout'll pick him up, Rig—if he's really cutting our trail."

"He is, all right," Rig growled. "Don't make no mistake. I had him spotted at midmorning. When you sent me on ahead this afternoon, I picked me out a pinnacle rock and climbed it. He's on our tail, for sure."

"Do any of the boys know it?"

"Not from me."

"Good. Don't say anything. I'll keep Darling at the mouth till midnight. Whoever it is won't get past him. This brush will stop him to the east, the mountain to the west." He paused, scowling. "Got a hunch who it is, Rig?"

"Not me. But if he ain't careful, he's going to get a slap over the head with a gun. He ain't even using sense about it."

"That's why it doesn't bother me. If he was bringing fight talk, or heading a posse, he wouldn't be so open about it."

"You can't tell," Rig answered as he turned away.

Curt scowled thoughtfully as he watered Blackie from his hat. Three days back, Curt and his men had shaken a posse, but not once had they let up. He wanted to clear out of the Estancia Basin, for he could read signs, and the signs told him bluntly that Curt Lessing and his men would meet trouble and plenty of it if they stayed.

He cursed softly, disgustedly. The whole raid on Estancia Basin—that strip of country that he hated—had gone wrong. Seven years ago he had left his ranch in Estancia Basin with two murder warrants out against him. They had been fair killings, but the word of a lying witness, a woman, and four hostile ranchers, he could not buck. He had turned outlaw. Once established, he made it a point to loot Estancia Basin every so often. Twice he had done it successfully. This time he had met trouble.

The trouble was in the form of Gil Keller, a cheap outlaw leader. Keller had ridden in from the west as Curt rode in from the east. Instead of raiding, stealing cattle, sticking up banks, Keller had burned and killed.

"Damn him!" Curt thought savagely. If it hadn't been for Keller's alarming the Basin, things would have gone all right.

As it was, Curt and his men rode up on a burning ranch house one night. They heard cries from the building and investigated. Three women had been locked in a room to die.

Curt rescued them, brought them out unharmed, but he knew what it meant. He was seen and he would have to leave the Basin. People would swear that Curt Lessing, famed as the woman-hating outlaw, had locked the women in the room, set fire to the house; then, when the women were half-crazed with fright, staged a last-minute rescue.

And he was right. By morning, a blood-mad posse had been on his trail, and Curt decided to clear out.

Most of this day they had ridden the bald, gaunt, waterless foothills of the Infiernos, a rocky, barren range of mountains that bounded Estancia Basin on the west. Tomorrow, he and his men would be safely on the other side, out of danger.

Thinking it over, Curt said aloud: "There's always another time."

But who was this single rider following them all day? Not that it mattered, for one man couldn't do much harm. Even if he did spot their camp, he couldn't pick up a posse before they were off in the morning. Yet he was trailing them, certainly. Curt resolved to drop a man back tomorrow morning—maybe himself—and see what this curious jasper wanted.

The men were filing into the rincon now. They were weary and thirsty and looking forward to a night of rest. The horses were watered, pegged out, a guard set over them, while the last of the jerky was taken from the saddle rolls and pooled. Coffee was boiled in three lard buckets, and the men dined off this meager fare.

Curt sat a little apart, his meal finished. He had purposely feigned a lack of appetite, so the jerky might go further. Rolling a smoke, he studied the men. They seemed not to mind much the last disappointing week. Rig was sprawled out, his cigarette pointing to the stars.

"Where do you reckon Keller is?" Rig blurted out suddenly.

Curt growled in his throat, and his gray eyes glinted a little. "I dunno. Once we cross the Infiernos, I aim to find out though. Reckon this country is getting a little crowded for him and—"

The crack of a shot, not close, brought him to his

feet. He looked at Rig.

"That whippoorwill," Rig said, and he was off in the direction of the canyon mouth.

The men glanced curiously at Curt, looking to him for a sign. Most of them were still eating, and they paused with food in their mouths, wondering if the shot were the prelude to an attack.

"Eat up," Curt said casually, and lounged back again. He told them of the man that had been following them that day. In the middle of it, he was interrupted by the return of Rig, who was prodding before him an unarmed and travel-weary stranger.

Curt stood up, and Rig and his prisoner stepped into the circle of firelight.

"He gave himself up," Rig volunteered.

"Lessing?" the man said, looking around at the group.

"Here," Curt drawled coldly. He sized up the man and a little smile of contempt played at the corners of his mouth. This was no cheap glory hunter; neither did he look as if he had come to throw in with an outlaw gang. He was young, with a clean-cut, innocently stupid face, and of medium height. One word described him—colorless.

"Are you the jasper that pulled them three women out of a burning house back near Mimbres wells?" the man asked.

"What if I am?"

The man reached inside his shirt and drew out a paper which he handed to Curt.

Curt accepted it hesitantly, a scowl on his face, then stepped close to the fire. Remembering himself, he said to the man: "You're likely hungry. Help yourself to what chuck we got."

"I'll do that," the stranger said amiably.

Curt squatted by the fire and unfolded the paper, first looking curiously at the wax seal that bound it. The printed letterhead informed him that it was from the office of the territorial governor. The message was brief, simply informing him that in view of the heroic work he had done in saving the lives of three women, the governor had seen fit to pardon him and all his men— providing that within forty-eight hours after receiving this letter, he had surrendered himself and his men to proper agents of the law.

Curt read it over three times, glancing at the signature, the paper, the seal, the fine, flowing writing of the secretary. It looked genuine.

"Well, I'm damned," he muttered softly, looking up at the messenger. "Do you know what this is?"

The messenger nodded, grinning, with his mouth full of food. "I reckon."

"How come?"

"Them three women was kin of a great friend of the governor's. After that posse left on your trail, them women got calmed down enough to talk. They said it wasn't you at all that locked 'em up, but it was you that saved 'em. Crockett—it was his wife and two daughters—was down at Las Cruces to meet the governor. They sent word to him, and I reckon he wanted to pay you back." ·

He indicated the paper. "I been on your trail for three days now."

The men were looking at Curt for an explanation. He rose and walked away from the fire, trying to hide the genuine amazement his face must have shown.

Far out of the circle of firelight, he sat down against a boulder. His mind was in a turmoil. It was like stumbling onto a fortune that was his for the asking. When he read the letter, there had been no doubt in his mind. He wanted to be a free man, to live like other men lived, unharried by the law. It was his now for the taking.

Three years ago he had tried to leave the owlhoot. He had bought a small spread down in the Mogollons. But his name and reputation followed him. He left an hour ahead of a sheriff, and since then he had been reconciled to his lot.

But now it was different. Pardoned by the governor, he could carve out the remainder of his life with toil, not with a gun.

But what of the men? Curt knew them well, and he thought he knew, too, what they would say. He had not picked killers in recruiting his men. He had checked up on their back trails and knew their stories, which were all of a kind: One drunken brawl, a shooting, and flight; or trying to buck a mean lawman. At bottom they were decent men, who had played in hard luck. And he knew that they would welcome a pardon, and the peace it would bring them.

Fighting down his visible exultation, he walked back to the fire.

His mind was made up. He tossed the paper to Rig, and told him to read it aloud. Squatting by Rig's side, he built a smoke, watching the faces of the men as they listened to Rig's laborious reading.

Finished, Rig laid down the paper, and looked up at Curt.

"Well?" Rig said.

"You've got a little money, each of you," Curt began, his tone impersonal. "You've got a clean slate; no man can arrest you or hunt you down. Each man of you here has got something to go back to, something to work at and build up. Are you going to take it, or are you going to cross the Infiernos tomorrow, slaughter a rustled beef for food, sleep with your guns, and wonder who's on your back trail as you fall asleep?''

"What are you going to do, Curt?" one of the men asked.

Curt flipped his cigarette away and stared into the fire. When he looked up at the speaker, his eyes were unwavering. "Clem, you got accused of a wet-cattle deal by a land-grabbing rancher by the name of Kennedy, didn't you? That's after you had a nice little start over in the foothills of the Guadalupes. You come to me, then, and I took you in. Is that right?"

"I never said so, but I reckon that's it," Clem said.

"If it hadn't been for Kennedy, you'd have stuck with your spread and tried to rod it into a big brand, wouldn't you?"

Clem answered immediately. "Right. And I'd of done it, too."

Curt shrugged. "That's my fix. I had a spread down here in Estancia and I was making good. A half-dozen, water-thieving polecats liked the looks of the grass on my south range. I was a kid, and they thought they could take it from me. They did, after I killed two of them."

He looked around at the men. "I liked that spread. I sweat blood with my old man building it up. But it was worth it. And I'm going to do it again."

Rig looked at him sharply. "Then you're going to take the governor's offer, Curt?"

Curt nodded. "I never chose the owlhoot. I was forced to it. So were you, Rig; so were all of us. If I didn't like it well enough to hunt it out, I don't like it well enough to stick to it when I've got the chance to leave it. That's how I stand."

A murmur of assent rose from the men. Curt had put it in words for them. The messenger watched the men with quiet, curious eyes, as if he were surprised that these could be the hired killers of Curt Lessing.

184

Rig was staring into the fire. "What about the rest of that there letter, Curt?"

"You mean about the surrender? I think it's on the level. The governor is a man that keeps his word, from all reports. If he's crossing us, I can say one thing: He won't live to cross us twice."

"Not that," Rig said. "I believe the governor." He looked up at Curt.

"What did he mean by surrendering to a proper agent of the law?"

"An elected sheriff, I reckon, didn't he?" Curt asked the messenger. The man nodded.

"I thought so," Rig said. "Have you figured out just what sheriff you can reach in forty-eight hours?"

"The one at Mica City," Clem put in. "That's about a two-day ride."

"And who is he?" Rid asked quietly.

A silence settled on the men, and they looked at each other.

"I'll tell you," Rig put in. "It's old Jupe Cronyn, the biggest whippoorwill that ever hid behind a tin star."

"Cronyn?" Curt asked softly. "I thought he was shot guarding Blind Lucy Mine payroll last year."

"He was shot, right enough," Rig growled, "but they never killed him."

"That's right," the messenger put in, "he's still sheriff."

Curt cursed tonelessly. Cronyn was the most hated sheriff in that part of the west, a gunman, not a gun fighter; a murderer who happened to wear the star of the law. More than that, he was a bounty hunter—and Curt had five thousand dollars' reward on his head, dead or alive.

Cronyn would likely shoot him on sight. Or, failing

that, he would take Curt, destroy the governor's letter, kill this dumb messenger, then lead a lynch mob and string up Curt and his men. After it was done and he was in line for the reward money, he would plead ignorance of any pardon, and, with the letter and messenger gone, it would be a foolproof excuse. And this was what they were walking into.

"What about it, fella'?" Rig asked the messenger. "Is the governor right set on the forty-eight hours? Another half day and we could make this Mex settlement across the mountains and give ourselves up there."

The messenger shrugged carelessly. "I reckon you can do anything you damn please, but the forty-eight hours sticks. When I left, the governor said if you wanted the pardon bad enough, you'd kill your horses getting to a county seat in forty-eight hours. And he said if you took your time, it showed you didn't want a pardon very damn bad."

"Wait a minute," Curt put in. "If we was close to a straight sheriff, that might be right. You can see how we're fixed. What's keeping you from stretching it a few hours? The governor'll never know the difference."

The messenger laughed shortly. "Why the hell should I lie for a bunch of outlaws that'll let a tough-talking law spook 'em?"

Curt took two slow steps to confront the messenger. His eyes were cold with contempt. "All right, fella'. Maybe you shouldn't care. You're carrying out orders—to the letter—so you're safe. But did you ever think that Cronyn might like to get rid of you before he starts collecting bounty on us?"

"What of it?" the messenger said carelessly. "I ain't afraid of Cronyn—not a damn bit!"

Curt said softly, "I'll remember that. We'll ride into Mica City—under forty-eight hours. And unless I'm way wide of my guess, you'll have a yarn to take back to the governor about the law in this territory. And we'll damned well show him how bad we want his pardon, even if there ain't any of us left to make use of it.''

"Suits me," the messenger replied indifferently. "I'm just riding back to him with the truth."

"If you're riding at all," Curt added briefly. He turned to the men.

"Saddle up, boys. If we ride straight through, we'll make it before dark day after tomorrow. That may make a difference, but I dunno what."

II

Forty-five hours later, Curt and his ten men plus the governor's messenger pulled up on the ridge to the south of Mica City. Their horses were almost foundered, and the men themselves were haggard from loss of sleep and more than a week's steady riding.

Curt looked over the town. It was a mean place, the county seat of a barren and poor county, and in the light of the setting sun, already behind the hills, it looked more shoddy than sinister. A single dusty street was flanked by squalid clapboard stores. The four corners held the hotel, the sheriff's office, the bank and a rather large and unused store building.

Rig spat sourly, and his gloomy eyes sought Curt, who was looking somberly at the double-walled adobe jail behind the sheriff's office.

"Let's get it over with," Curt said savagely. He turned to the men. "Boys, I may be leading you plumb into a hang noose. I don't like the looks or the sound of it, but"—he shrugged—"I'm taking a chance. The jail looks tough and the sheriff sounds tougher. What about it?"

"Go on, Curt. A dozen men ain't easy to lynch," one of the men said.

"There's one thing I can do," Curt drawled speculatively. "I can put the governor's letter away where he can't touch it." He laughed shortly. "If he ain't a jughead, that ought to make him think."

"With five thousand bucks on your head, Curt? I dunno," Rig said.

Curt straightened up and looked at the governor's messenger. "If you'll come with me into town, I reckon your job's over—you, too, Rig."

"Where you going?"

"Me? I'm taking out a little revenge insurance," Curt drawled, pulling his horse around and heading him down the slope. "Give me twenty minutes, boys; then drift into town in pairs."

With Rig and the governor's man siding him, he rode into town. At the bank they dismounted. Curt unbuckled his gun belts and looped them over his saddle horn in front of two or three curious idlers, hitched up his levis and walked into the bank, his two companions following him.

He was taking a long chance he knew, for the safety of them all would depend on the honesty of the banker.

The governor's messenger, utterly silent these past two days, suddenly waked up. He laid a hand on Curt's arm. "Wait a minute," he said slowly. Curt paused. "Let me get this right," the messenger continued. "You're going to lock up that letter from the governor?"

"I aim to," Curt said.

"I wouldn't. Give it to me. I'll show it to Cronyn, then take it with me when I ride back to bring your pardons."

Curt shook his head slowly. "Huh-uh. I ain't that dumb. Every whippoorwill deputy Cronyn's got would

188

be waiting for you in a dry gulch. As long as that letter's safe, Cronyn's going to think twice before he starts collecting bounty."

The messenger stared at him evenly. "Lessing, you must think I'm not growed up, and that there isn't any law in this country. If Cronyn touches me, there'll be troops in Mica City in two weeks."

"Same troops doing who any good?" Curt asked scornfully. "You'll be dead; I'll be dead. Cronyn will claim you joined up with me and we tried to raid the town. It may stick, and it may not, but I don't aim to give it a chance."

He shook his head, and smiled a bit. "Mebbe you are growed up—but you haven't growed any of it on the owlhoot. Never give a lawman an even break, mister. He may be straight, and he may be forked. I've got five thousand dinero on my head, and I'm fair game for a bounty hunter. To me, they're all forked."

The messenger shrugged, and smiled derisively. "It's your letter, Lessing. It's a pity you haven't got an old woman's long, black sock to hide it in." He sneered. "Outlaw, hell! A jack-rabbit fighter!"

Curt's eyes narrowed. He was through the bank door now, but he took a step out, facing the messenger.

"Hombre, I let you rawhide me into comin' here against my better judgment. But if you think I'm letting you rawhide me into handing over to you the only thing that keeps me from hanging, then think again. I'd rather have something between me and the hang noose besides a stuffed hat. You're just forty-eight hours of unnecessary talk, as far as I'm concerned. Remember it!"

He turned on his heel and walked into the bank. A clerk at the long counter had overheard the conversation, and he stood rooted in his tracks as Curt approached.

"Wh-what is this, a stick-up?" he stammered, his eyes wide with fright.

"Hold up, hell!" Curt snarled. "Get your boss—the president."

"He's inside," the clerk said, indicating the partitioned-off section at the front of the room.

"Go get him, then!"

The clerk retreated doubtfully. Curt knew he was recognized and he cursed himself bitterly. Should he make a break for it now, while he was still safe? He looked at Rig, calm-faced, capable and pessimistic. No, he'd see it through. He had ten men depending on him, ten men who deserved the chance to lead decent lives.

When the door opened and a short, square-faced man in a loose, black suit stepped out, Curt's spirits rose. In that full second of sizing up the man, Curt knew he was dealing with a stern man, but a fair one. A shock of white hair softened the banker's features, and when he spoke, his voice was not especially harsh.

"Yes? I'm the president."

"You got a vault in here—or a safe?" Curt asked civilly.

"I know you, young man," the banker blurted out, and his eyes held no fear. "You're Curt Lessing. I'm warning you, if you intend to stick up this bank, I'll fight you till I drop."

Curt smiled. "No call to get roostered. I'm not aiming to hold up your bank. You can see I'm not armed. All I want is to do a little business with you."

The banker's features suddenly softened. He looked at Rig and the messenger, whose guns were in their holsters.

"But you are Curt Lessing, the outlaw?" the banker asked.

"I am. And I'm not gunning."

"Then"—the banker suddenly appeared agitated—"you better go—now. I—You better leave immediately."

Curt scowled. "But I ain't sticking up the place. All I want, like I told you, is to do a little business with you."

"But—"

"Do it with me!" a voice boomed from the door. Curt whirled. Standing there in the doorway was a broad, heavy man, his twin six-guns trained rocksteady on the trio at the counter. He took a swift step inside, and four more men, their guns out, followed him. Even at this distance, it was easy to see the star on his vest. Cronyn!

"You two hombres cross your hands and flip them guns out on the floor. And do it slow." His voice was flat, with no edge to it, the voice of a man who approached a killing with the nerveless, calm blood lust of a killer.

"Better do it, Rig," Curt said softly.

"Cronyn, I made a mistake," the banker said. "My clerk misinformed me. These men are here on business."

"Misinformed hell!" Cronyn snarled. "Cooper, this is Curt Lessing, the outlaw."

Curt heard the banker sigh.

"Look here," the governor's messenger blurted out, "I'm from the governor. These two men have been promised safe conduct by me!"

"Sure, and I'm General Miles, too," the sheriff sneered. "Better hurry it up. My thumbs are wet with sweat and they may slip off the hammers."

Rig was no fool. Slowly, he crossed his hands, slid them to his holsters, drew out his guns and dropped them to the floor.

The messenger, his face flushed under the quiet scorn of Curt's eyes, did likewise. The sheriff came forward and kicked the four guns out of possible reach. Curt looked him over and his heart sank.

Legend had not quite done justice to Jupe Cronyn; he looked even uglier than his reputation. His face was heavy, utterly loose except for a tight, thin mouth. Flesh seemed to sag all over him, as did his clean, loose clothes. His pale eyes had no depth, and they seemed never to blink under the sweep of his big hat.

"Before I said much, I'd do a little listening," Curt drawled.

The sheriff whirled on him and jabbed a gun at him. "Hoist 'em!" he snarled.

Curt obeyed. The sheriff searched him for hide-outs and found none. He stepped back a few feet, contemplating them with an utterly emotionless face.

"Mebbe this'll learn some of you tin-horn badmen to stay out of Mica City," the sheriff said flatly. "I'll give you a tip, but it won't do you no good, Lessing. When you find a bank you want to stick up, be sure it ain't close to a sheriff's office. And look for wires running across the street. It's danged easy to jerk a wire in the bank office and have it upset a water pitcher in the sheriff's."

Curt looked at the banker, his eyes filled with quiet scorn.

Cooper shook his head. "I'm sorry, son. I did it on the clerk's say-so."

"You ain't apologizing for calling me in to capture a killer are you, Cooper?" the sheriff jeered.

"He's done nothing to me," Cooper said staunchly.

"What are you jaspers talking about?" Curt drawled easily. "If I was still an outlaw, it might make sense."

The sheriff's eyes narrowed. "Curt Lessing, wanted dead or alive. Five-thousand reward, dead or alive.

Don't that sound like you're an outlaw?''

"It was," Curt said. "Talk to this gent"—he indicated the governor's messenger—"and maybe he'll save you from making a bad mistake, Cronyn—a real bad mistake."

The four deputies and the sheriff looked at the messenger.

"You couldn't save me anything, except wasting my breath. What is it?"

"I'm from the governor's office," the messenger said. "I've brought word to Lessing here that the governor will pardon him and his men if they surrender to a proper agent of the law. Lessing's surrendered. At his word, his men will. That's straight, Cronyn. If you don't believe it, send a man over to Las Cruces to check up on it."

The sheriff waited a long moment before he spoke. Curt saw his eyes cloud over, saw the imperceptible change in his mouth. Curt hoped savagely that the men would stay out until this was settled one way or the other. If they rode into town and saw him a sheriff's prisoner, they would burn the town down to rescue him, and thereby spoil their chances forever of becoming free men.

"Lessing's men?" the sheriff asked. "Where are they?"

"Up on—"

"Cut it!" Rig commanded harshly.

The sheriff laughed. "Ed, go out and get a posse up, pronto. Tell Castle to send all the guns and ammunition in his store over to the old land-office building across the street. Fort up in there. Looks like we're going to have callers."

He turned to the messenger again. "Thanks," he said dryly. "Now go on with your yarn."

"You can't do that, Cronyn," Cooper put in hotly. "The man's telling the truth! You've got to find out, anyway."

"Yeah?" the sheriff drawled, his tone ugly. "I'll give him a chance."

He turned to the messenger. "I don't know you. As far as I can see, you're one of Lessing's men trying to run a sandy on me. What you got to prove you're the governor's man?"

Here it was, Curt knew. The only thing in the possession of the three of them that could back up the messenger's story was the governor's letter to Curt, and once the sheriff had that last bit of evidence, they were helpless. He would have to act now or never. He looked over at Rig. Rig's face told him nothing except that he had come to the same conclusion.

He felt his stomach ball up. It was a long chance. If he were lucky, he would make it.

"Why nothing," the dumb messenger said. "I'm telling you I'm Lew Scoggins. Been with the governor for three years now. I don't carry no papers. I don't have to."

Suddenly, he looked at Curt, and Curt knew it had come. Scoggins was going to tell about the letter.

"He's got plenty on him," Curt cut in. "I never believed him either, Cronyn, until he showed me his papers. They're in an inside pocket in his shirt."

Scoggins' mouth sagged in amazement, but the sheriff acted. Curt knew Cronyn wanted any identification papers on Scoggins and that he would do anything to get them and destroy them. The sheriff, in spite of his weight, moved like a cat. He rammed his right gun in his belt, reached out and ripped Scoggins' shirt front.

Then Curt dived for his sheltering bulk, slugging him in the kidney. Cronyn straightened up with a grunt as Curt's hand streaked for the gun in the big man's belt. He got it, whipped it out, and with both arms around the sheriff, he turned him toward the four deputies, who had been caught flat-footed.

Curt's iron grip on the sheriff's left wrist held the cocked gun straight at the deputies; his right hand held the other gun, pointed, cocked.

"You can shed them things any time," Curt drawled, "only I'd be quick about it."

The sheriff was helpless. If he struggled, his already numb left hand would let the gun off at his own men. They looked at him questioningly.

"Drop 'em. He's got you," the sheriff growled.

The deputies dropped their guns.

"Take his left gun, Rig," Curt ordered. Rig did so. Then Curt backed off. "Now, fat man, you wouldn't listen. I reckon I've got to make you."

To Rig he said: "Cut down on the first one that moves." And to the banker he said: "Where's your vault, Mr. Cooper?"

"Over there in the corner, son. It's open."

Curt vaulted the counter, then drew the governor's letter from his shirt. "Take a look at this, Cronyn, and remember what's in it. It's the governor's promise in writing. Sabe? One bad play and you got this to talk out of the safe."

He turned to the banker. "I got to do this, Mr. Cooper. It'll protect you and me both."

He strode over to the safe, put the paper in it, then shut the heavy door with a slam and spun the knob. Then he took his gun, stepped around the corner of the safe and shot five times at the combination dial. With each shot, the dial bent out, lost its shape.

Finished, Curt looked at the sheriff.

"Safe, fat man. Get outta that jam."

He was smiling crookedly when a voice from the

office—a woman's voice—said: "If you're through, put down that gun. It'll make it easier to believe your story."

Curt whirled, but Rig did not take his eyes off the sheriff and the deputies. Curt saw a girl standing in the doorway of the office holding a gun on him. She was young, deathly pale, and her gun hand trembled. But Curt noticed the set of her jaw was hard, her brown eyes unwavering. Behind the halo of her corn-colored hair, he could see the clerk's head. For a moment he held the gun, his surprise mastering him.

Then his jaw clicked shut, and his eyes were suddenly cold. A woman! Wherever you went, whatever you did, there was a woman messing things up. He was about to ignore her, but the cold accusation in her eyes checked him. He fought down his anger. She was right. She had heard it all and understood. She was another witness. The paper was safe until the vault could be opened. Let Cronyn do his damnedest.

He dropped his gun. "All right, Rig. Give 'em back," he ordered.

"You dead set on that, Curt?" Rig asked.

"If you don't, you're a fool," the girl said calmly.

"Do it, son," Cooper said.

Rig wilted. With a curse, he threw the guns at the sheriff's feet and stepped back toward Curt.

Like hounds let loose, the sheriff and his deputies pounced on the guns.

The girl waited until they had them, watching what they would do.

They boiled over the counter, the sheriff's big bulk surprisingly agile. His face was contorted with an uncontrollable fury, and he snarled in his throat.

"Cronyn, don't touch those men!" the girl whipped out.

For answer, Cronyn's gun rose in a swift arc toward

the girl.

Curt leaped, but even before he reached the sheriff, he heard a shot; then something hit him on the head and he knew no more.

III

When Curt woke up, it was night. He was in a cell. In the corridor, out of reach, was a lantern sitting by a small heating stove in a far corner.

He tried to raise himself off the cot, but he lay back, groaning. Every bone in his body seemed splintering, every muscle torn and aching. Lying there, he pieced together the story. Then this must be Cronyn's jail.

"And I collected me a plumb beautiful job of pistol whipping," he thought.

He managed to sit up and look around. Rig was lying on a cot in the other corner of the cell.

"Rig," Curt called softly.

"Huh. Woke up, did you?" Rig growled.

"Did they work you over, too?"

"Plenty, but not as bad as you."

Curt felt his head. His hair was matted with blood and dust and his skull was sore to his touch. One eye was swollen shut, and his clothes were stiff from blood. He put his head in his hands and tried to think. Suddenly, he laughed softly.

"Rig, this is funny. When a badman tries to go straight, this is what he gets."

Rig swore. "Not quite all he gets. This ain't the end of it."

"You think Cronyn's going to hang the deadwood on us, then collect the bounty?"

"Listen," Rig said.

They sat perfectly still. Curt could hear the steady *tap, tap* of metal on metal somewhere outside the jail. "What is it?" he asked.

"Cronyn's working on that safe. If and when he gets it open, we'll be a couple of sick-looking jaspers."

"He can't do that," Curt said softly, "or can he? What about Cooper? He ought to have something to say about that."

"We been in jail over six hours, and he ain't been near us," Rig said dryly. "They're working on the safe and that means one thing, don't it? Cooper figured it was less trouble if he forgot us."

Curt growled in his throat, stood up and began to pace the floor. "What about the men? Did they try to come in?"

"I reckon not—leastways, I haven't heard 'em. Clem must have been watching the bank and seen them take us out. Reckon he aims to hold off until the last minute."

He spat out some blood. "Take a look out that window."

Curt climbed on the cot and looked out the high, small window on the wall side of the cell. He whistled softly.

"They got every kid over twelve toting a gun," Rig continued savagely. "It ain't going to do the boys a bit of good riding into this place. They wouldn't get to the corner."

Curt sat down on the cot again. He wished bitterly that he could clear his head enough to think this out. But what was there to think out? Every minute brought Cronyn closer to the governor's paper, and once he had that it would be the end. Cooper had deserted them apparently, having made no attempt to see them or free them.

"Where's Scoggins?" Curt asked dully.

198

"Next cell." Rig laughed softly, bitterly. "Wonder what he'll think of territorial law when he wakes up?"

"They'll kill him, Rig. They'll fill him so full of lead he won't be worth burying."

"Sure they will. They'll take him first because he's the one that can give them away. Then they'll take us next. Five thousand on your head, two thousand on mine—that's split between them four deputies, the sheriff—and it looks like Cooper, too."

Curt remembered something and sat up with a jerk. "What about the girl, Rig?"

Rig misunderstood him. "No, not her, nor the clerk. They can scare the clerk into keeping his mouth shut. The girl I reckon they've already took care of. Leastways, I saw her go down. They'll blame that on to us, too. We ain't got a chance, Curt."

"You mean they shot her?"

"I saw her go down. That's all I know."

Curt stood up and strode to the bars separating him from the next cell. "Scoggins!" he called. The figure on the cot did not move. Curt kept calling his name until Scoggins roused with a groan and sat up.

"Did you see what happened to that girl?" Curt asked swiftly.

"Sure. The sheriff shot her," Scoggins growled. "I saw her go down before they slugged me."

"And they didn't do anything to Cooper?"

"Not when I got hit, they hadn't."

Curt went back to his cot, half-choked with horror and anger. He thought of the girl standing there in the door listening to the whole conversation. It would have been easier and more natural for her to have thrown in with the law, and with her employer, Cooper; for Curt was convinced now that Cooper, perhaps for a cut of the

199

bounty money, had sided with the sheriff. But she had waited until the letter was in the vault, then had simply warned Curt not to do anything foolish.

And now she was dead! It was certain that Cronyn would not stop until he had her out of the way, with the blame for it on Curt and his two killers. Curt felt a pity well up in him. Women had never meant anything to him because they seemed weak, spineless, always taking their opinions from the crowd and from cheap, mouthy jaspers. Yet this girl had been cool and courageous enough to believe the truth and fight for it.

He lay down on the cot. The steady hammering on the safe was consistent and dogged.

"Like driving the nails in a coffin," Curt thought in despair. He rolled a cigarette and smoked it down. Rig was asleep. So was Scoggins. Life seemed pretty good right now, too good to hand over to a bounty-hunting sheriff.

He was looking at the ceiling, tracing the streaked pattern of whitewash out of his cell to the corridor ceiling. Right around the stovepipe where it went through the roof, it was smudged in brown whorls from rains.

Suddenly, he sat erect, watching the pipe. Slowly, the top joint was being pulled apart, inch by inch. He watched it breathlessly. The two joints of pipe wavered, parted and the lower six-foot section swayed gently, as if it were going to crash, then settled steady. The other section disappeared through a hole in the roof.

He was at the bars now, waiting.

"Can you hear me down there?" a voice whispered.

"Yes," Curt called. It was a woman's voice, surely.

"Then get ready." Even as it spoke, something was lowered through the roof hole on a piece of string. It was let down about five feet.

Curt suppressed a shout of delight. It was gun belts and two guns, wrapped tightly with string.

As he watched, a gloved hand and shirt-sleeved arm reached down through the hole, and grasped the string. Then slowly, the guns started to swing, pendulumlike. There was six feet of space the arc had to cover before Curt could reach them. It took an eternity, and Curt was sweating as he watched. Slowly, but surely, the length of the arc increased, just missing each time the unsteady stovepipe.

At last, it was swinging wide, and Curt reached through the bars, grabbing frantically at it. He missed, cursing. The guns fell back, just touched the opposite wall, then swept toward him again. This time, he had his belt, an end in each hand. As the guns reached the limit of their arc, he flipped the half loop of the belt up. It caught the guns easily, held them.

Then slowly, the string was played out as Curt drew the guns to him. He reached out, got them, wedged them through the bars.

"Who is it?" he called.

No answer. The string was withdrawn. In a few seconds, the pipe came down through the hole, fitted on the joint, and there was silence.

Curt blinked. Had it happened? He looked down at the guns. Was it one of that whippoorwill Cronyn's tricks, so that Cronyn could claim he shot Curt in self-defense? Curt unwrapped the gun belts, examined first the guns, then the shells. They seemed all right. He looked up at the stovepipe again. Hadn't it been a woman's voice that spoke? It was hard to tell a whisper.

He woke Rig up and told him what had happened. When he was finished, Rig said: "Right behind here is a meeting hall of some sort. She could have dropped out of the second-floor window to the roof.''

"She? Do you think it was the girl, Rig?"

"I dunno. I'm only going on what you said."

But it couldn't have been anyone else, Curt thought. One of his own men would have told his name. And he had no other friends in town.

Scoggins was awakened. It was decided to toll a guard into the corridor, disarm him and get the keys, then leave the jail as quietly as possible.

"Understand," Curt said to Scoggins, "I'm doing this on one condition; that we ride to the governor and you give him this story straight."

Scoggins promised. They decided that Rig and Scoggins would start a noisy quarrel, hoping to draw in a guard from the outer room.

Curt sat down on the cot, the two guns beneath him. Rig and Scoggins started quarreling through the bars. Their voices rose in well-feigned anger. Rig's cursing was vicious, violent, almost talented.

The corridor swung open with a slam, and a deputy raced into the corridor, gun in hand.

"What the hell's going on here?" he snarled. He was a lean man, with no chin, and his face was ugly with strain and sleepiness.

"Put that jughead over in another cell," Rig growled. "I was asleep and I woke up to catch that thieving polecat trying to hook my boots." His tone was wrathful, peremptory, and it acted on the guard just as they thought it would.

"Yeah? Well, who the hell are you to give orders around here, fella'?"

"Get him away," Rig growled. "If he comes close to me, I'll choke them boots outta him."

"Mebbe a pistol whipping would take some of the salt outta you," the guard sneered.

202

"I never said it wouldn't," Rig answered sullenly.

The guard slashed out with his gun through the bars, and Rig skipped nimbly aside, smiling a little bit.

"Why, damn you!" the guard snarled, fumbling in his pockets for the keys. Curt waited. He wanted to be sure. And strangely enough, the guard found he did not have them on him.

He looked at Rig. "I haven't got the keys on me, hombre, but one more peep outta you and I'll get 'em."

He stood there glaring at Rig, who said nothing. Then he turned and walked out.

Rig waited five minutes, then he started in again. His voice fairly bellowed as he cursed Scoggins. It took the guard a good two minutes to come this time, but he came with the keys.

He was cursing under his breath and glaring at Rig as he unlocked the door with one hand, swung it open and waited for Rig in the corridor, a gun in his other hand.

But, nevertheless, he was cautious. "Step out here!" he commanded. Curt rose from the cot, a gun wedged in his belt behind him.

Rig stepped out under the deputy's gun and the cell door was swung shut. Curt drifted to the bars, looking out. The guard stood in the corridor, glaring at Rig.

"You asked for it, hombre, and you're going to get it," he snarled.

His gun curved up in a swift arc. Curt whipped his gun around and jammed it savagely in the guard's ribs.

"Don't move!" Curt ordered. "Don't make a sound!"

Slowly, the guard turned. He looked at Curt a long moment. His glance fell to the gun; then raised to

Curt's eyes.

"You haven't the guts to let it off," he said softly. "You'd bring the whole place down on you with a shot—or a yell."

"I reckon you're right," Curt drawled thickly. "Only, you ain't got the guts to yell and find out, have you?"

The guard did not move. "Have you?" Curt taunted. "Go ahead. Yell, or let that gun off."

It was a tense second, then Rig laughed. He walked over, reached for the guard's gun, took it and the holstered one; then, while Curt was covering the guard, he opened the two cell doors.

Rig was businesslike. He handed his guns to Scoggins, then took a swift, savage slam at the guard's jaw. The deputy melted to the floor. Rig bound him, while Scoggins gagged him; then they locked him in the cell, first taking his watch, which showed it was an hour till daylight.

"If we can clear outta here before daylight, we got a chance," Curt whispered. Above all the subdued noise of the street, they could hear the steady slogging at the safe in the bank.

Curt eased the corridor door open a few inches. The sheriff's office proper held two cots, a table, a gun rack on the wall, and two rickety chairs. A candle guttered on the table. One of the cots was empty; the other held a sleeping figure. Curt looked at the two front windows. The shades were down. He tiptoed across the room until he stood over the sleeping man; then he and Rig waked the man at the point of a gun, gagged and bound him and blew out the candle.

Inching the street door open, Curt saw what they had to buck. Every fifty feet out in the street, a guard was posted. A bonfire had been built at the four corners, so

204

as to afford light in case of a jail break. There was a light in the bank, where the sheriff was doubtless working.

Curt drew back; Rig looked out.

"It's shoot it out, Curt, and we got a fifty to one chance of ever reaching a horse."

Curt leaned back against the table, scowling.

"Why, dammit, let me go out there," Scoggins said. "There ain't but five people that saw me. They'll think I'm a deputy. I'll go get some horses, pull them up behind the office here, then you two rannies make a break for it."

"Nothing doing," Curt said shortly. "You're the only jasper we got between us and a noose or a prison term. If they kill you, we're outta luck."

"Well, how you going to do it?" Scoggins demanded.

"How many people saw us this afternoon, Scoggins?"

"Everyone in the bank—all them deputies, the sheriff, the girl, the clerk, and the banker and a bunch of kids."

"No one else?"

"I don't know. They got me just after you. But I figured the sheriff was in a hurry to get you away before anyone talked with you. That's why he never let anyone in the jail."

"Then let's walk out," Curt said, straightening up. "Any jasper that thinks it looks phony will see our guns and think we're one of the mob that's deputized."

"It's a long—" Rig began, when suddenly a voice started bawling out into the night.

"Help! Help! They've escaped!" It was the guard, inside the cell. Scoggins' gag had worked loose.

"Why—" Scoggins began, whirling and heading for the cell.

205

Curt yanked him back. "It's too late," he said savagely.

He swung the door open and stepped out onto the street. The guard toward the jail had dived back in the alley at the sound of the voice, and was running around to the back window instead of into the jail.

"That saves us for a couple of seconds," Curt growled. "Don't run. Pretend like you don't know there's anything wrong."

Casually, the three of them turned toward the corner. At the same moment, a figure slid out of the shadow of the bank and moved toward them at a swift pace.

Curt felt his insides go cold, and his hand dropped to his right gun.

"It'll start right with that jasper," he muttered.

IV

Rig wanted to cut down on the man coming across the street and he said so. Curt shook his head.

They were strolling the few feet to the corner. Swiftly, the man was approaching. There was a guard leaning against the corner of the sheriff's office, and Curt hung back a little.

Now the man was behind Rig. He stepped out around Rig, and walked past Curt.

"Follow me and slug the guard at the entrance," a voice muttered, and again it was a woman's voice. Curt nodded, not even turning his head and the woman passed him, walked beyond the guard without a word and headed across the street.

As she passed, the guard at the corner straightened up. Curt saw his hand drop to his gun.

"Wait a minute," the guard called after the girl. She

did not turn. The man whipped out his gun, and Curt lunged for him, streaking up his gun as he did so. The man whirled at the sound behind him, turning smack into Curt's down-clubbing guns. Curt yanked him back alongside the building, and the three of them strolled out into the street after the girl. The fire was bright and hot, and Curt wondered with a crawling back how many men had seen him slug the guard. But he did not hurry his pace.

The girl was paused at the dimly lighted entrance of the land office, talking to a guard. Apparently, they were arguing.

"Is she loco?" Rig muttered. "That's where they're forted up waiting for Clem."

But they were drawing near now. Curt saw the guard look up; it was one of the deputies.

Even as he did so, the commotion behind them at the jail had started. Yells and shots came from the side street.

It was enough for the guard. He brushed the girl out of his way, his hands blurring for his guns. But Curt was quicker. Still walking toward shelter, he streaked for his guns, swiveled them up; they exploded. The deputy was slammed against the store; then his feet slid out from under him and he sat down, head on chest.

"Run for it!" Curt ordered. As if the whole town had been waiting for the signal, a crash of gunfire from the bank boomed out. Curt, Scoggins and Rig reached the door just as a blistering fire slammed into the store front.

Inside, Curt saw the woman waiting. "Out the back!" she said swiftly, "then left and into the livery stable. Follow me."

As they worked their way through the building, Curt could see the preparations that had been made for

Clem's raid. The land office and a disused store building. Two counters had been dragged across the front and back. Cases of cartridges and a stack of rifles lay on the floor.

They followed the girl, who vaulted both counters, heading for the rear door.

Curt had just cleared the last counter in his effort to catch the girl when a vicious blast of gunfire through the rear door of the building lighted up the whole night. He saw the girl stagger and fall.

"Get back," Curt yelled to Rig. Then, on his stomach, he crawled up to the figure on the floor, and dragged her back and around the end of the counter.

Rig and Scoggins had lighted the lantern and were squatting behind the counter. Rig looked at Curt.

"We can still try and fight out the front," Scoggins said.

Curt shook his head. "Not with her. And I ain't leaving her. If you jaspers want to take the chance, go ahead."

"Like hell," Rig growled. He turned to the rifles. "Come on, Scoggins, load up. We've been bought into a real scrap," he added grimly.

Curt knelt by the figure. It was the girl from the bank all right, and she was so beautiful that Curt hesitated before he touched her. Her left arm was bandaged tightly. Just above the bandage, a red stain was spreading on her shirt.

Curt cursed silently, working feverishly. He stripped the shirt down to the shoulder, then, looking around, saw the pails of water that the defenders had carried in for just this emergency. He swabbed out the wound, a flesh crease, then bathed the girl's face with cold water. She roused.

Curt smiled. "Take it easy. I'll have you tied up in a second."

He could hear the steady sweep of gunfire which was being directed into the front and rear of the store. Luckily, the sheriff's forces had backed the counters with sacks of feed from the livery stable. They were safe for a while, Curt knew, but a rush would cut them down. They were trapped, three men and a strange girl—a girl who had risked her life more than once this day to save them.

He bandaged the shoulder, trying to show a confidence he did not feel.

When Curt was finished, she sat up. Scoggins at the rear, Rig at the front, had opened up now, their shots sounding just a little sharper than the street firing. The girl saw it and understood. Her gaze settled on Curt, and she smiled weakly.

"Who are you?" Curt asked her.

"Marge Cooper. It was my dad in the bank."

"What happened to him?"

"Dead," the girl said bleakly. "When Cronyn shot me, he must have killed dad. Anyway, I woke up in Doc Duffey's house with a deputy guarding me."

She shrugged. "Cronyn had already told doc that you had shot me and killed dad. He coaxed these men out of here for a meeting in the bank—trying to keep them from lynching you. He's trying to hold them off until he gets the safe open, so he'll destroy the letter, then collect the reward."

Curt's eyes clouded over. "Then it was you who slipped the guns to me?"

She nodded. "I stole some clothes and climbed out a window."

"But why?"

"You are innocent; you are trying to go straight. If poor dad had known it, he would never have given the signal to Cronyn to come over."

Curt nodded, feeling sick. The girl had done her valiant best to save them from a killer sheriff. And now they would die—the girl, too—for Cronyn would see to that. Curt was kneeling beside her, looking dully at the front of the building. He felt her hand on his arm, and he looked at her. She was crying softly, with a grief that strangled her.

"I—I know what you're thinking. Don't. I brought it on myself." And suddenly, she leaned on Curt's shoulder and wept as if her heart would break. Curt patted her shoulder awkwardly, listening dully to the roar of the gunfire that was slamming into both counters with a deafening tattoo. He was frantically casting about in his mind for some way to escape, some way to save her. He would have sold his life to get her to safety, but he knew it was hopeless. Gently, then, he put his hands on her shoulders and looked at her.

"Marge," he said huskily, "You don't mind dying?"

"No more than you," she said softly.

"I do. I mind it like hell," Curt said huskily. "Because tonight I've found something to live for, something I never knew there was before—a good, brave woman. But I don't mind dying for that either. I reckon I've lived to see what I wanted most to see—even if I don't live to have it—and love it."

"We have a little while, Curt," Marge said huskily.

He held her in his arms a bitter minute, the whole barren procession of his life forgotten, and now dead. He had found a woman he could love, and she loved him. That was all a man could ask. Then he broke away from her, his face bleak and stern and cold. Only his eyes were gentle.

"We'll sell out high, darling. And when we do, we'll have had this."

He looked at her a long moment, drinking in her beauty and goodness; then he turned from her, picked up a rifle and joined Rig. Without a word, Marge began to collect the empty rifles and reload them.

Curt looked out. Across the street atop the sheriff's office, fifteen men were forted up, pouring a scalding fire into the room.

"Wonder how long it'll be before they think of dynamite?" Rig asked.

"Not long," Curt said. "They'll rustle a bunch of axes from the hardware store, knock a hole in the roof, then drop it down on us."

"On the girl, too," Rig said softly. "Damn their black and cowardly hearts!" His face was dark with fury.

"Curt, ain't there any way out? Nothing? If they knock us over, can't we get the girl safe somewhere?"

Curt shook his head. "We're through, Rig. Even if Clem could get to us, he'd only stop it a little. It's curtains for us all."

"Then by Heaven, they'll remember us," Rig snarled.

They worked like madmen, trying to keep up a hot, telling fire. A pail was placed over the lantern, throwing the place in utter darkness. They moved from position to position trying to make every shot count. A savage fire directed at the roof of the sheriff's office drove the attackers back momentarily.

In a lull, they could hear a beating on the roof. Curt looked at Rig, then at the girl, who had not heard it, then back at Rig. He shook his head, and Rig nodded.

They were yanked to attention by a rush at the front door. Twenty men suddenly swarmed around the end of the building clawing through the wide windows into

211

the room.

The girl leaped to the counter to help. It was a frantic five minutes, the three of them pouring lead into the oncoming men. At this range, Curt and Rig used six-guns, firing them in one swift, chattering roar, then grabbing others from the pile Marge had stacked behind them.

It was an advance of death for the attackers. Only one hardy gunman reached the counter, and Curt clubbed him with the butt of a gun. The mob broke, scattered, and retreated.

Scoggins had kept his fire directed at the rear, so as not to have a loophole for another attack.

Rig was hit in three places, none of them bad. Curt had a bullet crease on his cheek, another in his ribs, and a hole in his shoulder which was bleeding badly.

The girl bandaged them, while they reloaded. When she touched Curt, he smiled up at her in the gloom. His face was powder-grimed and sweating, his shirt wet with blood, but his face was strangely composed and gentle. Scoggins and Rig were back at their posts and the girl knelt beside him.

"The next one will be the last," she whispered. "I know. They'll try the front and rear both, with more men."

Curt nodded. "I'm ready."

"So am I," Marge whispered.

Even as she knelt, the fire swelled. Curt leaped to his feet. The whole town seemed to be swarming into the building! A mob broke from the side of the sheriff's office, running for the land office! Around both corners of the building, men were pouring in! The whole night was lighted by the gun flares.

One last look at Marge, by his side, and Curt opened up. He jumped the counter, standing in front of her, six-guns blazing death!

212

Scoggins had waited for the rush at the back entrance, but it did not come. He ran to the front counter to side Rig and Curt and the girl.

This was the finish! Once the mob came, and they would overwhelm them by sheer force of numbers, Curt knew. But he fought with a drunken, savage elation. When enough of them got in the store, it would be over!

Then a thunder seemed to shake the building and rise above the snarl of gunfire! Curt looked through the gun smoke over the heads of the attackers.

A mob of horsemen had milled up in front of the place. Even now they were dismounting, shooting!

Clem! But where had he got all the men?

Curt whirled, and threw Marge to the floor with one powerful sweep of his hand. "Down, Marge!"

As he did so, his glance raised to the back of the room.

There, inside the room, guns already barking, were more attackers. And in the vanguard was the sheriff. They had crept in when Scoggins deserted his post.

Curt growled savagely in his throat, forgetting the mob in front. They were caught now between two fires.

He leaped the counter, and started for the back end of the room.

Already the sheriff was shooting, but Curt walked on, his guns hot and waiting. A blind, red rage seemed to cloud his eyes, but he knew that he would not be killed until Cronyn was dead.

A slug caught him in the leg, and he raised his guns. The sheriff was advancing, too, game to the last. All Curt could see of him was twin spouts of fire, two feet apart.

Then he opened up, still walking, his hot eyes looking only at the space between the color. Another slug caught him in the shoulder, but he advanced. Dimly, he saw that the three men with the sheriff turned and ran through the back door. But the sheriff kept coming!

Then Curt stopped. He had three shots left! Feet wide apart, his gun bucking savagely in his hand, he let the sheriff have it! The shots were so close together they sounded as one.

As he finished, Curt raised his right gun and with a cry threw it at the sheriff! The aim was true—but the sheriff was not hit by it.

He had slumped to his knees in a strange attitude almost like prayer; then he pitched his length on his face!

Drunkenly, Curt laughed. He turned, only now realizing that the gunfire had slacked. He staggered to Rig's side. He could see that the members of the mob had their hands high. They had got enough.

Curt dropped the rifle he had just picked up and looked around him. Then, on the floor, he saw her.

His blow had swept her to the floor, and she had hit her head in the fall. Trembling, cursing, praying, Curt got water and bathed her face.

Her eyelids shuttled back, fluttered; then, all Curt could see was her eyes. He held her to him.

Much later, Curt felt someone shaking him roughly. He looked up. There was Clem, grinning, a stranger, beside him.

"I been talking to you for ten minutes, Curt."

"Wh-what about?"

Why, telling you what happened. I rode over to the next county, trying to get some help. The sheriff happened to be over in this little town on business. I told him the story and brought him over."

"Sheriff?" Curt asked blankly. "He's dead."

214

"Why, dammit, man, you—" Clem began, half laughing.

"It's a nice night outside," Rig said meaningly. He took the neighboring sheriff by the arm and led him around the counter toward the front of the store.

Curt looked down at Marge. "Do you know what they were talking about, darling?"

"Something about a nice night, wasn't it?"

"They weren't half right," Curt murmured.

THE DOCTOR
KEEPS A PROMISE

In the seven years since Mason Weber stepped down into the thick dust of Warms' street and received the microscope, the roped trunk and the seven heavy medical books handed him by the freighter who had brought him, he already had made his fight and lost it. It was the kind of fight only a shy man can make and a sensitive one can realize he has lost. He lost it when the county elected Dr. Caslin as its coroner, leaving Mason Weber to wonder who the thirty-two people were who voted for him instead of for the older doctor.

He had found out in the two years since. They were the men in bib overalls, and their women, the farmers from the country out under the San Dimas bench where the big Spade outfit, the Bearpaw, the Seven X and the Bib K had shoved them. They were the Mexican families whose adobes had been pushed to the farthest edge of town and who still called Warms by its old name, San Antonio de Jacona. And they were two bartenders from different saloons, both old men, who came to Dr. Weber because he knew good whiskey from bad and demanded it of them in quart bottles.

Save for these two, the rest were humble people, mostly unwanted people, farmers in the cattle country.

The town, loyal to the big outfits that gave them a living and hated hoemen, had done something to these people who were Dr. Weber's patients. They were so little used to asserting themselves that unless he heard them ascend the steps to the tiny waiting room above Sais' harness shop and went out to them, they would sit there a whole afternoon, talking in whispers and trying to keep from shuffling their thick-soled shoes. But they were his people and he was their doctor, for the town and the big outfits had shoved him into obscurity, along with his patients.

He heard these steps this afternoon, however, and opened the door into the waiting room. The girl was standing away from the door and behind her the sun poured through the single curtainless window, so that he could not see her face.

He squinted a little at the glare and stood aside, a slim, not tall man in wrinkled trousers and a white shirt whose cuffs and collar had been twice turned. He had skipped yesterday's shave, so that the pale wedge of his face seemed more slack than it was, and its expression was musing and indifferent and faintly proud. With his free hand he buttoned his vest and with the other he made a gesture of half-remembered elegance as he said, "Step inside, please," in a voice that was still thick with sleep or whiskey.

"No, it's not for me," the girl said quickly. "It's— can you come with me?"

Dr. Weber closed his eyes and inclined his head in assent.

"No, you mustn't!" she said hurriedly. There was something so urgent in her voice that it made him pause as he began to turn and look at her. "I mean, nobody must see you. Can't you pretend you're going somewhere else?"

"Just where am I going?" he asked quietly. He had a dry, impatient manner of speech that antagonized people, and in that moment he realized it again and wished he had spoken more gently.

She did not answer for long seconds, and he took two slow steps into the room and to the side of it, so that he could see her face. Where she stood now, the sunlight cut across her chest in a hard and merciless way that did not flatter her. It brought out the spots on her cheap bombazine dress and raised the veins in her red and work-worn hands. Above the gash of sunlight was the kind of face with which he had come to be familiar, the face of a farm woman. It was too thin and too angular, as if its blood were used up before it could feed the flesh that lay beneath, and it had a dignity that was its own beauty. She was looking at him, wanting to speak and afraid to, her blue eyes gauging a chance that she was reluctant to take.

"Now, what is it you want?" Dr. Weber asked, and this time his voice was kindly, purposely so.

"I've got to trust you," she began. Her voice was calmer now, too. "I—he's in trouble, my—this man. I don't know what kind, only he's hiding and he's hurt."

"Gunshot?"

"Yes." She kept her eyes steady. "Will you help him, come to him?"

"All right. Where is he?"

"You can't come to him. That's just it." She took a deep breath and looked down at her hands and he saw the shudder move her body. "I guess the hiding is more important than the wound. He thinks so. You'll have to wait until dark."

"Where is he shot?"

"The chest."

"Then it can't wait."

She nodded, saying nothing. Dr. Weber went into

his dark office and got his bag. Before he closed it he corked the bottle of whiskey on the desk and slipped it in the bag, putting on his coat afterward.

She was still standing there, watching the door, when he came out.

"Maybe we can manage it," he said. "Where is he?"

"You don't understand," the girl replied. "I guess I shouldn't have come. You see, he says they'll be after him. And if they ask you where he is, you'll have to tell them, won't you?"

"Not unless I want to."

"Why wouldn't you want to?" the girl said with quick bitterness. "If he's done something they shot him for, why shouldn't you turn him in?"

Dr. Weber's voice was edged with asperity and impatience as he said, "I'm not a sheriff, miss. I'm a doctor. You've got my promise, for what it's worth."

She hesitated only a moment and then told him where to come. Afterward, he went out, leaving her there in the waiting room as she requested, so they would not be seen together.

Over on the street the wooden awnings caught and held the midafternoon heat, and Dr. Weber carried his hat in his hand. Passing Prince's Keno Parlor, he nodded briefly to the two punchers in chairs back-tilted against the wall, and they said just as briefly, "Hello, Doc." He listened for any note of hostility in their greeting and he could find none, only a kind of unbending indifference that was almost dislike. The sour, smoky scent of alcohol made a cool wedge of air in front of the swing doors as he came abreast them. Murdo McFie on his way back to his bank upstreet came through the swing doors in time to see Doc and to pause on the sill, letting the doors nudge his back. The pause was timed so that Dr. Weber had to go ahead, and Doc understood. He walked past without a check in his rather deliberate stride, and McFie said "Afternoon, Doctor," in the kind of neutral voice that Dr. Weber had come to accept. He was even smiling over it as he turned at the corner toward McGovern's stable.

Once on his horse he followed her directions, striking south out of town. When he was out of sight of it over the low ridge, he left the road, swinging west, the reek of the sage and dust hot in his nostrils. When he came to the arroyo, wide and deep and dry, he sloped into it and clung close under the right bank, cutting back toward town. Her landmark was a black and rusty stove dumped into the arroyo years ago when this was the edge of town. Beyond he took the next trail out of the arroyo and found himself in a clump of cottonwoods and seedlings, and he tied his horse among them, afterward crossing an irrigation ditch and walking through a small field toward a cluster of adobe buildings. The sun lay hot on each shoulder blade, so that he straightened up to ease the cloth away from his back.

A Mexican was squatting in the shade of a low adobe building, watching his approach. He rose and took off his hat and opened the door beside him and Dr. Weber stepped into a black, windowless room smelling of stirred dust. The heat here beat at his face, rushing past him as if glad to escape.

He stood there a moment, letting his eyes relax for the darkness, and then he discovered she was beside him. "Over here. On this corn."

"Haven't you a lantern?" he asked.

The girl spoke to the Mexican and he disappeared. Dr. Weber went across the room. The man was lying on clean blankets under which had been stuffed some hay. The bed itself was a heap of field corn leveled out.

There was a dry rustle of shucks underfoot as Dr. Weber took off his coat and waited for the lantern.

Then the girl stood beside him, and he looked at the man. He was a young man, in fever, breathing with a kind of rasping difficulty that sounded ominous. He had a tough, wild face, burned a ruddy bronze, and he kept licking cracked lips. Doc's glance took in the levis and blue shirt, washed and sun-faded to a gray and patched carefully with goods of the same faded color.

"Your brother?" he asked the girl.

"Yes," she said. "He's—" She paused. "He's young and foolish and—and desperate!" she said softly.

Afterward, he asked for hot water, and when it came he set to work. The brother roused fighting, but when he understood it was the doctor, he lay back unsmiling, fear in his eyes. The bullet had shattered the lower rib on the right side, and it was lodged deep in the muscles that flanked the spine. It was a wicked and long afternoon for the boy, and it took all the whiskey in the doctor's bag to numb the pain; and when the probing was done he lay there gaunt and gray and shrunken. He had not allowed himself a scream.

Dr. Weber was surprised to find it was dark when he was through. He was shaking and he wanted a drink, and he walked over to the door, reaching for his pipe. He had not looked at the girl, had not spoken to her, save to give her orders, but now she was holding his coat in her hands, waiting to help him on with it.

"That was pretty rough," Dr. Weber said, looking closely at her. Her nostrils were a little pinched, and her upper lip was beaded with sweat.

"Yes," she murmured huskily. "Is it always that bad on them?"

* * *

222

Dr. Weber hadn't meant it that way. In his inarticulate and gentle way he was trying to tell her that it had taken courage to watch it. But she contrived to shoulder aside his sympathy, and he smiled a little at it.

"You're not from around here," he said. "I haven't seen you."

"We had a place out under the bench, but we lost it," the girl said levelly. "I'm in the kitchen at the Stockman's House." She moved a little, pulling up her shoulders which were sagging. "Will he be all right, Doctor?"

Dr. Weber shrugged and said, "Get word to me if there's any change; I'll be here later tonight," and went out. The Mexican had his horse outside, and he mounted and rode back to town, this time by the dark wagon road that threaded its way to the main street. Through his weariness his mind kept thrusting back to the girl. It was not so much what she had said to him, for that was negligible; it was what she had left unsaid. There had been no reference to his promise of secrecy, and that was something a man would not have abstained from in her place. He turned this over in his mind, remembering those kitchen-worn hands, and he thought he knew why she hadn't spoken. Those poor farmers had to have faith in others, since they could not buy help.

He put up his horse at McGovern's and headed upstreet, turning into Prince's Keno Parlor for the drink that had been on his mind these many hours.

Almost the whole of the saloon was clustered at the bar when Doc entered. There was a monotonous argument going on, with almost everyone having his say. Tim Prince, who spotted Doc before either of his bartenders, came over and set the bottle on the bar, and then stood there, his gray head turned, listening to the talk.

Doc took his drink, and then a word spoken louder than the others narrowed his attention.

"Did they say holdup?" he asked Tim Prince.

"Yeah. The stage was stuck up last night just as it pulled onto the Bench. One robber. Gus Envers, he's the driver, threw down on him and hit him, and then this fella cut loose and knocked Gus off the stage top."

"Kill him?"

"Gus? No. The fall knocked him out. After he come to, he made it to the Spade."

Doc raised his eyebrows and looked down at his drink.

"Funny thing," Prince said slowly. "When the Spade boys come back to the stage the express box was looted. The robber got it."

"He couldn't have been hit bad then," Doc observed.

"He bled enough so the Spade boys tracked him back to town."

"Here?" Doc said slowly.

"That's right. He's here in Warms. So is the loot."

Doc said nothing and paid for his drinks and Tim Prince walked back to the group. Doc went up to the group and listened to them. Four dusty Spade riders, their backs to the bar, were arguing.

One of them said, "All right. Sure he could have went back up the arroyo. You can't track in blowed sand the way you can on the sage flats. Only if he went up it instead of into town, where'd he go?"

"He's here," another Spade puncher said. "Sure as hell, he's here."

"I bet he ain't," a new voice said. "I bet you could turn him up in some of them hoemen's shacks under the Bench."

"Are you sure he was hit bad?" a townsman asked.

"Gus heard the breath slam out of him, he says. He

224

grunted."

"A man'll do that when he's hit in the leg."

"No, he won't," the Spade rider said. "He'll howl or he'll swear. When he's hit bad, he may try to yell but he can't."

Doc cleared his throat. He cleared it in such a way that the puncher, who was going to elaborate, stopped in mid-gesture and looked at Doc. The others caught that glance and shifted their attention to Doc, too.

"That's nonsense," Doc said. His voice was dry and sharp, although he did not intend it to be. "If he was hit bad, he would not have stayed to rob. He would hit for the hills to hide."

He ceased speaking and nobody said anything for a moment. "All right," the puncher said, then. Again there was silence, and Doc turned on his heel and walked out.

Outside, he walked slowly, listening to a small warning voice inside him. This was narrowing down, and when it did he would not have the liking of these people to bolster him.

He went back to his office and lighted the lamp and closed the door into the waiting room. After two drinks of whiskey he took down his books and read all he could find on gunshot wounds.

He was reading this when he heard the steps on the stairway. He carefully picked up his lamp and was standing in the office doorway when they came in. There was Charlie Coulter and Ferd Willis, one from the Bearpaw and the other Spade's foreman. There was Hod Strosnider, the express agent. He was a Texas man, thin-lipped and bleach-eyed, and his bones were too big for the weight of him, and he stank of horses, not the way a rider does, but the way a dirty hostler does. And there was Murdo McFie, from the bank,

225

solid and square and deliberate, with level, curious eyes. They greeted Dr. Weber and he set the lamp on the table and Murdo McFie, their leader, sat on one of the two chairs in the room and put his hands on his knees. The rest stood.

"You can't all be sick," Dr. Weber said, smiling.

"Hardly," McFie said. He looked over at Ferd Willis and Ferd looked at the floor in a way that might have been his diffident manner, but Dr. Weber knew was not.

"You've heard about the holdup, Doctor," McFie stated.

"I heard," Doc replied. He let it go at that.

McFie looked down at his hands. "Dr. Caslin hasn't had a call for a gunshot wound today. I wondered if you had."

Dr. Weber shook his head. "No. That would be pretty obvious, wouldn't it?"

"Wouldn't it?" McFie echoed. He was watching Dr. Weber with a steady gaze. There was no judgment, one way or the other, in his square face. He said, "You didn't have a sick call today, then?"

"Yes. I had three."

"Out of town, I mean."

"Yes. Three."

McFie was silent a moment. "You should know a gunshot wound when you see one, shouldn't you?"

"They aren't easy to mistake."

"No." McFie rose. "If you are asked to handle one, you'll report it, of course."

"To the sheriff. Naturally."

McFie was still looking at him. "The bank lost a little money in that holdup, Doctor. It was insured by the express company, of course." He inclined his head toward Strosnider, who had not taken his gaze from Doc's face. "Still, it means higher rates in the future,"

McFie explained, and added almost as an afterthought, "Then there's attempted murder to consider."

"I'll report anything that looks suspicious," Dr. Weber said.

"Yes. Good night." McFie looked at the others. "Coming?"

Charlie Coulter stirred from the window sill where he was sitting and came toward the door.

Hod Strosnider leaned against the wall and said to McFie, "I think we'll stay and learn about gunshot wounds."

McFie looked at Dr. Weber and nodded and he and Charlie Coulter went out. They tramped down the stairs at McFie's solid pace and Dr. Weber heard it distinctly, for the others, Strosnider and Ferd Willis, were silent until the sound of footsteps died.

When Dr. Weber looked back at Strosnider, he saw something in the Texan's eyes that did not surprise him. It was something other than indifference and it was something beyond dislike; and it quickened Dr. Weber's blood.

Strosnider said meagerly, "Where were those three calls, Doc?"

Doc didn't answer. He was watching them, his face shaped in a still half-smile.

Ferd Willis lounged out of the shadow. "McGovern said you got your horse around four. And you bought a drink at eight."

"That's four hours you were gone," Strosnider said carefully.

"Four hours is a long time," Doc murmured.

"You could reach Bearpaw, but you don't go there," Strosnider went on. "You could've short-cut to Cotton's place, only you don't go there either. Or you could've made them hard-scrabble outfits under the

Bench. All in four hours. Which was it?"

"Let's call it the people under the Bench."

Willis smiled slowly. "You rode south, Doc. That's north."

Doc hesitated a minute. "So I lied," he said to them both.

Strosnider lounged off the wall and carefully removed the chair from in front of him before he spoke, before he looked up at Doc.

"I never liked you, Doc," he said quietly. "None of us do. You walk a little too proud for a man to buy you a drink, and you love them farmers a little too much." He took a step toward Dr. Weber, and Willis shifted his feet. "It wasn't McFie that lost that money. It was insured with me, with the express company." He paused, his eyes still and wicked, but when he spoke again his voice was mild: "You show us where he is. We'll find the money."

"Maybe you better find him, too, then," Doc murmured.

"Think a minute, before you get so stiff-necked," Willis said.

"I've thought," Dr. Weber said gently. "Get out!"

Strosnider hit him in the face. He staggered back against Willis, and then was sent to his knees by a blow behind the ear from Willis. He caught Strosnider's kick by rolling his shoulder, and then a rap across his skull sent him into a warm, wet, aching sleep.

Close to daylight, her brother's fever broke. He saw her, smiled, turned his head and died while she was still smiling at him. Afterward, because she had nobody to whom she could turn, she went to Dr. Weber's office. She found him in a corner on his back, his feet tangled in the rungs of a chair.

After she dragged him into the office and onto the

228

leather couch, it took her a long time to think of whiskey. Even when she did she was afraid it would choke him, but she tried it. Afterward, his eyelids shuttled back and he looked at her and then at the ceiling and then at her again.

She said, from down on her knees beside him, "Hadn't I better get Dr. Caslin?"

"You stay here," he said. Presently, he asked her to help him sit up and he grunted a little as she did. Afterward he took a tumbler of whiskey and held it in both hands while she cut away his shirt and bathed his back. She didn't talk and Doc was glad for that.

She got him a clean shirt from the bottom drawer of his desk and he thanked her through lips as thick as his fingers, and put it on. She stood in front of him then, her hands at her sides. "It was all because of Dave, wasn't it?" she asked.

"Dave who?"

"Bechdolt. That's our name. They beat you because you wouldn't tell them where he is."

"How is he?" Doc asked gently, his eyes musing.

"He died this morning," she said quietly.

Doc looked up at her weary eyes and then looked away. "Yes, I guessed he would. I'm sorry."

He took her hand and pulled her to the couch and she sat beside him. Neither of them talked immediately. Finally, she said, "I guess maybe that was the only way out, wasn't it?" in a dull, weary voice.

"He was too young," Doc said gently.

"Yes."

"Tell me about him."

The girl leaned back and closed her eyes. "There's nothing to tell. It's like a match that doesn't strike clean, only sputters. We took our money and tried to homestead out under the Bench. Some cattle outfit—

Spade, the Bearpaw, the Bib K—burned out our stand of wheat last fall. They did that to some others, too, but we had nothing to fall back on."

"So you got a job in town," Doc prompted.

"Yes. I tried to earn enough for seed this spring, but I couldn't. Dave couldn't get a riding job with any of the big outfits. They wanted to break us, drive us out."

"He held up the stage for seed money?"

She nodded slightly. "He was bitter. We couldn't get a loan because we weren't proved up and our only possessions were a team, a plow and a tent. Dave knew about the money shipments on the stage. When he held up the stage he wasn't going to shoot. He told me. But when the driver shot him, he thought he would be captured. That's why he shot at the driver, so he wouldn't be taken and drag me into it." She looked at Doc briefly, bitterly. "He wouldn't even let his friend, the Mexican, tell me he was hurt. The man did anyway."

"Money for seed," Doc murmured, anger touching his voice. He stood up, unaided, and walked slowly across the room. He noticed something now on the chair and he asked idly, his voice musing, as if he were not thinking of what he asked, "What's that canvas sack?"

"The money. All the money. It isn't touched." Suddenly, she started to cry, making no noise, only the tears rolled down her cheeks. Doc stood above her, helpless, slow fury making his lips tremble.

"They'll get their money back," Doc said slowly. "They'll get something else too. They'll get what I've been wanting to say for seven years."

She looked up at him, fear in her face. "But you can't take the money back now! Not after last night!"

"They think I'm in it already. They'll know it now."

"But why should you be punished?"

Doc smiled unpleasantly. "Let's see if I am," he murmured. He walked over to his desk and took out a six-gun and rammed it in his hip pocket. He put on his coat and took up the canvas sack, and all the time she was watching him.

Paused in the doorway, he said, "I guess I need you beside me." He hesitated, at once shy and stubborn. "Afterward, I mean. Will you wait?"

She nodded and saw him smile. He went down the steps, holding himself straight, breathing very gently against the fire that was in his ribs. The town was awake and on the street, but the people who stared at Doc didn't bother him. He went upstreet toward the bank, and saw Ferd Willis lounging in its open door. He came erect and put his thumbs in his belt as Doc approached and stopped. Ferd's face was bland and wary, cocked for trouble.

"Changed your mind, Doc?" Ferd asked.

"Not any," Doc said quietly. "He's dead."

Willis looked at him levelly for a moment. "Who was he?"

"You'll never know, Willis. None of you."

"Maybe some more of what we gave you last night would change your mind."

"It might," Doc said gently, "if I got any more. I don't think I will."

He shouldered past Willis, walked the length of the long counter on the right and found Murdo McFie in his office at the rear. McFie rose from behind his desk, his impassive face as surprised as it ever would be. He was about to speak and then changed his mind, and watched Dr. Weber put the money sack on the desk.

"There's your money. All of it."

"Thank you," McFie said in his spare voice.

Dr. Weber stood there waiting for McFie to speak,

231

but McFie was not going to.

"You want to know who stole it, don't you, Mc-Fie?"

"I did not say so."

"You said so last night."

McFie's glance dropped to the sack, then raised to Dr. Weber. "That was before the money was returned."

"But your friends want to know."

McFie shook his head slowly. "They were not my friends last night, Dr. Weber. I am a businessman entrusted with money. I tried to get back what rightfully belonged to me. But I would never beat up a man that way to get the name of a thief."

"From now on, no one else will," Dr. Weber said softly.

"I would not put my faith in that," McFie said gently. "This is a rough country, Dr. Weber."

Dr. Weber smiled through thick lips. "I have learned that. For seven years I have whispered, McFie. Now I am going to shout."

McFie's face almost broke into a smile. "I think you could."

"I can," Dr. Weber said. "I am going to in about three minutes."

He left the office, shouldering past Ferd Willis at the door. Willis said, "Doc," but Dr. Weber did not pause in his stride. A small knot of people across the street watched him swing under the tie rail and cut slanting across the street and go into the express office.

Hod Strosnider was behind the bare counter of the express office calculating something on a piece of wrapping paper. He looked up into Doc's gun.

"Come out from behind there," Doc said. "I'm about to answer your question."

"About the stage robber?" Hod asked suspiciously.

"Any question you ask," Doc murmured. "The answer will be that it's none of your business. Now come out."

Hod came out, his face sullen and scared, trying to get a clue to Doc's real temper from his one good eye. When he was facing Doc, Doc swung the gun barrel in a rising arc that caught Strosnider on the temple, knocking him down.

"That's how it feels," Doc said. He threw the gun through the open door and came over to stand above Hod.

"Get up!"

Hod scrambled up and Doc hit him with his fist. Hod crashed into the paned window, and then the sill caught him behind the knees and he went on through as the window collapsed in a bell-clear jangle of glass.

Outside, Doc saw him lying there on the boardwalk, his arms a little outstretched, palms up, his feet still inside the window. Doc walked over to the gun, picked it up, and swung to face Ferd Willis across the street.

"Did you have something to say to me, Willis?" Doc called.

Willis was utterly motionless for several seconds. Then he said quietly, "I don't reckon, Doc."

"Maybe you have," Doc said. "I think you and all the other big outfits are pirates, Ferd. I think you're dirty. I don't think you'll stand up to a shoot-out alone, Ferd. If you will, try it now."

Ferd Willis didn't move. Doc gave him ten seconds, and then he turned and walked back to his office and the girl.

When Murdo McFie went home for supper that night, he went straight to the kitchen of the big white house that was his home. He kissed his wife, who turned away from the stove to talk to him while he washed his hands at the sink. While he was soaping his hands, he said, "Agnes, do you think you're an important woman in this town?"

His wife was cautious. She could not see his face, and that meant he was hiding it. She smiled, "I'm the banker's wife."

"How do you feel?"

"I never felt better in my life. Why?"

"Could you develop a pain on a day's notice?"

Her friendly eyes narrowed. "What kind of a rowdy trick are you and Charlie Coulter going to play on Dr. Caslin?"

"It's not Dr. Caslin," McFie said, "and it's not a trick. We're changing doctors."

HIGH GRADE

Ames Littlepage, having yanked down his window blind in the hope of shutting out the heat of early evening and the mingled smells from the reduction mills, turned to contemplate the pleated-bosom shirt on his bed. Naked to the waist, jangling two buttons in his large, half-closed fist, he reflected that he was probably a composite picture of all single men an hour before a party.

When he put on his coat over thick, powerfully muscled shoulders, it was with a sheepish feeling. Downstairs Mrs. Donovan, who owned this boarding house, was laying out a second supper for the Union Consolidated men who had seven miles to ride from the mine after the six o'clock shift took over.

Phil Michelson, one of the crew, good-naturedly growled, "Hello, lucky," to Ames. It was the greeting of a hungry man who has waited too long for food, to one who has already been fed; and Ames, understanding it, grinned as he pushed through the door into the kitchen. His long angular face, glowing after his shave, held a curious mixture of toughness and reflection; there was a gravity in his dark eyes and his face held the faint marks of past fights as well as the hint of buried humor.

Mrs. Donovan's daughter, Lily, was kneading tomorrow's bread on the large kitchen table, her arms almost to the elbows in the yeasty dough. She was trying to push a wisp of wheat-colored hair out of her face with her shoulder as Ames came to stand just inside the door, his shape tall and wide.

"Lily," he said, a slightly embarrassed grin on his long face, "have you got a needle and thread—white thread?" And then when he realized what his interruption meant, he said quickly, "No, no, I don't need it now."

Lily laughed. "Buttons?" Her voice had a pleasant, friendly lilt.

"Yes."

"You'll have to wait a minute and I'll sew them on for you."

Ames settled his shoulder against the wall to wait, and Lily, glancing at him, said, "You might bring the shirt down."

Ames went upstairs, got it and came down again. Lily was drying her hands on the towel that hung above the sink. She took the shirt from him and he followed her out onto the side porch, which held only a small cot and her bureau, lighted by a bracket lamp on the wall. About her clung the good smell of yeasty bread, and Ames wondered idly if the reason her slim back was held as straight as a gun barrel was nature's compensation for the hours she spent in quiet, uncomplaining drudgery.

He leaned against the door frame. "This isn't right," he declared apologetically. "Room and board doesn't include patching up what a Chinaman butchers."

"You should buy some shirts," Lily said, bringing out her sewing basket and sitting down on the cot.

Ames watched her curiously as she looked first at the shirt collar, then at the cuffs.

"These need turning," she remarked. He said nothing and then she ran her hand up the sleeve. Two square inches of her palm showed through a hole in the forearm of the shirt, and she looked questioningly at him. Her eyes were blue, younger than his gray ones, but wiser and there was a friendliness in her mouth that was teasing and yet almost manlike. "And what about this?" she asked.

Ames laughed then. "No one will see it unless we play poker. And if they start poker, I say good-by."

"I can patch it."

"No, I'll slop acid on it again tomorrow, so why bother?" He paused, frowning a little. "Besides, I mean that about the poker."

"They say you can take care of yourself," Lily said, not looking up from threading her needle.

"Not with that crowd," Ames said shortly. "There's Haleman from the Piute Mills. He won't play under a fifty-dollar limit. And Herkenhoff and Wieboldt and that Pacific Shares crowd. They're owners. An assayer hasn't got any business bucking that kind of money."

"You can some day, Ames," Lily told him.

"You think so?" Ames asked quickly.

Lily smiled, but did not look up from her sewing. "What does your Cornelia think? Would she marry a man who couldn't protect himself among her own friends?"

Ames grinned faintly, and shook his head. "She has faith, all right, but damned little understanding, Lily. Being rich, she can't comprehend poverty." He paused, watching her swift fingers sew on the buttons. "But you," he went on slowly, "you're poor, and you know that poor people stay poor. And still you can encourage me."

Lily shrugged. "Rich men like you, Ames. That's all it takes in a boom town like this."

When she was finished he thanked her, smiling, and went upstairs to put on his shirt. He came down again almost immediately, his boots holding a dull polish, his black suit clean, his black hat brushed free of the mica dust that was a part of the air of this town. Lily, who was clearing the table after the last diners, waved and smiled to him as he went out.

The Donovans' boarding house lay just a block from the rutted main street of Piute Sink, and as Ames turned into it the color and noise and bustle stirred him. It was a bawdy, brawling town that talked of gold and shares, of melons and dividends and the stock market, of claims and pumps and judgments, of high-grade stuff, borrasca and bonanzas, of stock rigging and mine rigging—but mostly of gold.

It was young enough so that civic pride had not yet forced the huge, ten-team ore wagons to use the back streets on the way from the mines in the mountains beyond to the reduction mills; and yet it was old enough to contain a three-story brick hotel that stood less than a hundred yards from tent saloons.

Millions of dollars of the big money in San Francisco had been poured into Piute Sink's mines, its mills and their equipment, and still a man could not walk a block of the main street and keep to boardwalk. Welshmen, the Cousin Jacks, the Germans, the brawling and lusty Irish, and the Mexicans from San Luis Potosi all mingled cheek to jowl on its big crowded street.

Faro barkers were pushed to hoarseness by the din from the honky-tonks and saloons, and blooded horses rubbed noses with mules at the tie rails. Mad and rich and profligate as it was, it could get into a man's blood, and it was in Ames'. It was money—raw, brutal and

238

powerful, and he had none of it.

He stepped out into the road to avoid a brawl in front of Harman's Keno Parlor, and a couple of desert rats on the fringe of the curious whooping crowd saw him, waved and went back to watching the fight.

Ames' Assay Office was a slab affair downstreet past the thick of the saloons. He had a pair of defective scales and some choice pieces of ore as window decorations and that was all.

Beyond the window was his littered desk and a small third-hand safe bearing the legend on its door, "Seven Seas Whaling Co., San Francisco." He had never had the lettering changed, and it amused him to have people ask how he had come to switch professions.

The safe was backed against a partition, next to some sample bins, and beyond the partition were his tools of trade—retorts, carboys of acid, tables, sample crushers, sieves, molds, and sacks of fuel.

Ames locked the door after him, lighted the lamp, set it on the floor by the safe and began to fiddle with the safe's dial. There was a report inside which he was to deliver later that evening.

Before he had finished the combination, he heard a knock on the door, and twisted his head, his hand cupped above the lamp chimney to blow the light.

Then, making sure the safe was still locked, he rose and went over and opened the door. A burly man whose features he could not place, spoke from around a cigar. "Evening, Littlepage. Mind if I come in?"

Ames stepped aside, and the man walked straight on through to the sheltering darkness of the partition. "Let's bring the lamp back here, eh?" His voice had a resonant, slightly false note of geniality.

Ames lifted the lamp from the floor, stepped behind the partition and turned. "Name's Manley," Ames' caller said, holding out a thick-fingered muscled hand.

"Know me?"

"Can't say I do," Ames said, shaking hands.

Manley was a big man, almost as tall as Ames himself and thicker because he had gone to fat. Above a rubbery mouth and a small beaked nose his eyes were calculating and utterly without expression, save for a cold brassiness. His clothes were black and unpressed, but the heavy gold watch chain, a solitaire stickpin and the fine pair of boots, all signs of affluence on the frontier, did not escape Ames.

"Can you spare a few minutes to listen to a proposition, friend?" Manley asked.

"I can't think what it would be, but go ahead." Ames drew out his pipe and packed it, leaning back on a sample bin.

Manley was looking around the room, talking at the same time. "You're doing pretty good here, Littlepage. So-so, anyway. Well, that's all right. You got a reputation for absolute honesty in this camp." He turned his head to look at Ames. "Would you sell that reputation for fifty thousand dollars?" he asked in the same casual voice.

Ames scowled. "I don't get it."

"I know. Just think about the fifty thousand dollars a minute. Let me talk." Manley looked at the tip of his cigar. "You're going to marry Liam Costello's daughter, Cornelia, I've heard. Right?"

Ames said nothing, only watched the man intently.

"No offense meant when I say this, Littlepage, only that takes money. He's rich and you're not."

Ames gave a sudden, sardonic laugh, but Manley's face didn't change. "Suppose you had fifty thousand dollars to invest," Manley said carefully. "Keeping that in mind, let me tell you what I heard today. Costello and Herkenhoff are going to raid Pacific Shares' stock next week. Strictly confidential, you understand.

240

They'll dump their shares until Pacific Shares is quoted at ten. What if you bought five thousand at that price? You'd make money, eh, on Costello's little shenanigan?''

"Make it plain talk, Manley. What are you trying to say?''

"No. Not yet. First, I want to show you that if you made yourself a stake, Liam Costello could triple it for you in a week.''

"I know that.''

"Sure. Costello's a pirate. He admits it. He's the slickest stock-rigger in this camp.''

"What do you want?'' Ames asked tolerantly.

Manley laughed and lounged off the table. He started to prowl around the room, talking aimlessly. "Know those two claims north of the Vanity Fair?''

"The Golconda? Sure.''

"They're mine,'' Manley said. His back was to Ames, and he was fingering a pestle. "One hundred and eighty thousand square feet of low-grade gravel, rabbit holes, conglomerate and scrub cedar. It'll make us both rich.''

Ames smiled inwardly at the brass of the man. He knew Manley wanted him to ask questions, and he did.

"Both of us?'' he inquired ironically. "But I'm an assayer, not a promoter, Manley.''

"Wrong,'' Manley said whirling and stabbing a finger at him. "All I need to sell stock in that gravel pit is a favorable assay report, say, eight hundred dollars to the ton in gold and silver. You give it to me and we're rich.''

Ames shook his head. "Even a child wouldn't buy mining stock on an assay report.''

"Wrong again,'' Manley said. He strode over to Ames now, and faced him, his voice low and persuasive. "You're likely too modest to notice it, Littlepage, but you've got a mighty fine name with prospectors around here. I don't mean the swindlers and the stock-riggers; I mean the hardrock men, the discoverers. They like you. If I can show those old desert rats a good assay from you and prove you've bought some stock in the Golconda, they'll talk. They'll carry the word. Pretty soon, the small suckers, the riffraff, the gamblers, the honky-tonk girls, the Mexes, the freighters, all the small-money stuff, will take a ride on my fifty-dollars-a-share stock. I'll peddle it and duck out with half the loot. The other half is yours."

"Just a cheap swindle," Ames said slowly.

"That's it. Only not so cheap. I figure we can make a hundred thousand on it. And you'll be absolutely safe."

Ames looked at him closely. "How do you figure that? I'll have given a crooked assay on worthless ore."

"Oh, no," Manley said, smiling. "Oh, no. I wouldn't let you in for that. The ore I bring in to you will assay at eight hundred dollars a ton. Of course, that ore won't be from the Golconda, but you'd have had no way of knowing that."

"It doesn't ring true, Manley," Ames remarked shrewdly. "All you had to do to put this swindle across was bring me the ore. As you say, I wouldn't have known where it came from." He paused. "Why are you offering to make money for me when you could have kept it all yourself?"

Manley smiled disarmingly and dropped his cigar and stepped on it. "That's to the point," he murmured. "The reason I'm splitting with you is pretty simple. You marry Liam Costello's girl. He'll put you next to a dozen deals where you can make money. You're on top. All right, when you're there you won't forget me. When you rig up a really big swindle, you cut me in. Plain business. Favor for favor."

He held up a hand. "Don't say anything now. Think it over. And just remember a couple of things: You're protected, you take no risk. And the deal doesn't smell a bit more than Costello's or Herkenhoff's or Mathias' or any of the big boys." He smiled. "I'll send my samples around in the morning. Good night." He went out without shaking hands.

When the front door closed behind Manley, Ames did not move for a moment. He was waiting for the anger and the resentment to come. Somehow it didn't. Manley was a scoundrel, of course, but cynical enough to admit it. Ames laughed, picked up the lamp and went back to the safe.

Fiddling with the dial, Manley's words kept creeping into the front of Ames' thoughts. The scheme, of course was a swindle, but no worse than things Costello pulled, as Manley had said.

Suddenly Ames paused in his dialing, stopped by a memory. That Westwind King mine of Liam Costello's that had failed three months ago. On the rumor that a ledge of pure silver sulphurets had been uncovered, Costello had pulled in some big promotion money. For five months the mine had paid well, a dividend was declared, and then the vein disappeared. Or had it? Was the vein ever big enough or deep enough to warrant a huge stock issue?

Stockholders in London and Vienna, where the issues were floated, had gambled on Costello's name and luck. Wasn't it all a swindle, planned and executed in the realm of big money, where bluff, brass, wits and luck served for sagacity and acumen?

Ames shook his head as if in answer to some inner prompting, got the papers he wanted, closed the safe and stood up, a small anger and excitement crawling within him. In a few minutes he would be talking and drinking with these big stockriggers, and no guilt would show on their faces. They were good men, sober, generous, shrewd, industrious. And they were nice to him, liked him well enough to throw business his way when they could.

Blowing out the lamp, Ames looked around the dingy office and back room where he and his helper worked, and suddenly he was disgusted with it and a little ashamed. Out on the street he stopped at the nearest saloon for a drink, and then made his way up the crowded street to the Union House.

Ames climbed a spacious flight of stairs to the right of the lobby and paused at the door of Liam Costello's suite. He was admitted to a foyer by a Mexican maid who took his hat, led him through a short corridor where the smell of rich cigars eddied by him, and then into the large drawing room whose windows looked out onto the main street.

Of the half dozen women there, some of them young, Cornelia Costello was easily the most attractive to look at. She had been watching the door and she came over to Ames immediately, her walk so indolent that it barely stirred the full skirts of her flowered yellow silk dress. She was tall and slim and sulky-looking with her dark creamy skin and eyes that were sometimes brown, sometimes violet. Her mouth was arrogant yet full of humor, the lips generous and almost pouting. She had a kind of mocking, lazy way about her that could stir Ames to disapproval, then make him laugh with delight.

She kissed him, a little too affectionately for this time and place, and then led him over to the table of whist where the Herkenhoffs, man and wife, the Lowry girl with Wieboldt and his two guests from San Francisco, and Liam Costello were lounging.

Costello, a black Irishman, small and with a shrewd, humorous face, was holding up the game long enough to dare side bets on the next hand. He shook hands with Ames, quieted long enough to make introductions, and then resumed his jeering. When there were no takers, he excused himself, poured a drink from one of the bottles on the buffet, handed it to Ames, and then took him and Cornelia over to the young woman and two men who were looking out the window at the street below. It was a free and easy kind of gathering, informal, an almost nightly affair but one still exciting to Ames.

"Pity about the cave-in at the Hopeful last night," Costello remarked, looking down on the crowded street. "No mourning out there, though. How many men caught?"

"Seventeen," Ames answered.

"Why don't we turn our party tomorrow night into a benefit for the widows?" Cornelia asked. "It would be fun."

"It would be a brawl, Connie," her father said.

"No. Not that kind of party. We could make a nice german of it down in the lobby and dining room, with tickets at twenty dollars each, the money to go to the fund." Her eyes began to glow with excitement. "Would the hotel let us, dad?"

"They'd better," Costello said cheerfully, "or I'll vacate a floor for them."

"Would you like it, Ames?" Connie asked.

Before Ames could answer, the other girl, a stranger from the coast, said she, too, thought it would be fun. The group moved over to consult the whist players and Costello was left with Ames.

"Harum-scarum," Costello said. His gray-shot hair rode his tight little skull like a stiff brush. He mouthed a cigar with nervous impatience.

"I heard something tonight," Ames said carelessly. "Money talk. I wondered if it was true."

"What was it?"

"That you're going to raid the Pacific Shares bunch next week."

Costello peered up at Ames from under thick black brows, his glance curious, but giving away nothing. "Since when," he asked, "have you been interested in market talk? Going to get in?"

"Maybe."

"Then come to me, like I've invited you. A tip you pick up on the street is put there for a purpose. It's a lie—invariably." He paused, watching the younger man's face with kindly shrewdness. "Ames, I've tried to help you before."

"I've never had the money to start with," Ames said slowly, in a tone whose carelessness surprised even himself.

"You've got it now? How much?"

"Around fifty thousand." The minute he said it Ames knew the decision had been made when he left the office, and he felt a momentary doubt.

"Good. I'll double it in short order. I'll double that, too," Costello said, grinning. He regarded Ames with complete affection. "You're all right, son. You're proud. You wanted to make your stake first, and I don't blame you." He laughed. "For a while, I had you figured as timid."

Cornelia, who had come up to them in time to hear her father's last words, looked amused. "Ames timid?" she drawled. "He'll be a money man after your own cut, dad. You'll see." She smiled up at Ames with lazy friendliness, and Ames took her hand, strangely angry. This was all it took to make him one of them. Suddenly he had to ask a question of Cornelia, and he did, the urgency of it carefully disguised.

"Would you still have married me if I *had* been timid, Connie?"

She looked at him with gentle mockery in her eyes

246

and then squeezed his hand. "Bless you, I was going to, Ames." And then, as if to tease him she added, "But the pirate in you was obvious. I knew it would break through."

"Money," Costello said, "is simply the dividend of guts."

"Put coarsely," his daughter added.

Costello nodded grimly, arrogantly, smiling at her. "Why not? A slaughterhouse is coarse, and nobody denies it. So is making money, only you slaughter a different breed of sheep."

Herkenhoff, a bald man with a cunning expression on his soft, fat face, came over. "We've got enough for a table of poker, Liam," he said impatiently. "It's either that or I'm going to sleep in a chair."

Ames went home at five in the morning, his brain tired and fogged with smoke and liquor, his spirits depressed. Bare dawn had touched the desert to the east with a momentary coolness, and to the west the clean bare sweep of the Pintwaters was almost cold-looking. The sun was touching the tip of the highest peak when he let himself in.

Out in the kitchen he could hear the muffled clatter of activity. He paused at the stairwell, wondering at this depression, and not allowing himself to think of his decision to take up Manley's proposition.

Suddenly, he turned and walked through the dining room and opened the kitchen door. Lily, waiting for a hot fire, was taking the cloths off the pans of bread which had been set to rise during the night. She looked at Ames and said, "Morning. Going or coming?"

Ames couldn't raise a smile. "Coming, I guess. No, I'm not. I've got work to do today." He looked around him. "Got any wood to chop?"

"Cords of it."

"Good. It'll clear my head." He tramped through

247

the kitchen, peeling off his coat, and then he paused at the door and rammed his hand in his pocket. He brought out a handful of gold coins and jingled them, his somber eyes on Lily. She looked fresh and pretty as she came over and regarded the coins in his palm.

"You won," she said, her glance lifting up to his face.

Ames nodded. "I'm on a lucky streak."

"You always have been," Lily told him. "All you needed was to find it out."

She looked so pretty and so pleased at his luck that suddenly Ames felt a little sick. He recalled the whole hard drinking night against the background of his shoddy decision, and he felt miserable, shamed and in need of help. On impulse then, he took Lily in his arms and kissed her, and she did not resist him.

Finally, Lily pushed away and looked up at him, her eyes grave. "What was that for?"

"Didn't you like it?"

She answered levelly, "Yes, I did."

"Then why do you ask?" Ames asked roughly.

"Because you're engaged to a pretty girl and a rich girl. But all of a sudden you've got lucky and you're drunk. You kiss me. You're unhappy, Ames, when you should be happiest. Why?"

Ames couldn't answer. He scrubbed his face with the palm of his hand and then looked at Lily a long moment before he said, "I wish I knew, Lily."

"It's when you're happy you should kiss me," Lily said. "Then I could understand it."

In the face of her honesty, Ames felt a dismal shame. He shook his head and brushed past her, lurching a little from the liquor. He knew he had done something unspeakable; he had taken a shameful advantage of Lily's open love for him and had cheapened it. Had his decision to throw in with Manley begun an erosion of his character that had led to a drunken fondling of a decent girl? At the same time he denied this, he felt a self-loathing.

He attacked the wood pile and worked steadily for two hours. When he went in again, Lily was upstairs making the beds. He ate and went down to work, his head cleared but his spirits at rock bottom. At nine o'clock two big sacks were dumped in the alley behind the assay office. They contained the ore from Manley.

By mid-afternoon, Ames found that Manley had guessed right. The ore assayed at $700 the ton—$450 in gold, $250 in silver. He made out his assay sheet in detail, left it on a spike in the safe for Manley to call for it, and went home and slept.

Like any tight clan, mining folk take care of their own. Scarcely a night passed but what someone, quarreling over a claim, a table stake, a drink or a girl, was killed. Men stepped over his body to buy a beer, not even trying to remember the face. But let a drift cave in, killing the men who were working in it, and it was different, for there were ways and ways of dying.

When the hat was passed for the widow around the saloons and gambling halls, a gambler would cash in the stake of chips before him, scrape the gold in the hat, and wish the survivors well, not even knowing their names. A honky-tonk girl would contribute a night's earnings. A saloon would raffle a hat at twenty dollars a throw, selling every customer a chance, and turn over the proceeds to the fund. Or, like tonight, a dance at the Union House would be organized, where none was barred and the ticket of admission was twenty dollars. All, from the passed hat to the dance, were peace offerings on the altar of luck, made by a superstitious and open-handed folk.

Lily Donovan, in a blue silk dress that seemed to

249

touch her honey-colored hair with a thousand lights, went to the dance with Phil Michelson, a young engineer from the Union Consolidated.

Sweet charity was smiling so brightly that the Sage Hen, rotund duenna of twenty honky-tonk girls, shook hands with Connie, smiled modestly at Ames, and comported herself with the dignity of a duchess. The men of that woman-hungry camp were scrubbed and polished and sober enough to keep within the strict bounds of decorum. Whoever did not was ushered out swiftly by bouncers loaned from a half dozen saloons. It was gay and fun, completely democratic, perhaps because death, in whose honor it was really held, set the example.

Connie, in a white low-necked dress, was besieged from the start by all the young and personable men in the camp. Ames watched her billowing white skirt on the floor, and smiled with pride. When she passed him, her face flushed with excitement, she would wiggle her fingers in a little salute. After her partner returned her to Ames, following one dance, she said breathlessly, "Who are all these men? They're so nice and all good dancers."

"The broke and ambitious," Ames said, aware of his own membership in their class.

"I'm tired," Connie complained, taking his arm. "Who has the next dance with me?"

"Phil Michelson."

"I don't know him," Connie said carelessly. "Let's go up to the suite for some punch."

"Can't," Ames said shortly. "It's a contract."

Connie looked briefly at him. "Point him out to me."

Ames spotted Phil and Lily across the room, talking to Big Joe Hyde, a saloon owner, and his wife.

"He doesn't look interesting," Connie said when

Ames pointed to Phil. "Let's go up."

"But, Connie, I promised."

Connie searched his face. His obstinacy seemed to touch a spark of resentment in her. "But, darling, I don't want to. I'm tired. Will you come along?"

"He's a nice fellow," Ames said humbly. "I live with him."

"But you live in a boarding house, Ames. Do I have to dance with everyone in the boarding house? Now come along."

"I'll take you to the stairs, but I'm coming back," Ames said stubbornly.

Connie's face changed imperceptibly as she understood the implication. "Oh, you'd like to stay and dance with his partner?"

"Yes. It's custom, isn't it?"

"Who is she?"

"Lily Donovan. She runs the boarding house with her mother. She's my good friend, Connie," Ames explained. His voice was grim enough to warn Connie.

"I'll stay, of course," Connie yielded immediately, humbly, just as the fiddles swung into a schottische.

Phil and Lily came over, and the introductions were made. Connie smiled pleasantly at Lily, who regarded her with friendly, unimpressed eyes, and then the two couples separated to dance.

"She's very lovely, Ames," Lily said.

Ames nodded and then said in a low voice, "I'm sorry about this morning, Lily."

Lily looked up at him. "Why are you?"

"It must have seemed to you that I thought you were cheap and easy. I don't."

"Nobody will ever think I'm cheap and easy because I'm not." Lily's voice was low, her tone serious. "Let's say you were drunk, Ames. Just don't do it again."

"I wish I hadn't done it once," Ames said bitterly.

Lily tilted back her head so she could watch his face. "I'm glad you did."

Ames frowned, puzzled. "Why do you say that?"

"This will probably shock you," Lily said. "I'm glad because now I'll never have to wonder what it would be like."

The music stopped and they sought out Connie and Phil. Ames saw that Phil looked harassed and uncomfortable while Connie's face was bland and proud. She put her arms in Ames' as soon as he joined her. Lily murmured something about the size of the crowd.

"Tell me, Miss Donovan," Connie said curiously, "aren't you the girl who runs Ames' boarding house?"

"Yes," Lily answered easily.

"Isn't it hard?"

Lily smiled. "It's work," she admitted.

"Do you make much money at it?"

Lily was still smiling, and Ames looked down quickly at Connie. Lily laughed. "I had over eight hundred dollars in the bank this morning. A year's work."

"Really?" Connie said, genuinely surprised. "Why, I pay my maid more than that. Perhaps I could put you in touch with some of my friends who could place you in service."

For a moment Lily did not speak, and Ames could see the amazement and hurt well up in her eyes. He looked at Connie, almost ready to express his anger, and what he saw baffled him. Connie, too, had observed the hurt in Lily's face, and she was honestly distressed and bewildered. She glanced up at Ames, pleading for help and an explanation. What was wrong? —her eyes seemed to ask.

But Connie had tact, and she said no more. She put out her hand and Lily took it. "It was nice to meet you both," Connie said sincerely. "I have a headache. I think I'll go upstairs." She shook hands with Phil

252

Michelson.

Ames, as he left, pressed Lily's arm, and then turned away, Connie on his arm.

They went through the lobby and upstairs, not speaking, but when they were in the drawing room, Connie turned to Ames. "What did I say down there that hurt her, Ames? What did I do?"

"You don't understand?" Ames asked wonderingly.

"Do you think I would hurt a girl intentionally? Your friend? And I hurt her. What did I say?"

"You offered to get her a place as a servant with your friends, Connie."

"Shouldn't I have done that? I only meant to be kind, to help her." Connie's eyes were pleading for understanding and forgiveness, and Ames felt his anger drain away. There was nothing he could say, no way to explain the gulf that lay between them, but he was determined to try.

"Sit down, Connie." She sat in a deep chair and Ames stood before her, his brow wrinkled in a frown.

"Lily and her mother own that boarding house. Donovan was a mine super, killed in an accident like this cave-in at the Hopeful. Lily and her mother were left with a little stake, and they turned it into this boarding house. They're making out, all right, even saving a little money."

His voice trailed off in hopelessness. Connie was listening intently, had heard every word, and yet there was no understanding in her eyes, her face, her attitude.

"But she works hard," Connie said. "I only had to look at her hands. She's attractive, and Judy Herkenhoff would love her for a maid. Wouldn't it be better than taking in boarders? Wouldn't she make more money?"

Ames smiled ruefully, and said nothing. Connie

253

leaned back and covered her face with her hands. "I'm so sorry. But I can't understand what I've done, Ames."

"You're tired," Ames said. "Maybe you ought to get some sleep."

She agreed, and Ames kissed her good night and went downstairs, his step deliberate, his eyes musing. Lily and Phil were not in the hall. He got a drink at Harman's and went back to Donovan's.

The dining room was dark, and he tiptoed through it to the kitchen. There was no light there, and no light on the porch. He wanted to talk to Lily, to explain it all to her, tell her that Connie had not meant to hurt her.

But could he tell her that Connie had so little understanding that she could see no hurt in what she had said? Could he make Lily believe that money, the amount of it a person had, was all that counted with Connie? Either you didn't have it or you did. All the people who did have it, or were going to get it, like himself, were her equals; those who did not have it, should try and get it and were all one class, her inferiors, like her servants.

When Ames went down to get his shaving water before breakfast next morning, Lily was in the kitchen.

"Lily," he began, "about Connie last night."

"Let's not talk about it," said Lily. "I'd rather not."

"Let's do," Ames said grimly.

Lily glanced at him briefly. "You want to apologize for the woman you're going to marry, Ames. That's not right, and you know it. Why should you?"

"She didn't mean to hurt you."

"I really believe she didn't mean to, Ames. Can't we let it go at that?"

Ames reached out and turned Lily to face him, and then let his hands drop from her shoulders. "I asked

254

her afterward,'' he said, his glance steady on Lily's face. ''She said she really wanted to help you.'' His eyes suddenly avoided her. ''It's Costello's money,'' he murmured, with a bitterness he could not keep out of his voice. ''It's built a wall around him and Connie and their friends. Everyone who can climb that wall is welcome. Then they ask the stranger about the people outside—like Connie asked you last night.''

Lily laughed suddenly, a calm, easy laugh that dissolved some of the tightness in Ames' chest. ''But why be so earnest about it, Ames? It's you I know and like.''

''But I wanted you to like her.''

Lily looked at him keenly and then smiled her secret, wise smile. ''That never happens. Maybe it was never meant to happen.''

Ames understood that, and he nodded, but he was dissatisfied. Lily was wise, and knew instinctively the things of which a man was ignorant or which he was too stubborn to recognize. He was the one who had been anxious for Lily to meet Connie. Lily had never moved to meet her. Even last night, it was he who arranged the exchange of dances, not Lily, not Phil. And yet, it could have turned out differently, and he voiced this thought. ''When I've married and made some money and lost it, Lily,'' he said with wry humor, ''you and Connie will be friends.''

''Or when I've made myself rich, like I'm going to,'' Lily said lightly.

Ames grinned. ''You've decided to be rich, not a servant?''

Lily looked at him and laughed, and it was all right again. He put a leg on the table and sat down. ''Yes, I decided yesterday, Ames,'' Lily said. ''Or rather, Phil did for me. We're going to be rich.''

''Married?'' Ames asked, his pulse quickening.

Lily made a grimace of mock horror. ''Certainly not.

255

It's a friendly pool to make a million—and avoid the life of a lady's maid."

"How do you go about this?" Ames asked, strangely relieved.

Lily shrugged and raised her eyebrows. "You give a man money, and he gives you a piece of paper. Pretty soon, he comes and tells you that other people want to buy your paper, and you sell it for ten times what you paid for it." She laughed. "It's really very simple."

"Mining stocks, eh? Whose?"

"The Golconda. It's promoted by a man named Manley."

Ames lunged off the table and grabbed Lily by the shoulders and shook her. "Lily, you didn't buy stock!"

"Why . . . why, Ames, what's the matter? Yes. Eight hundred dollars."

Slowly Ames' arms fell to his side, and he stared at the floor.

"What is it, Ames?" Lily demanded.

"It's a fraudulent stock," Ames said hoarsely.

"But you made the assay on their ore. And your a stockholder. I saw it."

Ames looked up at her, his eyes tortured and miserable. "Yes. That's how I was going to get rich, Lily," he said bleakly. For one brief instant he saw the pity in her eyes, and then he tramped out of the kitchen. Upstairs he got his hat and coat and came down and went out, turning toward town.

After trying five saloons, he found Manley in the dining room of the Union House at a late breakfast. A few other people were scattered around the room at tables. Ames' face had settled into a tight, pale hardness. He paused by Manley's chair, and without returning the promoter's greeting, asked, "How much money have you taken in, Manley?"

"Why?" Manley looked shrewdly at Ames, unable

to gauge his face, and his eyes were suddenly crafty. "Why?" he repeated.

"How much?"

"Six, eight thousand."

"I'd like to see it," Ames said quietly. "I'd like to see the list of buyers, too. Come along. Have you got an office?"

"Yes. Wait till I finish my breakfast."

"Come along," Ames said flatly.

Manley rose, and Ames followed him out to the street, down it, up an open stairway to a room above a hardware store. The promoter opened a door on whose glass was painted GOLCONDA MINING CO., INC. Beyond was a spacious room, holding some easy chairs, a table, a desk and a safe. Manley turned to Ames as soon as the door was locked.

"Has somebody been talking about me?"

"Yes."

"Every dollar I've taken is in that safe!" Manley said hotly.

"Open it and let's see."

Manley went over to it, was silent a moment as he fiddled with the dial, then swung the door open and stood up. "Count it for yourself."

Ames walked to the stair doorway, unlocked it and opened it and then came back into the middle of the room. "Manley, you're through," he said in a voice edged with controlled anger. "There's a stage leaves at noon for Frisco. Take it."

For a long moment Manley stared at him, puzzled, suspicious. "What for?" he asked softly.

"At noon I'll announce this deal is a fraud and return the money. If you love your hide, clear out!"

It didn't take Manley long to decide. His hand streaked for the gun at his hip. Ames hit him in the face, and Manley crashed against the desk and went down. His gun fell to the floor, and he made a grab for it. Ames kicked it under the safe.

"Get up," Ames said in a choked voice.

Slowly Manley came to his knees, then lunged. Ames straightened him up with an uppercut, then drove a fist into his fat midriff, looped a right over and knocked him down again. Manley staggered to his feet, picked up a chair and threw it.

Ames ducked, then dived at him and they both went down. From there on it was a wicked fight, with no science, little skill and all savage anger. They tipped the table end over end, and Ames was knocked back against it. He met Manley's rush with his feet and then shoved.

Manley slammed back against the wall with such violence that a window sash fell down with a crash like the report of a gun. Ames was on him, then, and drove a blow at his shelving jaw, another at his chest, a third at his head. Manley tried vainly to kick, but he was dazed. Ames measured him, feinted with a right aimed at his midsection, and when Manley's guard dropped, looped over a left with a slap of knuckled studded bone on flesh. Manley went down, tried to rise, and rolled over on his back. Ames dragged him to the door and threw him down the stairs.

Afterward, Ames leaned both arms on the desk, gagging for breath. Then he went over to the safe and cleaned it of sacks of coin, a few notes and all the papers it contained.

Manley was gone when he went downstairs. Ames hesitated there, weaving with weariness, and then cut across to the Union House and mounted the stairs to Costello's suite.

It was only when the maid gasped as she opened the door, that Ames realized that he was bleeding, his coat ripped, his face bruised and thick-lipped. He brushed past her and into the drawing room, where Connie and Costello were sitting.

"Ames!" Connie cried. She ran over to him, but he did not look at her.

"I've come to turn down your offer to make me some money, Costello," he announced heavily.

Costello was motionless in his chair. "Why?" he asked presently.

"I haven't any. I was going in with Manley on a fake mine. No ore, faked assay and worthless stock."

"That was clumsy," Costello said wryly. "Do it better next time."

"There won't be any next time," Ames said, looking at Connie. Her eyes were wide, troubled, unsure. "Connie, I'm a poor man. Maybe I won't always be, but an assayer doesn't make much."

Connie smiled faintly. "You won't always be an assayer, Ames."

"But if I am?"

Connie only shook her head. "You won't, Ames. You'll make a fortune some day. You stumbled this time. You won't next."

That was all he wanted to know. He looked at the sacks of coins in his hands, then glanced at Costello, and then at her.

"Connie, you offered to marry me once if I let your dad help me. I wouldn't do it. I never will, not the way he means, and you mean. Will you still marry me?"

"You're too proud, Ames!" Connie cried. "It's absurd!"

"Will you still marry me?" His voice, his eyes, his manner was relentless.

"Ames, be reasonable!" Connie pleaded. "Don't be so hard, so angry!"

Ames regarded her a moment longer, and then nodded his head, as if agreeing with something. "That's all we've got to say to each other, I reckon. Good-by.'' He turned and started out.

"Ames!" Connie called imperiously.

He did not even hear her. He let himself out and turned toward Donovan's, almost running.

Lily was in the kitchen when he tramped in and put the sacks of coins on the table. She did not greet him, and made no comment on his appearance, only watched him with grave wide eyes.

His hand shaking, Ames counted out eight hundred dollars in double eagles and stacked them on the corner of the table. Then his glance lifted to Lily. "Put it back in the bank," he said grimly. "Pass the word to your friends that they can get their money back from me."

"I'm sorry, Ames," Lily said softly.

"I'm not." Ames' voice was low. "I've waked up, Lily. The money fever's gone. I'm a poor man and glad of it."

Lily smiled crookedly and shook her head once. "Costello will never let you be poor, Ames."

"I'm through with the Costellos, too. That's part of the fever I've licked."

"And Connie?"

Ames crossed over to her. "It would never work, Lily. I told her it wouldn't, but I never told her the real reason."

"What is the real reason?"

"You are," Ames said simply. "For months I've tried to tell myself that Connie and all she stands for is what I want." He shook his head. "I even staked my good name on it."

Lily said nothing.

"I haven't got much of a name now, Lily. I—"

"It's good enough for me," Lily said softly.

"That's what I was going to ask you," Ames said,

watching her. "Is it good enough for you to wear the rest of your life?"

Lily was already nodding assent.

TRUMPETS WEST

Ft. Akin's one-room hospital stood at a corner of the parade grounds. Out of respect for the newly-sown grass on the scuffed and piebald parade ground, a man who wanted to reach headquarters building in the center of the opposite side of the parade ground had been ordered to use the gravel walk.

On this late afternoon of an Arizona July, however, Lt. Burke Hanna stepped out of the hospital door and cut string-straight across the parade ground for headquarters building. He was a tall, unshaven and dirty man in a moderate hurry, and his field uniform was grimed a color closer to gray than blue.

Crossing the gravel drive, he went up the short walk of headquarters building. A hulking, barrel-chested Sergeant Major with a black short-clipped beard that reached almost to his eyes, was coming down the veranda steps now. He saluted and said, "Glad you're back, sir."

"Thanks, O'Mara," Burke said. His foot was on the bottom step when he halted and turned and called, "O'Mara."

The sergeant came back to him, and Burke said, "Did you see those ration requests I sent in by

Hardy?''

"Yes, sir," O'Mara said in the bland voice of an old soldier who knows his rights. "Captain Ervien wouldn't sign them, sir."

Burke said, "Right. Thanks," and went up the steps. His voice seemed dim with disuse to him and full of an unnecessary truculence. Standing in the big doorway of the adobe building was Lt. Abe Byas, a big man with a morose and homely face and so wide of shoulder that he nearly blocked the doorway—which seemed to be his intention now.

Burke hauled up, and Byas said with gentle mockery in his deep voice, "Counted ten, Burke?"

"I've counted ten thousand," Burke said grimly. "Let me past, Abe."

"Sure," Byas said, not moving. The two men regarded each other a long moment, and then Hanna drew a deep breath. "All right," he said patiently. He lifted off his dusty campaign hat and beat at his trousers with it. His black hair, ragged at the edges, was darker than the thick beard stubble sworled on his lean and weather blackened face. He saw, with a kind of hopelessness, that the soles of his cavalry boots were frayed at the edges, as if a dog had been chewing on them, and when he looked up now, his wide mouth was humorless. He said bitterly, "What's gone on here, Abe?"

Byas only shook his head in kindly refusal to answer. "Did Doc Ford see your cripples?"

Burke nodded, and said in the same bitter voice, "Two men half dead with dysentery. Raines' feet are cut to ribbons; so are Kahn's. A half dozen others crippled up, and another dozen starved and played out or sick from a diet of horsemeat." He paused. "Now can I get past?"

Byas stood aside, and as Burke passed him he laid a hand on his arm. "Look, don't go in there that way.

Get a cinch on your temper, will you?"

"Sure, sure," Burke said wryly and went across the bare room and said to the sergeant behind the desk, "Lieutenant Hanna to see Captain Ervien."

"He's got the Agent with him, Lieutenant, but he's expecting you."

"Yes," Burke said dryly. He paced once across the room and caught sight of Byas, huge in the doorway, watching him gloomily. Byas said, "Calla says come over for dinner tonight."

Burke said, "All right, thanks," in as polite a voice as he could muster. Byas continued to regard him now with a lessening gloom, and then spoke again, "Parade grounds is off limits now. It's sown with grass."

Burke's green eyes glared at him balefully; Byas grinned faintly at his anger and went out, and Burke turned his head and looked speculatively at one of the chairs. If he sat down, he would never want to get up, he knew.

The door in the wall ahead of him opened now, and a big, soft pale man in an oversize black suit stepped through, closing the door behind him. He and Burke saw each other at the same time; for a fleeting instant it seemed as if there would be no recognition, and then Burke said idly, contemptuously, "Hello, Corinne."

The Apache Agent smiled now and said with a false heartiness, "How are you, Hanna?" nodded courteously to the sergeant and went out.

Burke crushed his dusty campaign hat under his left arm, knocked firmly on the door Corinne had just closed, opened it, and went inside.

Captain Ervien was at his desk, which was set across the corner of the room between two windows. The American flag and the squadron standard were stacked behind him. He did not look up until Burke was almost in front of him, and then he watched Burke come to attention and salute and say, "Lieutenant Hanna reporting, sir."

Ervien returned the salute, and then leaned back in his chair, regarding Burke's appearance with a dark and cynical amusement that Burke, from three years of service with him as a junior officer, knew was sincere. Whatever ease there had been between the two men had vanished long before Ervien, upon Major Drummond's death, had been appointed commanding officer. Ervien, with his well-tailored uniforms, his thorough and calculating knowledge of Army ways and the dark handsomeness of thirty-five, had elected the course of the garrison soldier. Burke saw the nostrils of his nose twitch faintly, and he thought, *He's smelling horse for a change.*

Ervien said now, "Burke, I saw you bring in K Troop." He shook his head in disgust, and added almost irrelevantly, "The lot of you looked more like a bunch of Mexican army deserters than soldiers."

"Maybe that's because we've been treated like Mexican deserters, Phil," Burke answered.

Ervien blandly ignored that; he said, "You were afoot. The only officer—walking, just like a damned infantryman. Why?"

"We lost fifteen horses. Ate some, too."

"But not your own. Your sergeant was riding him."

Burke nodded shortly. "Raines had walked half the distance from Ojo Negra. His feet are badly cut. The whole Troop walked half way, turnabout." He added with an edge to his voice now, "That's the only way we could get back here."

"You had rations and forage for five weeks," Ervien said flatly. "Enough to find that renegade Ponce and his band, fight them if you had to, send them back to the reservation and extend your patrol. Those were your orders, weren't they?"

"My dispatch to you explained that," Burke said with a mounting aggressiveness. "We shared all our supplies with Ponce and his Apaches. That's the only way we could get them back alive."

"He got to his hideout without Army rations!" Ervien flared. "Let him get back without them! Who are you to be giving away Army supplies? Let the black devils starve!"

A blazing anger left Burke inarticulate for the moment, and Ervien leaned his elbows on the desk. "Once you'd sent Ponce back, I suppose you sat there eating up your remaining rations and waiting for more instead of extending your patrol, as you were ordered."

"We sat six days," Burke retorted heatedly. "And why not?" His voice thickened with anger now. "Good God, Phil, why didn't you send the forage and rations and take it out of my pay if necessary? Instead, you sent a refusal and ordered the patrol!"

"You made the patrol, didn't you?"

"With half my Troop afoot and sick from horse-meat!"

Ervien said distinctly, tapping the desk with his soft forefinger for emphasis, "You have been gone four weeks and three days. You were issued rations for five weeks. I know that, because I just checked the supply records with Sergeant O'Mara. If you and your men suffered, you've nobody to blame but yourself."

There was, Burke knew savagely, no rebuttal open to him. Technically, Ervien was right, and yet Ponce, the Apache subchief he had been ordered to send back to the reservation, could not have brought his half-starved band through that poor country without Army supplies.

Ervien leaned back and laced his fingers atop his curly chestnut hair and surveyed Burke. He said dryly, "You feel abused, Burke?"

267

"I feel my men have been treated like dogs."

"Like troopers," Ervien said sharply, "and damned poorly officered troopers." He sat erect now and said matter-of-factly, "We've got word that Federico, Ponce's nephew, is skulking around the Mogollon Rim north, waiting for Ponce to get fed and supplied by the Agency here. When he's rested, Ponce intends to break and join him, and raid the Navajo country with him." He paused, isolating this. "Tomorrow, suppose you draw rations and forage for two weeks and take K Troop up there and confirm Federico's presence or absence, and return in two weeks. See if you can turn in a satisfactory job this time."

A stunned anger rose in Burke then. He thought of his Troop, a dozen hospitalized, the rest sick and exhausted, and he knew Ervien knew this. He said slowly, "You mean that, Phil?"

"Those are your orders."

Burke still had a grip on his temper, yet it was failing fast. He put both hands on Ervien's desk and leaned on them. "Phil," he began in a shaky voice, "this will make the fourth consecutive patrol for K Troop. In the past six months, we've been out all but nine days. I suggest you send another troop."

"Those are your orders," Ervien repeated.

Then the rage came, and with an appalling swiftness. Burke slowly straightened up to attention, and said with a savage formality, "I refuse to obey them, sir."

There was a long moment of on-running silence, during which Ervien eyed him shrewdly. Burke knew Ervien was casting up the probable results of a court martial, and when Ervien spoke now, it was still with confidence. "Want another chance, Burke?"

"No sir," Burke said. "My only way of protesting that treatment of sick men is by refusing to obey your order. I do refuse."

268

Ervien sat erect and said with a cold formality, "Very well, you will consider your self under arrest and confine your movements to the limits of the Post, pending further action, Mister Hanna."

"Very good, sir," Burke said woodenly. Again he saluted, again had it returned, about-faced and was half way to the door when Capt. Ervien said, "By the way, Mister Hanna," in a soft, commanding voice.

Burke paused and looked at him. Ervien picked up a sheaf of papers from the corner of his desk and tapped them. "I've read your report on the alleged offenses against the Apaches committed by Mr. Alec Corinne, their agent. I've just discussed the matter with him, and I have only one comment."

Burke waited silently.

"You seem to have a difficult time learning the soldiering profession. I suggest you study it and listen less to gossip. Let the Indian Bureau discipline its agents. That is *not* the Army's business." He tossed the paper into the wastebasket and Burke went out.

The late afternoon sunlight lay still and blazing on the parade ground, and the young trees lining the gravel walk rustled in the hot breeze; the blue line of the Ragged Top peaks to the west shimmered in the sun. Burke tramped down the steps and turned right up the gravel walk, thinking oddly that here in this long rectangle surrounded by neat plain buildings, there were more trees than he had seen in a month. The rage was still in him, a live thing that almost sickened him. He had, he knew, been systematically harried and ridden until he had rebelled—and now Ervien had him. Nor did he have to look for the reason; you didn't write blistering reports about a crooked Indian agent and submit them to a superior officer who was engaged to marry the Agent's daughter, as Phil Ervien was going to marry Vinnie Corinne.

269

He turned up the short walk leading to the low out-size adobe building that was the unmarried officer's quarters and went in. The lounge was empty, and he went on down the corridor to his bare and simple corner room at the rear of the building.

He sank wearily onto the plain iron bed and sat motionless a moment, stupid with weariness.

This, then, was his homecoming—on which he had planned to be married. The prospect of seeing Calla now brought a strange reluctance to him. In a matter of minutes now, Lucy, Abe's wife, would have learned of his arrest and would have told her sister Calla. News traveled like that in a remote post. And Calla, with everything set except the marriage day, which Burke was supposed to have settled with Ervien a moment ago—what would Calla do? Tiredly, Burke pulled off his boots. She couldn't marry an officer under arrest, a man who could not wear a sword at his own wedding because he was forbidden now to carry arms, or leave the designated limits of the Post. Or command troops.

Burke swore darkly, thinking, *Thirty is too damned old to let myself be baited into a fight with a CO*, but he knew that wasn't right either. Rising now, he stripped out of his torn and filthy uniform, put on slippers and robe and went down the corridor to the big bathroom. There, he shaved and bathed with the slow thoroughness of a man who has done neither for many weeks, and afterward started back to his room.

Before he reached the door, he halted and raised his head and sniffed. Only one man he knew smoked the black and vile Apache trade tobacco that he was smelling now; he went on, and in the doorway, before he looked, he said gloomily, "Hello, Rush, you damn carrion crow."

Rush Doll was seated backtilted in the chair at the foot of Burke's bed, his feet on Burke's blankets. He

270

grinned sparsely around the long cigarette pasted in the corner of his mouth, a man of fifty, graying and dried by decades of Arizona summers. He wore a cast-off Army shirt, denim pants and Apache moccasins, and was, unqualifiedly, the best packmaster in the West and Burke's friend.

He jibed now by way of greeting, "Footed it back, I hear."

"On horsemeat," Burke said wryly. He opened a drawer of the chest in the corner and took out some clothes.

Rush said presently, "What's a general court martial?"

Burke turned to look at him. "So it's out, is it?"

"You wouldn't go on patrol tomorrow, they say."

Burke nodded and savagely slammed the drawer shut. He said morosely, "The need for Lieutenant Hanna, and only Lieutenant Hanna, on patrol is what gravels me." He glanced obliquely at Rush. "Remember that report on Corinne you helped me with?"

Rush shook his head. "No. That's not the reason."

Burke was about to sit down. Now he didn't; something in Rush's tone held him motionless.

"Things have been happening since you left," Rush murmured. "He wants you out of the way."

"Things like what?"

"Your report accused Corinne of long countin' the 'Paches so he could put their rations in his pocket, didn't it? Well, he's quit that. For the past month he's been busy tradin' the fat government issue beef for all the scrub cull beef anyone brings him. He trades at the rate of two fat beef for three culls."

Burke sat down slowly on his bed. "To issue to the Indians? That won't do him any good. The beef is issued to the Apaches by weight, not by count."

"What if he's rigged the agency scales to weigh out

every beef at six hundred pounds or over, even if it really weighs three hundred?''

Burke only stared at him and Rush went on, ''Say he gets three hundred fat beef for issue. He trades two hundred of 'em off for three hundred culls. He issues the three hundred culls weighed on his rigged scale, then sells the hundred fat ones left and pockets the money.''

Burke said nothing, only stared down at his bare and bruised feet. Ervien's order made sense now. There was only one man in either Post or Agency who cared enough about the Indian's welfare to keep their agent honest, and that man was himself. And his reason was simple enough; he was tired of seeing Apaches starved into breaking out and then having to fight or capture them. Now Ervien, protecting his prospective father-in-law, wanted him out of the way, and he had him out of the way.

As Burke reached for his socks now, a thought came to him. He asked Rush, ''What about Ponce's bunch I sent back? Have they been fed well and issued rations?''

''They ain't had a square meal since they hit the reservation,'' Rush said flatly.

Broodingly, Burke dressed, silent now. He had forgotten Rush when Rush said searchingly, ''You goin' to put that in your new report?''

Rush had risen and had his shoulder against the doorjamb. Burke said unsmilingly, ''You think Ponce would talk with me tonight?''

''How?'' Rush asked. ''You can't leave the Post, and he ain't allowed to come on it after dark.''

Burke thought a moment and said, ''You bring him over to the blacksmith shop after dark. That's Post limits. We can talk there and neither of us will be disobeying orders.'' He looked levelly at Rush. ''I promised Ponce we'd treat him right if he came back. If we don't, Rush, he'll bust out and gut this country. And," he added slowly, "I wouldn't blame him."

When Rush agreed and left, Burke hurriedly dressed. As he was struggling into his blouse, Lieutenants Umberhine and Cavanaugh poked their heads in to say hello. They made no reference to his arrest. Finished dressing, Burke picked up his garrison cap and pistol belt, and then, remembering, he hung the pistol on the wall. He could not carry arms.

He stepped out onto the walk and cut across the parade ground, heading for the third square brick house in the row of married officers' homes opposite. Absently, he glanced at the twin row of barracks at the south end of the parade ground. Men were free for the day now and were lounging on the barracks stoops, some talking, others watching wrestling matches. The clanging sound of horseshoes being pitched came to him with regularity, and as he listened, trying to catch the degree of expertness of the pitcher, he thought of Abe Byas. Should he tell Abe of Rush's revelation? He decided against it; Abe was Ervien's adjutant, honor bound to be loyal to him, and there was no use troubling Abe until he had proof.

Byas, bareheaded, was waiting on his walk when Burke crossed the drive and came up to him.

"Look," Abe said mildly in greeting, "I'm adjutant of this post. You want to appear before me tomorrow morning for disciplinary action?"

Burke hauled up. "What for?"

Abe pointed to the parade ground. "It's seeded," he said carefully, distinctly. "Stay off it, now, will you?"

Burke grinned. "I forgot."

Abe turned and they went up the walk, and now Abe looked reprovingly at him. "Well, you did it up brown, didn't you?"

"Didn't I?" Burke murmured.

"You'll learn," Abe said. "Just keep chewing his ears until you're in real trouble."

Burke didn't reply, and Abe mounted the steps. His house was a square brick affair with a small porch and an iron railed widow's walk surmounting its sloping roof. Abe went in first and waved his right hand toward the parlor, saying, "Sit down. I'll get Calla," and went on through the hall toward the back rooms.

Burke looked around the pleasant parlor, whose contents had been freighted half a thousand miles. Through the open window he caught the brassy, saucy sound of mess call being sounded, and he wondered gloomily what he was going to say to Calla.

Hearing a sound, he turned just in time to see Calla, apron over her dress, come into the room. She didn't pause, didn't speak, only came into his arms and kissed him. After she had kissed him twice more, she hugged him and said into his ear in a low, shaky voice, "I've got to get used to missing you, Burke."

Burke smiled faintly and held her from him, looking hungrily at her. The grave and mischievous amber eyes told him nothing except she was glad to see him. Her wide mouth, soft and smiling, was happy enough. She had been fussing with her thick golden hair; it was done differently atop her head, and he thought it beautiful, just as, without knowing why, he thought her gray dress, through the sleeves of which he could feel the rounded softness of her arms, new and delightful. He said, "If that's what they call a soldier's welcome, I'm for it."

He held her to him a moment, and then said quietly, "Did Abe tell you, Calla?"

She drew back and looked gravely at him. "About your arrest? Yes. I'd have hated you forever if you'd taken your Troop out as Ervien ordered." She frowned

274

quizzically. "Did you really think I'd mind?

"Idiot. Would you marry a girl who did mind?"

"Well," Burke said slowly, "I wouldn't blame a girl for being a little mad over a postponed wedding."

Calla said, alarm in her eyes, "Who said it was postponed?"

"Look, honey," Burke murmured. "You can't marry an officer when he's under arrest. I couldn't even wear a sword at the ceremony."

"Do you think I care about a silly sword?" Calla flared.

"I do," Burke said grimly. "I want to know whether you'd be marrying a soldier or a civilian. So do you."

Calla sighed in mock exasperation, took his hand and led him over to the sofa and pulled him down beside her. "Burke, let's be practical. If you hadn't sassed Captain Ervien, you'd be on patrol tomorrow, wouldn't you?"

"I suppose," Burke admitted.

"Then, for heaven's sake, you're here now. You will be until the trial. It's the only chance he'll give us to be together. To hell with your arrest!"

Burke looked faintly shocked, and Calla said swiftly, vehemently, "I mean it, Burke. I'm tired of being Mrs. Hanna-to-be! The chapel is on Post limits, isn't it?" Burke nodded, and Calla said promptly, "Then let's get married tomorrow. In private or public, I don't care. It's nobody's business but ours." She smiled now at her own vehemence. "Speak up, soldier."

Burke grinned. "I kind of like the idea," he murmured. "Of course—" He paused. He had just caught sight of Abe standing in the doorway. Burke said, "You've got a wife. Let me get one, will you?"

"Later," Abe said calmly. "There's a trooper at the back door. He wants to speak to you."

Burke swore under his breath and rose and started

for the door. He came back, leaned over and kissed Calla, and then went into the hall toward the kitchen. *That's how much you know about the girl you'll marry,* he thought wonderingly.

Lucy Byas, an older and smaller and more placid version of Calla, was in the kitchen, and she looked over her shoulder at Burke's entrance and said, "Hello, you wild-eyed Mick." Although she had a dish in each hand, Burke hugged her in passing, and then went on to the back door.

"Hello, Carney," he said to the beardless trooper on the steps, and then he saw the restrained excitement in the soldier's face. "What's the trouble?"

"I thought the lieutenant ought to know, sir. Raines and O'Mara are buildin' up a fight over issue of mounts down at the corral."

Burke scowled. "I left Raines in the hospital."

"He's on crutches, sir. Doctor Ford let him out."

Burke swore and went down the steps. "You go along to supper, Carney. And thanks." He strode down the alley, cut left down the short street lined with the homes of the married enlisted men, and at a trot, passed A stable. Raines, K Troop's first sergeant, was a tough, tobacco-chewing bantam of a man with an aggressive loyalty to his officers, his men and his horses. And when Burke thought of him fighting with O'Mara, the squadron bully, the sly toadying Irishman whom anyone but Ervien would have broken and kept broken, he was worried. And Raines was on crutches.

Passing B stable at a run now, he saw the place was deserted; all the troopers were at supper call. He cut in through the forage shed that lay between B stable and the corrals and saw a big supply wagon blocking the far door.

Ducking around it, he hauled up. There, in front of the corral gate in the slanting sunlight were O'Mara and Raines. Raines, on his bandaged feet, had backed against the corral poles beside a stack of forks and shovels, and was swinging his remaining crutch in a half circle, trying to fend off the squat, long armed O'Mara. Even as Burke saw this, O'Mara moved inside the arc of the crutch, and he smashed savagely at Raines' seamed face with the swift pawing motion of a bear striking. Moving in, and pulling Raines to him, he stamped savagely on Raines' bandaged feet and then, half turning, he picked up the smaller man whose fists were flailing at his bearded face and slammed him to the ground, falling with him and on top of him.

Burke vaulted the wagon's tongue; his foot caught in one of the loops of a long stay chain festooned on the tongue, and he fell heavily and came up again, running. He saw O'Mara's fisted hands drive squarely into Raines' face again and again, and then Burke pulled up.

"O'Mara!" he said in an iron voice. "Get up!"

O'Mara thought he was alone; the voice of authority startled him, and he turned to see Burke beside him, and he was already rising. He paused, his knees half flexed and then slowly sank back on Raines.

"Lieutenant, you're under arrest, with no authority for anything," he said gently.

"Get to your quarters!" Burke said.

O'Mara stared quietly at him with his small red-rimmed eyes, which were calculating and sly and arrogant and then he said in his strangely gentle voice, "Off with you, Lieutenant. I've this to finish." And he slashed savagely at Raines' face.

Burke hit him, then, in the face, a driving blow that knocked him off Raines and into the dust on his back. O'Mara sat up, raised a thick and meaty hand to his jaw and said mildly, wickedly, "You struck an enlisted man, Lieutenant."

"Get to your quarters, O'Mara," Burke repeated.

O'Mara came to his feet with a slow, sure indolence and when he was erect Burke saw his massive blocky shoulders had burst the seam of his blue shirt. No fear and no respect, only a kind of animal cunning was in his eyes now; he rubbed his beard gently with the back of his hand and said, "It'd be a fine thing to smash you, Lieutenant—you under arrest, and not allowed to order me. It'd be your word against mine."

"I wouldn't try it," Burke advised mildly.

O'Mara looked around the lot in one swift glance to make sure there were no witnesses, and in that moment Burke knew that O'Mara's hatred of authority and the whole officer system, plus his sharing Ervien's dislike of K Troop in its entirety, would drive him to attacking. And he would not be penalized for it.

O'Mara glanced at Raines, then moved over and kicked him in the temple. "No help there, Lieutenant," he said. Then, in a crouch, thick arms outthrust, he came slowly at Burke. He came out of his crouch like a spring uncoiling, and Burke hit him once in the throat before O'Mara's massive arms wrapped around him. Burke stamped savagely on O'Mara's feet, but O'Mara squeezed him with a breath-stopping strength. Burke felt his chest constricting, felt O'Mara's wiry beard pricking through his blouse against his shoulder. Now O'Mara heaved to lift him off the ground, and Burke brought his knee up into O'Mara's groin with a murderous violence. O'Mara whined, and his grip loosened, and Burke turned sideways, jamming the point of his shoulder into O'Mara's face. O'Mara's hold broke now, and Burke, when an arm was free, looped an overhand, chopping blow into O'Mara's face. As they broke away now, Burke kicked him solidly in the pit of the stomach, and O'Mara, off balance, backstepped until he crashed into the corral fence and fell heavily on his side among the clutter of stable tools. Burke was breathing deeply, impressed now by O'Mara's great strength, and wary of it.

On an elbow now, O'Mara pawed the blood away from his nose and his movement stirred the tangle of tools. He seemed now to notice them for the first time. Looking wickedly at Burke, he pawed among them until he found a wide-tined pitchfork. Supporting himself with it, he came unsteadily to his feet, and Burke, knowing intent to murder when he saw it, reached for his pistol. He was not wearing it, he remembered then, and in the same moment, he began to back slowly away.

Now O'Mara lifted the fork like a spear and came shuffling toward him. Burke wheeled, looking for a weapon. Across the lot, he spied the stay chain on the wagon tongue that had tripped him, and he turned and ran for it, and O'Mara ran too. As Burke neared the wagon, O'Mara, fearing his intention, raised the fork over his head and hurled it like a spear. Burke fell and rolled under the wagon tongue, and the fork drove into the double tree, and then boomed into the wagon box.

O'Mara was charging again now, and Burke, on his knees, unhooked the heavy stay chain. As O'Mara was on him, Burke slashed backhanded at him with a short length of the chain, and the murderous weight of it raked across O'Mara's chest, tearing the shirt away and leaving a bloody furrow in the matted hair of his huge chest.

The force of O'Mara's charge was halted; he staggered back one step, caught his balance and lunged to close. Burke had risen now, and he backed up a step and raised the chain and savagely slashed it down across O'Mara's shoulders. The chain's bludgeoning weight beat O'Mara to his knees, but even then he groped out and his bloody fist gripped Burke's ankle.

Again Burke brought the chain down, this time across O'Mara's black, round skull.

O'Mara fell on his face, not stirring. Burke stood over him a long minute, breathing deeply, and he thought he had killed the man and did not care.

Stepping around O'Mara, then, Burke went over to Raines, who was lying on his back just as O'Mara had left him. A cud of tobacco pouched his dry and leathery cheek, and Burke felt gingerly of his jaw to see if it was broken. A livid bruise was rising on Raines' temple, and the gentle slapping Burke gave his face would not bring his eyes open.

Burke was hesitant a moment, then he picked Raines up in his arms, turned and tramped through B stable. Between B and A stables, he met two troopers, and called them to him.

"Take Raines to the hospital," he ordered them. "Then one of you go over to the officers' mess and get Dr. Ford."

Soberly, the two troopers he did not know took Raines, and Burke watched them disappear behind A stable. He stood there in the cool, reeking stable smell a moment with a quiet despair, brushing the dust from his uniform, and he was thinking, *This is real trouble, now.*

There was nothing to do except report it, he knew; he turned wearily up toward the parade ground.

He had passed the barracks and was approaching the sutler's post which housed the officers' club when he saw Captain Ervien leave headquarters building and turn toward him.

Increasing his pace, Burke reached the long veranda of the Post trader's first. He waited, and as Ervien approached, Burke saw the frown come to his face. Burke was hatless, his uniform stained and dusty, and as Ervien paused and returned Burke's salute, there was a look of distaste in his dark face.

"Sir," Burke began formally, "I think I've probably killed your sergeant major."

Ervien's mouth opened slowly, but no words came.

Burke went on, "O'Mara was roughing up Sergeant Raines. When I ordered him to stop, he refused, saying I had no authority to issue orders. I hit him to keep him from hurting Raines. He thought that gave him the right to attack me, and he did. I think," he finished, "I may have killed him."

There was a long silence, and Burke saw the wicked anger mount in Ervien's dark eyes. Ervien said then in a dry and savagely formal voice, "Mister Hanna, you seem to get in trouble even when confined to the Post. Confine yourself to quarters and mess until I have the particulars."

"Yes, sir," Burke said, and Ervien brushed past him.

Back in quarters, Burke paused long enough to send the orderly over to Byas' explaining his absence, and then went on to his room. Abe, he reflected wryly, would probably be pulled away from his supper to investigate, since he was adjutant.

In his room, Burke closed the door and sank wearily to his bed. He wondered idly what Raines and O'Mara had quarreled about, and then he thought of his own predicament. Outside of having to face the very serious charge of striking an enlisted man, there was Calla to think about now. Even Calla, badly as she wanted them married, couldn't be married in the lounge of bachelor officer's quarters. Burke swore under his breath when he thought of it.

A knock at the door proved to be the orderly who had returned from Byas' with a tray of food—the supper he was to have eaten with Calla and Abe and Lucy.

Burke ate hungrily, and afterward loaded a pipe and

281

lay down on his bed, staring gloomily at the ceiling in the lowering dusk. Either he could broodingly count his sins, or what were called his sins, or he could forget them; there was no changing anything now. He swung his feet to the floor and rose and prowled restlessly to the window and came back. There, lying on the corner of his desk and covered with five weeks' dust was his black notebook. A hundred hours of friendly argument with his fellow officers about cavalry tactics and Army practice had led him long ago to fortify his views by writing them down. He opened the notebook, and then closed it with disgust. What did it matter if he contended, against cavalry practice, that a mounted charge against hostile Indians was not impossible? Or that a native pony who lived off the land was a better mount than a grain fed Army horse?

He turned away in distaste, and at that moment with a sobering shock, he remembered, *Ponce. I can't see him tonight!* Standing in the middle of his room he let his pipe get cold thinking about this. He had to see Ponce, not only to confirm Rush's information that his band had not been fed since their return, but because Ponce dissatisfied meant trouble—and real trouble.

Stirring himself finally, he saw that it was dark, and he moved over to his desk. He struck a match and lighted the lamp, and was adjusting the wick when the soft knock came on his door.

It opened immediately, and Rush Doll stepped in. Rush put his shoulder against the wall, and Burke straightened up and looked at him.

"You confined to quarters, like they say?"

Burke nodded. "How's O'Mara? Have you heard?"

"All right. You can't kill a brute like that. He's in the hospital. Raines is all right. He's left."

"Hear what they fought about?"

"O'Mara was tryin' to work off his crowbait mounts

282

on K Troop replacements, and Raines wouldn't take 'em.'' Rush straightened up. ''Well, I better go send Ponce back.''

''He's there?''

Rush nodded. Burke stood hesitant a moment. He was on his honor as an officer and gentleman not to break arrest. But if he didn't meet with Ponce and somehow persuade him to patience until Ervien could be convinced of the necessity for making Corinne feed his people, then he would be criminally liable.

He came to his reckless decision then and said, ''Hold him there, Rush. I'll meet you at full dark.''

Rush went out and Burke blew the lamp. Moving to the back window, he waited until he saw the slow pacing sentry on his beat past the rear of the line of buildings fronting the parade ground. This sentry probably wouldn't know of his being confined to quarters, but Burke couldn't take the chance. He waited the few moments until full dark, then raised the window gently. When the sentry passed, Burke climbed over the sill and dropped to the ground. Quietly, he walked ahead until he was in the friendly shadow of the laundry. Once there, he turned and skirted the sutler's post, the barracks and A stable, and cut down toward the blacksmith shop, which marked Post limits.

A pair of troopers were doing some work there by lantern light on a wagon wheel; the nearby stable guard, carbine slacked under his arm, was peering off in the darkness. As Burke approached the guard saw him and turned to stroll away. Beyond, in the half light of the lanterns, Burke saw the two figures of Rush Doll and Ponce.

Burke approached the guard, whom he recognized now, and returned the guard's salute. ''Bellows, I'm under arrest, you know,'' he began.

''Yes, sir, I heard it, sir.''

Burke pointed to Doll and Ponce in the darkness. "I have to talk with that 'Pache. He's not allowed on the Post after dark and I'm not allowed off it. Suppose we meet on the line and you watch us."

Bellows grinned. "As long as nobody crosses, I'm obeying orders, sir."

Burke went on, and paused at the line of the blacksmith shop's wall. Rush and Ponce came to meet him, and in the dim light of the lantern, Burke looked searchingly at Ponce. He was taller than the average Apache, perhaps thirty-eight, with squarish flat features holding a subtle blending of fierceness, pride and cunning that had made him Tana's subchief—and a rebel. He was dressed in a dirty blue calico shirt, worn tails out, breechclout and high leggings and moccasins. Gravely he extended his hand to Burke and shook hands.

This was hardly the time for ceremony, Burke knew, but he offered Ponce a cigar from his pocket, and it was accepted and lighted. Burke and Rush knelt while Ponce squatted silently in the dim light. He spoke now in Apache to Rush, who interpreted to Burke, "He says he's sorry you got in trouble for giving him and his band food."

"Tell him I'm his friend," Burke said. "My friends don't go hungry."

Rush interpreted and Ponce answered quickly, almost with hate. Rush said dryly to Burke, "He asks if you're still his friend, because he's hungry and so are his people. They've been hungry since you sent them back—as hungry as they were before."

"Ask if he hasn't been included on weekly ration issue, along with the others."

Rush and Ponce conversed a moment, and then Rush said, "He says Corinne is punishing him for breaking out last time. They receive short rations, not

284

as much as the others. From lack of meat they're getting weak and sick. It's hard to hold the young bucks in, he says, and he wants to know how to get more meat. They're killing their ponies, he says—and he's lying on that point, of course.''

''Don't they get beef?''

Rush spoke again to Ponce, was again answered sharply, and Rush looked at Burke, irony in his eyes. ''Sick beef, starved beef, with no meat on their bones. With the fat beef they used to get, there was a little for everybody. Now there isn't even a little.''

Burke said, ''Tell him I'll talk to Corinne.''

Rush passed on this information, and again he received a quick and flat reply. ''Tomorrow,'' Rush repeated, ''is issue day for beef. He has told his young men to wait, to see what tomorrow brings. If they get the same sick, scrub beef, Ponce ways he isn't sure if he can hold them in.'' Rush paused. ''He's threatening you, Burke. Those young men of his are pretty handy to put the blame on. He's mad, and he's threatened old Chief Tana he'll break if his people aren't fed better.''

Burke said slowly, ''Tell him if he breaks, I'll hunt him down, and this time I'll kill him and every man that breaks with him.''

Rush hesitated a moment before translating. When he had, Ponce glanced levelly at Burke, and Burke held the glance. There was a challenge there and Burke saw it. Finally, Ponce spoke and Rush translated.

''He says you can't hunt him down. You're under arrest. The rest of the soldiers he's not afraid of.''

Burke rose now, signifying the end of the parley. He waited for the customary *enju* from Ponce, which signified ''All is good,'' but this time it did not come. Ponce gravely shook hands and turned and vanished noiselessly in the night.

Burke watched him go, and then, looking at Rush,

he surprised a look of gravity in his eyes. "He's made up his mind to break, already," Burke said slowly.

Rush cursed viciously. "That damn Corinne!"

Burke stared out into the warm star-studded night. He would go to Ervien now and tell him what Ponce said, pointing out that Corinne's weekly short-weight swindle tomorrow would touch off the explosion. But Ervien would either reprimand him for not minding the Army's business, or deny that Corinne was engaged in sharp practice. Only by being confronted with the evidence of Corinne's crookedness could Burke drive him into correcting it in time. And reluctantly, he knew what he was going to have to do. It would have to be done alone, without Rush, for he could not risk dragging Rush into a scheme which, if it were discovered, might cost him his livelihood. And Rush would hate him for what he would say now. He said resignedly, "All I can do is warn Ervien."

"That won't do it, Burke!" Rush said vehemently.

Burke shrugged. Rush looked bitterly at him a moment and sighed, and said curtly, "I suppose you're right. The hell with it. Good night."

He turned and walked off stiffly, angrily into the darkness toward the distant lights of the agency a half mile to the south across the flat. Burke strolled back to the deep shadow of A stable and then hauled up. He knew that what he was about to do would have far graver consequences than anything he had done thus far, and for a moment, watching the stable guard on his round, listening to the night horses of the Post, he reckoned the risk and knew he must take it.

Presently, a couple of troopers joined the two already at the blacksmith shop. There was a parley there which Bellows, on his round, paused to join.

This was the chance Burke had been waiting for. Circling far outside the light of the shop lanterns, he noiselessly crossed the Post limits and set out toward the agency lights. He was going to see for himself if the agency scales were rigged, as both Rush and Ponce said they were.

He kept well away from the road between Post and agency, crossing it only once in his circle which skirted Corinne's big store and the agency buildings clustered around it. The corrals, he knew, were on the flats behind the agency buildings, and he supposed cynically that Corinne had watered the cattle heavily tonight and had penned them in the huge issue corral.

Once in the shelter of the agency's adobe stables, he halted and listened. He could hear the occasional bawling of restive cattle in the corral ahead. *Probably hungry,* he thought, and he wondered if Corinne had put out a night guard. He'd have to take that chance. From watching past issues, he knew where the scales were. An issue-chute was set up leading across the scales from the corral and it was here that each Apache head of family or clan leader presented his ration ticket, had it stamped, watched his beef weighed, and received it.

A pack of dogs around the distant Apache *wickiups* started a fight. Under cover of their yammering, Burke made his way in the deep blackness toward the big holding corral. Once there, he moved to his right until he saw the high oblong box housing the scale machinery outlined against the sky among the chute rails.

Approaching it, he knelt and felt along its board panels for the handle of the door that gave access to the adjusting mechanism. His hand touched a hasp and then a heavy padlock. Corinne, evidently, wasn't taking chances.

Burke rose, cursing, and started beating about for a piece of iron with which to pry off the padlock. His boot hit something and he leaned down, and as he did so he heard the hoofbeats of horses at a run.

Rising, he looked off toward the dark stables, and at that moment he heard a sharp command given. "Spread out and cover the corral, men!" The voice was Ervien's.

Burke knelt, listening to the mounted troopers beating toward him. He turned and ran, then, hugging the corral fence, but the troopers fanned out quickly in the darkness, cutting off his escape. Halting, he saw a pair of troopers now rounding the stables, and each held a lantern.

Burke debated vaulting the corral and hiding on the other side, but he knew his presence there would spook these wild range cattle inside. Either they would attack him, or give away his presence by their actions.

Kneeling there, a gray despair touched him, and he thought, *He knew where to come for me.* Ahead of him a trooper had turned his horse and was carefully scouting the base of the corral. The troopers with lanterns had split now, one going to either side of the corral. Ervien had halted midway between the corral and the stables.

Burke waited with a kind of fatalism, and when the trooper with the lantern approached, Burke stood up and said, "All right."

"Here he is, captain!" the trooper called.

Burke waited there, blinking against the lantern light, as the platoon collected. Ervien rode up slowly and reined in, and for a moment he and Burke looked levelly at each other. Burke said recklessly, then, "You knew where to hunt for me, didn't you, Phil?"

Ervien said coldly, formally, "Mister Hanna, I went to your room and found you had broken arrest. Consider yourself a prisoner."

Burke said, forgetting caution, "Dismount three of your smallest men and weigh them together on that scale, Phil. See if they don't weigh over six-hundred.

Are you afraid to?"

Ervien's voice was shaking with rage now as he leaned over and pointed accusingly at Burke. "You have broken your word of honor as an officer, Mister Hanna. Now come along, or we'll bind you and carry you!"

"Sure," Burke said slowly, hopelessly, knowing he was beaten. He began to walk toward the stables, and the troopers, at Ervien's orders, flanked him. Ervien silently rode on the right flank.

They went on past the stables, between the agency buildings and turned into the road that ran in front of Corinne's store to the Post.

A brace of carriage lamps lighted the store's deep veranda, and Burke saw Corinne, soft, gray and formless in his baggy black suit, watching silently at the top of the steps. A scattering of Apaches and agency employees were seated on the veranda benches watching wordlessly.

As they drew even with the steps, Burke halted and looked balefully up at Corinne. Ervien, sensing trouble, said, "Forward, Mr. Hanna!"

Burke didn't move. He raised his arm now and pointed at Corinne and said slowly, "Corinne, if you short weight that beef you issue to Ponce tomorrow, he'll break. He told me so tonight. And every drop of blood it takes to get him back here will be on your head!" His hand fell now.

"Forward!" Ervien roared. "Sergeant, put a carbine on that prisoner and if he refuses to move shoot him!"

Burke had never ceased looking at Corinne, who did not move. Now he looked over at Ervien. "You heard it, too. I'll go now."

Burke tramped on, and was soon in darkness. The troopers flanking him were quiet, awed into silence by the gravity of their errand. Later, at the sentry gate, the sentry silently presented arms, and afterward Burke tasted the full measure of this calculated humiliation. He was an officer being brought back afoot by the commanding officer and guard, a prisoner who had broken arrest. They filed past the sutler's post where loitering enlisted men, baffled and wondering, watched them in silence.

It was here, at the corner of the parade ground, that Ervien at last spoke and a score of men heard him. "Sergeant, put him in the guardhouse, and double your guard."

Sometime after ten o'clock next morning, Burke, fed and rested, was lying on his bunk trying to pick out the separate sounds of a post working through a July morning. His barred cell was a big one, occupying half the small adobe building that lay between the two barracks. A pair of troopers were sleeping a drunk off in the cell opposite.

Burke turned his head at the sound in the passageway and saw Abe Byas being let in by the sergeant of the guard.

Burke swung his feet to the floor and Abe, closing the cell door behind him, said, "Hello, Burke," with a morose lack of enthusiasm. He put his huge bulk gently on the foot of Burke's cot, and regarded Burke a moment and shook his head. "Since the middle of supper last night," he said, "I've been looking around for the pieces of all the regulations you've broken. Did you miss one?"

Burke's long face broke in a grin, and Abe regarded him unsmilingly. "Ervien has me drawing up the list of additional charges this morning."

"I added some," Burke murmured.

"For God's sake, why did you have to break arrest?

290

Why were you at the Agency?''

Burke said dryly, ''I'm a kind soul, Abe. I wondered if Corinne watered his beef.''

''Dammit, can't you be serious?''

''I am serious,'' Burke said gravely. ''Either I'm out of the Army or he's out, after the court martial. Let's let it go at that.'' He wasn't going to tell Abe of his certain belief that Ervien was winking at Corinne's cheating the Apaches. Abe would be torn between his loyalty to him and his duty to Ervien and, if he became involved, would have to risk his career.

''How is Calla?'' Burke asked, almost reluctantly.

''She's crazy,'' Abe growled. ''I mean she isn't even worried.'' He looked at Burke. ''I couldn't help but hear your plans last night. Happy wedding day.''

''Thanks,'' Burke murmured.

Abe stood up. ''Anything you want, outside of a change of clothes and razor? Any statement to make?''

Burke shook his head. ''When'll the court martial sit, Abe?''

''In two weeks maybe. When I've heard all the witnesses the case will be forwarded.'' He looked down at Burke, puzzlement in his face, ''I hope you know what you're doing.''

''I do. Thanks.''

When Abe was gone, Burke lay down again, and he found himself thinking of the coming court martial. He had only to plead justification and state his case, but that case must be proven. He saw now that he must do two things: he must prove his charge of crookedness against Corinne; and he must prove that Phil Ervien knew of Corinne's swindle and was abetting it. *If I can't I'm cashiered,* he concluded bleakly.

Sometime later he was roused again by the sergeant's footsteps. Glancing over, he saw Calla, a covered tray in her hands, standing by the cell door. He rose, and

Calla came in; before she put the tray down, she kissed him.

"Happy wedding day," Burke said gravely.

"You wait," Calla said, a kind of merriment in her eyes. "You can't dodge it by going to jail."

Burke grinned. "Why did they let you in here?"

"I asked permission of your Captain Ervien," Calla said, and added slyly, "He's a charming man, really."

She was wearing a flowered green dress, cool and fresh as new grass, and Burke didn't wonder at Ervien's gallantry. He put the tray on the floor and pulled her down beside him, and she half turned to him, regarding him soberly. "How much of what Abe says they say you did, did you do?"

"I can't unravel that," Burke said, and then, when he saw she was serious, he became serious, too. "All of it."

"Can you justify it?"

"All of it," Burke repeated. "Either I don't belong in the Army or he doesn't, Calla."

She reached for his hand and Burke knew that she believed in him completely.

He said then, "Calla, how much of the money I gave you for our house stuff have you got left?"

"Three hundred dollars or so. Why?"

"I'm going to buy us a wedding present," Burke said musingly. "A couple of ugly, brindle, half-starved cows." He smiled at her look of puzzlement, and then, speaking in a low voice, he told of what had happened last night, and why. He held back nothing, and finished by saying, "I never saw the scales, Calla. I can't prove anything on Corinne—and I've got to."

Calla nodded. "But what have two cows got to do with it?"

"You get our money and take it to Rush Doll. The beef issue is going on right now. Tell Rush to pick out

292

a couple of Corinne's issue beeves—cows that are marked or disfigured, so if a man saw them once he'd never forget them. Tell Rush to buy or trade for them with the Apache who was issued them—and that Apache must be a member of Ponce's band. Does it all make sense?''

''Yes,'' Calla said quickly. ''Either Corinne fixes the scales and weighs Ponce's beef right, or he short-weights him—and you have the evidence. If Ponce breaks, you can prove why. Oh, Burke, he won't break, will he?''

Burke shrugged. Calla stood up quickly. ''I'll go now, Burke. I don't know if I can come again.''

Burke kissed her and called the sergeant, and afterwards he stood looking through the bars at the door Calla had just passed through. When he turned back to his lunch, there was a quiet glow of pride and contentment in his face.

Early that evening, the sergeant of the guard gave him a note. It contained one word, *Enju,* and was unsigned, and Burke knew Rush had succeeded.

He got to sleep late. At 4:30 next morning, at bare dawn, the bugle woke him. It was sounding Call to Arms.

Burke lay there wide awake, hearing the sound of men running and their talking. Ten minutes later, the sergeant of the guard poked his head in and said, ''Thought you'd want to know, sir. Ponce's busted loose again.''

Burke sank back on his cot. So it happened, just as he had warned Ervien it would. A hot anger came to him; men would die, ranches would be ravaged and burned, and a whole countryside thrown into terror until Ponce was brought in again. And this time, Ponce would fight. He had trusted the white man's word, and been betrayed. And all of it was on Corinne's head.

293

Burke dressed then, listening, hoping for more information, but in the business of preparation, he was forgotten. The trooper who finally brought his breakfast told him that Ponce had killed an agency policeman in his break. The trooper didn't know how many bucks had broken with him, but they were headed west for the Tonto Rim.

Burke was almost through his breakfast when the corridor door opened and Captain Ervien, followed by Lt. Byas, stood aside to let the sergeant unlock his cell.

It was full light now. Burke put his tray on the floor and came to attention.

Ervien looked haggard and worried, as he returned Burke's salute, but a kind of pride in the man would not let him relax.

He said stiffly, "At ease, Mr. Hanna."

Burke relaxed a little, glancing at Abe's sober face.

"Mr. Hanna," Ervien began, "I have come to a decision I think is a fair one, and I have disregarded my personal feelings in the matter."

Burke said nothing, and Ervien said, "I am releasing you from arrest, Mr. Hanna. You are to assume command of K Troop immediately, and prepare to take the field."

Burke glanced at Abe, who only nodded in confirmation. Burke said slowly to Ervien, "What's the reason, sir?"

"You are our most experienced commander in the field," Ervien said simply. "You know Ponce, you know how he fights. You've campaigned longer and more ably than any man in the squadron. You are needed." He added stiffly now, "It's your privilege to refuse, of course. It will not influence your record. Neither," he said bluntly, "will your acceptance."

"Why, I'll accept, of course," Burke said promptly.

"Very well. Assembly will be sounded in half an

hour. Have your troop ready."

Ervien went out, and Burke stared unbelievingly at Byas. "What's behind it, Abe?"

"Nothing. He said it all. We need you."

It was midday of the second day out of Ft. Akin when Burke, topping the Tonto Rim, led K Troop in a circle and ordered dismount. Abe Byas, who had turned over his I Troop to his second lieutenant in order to join Burke's advance party, stepped heavily out of the saddle and sought the closest shade. The troopers eased from their saddles and loosened cinches that had been tightened for the long ascent, then sought shelter from the blasting midday sun under the pines that grew almost to the edge of the Rim.

Burke loosened his cinch and, seeing Abe was flat on his back in the shade, moved over to Abe's horse and loosened that cinch also. A faint excitement was running through him now. Last night, Nick Arno, the chief of scouts, had climbed close enough to the top of the Rim here to see Ponce's campfires. Ponce would know that, and would make his stand sometime today. Burke thought he knew where it would be, and he impatiently waited word from Nick, whose scouts were well to the front and flanks.

Byas said dreamily now, "It's hell to carry as much weight as I do, Burke."

"It's hell on your horse, too," Burke jibed, and walked back to the edge of the Rim, passing among the resting blue-shirted troopers. At his call for volunteers from K Troop, every man passed by Surgeon Ford as able to sit in a saddle had volunteered, and now he looked at them, along with his few replacements, trying to gauge their temper. They were silent, preoccupied; having just come off the grinding patrol of sending Ponce back to the reservation, they had a personal interest in finishing the job now, Burke knew. Sergeant Raines was cruising silently by himself among the troopers, his campaign hat turned up at the back and in the front, his tight, leathery face pouched in the right cheek by his ever-present cud of tobacco. He had borrowed a pair of oversize boots to accommodate his bandaged feet, and Burke knew he felt ridiculous and therefore touchy.

At the Rim, Burke halted. A thousand feet or more below him perhaps two miles away on the backtrail, Troops I, L and M, comprising two hundred men, toiled antlike up the first lift of the trail; and behind them a string of crawling black beads told him Rush Doll's mule pack train was coming along. For a moment, the panorama of the basin caught and held his attention. He had seen it many times from this point, but never twice alike. Now it was gray, stippled with green and brown, with great pools of black cloud shadow moving majestically across it like lakes of cooling lava. An almost unbearably hot draft of wind lifted ceaselessly over the Rim.

"Lieutenant, sir."

That was Raines. Burke turned, and saw Nick Arno, the young half-breed Apache who was chief of scouts, trotting silently through the resting troop. From the waist up, Nick was dressed like a white man, wearing a dun calico shirt, neckerchief and black campaign hat; from the waist down, he was Apache, with breechclout, high leggings and moccasins. The cast of his broad features was Apache, but his pale, coffee-colored skin bespoke white blood.

He hauled up before Burke, not breathing hard, and Burke waited.

"He's gettin' ready to fight, Burke," Nick said. "He's run far enough."

"The far bank of Quartermaster Creek?" Burke

asked. This was his hunch, and he saw it confirmed by Nick's nod. "How many?"

"Sixty or seventy, not counting women and kids. They're holed up in rocks on both sides of the trail!"

Burke looked beyond the resting troopers and up the timbered trail to the country ahead. The trail, he remembered, climbed over the near ridge he could see, sloped down and crossed an open park to climb again for a higher ridge before it dived steeply into the wide and sandy waterless wash that was Quartermaster Creek. It was on the far bank of the creek, among the vaulting boulders, that Ponce had forted up, and now he said to Nick, "Don't cross the creek, Nick. Scatter your boys to the right of the trail along the ridge and open up on them. Hold them there, and when you're set, start back and I'll meet you on the trail."

Nick nodded and swung into an easy trot past the troopers and Byas and up the trail. Burke went over to Raines who, along with a dozen other troopers, were watching expectantly.

"Raines, you ride," Burke said. "The rest of us will walk. No smoking, no talking. Ponce's about three miles ahead. Let's get going."

With Byas silently plodding behind him, Burke led the file through the timber to the ridge and over it. The humus of pine needles silenced the footfalls of the horses, and there was only the hushed sound of creaking leather. On the downslope as the timber thinned, Burke saw the open grassy park he had promised Ervien would make a suitable assembly point lying still and deserted in the sun.

Once there, Burke almost absently gave the command to fall out while he studied the park. His glance passed over and then returned to the left of the trail at the far edge of the timber.

Byas, from beside him, was studying the park too; he

297

said, "I feel awful naked here, Burke. I keep thinking I see Indians behind trees."

Burke only grinned and beckoned Raines over to him. Burke told him to take Callahan and see if they could make their way mounted down the wash, and he pointed to it, adding, "I want to know if we can get through there mounted to Quartermaster Creek without being seen. If there's been anybody down it ahead of you, pull back and we'll forget it."

Raines shouted for Callahan, and the two of them set out, Callahan, a gaunt and taciturn man, holding back to let Raines precede him by fifty yards, the seasoned trooper's precaution against ambush.

Burke stepped into the saddle now, as Byas said, "Hell, Ponce's got that wash spotted, Burke."

Burke shook his head in negation. "If we were 'Paches, he might have, Abe, but we're only dumb soldiers. A goose-trap ambush on the far bank of the Quartermaster is good enough for us. It's worked on us before, and he thinks it'll work again." He lifted his reins, just as the sound of distant scattered fire came to them. Burke listened a moment, then turned to Abe and grinned. "See?"

"Quartermaster Creek?"

"Far bank." He put his horse into motion, calling over his shoulder, "Post lookouts, Abe, and take over, will you?"

He put his horse across the park and into the timber, and the trail climbed gently again. He felt a curious impatience to examine Ponce's position, now, although he already pictured it. He knew, without any cynicism, that Ervien had elected him to pull his chestnuts out of the fire, and he was willing enough. For this was his chance to settle his score with Ponce, as he promised him he would.

A ten minute ride brought him just short of the timbered crest where Nick was waiting, standing beside the trail, facing the sound of firing and listening intently.

Dismounting, Burke picketed his pony off the trail and joined Nick, who wordlessly led him angling to the right of the trail into the thinning timber of the crest. Nick crawled up behind a windfall lying across the hump of the ridge; Burke came up, hatless, and bellied down beside him.

Before them, the timber ceased almost abruptly; a field of jagged and tumbled boulders sloped easily down to the steep bank of Quartermaster Creek forty yards away. To his left, and across the wide sandy and waterless wash, Burke saw the trail rising steeply to vanish into the boulder field piled high and vaulting on the far bank. Behind the rocks a bare and level sage flats stretched for several hundred yards until the thick timber began again. It was among these boulders on the far bank that Ponce had placed his men on both sides of the trail, waiting contemptuously. Now Burke could pick out the sharp flat crack of Ponce's Winchesters, which were answered by the muffled, heavier bark of the scouts' cavalry carbines to his right on this bank.

Nick touched his arm and pointed across the wash to the right and rear of Ponce's position. Burke saw a column of dust lifting in a slow spiral above the pines, and he knew it was Ponce's pony herd. *He's keeping them moving in a circle*, Burke thought. *Bait for us.*

Nick said then, "Ponce thinks you're in jail, Burke. That trap is for the others."

Burke grunted assent; he'd forgotten that, and it would help. He told Nick to keep the scouts in position and firing, so as to make Ponce waste ammunition, adding, "If they move to our left across the trail, send back word."

Returning to his horse, Burke mounted and turned

back down the trail. The rightness of the plan he had half-formed in his mind was confirmed by what he had seen. If only Raines' report was favorable. Impatient now, he lifted his horse into a canter down the trail to the assembly point.

As he rode into the park, he saw that I, L and M Troops had arrived and dismounted, and were scattered across the park in the hot sunshine, roughly holding formation. The officers, dismounted beyond his own K Troop in the middle of the park, were gathered in a loose circle around Ervien, who was still mounted.

Burke rode straight for his troop and saw Raines break away and come toward him. Reining in, Burke said, "What luck, Raines?"

Raines shifted his tobacco before he spoke. "We got down the wash without any trouble. There's been nobody over it, lieutenant."

"Can a troop get through unobserved?"

"In a column of troopers, yes sir."

"Did you scout the other side?" Burke asked hopefully.

Raines nodded. "Yes sir. We found a wash and went up it into the boulders."

Burke felt a quiet elation now, and he asked, "What's it like on top?"

"Past the boulders, it's mostly level, with sage and rabbit brush flats clean to the timber."

Burke's face broke into a faint smile. "Fine work, Raines. Thank you."

"Sir," Raines said ominously. "O'Mara's along!"

"Keep away from him. We've got other business, Raines." Then he understood that this might be Raines' way of warning him. He looked levelly at Raines, and said again, "I see, thank you, Raines."

Pulling his horse around, Burke rode over to join the officers, and as he approached he heard Ervien say fretfully, "I still think it's unwise to move until Doll's pack train is here." He caught sight of Burke then, and swung out of his saddle. Without his blouse and in his shirtsleeves, Ervien seemed somehow frail, soft and ill at ease. A day of beard growth blurred the edges of his sharp face; his uniform was dusty and his shirt was staining with sweat at his belly and back. He contrived to hide his harried expression from only the closest observer as he said stiffly, "Well, Mister Hanna. You're advance party. What have you found?"

Burke swung down and looked at the ground about him. He found a bare patch of clay a yard or so to the right of him; stepping over to it, he started to kneel, then looked up at Ervien. "You want your first sergeants to hear this, sir?" he asked.

"Very good idea," Ervien murmured.

Byas turned and shouted, "Pass the word. All sergeants assemble here!" Burke knelt and smoothed out the clay, then began to draw his map with his finger. The officers collected about him in a loose circle, and the sergeants as they came up, fell in behind them.

Burke, waiting for the laggards, looked up to see Sergeant O'Mara, his nose swollen but his face otherwise unmarked, watching him with bland and arrogant eyes.

They were all watching now, and Burke explained his simple map, giving Ponce's position, the locations of the pony herd and the disposition of the scouts.

Finished, he looked up at Ervien. He had, he saw immediately, done the wrong thing, for Ervien was looking at him with an air of expectancy mingled with relief, as if the burden of decision had been lifted from him. The harried expression returned to Ervien's face now; he looked awkwardly about him, and saw the other officers watching him. He cleared his throat and said formally, "Any suggestions, Mister Hanna?"

301

"Yes sir," Burke said bluntly. "It's the usual sucker's trap he's set. I propose we don't oblige him."

Lt. Umberhine laughed. Ervien looked reprovingly at the stocky officer and then at Hanna. "None of us want to, I assure you. Go ahead."

Burke looked over at Umberhine, now. "You laughed, Brad, and you're right. Ponce expects us to fight across the wash and make for the pony herd he's labeled for us, so he can butcher us in that wash where the trail crosses."

"What's your scheme?" Byas said.

Burke told them of Raines' reconnaissance, which offered a covered route around across the creek and behind Ponce's flank. One troop, Burke said, should reinforce the present line of scouts at the wash; a second troop should take Raines' route, while the other two troops should swing around to the right to make a demonstration against Ponce's other flank as if to cut between him and his pony herd.

"Is this a fake demonstration, Mister Hanna?" Ervien asked sharply. "You just told us Ponce expects us to do that."

"No sir," Burke said. "That's where we ram home the first hard attack—a quarter mile to the right of the trail where the banks are lower."

"Approximately where Ponce expects us to," Ervien said dryly. "Be consistent."

"I am," Burke said flatly. "We don't ram it home until the troop that's crossed the wash and hidden on his other flank is all set and firing. When Ponce sees his pony herd threatened and moves to protect it, the hidden troop will take him from the rear and cut off escape into the timber." He looked at the circle of attentive faces now. "With eighty men, he can't fight two ways. The two troops on the right will cross between him and his pony herd, then wheel and cut into him."

302

Burke rose now, and Ervien stepped forward, knelt, and studied the map. Sergeant O'Mara behind him leaned hands on knees and looked over his shoulder, while the other officers crowded up and regarded the map in silence.

After a long moment, Ervien rose. "We'll accept that, Mister Hanna. It's very good," he acknowledged. Now, regarding each officer in turn, Ervien was once more the sharp garrison soldier. His work was done for him. To Lt. Umberhine, he gave command of Troops L and M and they were to force the crossing on the right. To Byas fell the command of Troop I, which was reserve, and of the scouts at the trail crossing.

To Hanna and K Troop fell the mission of crossing the Quartermaster unobserved and coming in behind Ponce, and Burke, hearing this, felt a grim satisfaction. Ervien himself, as commanding officer, elected to take his position behind Lt. Umberhine's main attack.

As the group broke up to scatter for their horses, Ervien called, "Good luck, gentlemen. I will post a lookout to our right and rear."

Burke fell in beside the lumbering Byas as they sought their horses. Abe glanced at him and said, "You earn your pay, don't you?"

Burke didn't answer; he said quietly, "Abe, your troop won't need pistols. I want to borrow them."

Byas said slowly, "All right. But why?"

"This is one time," Burke said grimly, "we'll get more than ponies and squaws. I'm after the bucks."

"At short range," Byas said.

"As short as I can make it," Burke murmured.

While the pistols of I Troop were being handed over to the K Troopers, Burke looked across the park at the orderly confusion of troops mounting and forming up. Ervien, with O'Mara at his side, was still studying the map, and Burke saw him point to it gesturing

303

vehemently. Ervien, he supposed, would keep O'Mara, which was satisfactory to K Troop, he knew.

Burke let Raines and Callahan precede him into the wash, then giving K Troop the order to mount, he led on. The issue of extra pistols was causing comment, he knew, and he would give his Troop the reason in good time. Soon the high clay walls closed about them, and the heat was stifling, so that when they came into the blazing brightness of the Quartermaster Creek's sandy bed, it was almost a relief.

Here Raines' trail, hidden from Ponce's view by a sharp bend in the stream bed, crossed and dropped downstream a hundred yards, then headed up a wide sandy draw through the boulders that climbed steeply as it narrowed to little more than the width of a horse.

As Burke pulled out of the arroyo in one last steep climb, he saw immediately to his right Callahan holding his own and Raines' horses. Beyond Callahan, a long low clay dune that cut toward the creek screened his view of Ponce's position.

Raines, his dusty blue uniform almost the color of the clay, was bellied down below the crest of the ridge, which was covered with rabbit brush and sage.

Forming his troop in line below the crest, Burke quietly gave the command to dismount and joined Raines.

The wide sage flats lay in front of him now, separating the timber to his left from the boulder-studded canyon rim to his right. He could tell that L and M Troops had joined the engagement by the increase in volume of fire and, watching carefully, he caught an occasional glimpse of a trooper, small in the distance across the creek, edging his way forward.

Leaving Raines in observation, Burke pulled back behind the dune and called the Troop together. His old troopers were watching him expectantly; only the volunteer replacements showed any uneasiness.

Burke began easily. "This is one time a soldier gets in the first shot with an Apache. They haven't seen us." The troopers grinned at that. "We're going to scatter down this ridge at ten yard intervals and fire two volleys from carbines. That lets L and M know we're in position, and it tells Ponce he's outflanked. Then you'll fall back to your mounts."

There was a puzzled silence at this last piece of information. Finally, Callahan said, "Beg pardon, sir, but these extra pistols. What are they for?"

"A mounted charge," Burke said quietly.

An even longer silence followed, and Burke saw the old troopers were mulling this over in their minds. He glanced up the ridge and saw Raines looking at him. He thought Raines was grinning, but he couldn't be sure. A mounted charge against Indians, of course had been given up by the cavalry long ago as impossible, and Burke knew the older troopers were remembering this.

He said then, "When we volley at Ponce's rear, he'll have to pull out of those rocks or die there. Once he's in the open and afoot, you'll have a horse under you, twelve shots in your pistols and five in your carbines. If you're tired of fighting Indians like an infantryman does, here's your chance. We're going to wind this one up without a footrace."

The men laughed at that, and Burke said, "All right, move forward. Open fire when I do."

The Troop scattered down the ridge now, and Burke pulled his carbine from his saddle scabbard, and climbed the ridge to belly down beside Raines. He surveyed the boulder field now, and catching a movement there, he shot carelessly at it. A ragged volley followed; men were reluctant to shoot without targets, and the Apaches were well hidden.

The second volley, sweeping nearly the whole of Ponce's line beyond the trail, stilled Ponce's Winchesters. Then, as Burke had hoped, there was a stir of activity in the rocks. Several bucks changed positions; a handful stood up briefly, staring at the dunes. He heard angry and excited shouting, and one buck broke for the long run to the timber and, thinking better of it, dropped behind a clump of sage.

The overtone of L and M's fire dropped off now. Burke thought, *They're crossing,* and lifted his glance to the bare bank of the creek. What he saw puzzled him. Blue clad troopers were pulling out of their positions along the rocks of the creek bed, and were hastily retiring up the slope and over the crest.

Raines, seeing it, spat, then looked quizzically at Burke. "What's that for?"

Burke shook his head in wonderment. If they were reforming for a dismounted charge, they'd better hurry.

And then his attention was yanked to Ponce's band. They were drifting out of the rocks now to face this new threat to their rear. There was no concerted movement; here a naked buck, mud-smeared, bent over and running would show himself a second and drop, and another would rise after him. The direction of their movement was obliquely across K Troop's field of fire, and Burke thought, *He's trying to get between us and his camp in the timber. If he reaches timber, he's gone.*

He said, "Come on, Raines," and turned and ran downhill for his horse, raising his arm in the signal to the waiting troopers to mount. Riding immediately to his position in front of center, he ordered, "By the right flank," and rapidly moved the Troop, still hidden by the dune, toward the creek. When the lead trooper had almost reached the rocks, Burke pulled his pistol and signaled, "By the left flank."

The Troop turned into line, labored up the short

climb, reached the crest and, as if heeding a signal unspoken, boiled down the far side and out onto the flats at full gallop, yelling wildly.

A hundred and fifty yards ahead was the scattering of Ponce's bucks who had broken from the boulders. At sight of the charging line of mounted troopers, they remained motionless, momentarily stunned with surprise. This was not the way they fought; nor had they ever fought mounted soldiers before. Then the panic hit them. A pair of bucks broke and ran for the rocks; then, seeing they would be cut off, dropped to the ground. Burke knew their confused milling was real panic, and he rode hard for the center of the band. Wild and inaccurate shooting came at them now.

Holding his fire until he was almost on them, Burke chose a frightened young buck as his man and rode him down. The impact hurled the buck into a kneeling Apache ahead whose Winchester was already leveled at Burke. The gun went off and Burke saw the Apache raise his gun as a pike and thrust savagely at him. With his pistol arm, Burke fended off the blow, and then he was past, and turning in his saddle he leveled and shot almost over his horse's croup into the Apache's side.

His horse swerved then, almost unseating him, as Trooper Breen, still mounted, cut across his path. Burke saw the reins of Breen's horse flying; the man had both arms folded across his belly, and was swaying drunkenly in the saddle. At the impact of Burke's horse, Breen pitched sideways and fell, and Burke's horse caromed off to the right. Wheeling, Burke rowelled his horse to complete the circle and found himself almost alone in swirling dust. The momentum of the first charge had taken the troopers past him, and now he saw the half dozen desperate Apaches who had withstood the charge firing at the galloping troopers, some of whom had fallen. A score of downed Apaches lay scattered in the choking dust raised by the charge. Burke had already chosen the nearest Apache when he heard the terrified protesting moan of a man to his left. Burke swiveled his glance in that direction and saw two Apaches, one stripped, the other in a dirty calico shirt, savagely clubbing a downed trooper with their gun butts.

Pulling his horse half left, Burke shot once, and the Apaches, unhit, dropped to the ground. A returning trooper galloped across in front of him, but before the two Apaches were hidden from sight, Burke saw that the buck in the calico shirt was Ponce.

Rowelling his horse, he shot again, and this time Ponce's companion rose and ran. Two more troopers, both mouthing the Rebel yell, cut in front of him, heading for the remaining Apaches. Burke had to pull up to avoid collision. As the two riders cleared him, he saw Ponce, dropped on one knee, some thirty yards away, his Winchester slacked hesitantly in his arms. As soon as he identified Burke, he raised his gun and Burke was looking into its muzzle. Instinctively, Burke flattened out on the neck of his horse. The shot came immediately, and Burke felt his horse shudder at the impact. As if propelled from a sling, Burke was catapulted over his horse's head. He landed heavily on his chest in the dust, and the breath was driven from him. Gagging, he rolled on his left side so that his pistol arm was free, and now Ponce shot again. The noise was deafening, and Burke felt the sting of the powder. Burke bent back his head and saw, not ten feet away, Ponce's squat figure half hidden in dust, levering a shell. Burke was lying on his side; with no time to roll on his belly, he streaked up his pistol swiftly and shot immediately at the dust-blurred outline of Ponce canted awkwardly in his vision.

He thought he missed; he rolled over, panicked,

expecting Ponce's shot, but the barrel of Ponce's gun slowly tilted down, halted, was inched up again, as if he were lifting a great and ponderous weight. The calico shirt began to stain redly at the belly and Burke shot at the stain. Ponce went over backwards, his knees still unbending, and fell heavily and lay still.

Burke rose now and was immediately aware that something had happened. The close handfighting was over; the troopers scattered over the flats who were herding their prisoners back were now under fire themselves from the rocks, and from the dunes, behind which the Apaches had filtered. Raines and a half dozen dismounted troopers were fighting their horses quiet, and kneeling to minimize the target they presented. Even from the timber came shots from the bucks who had taken refuge there.

Burke looked bleakly off across the creek, and a hot sense of betrayal was in him. Where were L and M Troops? K had been left to make the fight alone, and unless they got out of here, the table would be completely turned on them. They were exposed now.

Burke saw one of the volunteer replacements sitting up in the dust a few yards from him, flexing a bloody arm with a look of bafflement in his young face.

Burke ran to him, helped him to his feet, and then half dragged, half carried him toward Raines and the men guarding the prisoners. Lagging troopers were racing toward the same point.

Burke called sharply, "Callahan, take your squad and mount the wounded men. Raines, take the second squad and bind those prisoners. The rest of you scatter and make a run for the rocks. When you get there dismount and get into action."

As the troopers dispersed and rode for the boulders, enough fire was drawn off the wounded to allow Burke and Callahan to mount them. Raines left, directed by

Burke to hole up close to the trail, and presently, still under inaccurate fire, Burke mounted the dead trooper Breen's horse and headed for the rocks, bringing up the rear.

Fifty feet into the tangle of high boulders, Callahan and two troopers had already found some shade and were making the wounded men comfortable. Burke, stepping out of the saddle close by, heard his dismounted troopers firing, and he felt a savage and wicked anger at this bungling. L and M had never tried to cross. These rocks held the blasting heat of the overhead sun, and he took off his hat and wiped his brow with his sleeve. Looking back over the flats now, he caught occasional glimpses of running Apaches. Keeping to cover, they were rallying to attack again knowing they could win now. These rocks, Burke knew, had won K Troop only temporary respite; this sort of cover suited the Apaches best, and they were shrewd enough to know if they could corner this scattering of deserted troopers here, the soldiers would die. *We've got to get some help,* Burke thought narrowly. There was the trail down to the Quartermaster and across it along which the ambush was originally laid. Was it still held by the Apaches?

He called, "Callahan," and, while Callahan made the last of the wounded comfortable, Burke thought stubbornly, *Damned if we'll run. I Troop must come to us.*

"Yes, sir," Callahan said from beside him.

"Callahan, we've got to get word to I Troop to cross the creek and reinforce us. The trail over there is the only way to them, and God knows what's down there." He paused, sobered by the thought of what he had been going to ask of this man.

"You want me to try it, sir?"

"I guess not," Burke said slowly.

"I'll make it, sir. Let me try."

Somebody must go, Burke knew, and he steeled himself and said, "All right. Tell Lieutenant Byas we're clearing out both sides of the trail, and it'll be safe for him to bring I Troop across. Tell him to hurry it. Good luck."

Callahan mounted and rode out of the rocks and turned left, and was lost to sight around the boulders.

Burke now posted the two troopers among the rocks with order to fire at will and mounted out and turned through the rocks toward the trail. He had traveled only a hundred feet or so when he found Raines and two more troopers hidden back among the rocks. Raines had their prisoners lying flat on the ground, face down, and was directing the fire of the other two troopers.

Dismounting, Burke briefly told Raines his plan, and Raines ordered the waiting troopers to go out and pull in both flanks to the edge of the trail.

When they were gone, Burke stood looking at the half dozen naked and sweating Apaches stretched belly down on the ground. They were watching him carefully, a hot hatred in their eyes, and he knew however this fight turned out today, it would settle nothing with these people; they had a grudge deep and nourished by the actions of men like Corinne.

The sound of an approaching horse roused him, and he looked over his shoulder. There, among the boulders, stood Callahan's horse; and it was riderless, and the horse's rump was bleeding from a long gash.

Burke and Raines glanced dismally at each other, and Raines said around his tobacco, "You hold these monkeys, Lieutenant. I'll go."

Burke was touched with a gray despair, and he slowly shook his head. "No. You know what's got to be done, Raines. Hold that trail open for us; either kill those devils guarding it or keep them down until we're through."

He stepped into the saddle, just as the slug from a searching shot ricocheted off a nearby boulder. Time was precious now, he knew. A couple of troopers afoot ducked into sight and sweating and swearing, headed for Raines.

As he rode on toward the trail, Burke put as many rocks as he could find between him and the Apaches on the flats, but the shooting was uncomfortably close.

When at last he picked up the trail, and turned into it, he saw troopers already forted up behind rocks on either side and shooting.

And then he gave his attention to what lay ahead. The trail, he remembered, twisted and turned between towering rocks, dropping steeply for fifty yards to the bed of the creek, and every rock was big enough to hide a dozen Apaches.

Pulling his pistol now, he urged his horse into a trot and then rowelled him into a run. Timid at first, the horse finally plunged into a reckless run, and Burke, leaning flat on his neck, gave him his head. He was going to run through somehow.

Rounding the first twist in the trail, Burke's knee was raked savagely against a jutting boulder, but he did not rein in. His horse stumbled once, recovered in time to hurtle around another boulder and take the steep drop beyond in a lunge that almost unseated Burke. And then, coming around a sharp curve, Burke saw what he had been expecting. Callahan lay in the trail between precipitous walls. The two Apaches cutting his already mutilated body had had no warning of Burke's presence, and, now they looked up to find horse and rider hurtling down on them. One buck clawed at the rock in his haste to get out of the way, then turned and ran down the trail. Burke rowelled his horse savagely at the other Apache flattened against the wall, drawing his knife.

Burke shot him in the face, and in falling the buck came under the pony's hooves and was rolled along the trail. Burke raised his pistol again now and shot at the buck running ahead, and his hammer fell on an empty chamber. He had used his spent pistol. Kicking his foot out of the stirrup now, Burke waited until his pony was even with the Apache, and then he kicked solidly, catching the buck between the shoulders. The buck went down between the pony's legs and his scream was cut off sharply. Burke yanked his reins up as the buck, tangled among his pony's legs, tripped him. For a moment, Burke thought the pony would go down, and then he was free, and running again.

Two more lowering curves in the trail, and Burke saw ahead the gleaming sand of the river bed. From somewhere up the rocks on the right a futile shot searched for him, and then he was in the deep sand of the wash.

Under Burke's urging, his pony labored through the deep sand, as an erring marksman among the rocks kept firing swiftly and inaccurately at them.

At the far bank, Burke reined down to a walk for the climb. Pulling onto the bank, he saw Abe Byas and two troopers waiting for him behind a rock.

Burke swung out of the saddle and said shortly, "Bring your men over, Abe. And make it fast."

Byas hesitated and Burke's ragged temper flared. "Dammit, man, you're reserve and I'm calling on you!"

"Take it easy, Burke," Abe said. "I was wondering about the trail."

"It's cleared," Burke said. "Make it fast, Abe, or I'm all that's left of K."

Abe gave orders to his sergeant and then turned to regard Burke.

"What happened to L and M?" Burke demanded angrily. "Did they ever cross?"

Byas only shook his head. By now, the first of Nick's scouts came at a jog down the trail, and Burke halted them long enough to tell them what he wanted. The trail was being cleared by K Troop. He would lead the scouts and I Troop, dismounted up the trail, where they would split, travel the edge of the boulder field in both directions for five hundred yards, then, flanking the Apaches, dig them out of the rocks.

Walking across the bed of Quartermaster Creek was a slogging, exhausting job, and Burke found his legs trembling with weariness as he achieved the other side. Without a pause, he started up the trail, Nick ahead of him, Byas behind him. Only a scattering of shots had harassed them as they crossed. There was steady fire now above them in the boulders on both sides of the trail but none of it was directed at them, and Burke knew Raines was obeying instructions to keep the Apaches down.

Reaching the top, Burke and Byas divided the squads, two to each side of the trail, and the hunt was on. But it lasted only a matter of minutes. The reinforcing I Troopers, hunting in pairs, and pushing the Apaches from the flanks toward the center where K Troop was waiting, were too much. The Apaches were killed, or gave up, seeing the hopelessness of their position.

When the first scattering of sullen prisoners began to trickle in, Burke sought out Byas, and found him looking over the wounded men. Burke, bone weary and exhausted and wet with sweat, was leaning up against a rock in a piece of shade when Abe approached.

"You feel like turning over the clean-up job to a junior officer, Abe?"

"All right. Why?"

314

"Then come with me," Burke said grimly. "Somebody's going to answer my questions."

Byas knew he was referring to L and M's disappearance. They borrowed two horses, mounted and rode down the trail and across the river. When they had achieved the timbered crest on the far bank, the trail widened, and Burke reined in to let Abe come abreast of him.

"What happened, now, Abe?"

"I never made it out," Abe said wearily. "L and M started to cross after your volleys, when they were pulled back. I sent a runner to Ervien asking what was wrong. He came back with the answer that dust had been sighted to his right and rear, that he was pulling back to protect our flank, and for me to have the reserves ready to move."

Burke's baleful glance settled on him. "Did you hear any shooting back there?"

"Not a shot," Abe said grimly.

Burke was silent a moment and then murmured, "It better be so."

When the timber thinned out and they could see the park where the assembly point was, Burke saw that L and M Troops had come in only minutes before. Some of the troopers were still unloosening cinches. Beyond them, Rush Doll's packers were just beginning to unload the mules in the shade. The sun to the west now, giving some shadows. And then Burke saw Ervien. He and the officers of L and M Troops were kneeling in the sun just where he had left them over his map of the battle plan in the center of the park. Rush Doll, hands on hips, was looking over Ervien's shoulder.

Burke and Abe rode directly up to them and dismounted, and Burke saw instantly by the faces of these officers that a bitter argument had been interrupted.

Ervien seemed shocked by Burke's dust-grimed appearance. He rose now as Burke dismounted, and said crisply. "Well, Mr. Hanna, what have you to report?"

Burke said with an ominous quiet, "Ponce's dead, twenty-three of his men are dead, and the rest have surrendered. Three dead and three wounded from K Troop." He paused. "How many dead and wounded in L and M, sir?"

"Look, Burke," Lt. Umberhine said hotly. "I was—"

"Let your commanding officer answer, Brad," Burke murmured, watching Ervien.

Ervien's sunburned face flushed a deeper red. "I countermanded Brad's order to advance across the creek." His voice was quiet, almost arrogant.

"Why, sir?"

"Abe has probably told you. The lookout I posted saw dust clouds to the rear and right of our position. I couldn't risk leaving our flank open, so I ordered L and M back to protect our position."

"And were they hostiles, sir?" Burke said evenly.

"As it turned out, they weren't," Ervien said.

"It was me," Rush Doll drawled. "My pack mules stirred the dust."

Burke frowned. "What were you doing to the right and rear of L and M, Rush? This was the assembly point."

"I got order from the captain through O'Mara," Rush said slowly.

Ervien nodded. "That's right. L and M were the bulk of the troops to be supplied. Doll could have followed our advance across the creek much easier than waiting here to move across."

"You didn't tell me that, sir," Umberhine said angrily.

Ervien looked calmly at him. "An oversight. I apologize, Brad."

Burke said slowly, "If you knew Doll was coming that route, the dust shouldn't have surprised you."

"I didn't see the dust or its position. It was reported to me by the lookout."

"Let's talk to that lookout," Burke said. "Who was he?"

Ervien hesitated only a split second, and then said, "Sergeant O'Mara."

Umberhine shouted for O'Mara. Burke glanced fleetingly at Byas, who was studying Ervien with a sober puzzlement in his face.

O'Mara broke away from a cluster of troopers, approached and saluted. Ervien began, "Sergeant, tell—"

"One moment, sir," Burke said flatly. "I'm going to ask him." He looked levelly at O'Mara and the sergeant blandly returned his stare. Burke said, "You knew Doll was coming up on L and M's flank. Who did you think raised that dust?"

"I only reported it, sir," O'Mara said in his gentle sly voice. "I was not asked my opinion."

"If you had been, what would you have said?" Burke asked dryly.

"I'd have said we should protect ourselves till we were sure," O'Mara replied blandly.

Burke shifted his glance to Byas and said slowly, "There you are, Abe."

Ervien said sharply, "There who is, Mister Hanna? Since when are a commanding officer's orders subject to discussion?"

Burke's hot and wild glance settled on Ervien now. "Since today, Phil. You pulled out of the fight and left K Troop to be massacred. If we didn't have the luck of the damned, the lot of us would be dead now. We aren't—thanks to I Troop." He looked hotly at the group of officers around him. "Now hear me. Abe, you're adjutant and next in command. I demand you place Captain Ervien and Sergeant O'Mara under arrest for dereliction of duty."

"I demand it, too!" Umberhine said flatly. "Damned if I'll let any man make me a coward!"

Byas said slowly, "I'd like it better if I knew the reason for this, Burke."

"I'll give you that, too," Burke said. "Corinne has cheated the Indians blind, and Ervien has protected him. When I recommended Ervien report Corinne's dishonesty, I got sent on six months of patrol. And when Ponce broke out, Ervien knew he was in trouble, because I warned him Ponce would break." He looked around at his fellow officers. "You all saw that plan of battle I submitted. You saw where K Troop, myself commanding, was placed. If anything slipped, we were in a fair position to be wiped out. It slipped, all right— and I say Ervien, in collusion with O'Mara, planned to kill me and my Troop."

"But proof, man, proof," Abe said gently.

"Of Corinne's crookedness? I've got it at the Post. The rest will come out in the court martial—his or mine."

There was a long moment of silence, and it was broken at last by Ervien. "Mister Hanna, you are now under arrest—again."

Abe Byas said gently, "No, Captain Ervien. It's my duty as senior officer to place you under arrest, and assume command."

Ervien looked arrogantly about him. "Very well. All of you will undergo a court martial for mutiny."

The victors of the battle of Quartermaster Creek reached Ft. Akin a little after nine o'clock the second night after the battle. The Post was ablaze with lights, and the veranda of the sutler's post crowded with the garrison sol-

318

diers and the womenfolk of absent men.

As the troopers were wearily scattering to their barracks five horsemen entered through the north sentry gate and rode along the parade ground to dismount at headquarters building, whose lamps were lighted.

Lt. Byas led the way into the building, spoke to the sergeant, and went immediately into Capt. Ervien's office. He spoke courteously to Mr. Corinne who had been sitting at the chair beside Ervien's desk, then stepped aside to let Capt. Ervien, Lt. Umberhine, Rush Doll and Burke Hanna enter.

As Burke closed the door, Corinne said irritably, "Phil, I ought to be over checking in that pack of Ponce's scoundrels. Can't this wait?"

"No," Ervien said bluntly. He walked over to the desk and sat on its edge, and glanced at Burke. "Go ahead, Burke."

Corinne's glance flicked to Burke, who was already looking at him.

"Corinne," Burke said, "Rush Doll has two cows over in his corral. They were issued by you to Klin at Saturday's issue. Klinse's kept his ration slip—with your figures."

He paused, and Corinne said nothing. Burke went on, "Then we're going over and weigh them on the agency scales."

Corinne looked at Ervien, and only now did he begin to suspect something was amiss. Abe's message summoning Corinne tonight was delivered by a trusted trooper who had been told to explain nothing of what had passed at the assembly point. Corinne said dryly now, "Are you the commanding officer now, Mister Hanna?"

"Lieutenant Byas is."

Corinne looked again at Ervien, and Ervien nodded. Corinne's already flabby face seemed to sag; he looked despairingly at Burke and said, "Our scales were broken, Mister Hanna."

"Give it up, Alec." Ervien's voice was quiet, sardonic; and every man in the room looked at him. He only shook his head at Corinne and said to Byas, "You're kicking him out?"

"As fast as he can pack up," Abe said grimly.

"What'll satisfy you completely. If I get out too?"

Byas was about to answer, and then glanced questioningly at Burke.

"Yes," Burke said implacably. "Get out. You're scum. Resign - or face a court martial—if Lieutenant Byas will let you. He doesn't have to."

Abe rose from the desk and indicated the chair. "Write it out."

Ervien sat down wearily and Byas strode past Burke and went out into the anteroom, leaving the door open behind him. Burke heard him say, "Sergeant, before you close up, fill out papers reducing Sergeant O'Mara to private on stable police."

When he came back in Ervien looked up from his writing. "Would you like me to give a reason?" he asked Byas.

"You've been given it," Byas said quietly. "You're scum. Officially you can say 'for the honor of the service'!"

Ervien's face flushed, and his glance dropped to the paper. He signed his name, rose and extended the paper to Byas, who put it on the desk without looking at it.

"Get out of that uniform. Your transportation will be ready in an hour," Byas said. "We'll send your stuff to Corinne. You," he added to Corinne, "hand over your books to Lieutenant Hanna tomorrow morning at eight o'clock. Don't try to go to your office. It's under guard."

Some minutes later, Burke and Byas said good night to Rush and Umberhine and wearily headed for the lights of Byas' house. Halfway across the parade ground, Burke said, "Abe."

"What?"

"I'm on your grass seed. So are you."

Abe laughed. "Hell with it. As the commanding officer, I can walk where I want."

At the house, Abe opened the door and stood aside to let Calla come into Burke's arms, afterwards going past them and inside to greet his wife. Minutes later, when Burke with Calla, came into the living room, Abe and Lucy were standing in the middle of the room arm in arm. Abe said, "Calla, do you want the chaplain tonight, or would you rather be married tomorrow in your own house?"

Calla grinned. "I can wait. But where's my own house?"

"You're standing in it. I'm taking over Ervien's house tomorrow. He's resigned."

Calla looked up at Burke, and then glanced at Abe. "Make it early, will you please?"

COURT DAY

The closing arguments were finished and, after instructing the jury and watching it file out, Judge Morehead recessed the court and went over to the Stockman's House for a beer. The courtroom spilled its crowd onto the hard-packed adobe yard. A March wind that had been pelting sand against the courtroom windows and shaking them was a wild thing out in that thin sunlight, and the crowd of ragged nesters hugged the sheltered east face of the adobe building, as silent and patient in waiting as their teams that lined the tie rails.

Ernie Manners, his worn jumper gray and paper-thin over his thick shoulders, walked with a solid and deliberate step as far as the cast-iron watering trough by the tie rail and sat on its edge. Beyond him across the road and under a leafless cottonwood, the Socorro stage was waiting. It had been there since court convened this morning, and it would leave as soon as the jury returned a verdict and Joe Williams was either freed or put aboard it for the journey north to Santa Fe.

Trouble had ridden Ernie Manners and gentled him, so that his square weather-scoured face was almost impassive as he looked at the stage. To the other small ranchers it was a token of their and Joe Williams' defeat, soon to be made public.

Tim Bone came down the walk and stopped by Ernie and said, "Don't look like anyone ever doubted that jury, does it?"

"No."

"Are those Spade riders with the driver?"

"Yes. Guards," Ernie murmured.

Tim Bone laughed shortly, without humor, and fisted his hands in his hip pockets. He was a middle-aged man and wifeless, his face shaped with a strange violence that danced wicked little lights in his eyes and made his speech aggressive. "Don't look like Bill Friend had any doubts either," he observed, quietly for him.

A bailiff left the courthouse door and walked over to the Stockman's House, the crowd's murmur following him. Almost immediately, Judge Morehead came out before the others and crossed the dusty road ahead of a team, waving at the driver. The others followed. To Ernie Manners and to all those small ranchers of the San Jon basin it was a roll call of their victors. There was young John Comer, the deputy sheriff, who walked alongside the Spade foreman, Ferd Willis, as far as the near walk, and then stopped and waited for old Bill Friend, the Spade owner, and Martha Friend, his daughter.

Comer didn't need to stop, Ernie knew. Ferd Willis knew it too. Where it would have been easy for Ferd to walk past that clot of hostile men and women, ignoring them, it was not easy to stand and face them. But it was a concession he made to John Comer's arrogance, and Ferd stood there, idly scraping a circle in the dirt with the toe of his boot, looking down at the ground to avoid the stares.

Afterward, he fell in beside Bill Friend, while Martha Friend walked along with John Comer. Of those four, only Martha tried to greet the loose rank of nester men and women watching. Ernie saw her nod occasionally, saw the womenfolk nod in return and less often a man raise a hand to his worn hat. Bill Friend looked straight ahead, erect and unbending and implacable. John Comer whistled softly, his walk slow and unconcerned and somehow wary.

When they entered the door, Ernie looked down at his hand and then wiped it on his leg.

"Maybe we ain't ready yet," Tim Bone murmured. "Maybe we better wait and see what they do to Joe."

Ernie looked up quickly and Tim's glance slid away.

"Don't be a fool," Ernie said quietly. "This'll turn out short weight for us, but don't make the mistake of trying to fix it that way."

"Sure," Tim said, disbelief in his voice.

The crowd broke and filed back into the courthouse. Ernie was the last one in. What happened then was news to none of them. For the crime of killing and butchering out a Spade beef with which to feed his family, Joe Williams was found guilty by a jury of townsmen and sentenced to ten years in the Santa Fe penitentiary.

But by the iron watering trough again, Ernie saw the arrangement of these waiting men was a little different this time. If trouble was coming, it would come now, and he hated the thought of it. It was patience that saved men, patience and waiting, and he wondered if these men would wait.

When the deputy came out the door with Joe Williams, it was Comer whom Ernie watched. The crowd stirred, gauging Comer's hand. It was a good one. Joe Williams, handcuffed, walked beside him. On Joe's other side was Ferd Willis, and on the stage top across the street were three Spade riders, rifles in hand.

Comer was so sure of himself that he paused to touch a match to his cigarette, a big man with thick shoulders and a proud way of carrying his young head.

In front of Ernie, Joe Williams said to Comer, "Can I talk to Ernie a minute?"

Comer liked the risk. He nodded and signaled Ferd Willis to step aside and then coolly surveyed the courthouse yard, knowing he and poverty had these silent men whipped.

Joe Williams said to Ernie, "She's going over with the Littlefields, Ernie."

"She'll be all right there, fine."

"She can raise a garden. Pay for her keep."

"Sure."

"Look," Joe's face was curiously attentive. "If she runs into any hard luck, you'll know it, won't you, Ernie?"

"I'll look out for her."

"That's what I mean. Thanks."

Ernie put out his hand and Joe took it wordlessly, a little of the bitterness and desperation in him mounting to his eyes.

Ernie said, "You find someone up there that can write, Joe. Keep the letters coming. We'll take care of her."

"So long," Joe said. Comer, seeing they were finished, threw his cigarette away and stepped up to Joe's side.

Tim Bone, from behind Ernie, drawled carefully, "Joe, you break out up there and I'll hide you."

Comer's gaze whipped to Tim. "Easy," he said.

"Mind now, Joe," Tim drawled.

Comer touched Joe's arm and they stepped into the street and crossed to the stage. Seconds later it rolled out and Ernie said to Tim, "Goin' upstreet?"

"In a minute," Tim murmured. He was watching Comer and Willis, who had turned and were coming back to the walk. Slowly the crowd was breaking up, drifting toward the stores.

Ernie sat down on the watering trough again, his sober and homely face watchful. Comer passed him and stopped in front of Tim. "Your advice is likely to get him shot," Comer observed.

"I'd liefer get shot than spend ten years in Santa Fe. So would Joe," Tim drawled.

"If the rest of your friends feel that way about it, then tell them to leave the Spade stuff alone."

"You might tell 'em yourself."

"I'll do that," Comer said quietly. "Now move on."

Tim showed no intention of moving.

"Move on, I said."

"I heard you."

Ernie's quiet voice interrupted them. "I want to talk to Tim, John."

It was a graceful exit for Comer. He nodded and walked up into the courthouse, big and confident.

"Come on," Ernie said, and Tim joined him.

Court day always brought a crowd to Warms, but today there were horses at the tie rails whose brands hadn't been seen in town since last fall. They had come to see what Bill Friend would do to one of their own people, and they had found out.

Ernie stopped in front of the Emporium and Tim said, "See you down at the saloon?"

"Later, I guess," Ernie said. Inside, he bought a sack of groceries and some dress goods with five of his last ten dollars and later, when nobody was looking, he left them in Littlefield's buckboard and went on downstreet.

* * *

Deputy Sheriff John Comer was talking to Martha Friend in front of the express office as Ernie hit the sidewalk, heading toward them. For a brief second, Ernie contemplated turning around, and then he gave it up. But he didn't want to see Martha after today's happenings. Before Comer had come he had seen something of Martha, taken her to dances, and once he had taken her to the Fourth of July barbecue out on Tuesday Creek. But when old Bill Friend made it plain that Ernie was no different than any other range-stealing nester, Ernie quit seeing her. Martha saw him first, and the surprise on her face was pleasant, Ernie saw. She smiled quickly, bent her arm at the elbow, raised her hand and wiggled her fingers in a wave to him. Ernie felt a flush of pleasure. He touched his hat, not intending to stop.

"Ernie," Comer called.

Ernie paused now, wheeled and walked over to them. Martha put out her hand and smiled again and said, "You're almost a stranger now, Ernie."

"It's along ride from the San Jon, Martha. How've you been?"

She said fine and Ernie saw she was lying. Behind the welcome in her eyes lay a sadness that Ernie had seen once before, on the night when she listened to him and her father argue whose was the rightful side in the division of the San Jons basin range. He wanted to say more, but there was nothing he could say without bringing in today's trial, so he looked up at Comer.

"I've got a favor to ask, Ernie." It was more like a command, and Ernie studied the man's face. It was not a kind face, not cruel either, only hard and lean and determined, almost humorless. "I'd like to have you move your boys out of town before dark," Comer went on.

"My boys?" Ernie echoed.

"Yes. All the small outfits lined up against Spade."

Ernie watched him until he was finished and then looked at Martha. Her eyes avoided his, and he returned his attention to Comer. "Why me?"

"You're the only level head in the crowd," Comer said. "They'll listen to you."

"Not when I talk that kind of foolishness," Ernie said quietly.

Comer rubbed a finger along his lower lip and said just as quietly, "It's not foolishness, Ernie. I mean it. They've got to be out of town at sundown."

"Why?"

"Spade is here in town and there'll be trouble."

"Ever think of movin' Spade?" Ernie murmured.

Comer looked thoughtfully at him and then shrugged. "All right. Don't bother."

Ernie's temper was crowding him and he knew it and didn't care. "How long you been here, Comer? Four months, isn't it?"

"Five."

"You aren't a Basin man," Ernie went on slowly. "When old Sheriff Baily died Bill Friend saw a chance to buy his own law. One way or another, every commissioner on that county board was in debt to Bill, so they voted with him. They voted to bring a man in from outside and they got you." He paused. "Begin to understand?"

"No."

"You were appointed, Comer, not elected. You're not our man. We'll take somethin' like happened today. It may take us five years to swallow it clean, but we will. Just don't crowd your luck until you know us, that's all."

He looked at Martha and touched his hat and left them.

* * *

329

The wind sent a rising sheet of grit against Budrow's saddle shop across the street. It caromed off the false front and raked the Spade ponies tied in front of Prince's Keno Parlor and Saloon. Ernie walked past them and beyond Grant Avenue, toward Dick Mobely's Gem Saloon, his tramp deliberate as always. His anger had already dried up, and in its place was a deep knowledge of defeat. If he carried Comer's word to the men down there at the Gem, all his work, all those patient hours of reasoning with them, would be canceled. Men, even men ground to the ways of poverty, would take only so much. He had nursed their pride along with his own, had reasoned them into taking the long view in the face of the knowledge that Joe Williams would doubtless be convicted. They would be angry now, but he could swing them to his side again—but not if he carried the red flag of Comer's word to them.

They were all here, clotted at the bar or sitting in chairs hauled over from the poker tables. There was no drinking, for drinking took money and they had none.

The talk didn't stop as they made way for Ernie. He packed his pipe and then dragged up a chair to the edge of the circle. Ed Horstmann, from out on Tuesday Creek, was speculating on just how much nerve it took for Comer to bring Joe Williams out to the stage in front of the crowd. Miles Overbeck regretted that they hadn't made a try for Comer, and Tim Bone laughed.

"Hell, it takes just one bullet," he said quietly, looking at them. "Just one bullet." When he came to Ernie, his glance passed him quickly.

"Maybe that's what we ought to do," Ed said. "Draw straws, maybe, or cut cards for him. Anyway, have a try at him. Or somethin'."

Ernie said, "You do, Ed, and you'll see your kids carrying this fight."

Ed laughed. "The oldest is only six."

"That's what I mean."

Ed looked over at him and opened his mouth to speak. Tim Bone put a word in before him. "It's either that or pull stakes for most of us, Ernie. You too."

"There's an election coming," Ernie pointed out, as he had done before.

"Next fall," Miles Overbeck said. "Hell. I ain't even got alfalfa to boil up for grub. Bill Friend sent a rider out last week while I was away, to stake my well for a homestead. The corner come right on the floor of my shack and damned if he didn't tip over my stove to drive his stake. I can't even drink."

"I know," Ernie said.

"You don't know," Tim said harshly. "If you did, Ernie, then why you arguin'?"

Ernie shifted in his chair. They were willing to listen to him; they always were. "You feel that way about it, pull up into the San Jon and live off the country till election time," he said. "Don't sell your places; don't give Bill Friend a claim; just pull out and wait."

"The other way's easier," Miles said.

"You know how it's comin' out," Ernie said slowly, repeating the old argument. "Why don't you wait? We'll vote Comer out next fall. After that, we'll give Bill Friend enough water and range for his needs and then it's done. But go at it with guns, and he'll drive the lot of us over the mountains for good."

Tim Bone said, "Hell!" and walked out.

Max Troutman said, "Ernie, why you figure to play it that way? You was never afraid of a fight." Ernie knocked his pipe out on his heel and pocketed it and then looked up at Max. He was back in the groove of the old argument, and he recited it as if it were new.

"We start pickin' and choosin' the laws we like and we ain't got any laws at all." He watched Ed Horstmann's face, which was eager to believe. "We got votes. We're Americans. And we elect our sheriffs by votes. If we can hang on this summer, we can vote Comer out—legal. And we'll vote in a fair man in his place. After that, Bill Friend will pull in his horns and leave us alone. But if we let Comer crowd us into gunplay, we're done.'' He looked at their faces. ''What's the matter? Ain't you got the guts to starve a little for your places?''

Ed Horstmann said, ''You're damn' right,'' and the argument started anew. Ernie knew how it would go. After an hour of talk Miles Overbeck would rise and say to Horstmann, ''You goin' home, Ed?'' and the meeting would break up. Safely, Ernie hoped, looking out under the swing doors to see how long the shadows were.

It worked out that way. Miles was on his feet, waiting only for a break in the talk to speak to Ed when Marty Beshears walked in. He came straight to the chairs and something in his face made Max Troutman cease talking. They all looked over at Marty.

''I just saw Comer,'' Marty announced, his eyes hot, his voice contained. ''He's givin' us till sundown to clear out of town.''

Nobody spoke for a minute. Ernie found them watching him, but he kept silent. There are times you can advise men, and there are times you can't.

''Well?'' Marty said.

''Is that so?'' Ed drawled. He tilted back his chair, turned his head and spat into the sawdust. Then he stood up. ''I'm goin' up to Prince's and watch the games for a couple of hours.''

A voice from the door, a cool commanding voice, said, ''I don't think so.'' It was Comer. He had both thumbs in the top of his wide leather gun belt. Ernie felt his stomach coil hotly. The fool! The whole sorry mess would blow up in their faces now. Comer would be killed and so would a couple of others and the war would come out in the open. Ernie opened his mouth and saw it was no use and shut it again.

Ed Horstmann said quietly, "Stand over, Marty, and let him open the ball."

Ernie slid off his chair toward the wall, his hand falling to his side. It was then that Tim Bone shouldered through the batwing doors. He had a gun in his hand and he came to a full stop some five feet inside the door, gun leveled at Comer, and said, "Hold it!"

Comer watched Ed Horstmann for a full three seconds, and then swung around to face Tim Bone. There was something in his face that told Ernie he knew he had made a mistake, and that he wasn't backing down.

"That's right," Tim drawled. "Turn around and take it in the belly."

"I said you're leavin' town by sundown," Comer said quietly. "Now get out of my way."

Tim Bone only said, "I don't reckon."

Comer didn't move. His iron bluff had failed, and a kind of panic crawled up into his face and was smothered. He shuttled his glance to Marty Beshears and got no help, and it was then he knew he might as well make his try for what it was worth, which was exactly nothing.

Ernie said sharply, "Tim, wait!"

Even as he spoke, he walked forward, knocking over a chair in his haste. He swung his body in between Comer and Tim and flipped both Comer's guns onto the floor. Then he reached up and took Comer's badge between his fingers and roughly ripped it off his shirt, taking a triangle of cloth with it. He grabbed Comer's upper arm and swung him roughly into a chair facing a table, and before Tim Bone could protest he turned to Dick Mobely behind the bar. "Paper and pen, Dick."

He got them and put them before Comer. Nobody else had moved. Ed Horstmann had his gun unlimbered now, and was scowling.

"That's for your resignation," Ernie said swiftly, pointing to the paper. "Write it out to Bill Friend. When you're through with that, write another to him and tell him to move Spade out of town right now!"

Comer picked up the pen, twisted the wad of inky paper from the ink bottle, dipped his pen and wrote in quiet haste.

When Comer had signed his name, Ernie ripped the sheets off the tablet, wheeled, and said to Tim Bone on his way out, "Just wait a minute, Tim."

Bill Friend was in the Stockman's House lobby talking with Judge Morehead over in a corner. Ernie walked straight to him, tossed Comer's badge in his lap and shoved the papers at him.

Bill Friend's tired face was wary. He took out his spectacles; then, sensing the urgency in Ernie's manner, he forgot to put them on. Holding the papers at arm's length, he read the first one. Without comment he turned to the second. His eyes were hard and speculative. "Where is Comer now?"

"Down at the Gem with a gun to his ear," Ernie said quickly. "All you got to do to get him murdered is sit there and ask me questions."

Bill Friend scrubbed his mouth with the back of his hand.

"Murdered?" Judge Morehead murmured.

Ernie didn't even look at him. He was watching Bill. He said, bitterly, "Ain't you rubbed it in enough for one day, Bill?"

Bill Friend didn't look at him. His glance roved the lobby, settled, and he called, "Ferd."

When Ferd Willis came over, Bill Friend said, "Get the boys together and go on out. Now."

334

Ferd looked at Ernie and grunted and went out. Ernie turned his back to Bill Friend and followed Willis as far as Prince's, where Ferd turned in. Dust was settling rapidly and the wind was dying.

At the Gem, Comer was still sitting in his chair. He had peeled a sheet of paper from the tablet and it lay torn in small pieces on the table top. Sweat runneled his cheekbones; he looked hard at the table.

Ernie stopped in front of him and he looked up.

"You're through," Ernie said mildly. "As soon as Spade gets moved out of town you better get your horse and ride out in the other direction."

He poked around for a chair and hauled it up to the table and sat down across from Comer, hearing the scrape of leather as Ed Horstmann holstered his gun.

"Damn you," Ernie said mildly, putting his elbows on the table, "I don't mind jumpin' on a man when he's down. Not on you anyway. If you don't clear this country by tonight you'll walk into a bushwhack inside another twenty-four hours."

He rose and walked to the door and stood in it a minute, his gaze directed upstreet. Tim Bone watched him, his gun sagging a little.

Ernie turned his head and said, "All right, get out."

Comer rose and walked past Tim without looking at him, his boot scuffing one of his own guns on the floor as he went. He passed Ernie and turned upstreet, his walk a little less hurried.

Ernie felt a little sick with the slackened tension. He let the door swing to and walked over to the hitch rail, placing both hands on it and hanging his head. The sudden explosion of voices from the inside welled out, and he turned away. There was a chance now. It had taken that threat of violence to crack Bill Friend. He had made a concession in moving Spade out of town,

335

and if he could make one he would make more.

The court-day crowd had left town. Blank spaces gaped at the tie rails, and the street was quiet.

Ernie found himself walking toward the Stockman's House, and checked himself. He was ravenously hungry, but the meal at the hotel cost a half dollar. Too much. He fingered the coins in his pocket and then turned back and went into the Palace Café. He was alone, and glad of it. Thinking back on this day, there was some order to it, some hope come out of it. If Comer would leave, if it was in the man to see wisdom, then there was something to work with and build on.

Finished, he stepped out of the Palace and paused on its step, reaching for his pipe. A rider passed, his face turned toward Ernie, the muffled clopping of his horse's hoofs in the thick dust the only sound. It was Ferd Willis, and he turned his head quickly, without speaking. Someone cursed a horse down the street.

Ernie stepped down onto the boardwalk. From across the street in the darkened doorway of the express office, someone called, "Ernie!"

Ernie stopped, half-turned. Ferd Willis pulled up his horse and looked over his shoulder, for something in this voice was urgent and angry.

John Comer swung under the hitch rack and stepped out into the street. "Make your brag again, Ernie," Comer taunted, walking forward.

Ernie didn't move. He watched Comer as he came to a stop in the middle of the street, and he wondered at the savage anger in the man's voice.

"You heard it," Ernie said quietly.

"I thought I did," Comer said. He reached down and pulled out his gun, and Ernie heard the distinct click of its cock. A wild haste seemed to be pushing Comer. He shot as the upswinging arc of his gun was only half completed, and the bullet smacked against the

336

boardwalk, shaking it. His second shot was higher, and it slapped into the glass front of the store. The whole pane collapsed, jangling to the boardwalk.

Ernie reached down and brought out his gun, his breath held, and swung it up, moving smoothly. When the sight caught the light shirt of Comer, he fired. Comer shot once more, his slug rapping hollowly on the false front of the building, and in the same motion he sat down in the road. He put both hands to his chest and gagged, and then tried to get up and fell on his side, later rolling on his face.

Ernie walked over to him. Ferd Willis put his horse around and walked it back. Someone from Prince's ran up and then knelt by Comer, and by that time there were two more men there. Ernie looked up at Ferd Willis. "What's your story, Ferd?" he asked quietly. Tim Bone, breathing hard, stepped over to Ernie's side.

"There's no question," Ferd Willis said quietly, without fear. "Comer tried to get you."

Ernie's glance shuttled to the low porch of the Stockman's House. A cluster of men stood on the steps, among them Bill Friend and Martha. "Maybe you better tell Bill that right now," Ernie said. "Come along."

Ferd Willis put his horse in at the tie rail, and Ernie joined him. There were others now following.

Ernie stopped on the walk, and suddenly remembered he had his gun still in his hand. He holstered it, listening to Ferd Willis' steady voice. When Ferd was finished, Bill Friend said nothing, looking out at the people gathering in the road. Both he and Martha were facing Ernie, so that their faces were shadowed from the light behind them. It made a little golden halo around Martha's head as it touched her hair.

"Yes," Bill Friend murmured.

337

Tim Bone said quietly, "There's one of your deputies, Bill. How many more we got to fight?"

"None," Martha Friend said firmly. She put her hand on her father's arm and he looked at her in a tired way and did not speak. Martha said to them, looking at Ernie, "This never would have worked and we all know it. It's an election you want, isn't it? For sheriff?"

"Yes, ma'am," Tim Bone answered.

"And the commissioners can set a date for it?"

"Any time," Max Troutman said.

"Then they will," Martha said. She looked up at her father. "Can you give them your word for that, Dad?"

Old Bill Friend never looked more weary. He watched Ferd Willis for several seconds, his eyes speculative, and then shifted his gaze to Ernie. "Yes, I can promise that."

Those on the steps, all except Martha, walked out in the street to look at Comer, leaving Ernie to face her.

She stepped down to the walk, watching the men clot around the spot on the road, and her face was grave. Then she looked up at Ernie. "It's been a long wait, hasn't it?"

"Long enough," Ernie said.

Martha was silent a moment, and then she said, "Do you remember how it used to be, Ernie—before all this started?" Ernie nodded, mute.

Martha put a hand on his arm, and smiled fleetingly. "It's been lonesome for me too, Ernie."

Ernie watched her closely. He parted his lips to ask, "But what about Comer?" and then remembered that figure out in the road. Martha shook her head slightly, as if she understood what he was about to ask and was forbidding him to ask it. "Good night, Ernie," she said, and went quickly up the steps.

Ernie Manners thought he could see an end to pa-

338

tience, then. He put on his hat and went out into the road, steeling himself against the questions he would be asked. There would be an end to them, too, some day, because there was an end to everything a man hated to face but faced anyway. He had learned that again from her.

PAYOFF AT RAIN PEAK

I
MYSTERIOUS VISITOR

It was on the night of the day the decent folks in Waterman County lost the election that old Murdo Sayles saw this man. Murdo cast his vote and left Cobalt, the county seat, at noon, gloomily certain that law and order didn't have a chance. A high and inaccessible mountain country means hide-outs, hide-outs mean riffraff, riffraff means graft money and graft money means crooked lawmen. It was all that simple to old Murdo. Only he was inclined to carry his reasoning one point further. Crooked lawmen meant the end of his Happy Day Mine.

Murdo bucked a growing blizzard during the last hours of daylight, and even the tall timber of the slope didn't afford much protection. When he pulled into the clearing where the mine shacks were, he circled them to the corral and barn beyond.

After putting up his horse and forking down hay for him, he stepped out into a dusk made gray by the snow.

And then he saw this man. He was sitting motionlessly on a sleek, long-legged pony, a tall dim figure in the saddle.

Murdo put his hand on the gun under his mackinaw and walked slowly toward the figure, which did not move.

"You gonna fight or ain't you?" Murdo growled, certain that this man was the first of many unpleasant visitors to come.

"Fight what?" a low voice asked.

"Me. Else what do you want up here?"

There was a moment's silence. "Ever get rolled out of your blankets by a grizzly?" the man asked.

"What if I didn't?" Murdo asked shortly.

"I did, this mornin'. Up on the Rain Peaks. I'm cut up a little and hungry."

Murdo walked closer to regard his visitor. "You're a liar on two counts," he observed gravely. "Grizzlies has been holed up for a month. And the devil hisself couldn't get over the Rain Peaks this time of year."

The man pulled his horse around. "Thanks," he said dryly. "If I can ever do you a bad turn, let me know."

"Wait!" Murdo called. The man stopped and Murdo went even closer this time. He could see now that the man's left arm was in a sling made out of flour sacking. He could even hear the rider's teeth chattering in that slow cold snow.

Immediately Murdo felt ashamed of himself. "Light," he invited abruptly. "I thought you was someone else. You're welcome to shelter and food."

The man's face broke into a smile that Murdo didn't see. "Reckon I got to be helped out of the saddle," he said.

Murdo lifted him down. It was obvious now that the man was hurt, for his levis were torn and stiff with frozen blood. In sudden panic Murdo bawled, "Linnet girl! Linnet!"

342

Then he turned to the rider and said gruffly, "Why didn't you say so sooner? You set there talkin' like you was figurin' on borrowin' a match."

He guided the stranger across the snow toward the door, and now he saw that the man was young, somewhere close to six feet tall, and apparently hurt badly.

Halfway to the shack the door opened and a girl holding a lamp stepped through the doorway. She had a shawl around her shoulders and when she saw her father and this stranger her mouth opened a little in surprise.

"Get some hot water ready!" Murdo ordered. "This man's hurt!"

And indeed, Jeff Bleeker was. When he was seated in the small living room of Murdo's shack, Linnet and Murdo Sayles took a look at him. The sight of his leg made Linnet a little sick. Her small oval face, touched with healthy color on each high cheekbone, turned pale at the sight, and her blue eyes clouded over.

Jeff Bleeker saw it and he said, "You just bring me some hot water, miss. I'll make out by myself."

But that wasn't Linnet Sayles' way. She ordered her father to rouse Joe and a couple of the boys and look after the stranger's horse. Then she brought hot water and set to work.

Bleeker's right leg had been clawed, but luckily the sweep of the grizzly's paw had been down the curve of the muscle. To stop the bleeding he had poured flour over the wound and let it cake, so that it was sterile enough.

His tanned narrow face turned a little green while Linnet was washing the wound, but once it was done he grinned. And when she rebandaged his left arm, which showed five deep claw marks, he was almost smiling. His black hair was matted with the sweat that had

343

poured from him during those long hours of pain in the saddle, but he had a clean, wholesome look despite the smeared blood on his beard-stubbled face.

Murdo Sayles helped his daughter as well as a clumsy man could. Short, burly, with a grizzled thatch of iron-gray hair, he was a man whose face was incised with the lines of trouble, and lately suspicion had mounted into his eyes to stay there. He knew this himself, and the knowledge prompted what he said after Linnet was finished.

"I'm a mighty sorry man for what I said out there."

"That's all right," Bleeker replied. "My story did sound funny."

"You really did come over the Rain Peaks?"

Jeff nodded.

"Why?"

"Ignorance, I reckon."

"And what was a grizzly doin' out in this weather?"

Jeff shrugged. "I've heard of men that's seen 'em in winter, but I never believed it up till now. Anyway, this one went through my grub and then come over to me. I woke up with somethin' cold and wet sniffin' in my face. This first move I made for my gun, he was on me. He didn't get rough, just curious, I reckon. But it was enough to make it sort of hard for me."

Murdo nodded and Linnet came into the room with a tray of food which she placed across the arms of Jeff's chair. He ate ravenously, and they left him there to eat their own supper while they retired to the tiny kitchen.

Murdo, now that his conscience was no longer troubled, settled down into his usual gloom, and Linnet asked him about the election. They talked idly all through the meal, and the words came distinctly through the kitchen door to Jeff Bleeker.

"This is the end," Murdo said finally. "At six this mornin' every saloon was boomin'. Every hardcase in

344

the country was in town, had been all night long. When it come time to vote, they done so with a gun. If an election judge wanted to live, he just didn't challenge any votes. They was mostly voted by ten, and I'd say that roughly the votin' was six to one against us.''

"Then Tim Morehead is sheriff?"

"Yeah. And will be for the next six terms."

"What do you aim to do, dad?"

"Sell out," Murdo said bitterly. "It's either that or get robbed blind."

"But who could you sell to?"

"Murray Lowden," Murdo answered slowly. "At least I'll have the satisfaction of knowin' it's goin' to a decent man. I don't know how he does it, but he's got them hardcases to let him alone."

"Murray's a fighter."

"Aye." He looked up fondly at Linnet. "There's no chance it'll stay in the family at the same time, is there, girl?"

Linnet flushed. "I—I don't know, dad. I think so, maybe. I like Murray awfully well."

Murdo grunted. "So do I. Still, the Happy Day is no reason why you should marry him if he don't suit you."

"But—I think he does, dad."

Linnet suddenly remembered the stranger, and she went over to the kitchen door to see if he had overheard. But Bleeker's head was bent over his tray, and he appeared to be sleeping the sleep of utter exhaustion.

Linnet took his tray and got a blanket and threw it over him. The room was warm, heat from the open fireplace before which his chair was drawn making it almost uncomfortably hot. She looked at his relaxed face a moment, then went back to the kitchen.

Murdo smoked in silence. Linnet knew how this turn of events hurt him. With a blind bit of faith, he believed in the future of the Happy Day. Refusing all help, all financing, he had developed it himself, raising it from a one-man diggings to a fifteen-man mine. A stamp mill had been his latest innovation, and every cent that they made from the Happy Day went into new equipment and new inventions. It was low-grade ore, but there was a lot of it, and it was getting richer as they worked. Some day, Murdo Sayles was certain, he would have a real proposition. And now, just when the future looked bright, a set of crooked county officers had upset everything.

Waterman County was some four hundred miles from the capital, a forgotten corner of the Territory on the long and rugged slope of the Rain Peaks. Too barren for widespread ranching, it was poor country, spare in worthwhile population, but dense with the impermanent sort, the kind that made the town of Cobalt intolerable for decent folk.

And now that this lawless element had triumphed at the polls, nothing was safe. If a man had a mine, he had to ship gold. And Murdo saw the handwriting on the wall. With the hills filled with outlaws, a man couldn't ship a single bar of bullion. And once that word got out, it wouldn't be long before riders raided the mine itself.

A knock on the door roused Murdo and he went to open it. His face lighted with pleasure at the sight of his visitor.

"Murray! Come in, son."

Murray Lowden came in stamping the snow from his boots. He was a big, broad-shouldered man, with a full aggressive face. He gave the impression of power—an attribute that somehow seemed at odds with his apparent modesty.

"I came up to mourn with you," he said with a slow grin for Linnet. "The news is all bad."

"Morehead is in?" Linnet asked.

346

"Seven to one," Murray stated. Murdo helped him off with his coat, as he continued: "I reckon it's a lot like a wake, Murdo, comin' up here to ask you about your mine at this time. Still, I want it. Business is business for you, just like it is for me." He looked at Murdo from black, flashing eyes. "You still want to sell?"

"What else can I do?"

"That's up to you," Murray said gravely. "Personally, in your place, I wouldn't consider it. It's too good a proposition."

"I'm too old to scrap around with hardcases."

Murray smiled and rubbed his hands together. "Well, I'm not. I'll think I'm a lucky man if I get a chance to fight to keep this mine. If you want to sell, Murdo, name your own figure."

Linnet said, "Let's go in by the fire."

They went into the living room and the first thing Murray saw was Jeff Bleeker. He paused and said softly, "Who's this?"

Jeff roused at the sound of his voice, and Murdo explained what had happened, introducing Jeff.

When he was finished Jeff said, "I'll just step out, if you'll excuse me."

"You'll stay right there," Linnet said firmly. "Dad's going to talk over business with Murray, and there's no reason why you shouldn't stay where you are."

Jeff subsided under her orders and the talk soon switched to the mine. Bleeker sat there and listened, saying nothing, smoking his pipe. Linnet sat off in a corner and listened too. Murray Lowden made his proposition, which was a complicated one having to do with the payments for machinery, the size of the down payment, and other details. Murdo Sayles expressed satisfaction with the offer and Murray then drew a prepared agreement from his pocket and they signed it. Linnet was the first witness, Jeff Bleeker the second.

When he came to witness it, Jeff said, "Mind if I read it over?"

"Never sign anything you don't read," Murray Lowden said with a grin. "Go ahead."

The talk turned to the election again and Jeff read the agreement. Finished, he laid it on his lap and packed his pipe again, watching these three carefully. He struck a match and raised it to his pipe, and then something they were saying attracted his attention. He didn't seem to notice that his match had fallen on the deed and had set it afire.

Linnet was the first to see it. She gave a little cry that startled Jeff Bleeker, then jumped to her feet and rushed toward him. He looked surprised, and then, apparently for the first time, the tiny flame in his lap attracted his attention. He slapped at the fire, half rising in his seat as a shower of sparks fell to the floor. When it was finally extinguished, Linnet took the paper from him and held it up. A little less than a third of it remained.

Bleeker's face reflected misery and embarrassment as he looked at Murray Lowden.

"I'm certainly sorry, mister. I shouldn't have tried to light that match. I reckon my hand was so shaky the match slipped out."

Murray looked at him with murderous eyes. "I'm sorry, too," he said curtly. "Now I'll have to make another trip up here from town."

"I oughta be kicked," Jeff said morosely, adding, "Can't you remember what it was and write it out?"

Murray said, "Stranger, I let a lawyer do my legal work. I'll have to get him to make another."

Jeff hung his head, ashamed.

Murray Lowden's visit was spoiled. He settled into a half-surly silence that made old Murdo uneasy and brought a worried frown to Linnet's face. But it was soon over, for Lowden rose and said he would have to be getting back to Cobalt if he didn't want to be snowed in.

He didn't offer to shake hands with Jeff as he went, and Linnet, almost relieved that he was going, said good-by to him at the kitchen door while Murdo went out with him to the stable.

Linnet came into the room after he was gone and went directly to Bleeker.

"You did that on purpose, didn't you?" she asked angrily.

"What?"

"Set fire to that deed."

Bleeker's grin was slow, friendly. "Yes, ma'am," he said, surprisingly.

Linnet's eyes opened wider. "Why?"

"Somethin' about it smells."

"You mean Murray Lowden is crooked? He's not! You don't even know him! How do you dare say such a thing about my friend?"

Jeff held up a hand. "Easy, Miss Sayles. When I was eatin' supper in here, I couldn't help but hear your dad. Didn't he say that Murray Lowden wasn't havin' any trouble with these Waterman County hardcases?"

"Yes. What of it?"

"Don't that look sort of queer?"

"Why should it?"

"What does Lowden do?"

"He's a cattle buyer."

"The very man that would suffer most from a bunch of outlaw riders."

Linnet frowned thoughtfully, but Jeff wasn't going to give her a chance to protest. "Another thing, miss. This is none of my business, but I overheard it and I want to say it. Murray Lowden wants to marry you?"

Linnet flushed, but nodded her head.

"I've had girls," Jeff said slowly. "I never wanted to marry 'em, but I liked 'em. And when I called on 'em, I didn't talk business to their fathers. If I want to talk business, I'd save that till later, after I'd really said hello to my girl. Lowden just nods to you and starts in talking about buyin' the mine."

"He—he was excited," Linnet protested.

"Yeah. He'd rather have the mine than a wife."

Linnet said angrily, "That's not so!"

"Another thing," Jeff went on implacably. "Why didn't he draw up a new deed? You got pen and paper. But no, he wants to go to a lawyer and make it airtight." He leaned forward. "For instance, miss. That clause about payin' so much per month providin' the mine pays out so much per month. If the mine don't make the quota, he don't pay."

"But it does make the quota!"

"Under you, yes. Under him, I bet it wouldn't. Is your dad goin' to keep a bookkeeper watchin' him?"

Linnet said nothing, watching Bleeker's dark face. Jeff leaned back in his chair. "No, ma'am. Your dad's walkin' right into a trap. He's suspicious, but he's likely suspicious of the wrong people. If you let him sign that deed he's never goin' to get paid for that mine."

Linnet's eyes were really angry now. "But he will sign! What do you know about it?"

"Enough that if you give me time, I can prove this Murray Lowden is crooked. Will you keep him from signin' until I can prove it?"

"Certainly not!" Linnet said angrily. "And I think you're a conceited, skeptical saddle bum! Good night!"

She went into her room. Sayles came in later and offered his room to Jeff, but Jeff told him he'd rather sleep in the chair. They said good night.

Next morning Jeff Bleeker was gone.

II
DANGER TRAIL

Cobalt was getting the tail end of the blizzard, but here it was nothing compared with the storm in the mountains. If Jeff had waited an hour longer he would have been snowed in at the Happy Day. As it was he was out, and Murdo Sayles and his daughter were walled away from Murray Lowden, who was certain to return as soon as he could with a new deed. Whatever was done would have to be done before a trail could be broken to the Happy Day.

Cobalt's streets were a mire of slushy mud, and a thick snow drifted down to dissolve in it and make it even soupier. The falsefront stores that flanked the wide single street had wooden awnings the tops of which were frosted with the new snow. Store lamps burned at midday against the gloom of the storm, and Jeff had to watch carefully to avoid riding past the hotel, which was wedged in between the sheriff's office and the Cobalt Emporium.

He left his horse at the feed stable nearby and made his way back to the hotel, limping painfully. His leg still hurt, and wisdom told him to rest up. But the image of Linnet Sayles and her father about to be done out of the Happy Day would give him no rest. All the way down from the Happy Day he had been turning this over in his mind. He was strangely convinced that Murray Lowden was crooked—but how could he convince the girl and her father? Last night's appeal to the girl had been useless. She didn't love Murray Lowden, and it was only the old man's blind conviction that Lowden was one real man among a hundred crooks that influenced her. And if he was to prove Lowden a crook, it must be before that handsome, oily-tongued hombre had a chance to get back to the Happy Day with a new deed. Turning into the hotel lobby, he thought he had the plan.

Three men were sitting in the lobby, and at his entrance one of them drifted out to the street. The other two watched him. When he paid his dollar and a half and went up to his room, he paused at the head of the stairs long enough to hear the two men walk over to the register.

"Jeff Bleeker," he heard one of them murmur. "Ain't he the one?"

"Sure. Couldn't have left more'n a few hours after Murray."

"Better go catch Ed and tell him this gent's name."

Jeff went to his room, smiling a little. Unless he missed his guess something was going to happen, and it was going to happen shortly.

He was shaving in front of the mirror when the knock came on his door.

"Come in," he called, without turning around.

The first man in held a gun and wore a star that showed when his sheepskin coat parted. He was a heavy man, with a drink-flushed face that sagged at the corners of his loose mouth. He looked around the room suspiciously, then stepped aside to let in another man, one of the lobby sitters.

"Mornin' gentlemen," Jeff said mildly. He went right on shaving.

The sheriff cuffed a greasy Stetson back on his head and said, "Well, well, if this ain't luck."

"Why? Ain't you ever seen a man shave before?" Jeff said in mock surprise.

"Don't be funny," the sheriff said, "I'm talkin' about my luck and your hard luck. It ain't often that a sheriff has a chance for an arrest like this the day after he's elected."

"Especially when he's been so drunk durin' the

352

night that his eyes are still a little off center," Jeff retorted calmly.

"Not so off center they can't read reward posters," the sheriff growled.

Jeff turned and said slowly, "Meanin' me?"

"Meanin' you."

Sheriff Tim Morehead came over and slipped Jeff's gun from its holster.

Jeff said, "I always figured I was due to be famous. But I can't remember ever bein' asked for my name to have it circulated in every tank town sheriff's office."

"You got a poor memory. Ever hear of a murder of a United States marshal in Miles City by the name of Courtney?"

"Never did."

"Then your memory is poorer than I reckoned, Ed Sholto."

Jeff had his face turned to the mirror again, and he grinned. He was familiar with this bluff. When a crooked lawman wanted another man out of the county, all he had to do was dig up a reward dodger with a description roughly corresponding to that of the innocent man. Then all that remained was to arrest the innocent party, ship him out of the county—or shoot him, pleading that he tried to escape.

"My, my," Jeff drawled. "How a man's past catches up with him. Or some other man's past, should I say?"

"You're comin' along with me, Sholto, whatever you say," Morehead growled.

"Can I finish shavin'?"

"No."

Jeff's eyes narrowed. "Sheriff, you're goin' to regret that."

"Wash your face and come along," Morehead sneered. "And be quick about it."

353

He stepped forward and rammed his gun in Jeff's back. Jeff shrugged and laid down his razor, then leaned over the basin, dousing his face. He looked under his arm and saw that the sheriff's gun had moved off center and that he was holding it a little toward the left.

Jeff picked up the basin, the movement hidden by his body, and moved imperceptibly to the right. Then in one swift movement he sent the basin of soapy water over his left shoulder into Sheriff Morehead's face.

The gun went off just as Jeff wheeled out of the way. He whirled, threw his arms about the sheriff's fat body, and reached down for his gun, which the sheriff had rammed in his belt.

The movement was so quick that by the time the deputy had his gun out, Sheriff Morehead's broad back hid Jeff completely. Once he had his gun, Jeff rammed it in the sheriff's side.

"Drop your gun," Jeff said quietly, and stepped on the lawman's toe to emphasize his point. The gun clattered to the floor and then Jeff whirled the sheriff around and still protected by his body drawled, "Tell that stuffed shirt to put in his chips or get out of the pot. Whatever he does, he better do it quick, too."

"Put it down, Ed," Morehead ordered weakly. The deputy hesitated, then complied, and Jeff shoved the sheriff away from him. Now that immediate danger was past the lawman started to swear, and stooped down to rub the toe of his boot.

"I reckoned you might like that," Jeff drawled, grinning. "You've had your foot on a bar rail so long you got oversize arches, sheriff." He paused, regarding the two of them. "A couple of jokers if I ever saw any. Now what's the gag, sheriff?"

"What gag?"

"What am I bein' run out of town for?"

"I told you," Sheriff Morehead answered sullenly. He added, "You ain't got a chance, mister. Better turn over that gun and we'll forget you tried to escape."

"Answer my question," Jeff said stubbornly. "What have you got against me? I've only been in town an hour."

"I set a man in the lobby a-purpose for this," Morehead growled, "a man with a memory for faces and descriptions. You're Ed Sholto. What you tryin' to dodge it for?"

Jeff's grin was slow, amused. "So Murray Lowden don't like me, huh?"

The expression on Sheriff Morehead's face was transparent. He even knew it was and grinned weakly.

"That's it," Jeff went on. "Thought you'd accommodate a friend."

"Listen," Morehead said earnestly. "Take a tip, mister. I never saw you before. But Waterman County is for Waterman County folks. You stuck your face in somethin' last night that wasn't none of your business. I just aimed to ease you out of the county."

"At Lowden's orders?"

"Call it that if you want."

Jeff said, "Where'll I find Lowden?"

But Sheriff Morehead wasn't a fool. Here was a man with a gun and a grudge, but without knowledge as to the whereabouts of his man. He smiled more confidently now and said, "Suppose you find out."

Jeff's eyes narrowed. He walked over to his sheepskin coat and put it on. Then he picked up the two guns from the floor, threw them out the window and put on his Stetson.

"I asked you a question," he said softly. "Do I have to kill one of you to get the other one to talk?"

"I reckon you do," Sheriff Morehead said. As that last word was spoken, Jeff let the hammer slip. There

355

was a roar that was deafening, and the sheriff's hat vanished behind him.

"Next time I'll come closer," Jeff murmured. "When I ask a question, I aim to get an answer. Where's Lowden's office?"

Sheriff Morehead was a stubborn man, but not suicidally stubborn, and the expression on Jeff Bleeker's face was not pleasant.

"On the corner above the saddle shop," he growled. "If you go there, I'll cut you to doll rags before you get down his stairs."

Jeff said, "You come over and I'll cut Lowden to doll rags before you get up 'em. Just remember that."

He put his hand on the window sill and glanced below him. There was a ten-foot drop to the sloping roof of the next building—a risky fall for a man with a bum leg.

Already, Jeff could hear footsteps pounding down the hall. He went over to the door and locked it, tossing the key out the window. Then saluted the sheriff and deputy and climbed out on the sill.

"See you again," he said and jumped. He landed on the snowy roof and immediately lost his footing and began to slide toward the eave. Sheriff Morehead appeared at the window, cursing, and threw the wash bowl at him just as he slipped over the trough of the eave and dropped to the ground. His leg pained, but not badly.

He made his way to the street, cut across it for the saddle shop, and mounted the stairs that were built against the side of the building. There was only one door at the top of the stairs and he didn't bother to knock. Already, he could hear the shouting in the street.

Murray Lowden was seated in a swivel chair at an untidy rolltop desk. A barrel stove in the corner made

356

the room uncomfortably hot. The office was furnished with several old calendars, a huge double pile of Stockmen's Gazettes, two rickety chairs and a small square safe. Jeff glanced around him, then closed the door and slipped the bolt home.

When he turned, he was looking into Murray Lowden's gun.

"Put that away," Jeff drawled. "I've got that jugheaded sheriff on my tail now. He's dumb enough, but I didn't think you were."

Without paying any attention to the gun, he crossed over to a chair and sat down.

"What do you want?" Lowden asked in a cold voice.

"Send that sheriff away when he stumbles up here. After that, we'll talk business."

"What kind of business?"

"Gold," Jeff said.

Lowden narrowed his eyes at the word, but his attention was shortly taken up by a hammering on the door. He rose, undecided, then went over to the door and said, "Hang around downstairs, Tim. I'm talkin'."

"You all right?" came Morehead's voice.

"You fool, of course I am!" Lowden said snappishly. He returned to his chair and Jeff could see that his eyes were red from a night without sleep.

"Now talk," he commanded, the gun still on his lap.

"It's about this Happy Day Mine," Jeff began.

"Of course it is! What else could we talk about?"

"You want it?"

"You heard me offer to buy it. You saw me buy it, in fact, before you burned up the deed." His eyes narrowed. "What's the play, cowboy? You can't get away with that kind of stuff forever. Who are you?"

"Never mind who I am," Jeff drawled. "Just a saddle bum that got took in and fed. I was there only an hour before you came. But I reckon I know more about that Happy Day business than you do."

"For instance?" Lowden sneered.

"For instance, when did old man Sayles ship bullion last?"

"How should I know?" Lowden said cautiously.

"I think you do know if you'll try real hard to remember," Jeff said.

Lowden stared at him a long moment. "About a month and a half ago," he said.

"Correct. There's about a month and a half's gold output up there now. You reckon they aimed to give it over to you when you bought 'em out?"

"No."

"All right. They're goin' to ship it, then."

"What of it?"

"What of it!" Jeff echoed, his face expressing surprise. "Why, you ain't got good sense, Lowden. Why buy the mine right away? Dicker around a week until this snow melts down. By that time, they won't be sure you're goin' to buy and they'll have to get that bullion shipment on a train."

"What does that mean?" Lowden asked sharply.

"It means you'll get a lot of the Happy Day gold before you buy the mine. If you bought the mine, they'd weigh the gold and turn it over to you for market price. This way, when they're not certain you'll buy, they'll ship the gold and you hold up the shipment."

"How do you know they'll ship?"

"I heard 'em say so."

Lowden leaned forward. "Just how did you happen to hear that?"

Jeff told him about being taken in and bandaged and fed. The conversation in the kitchen he told word for word, including mention of Linnet's affections for

358

Lowden. The only untruth he told was about the gold shipment.

"That's why Murdo was so glad to see you," Jeff concluded. "That gold shipment has been worryin' him. He knows the longer he keeps it the less chance he has of gettin' to the railroad. He's even afraid of being raided there at the Happy Day."

Lowden settled back in his chair, his eyes speculative. "What did you come to me for?" he asked abruptly.

Jeff smiled faintly. "I've knocked around too long not to know a good thing when I see it, Lowden. You got a good thing here, and you're playin' it down to the last white chip. That's all right. But if I can show you how to get a few more chips out of it, I can make a little money."

"How much?"

"How many men you got workin' for you besides the sheriff and his gunnies?"

Lowden hesitated, then said, "Lots."

"How many?" Jeff insisted.

"What's that to you?" Lowden asked.

"Just this. If you name the number of men you'll need to hold up the bullion shipment, I'll know what kind of cut I'll get. I don't know the amount they're sendin', so that's the only way we can work it."

"I'll send ten men."

"And I'll take two shares."

Lowden thought a moment then nodded. "That's all right, so far as it goes. But how will I know when the stuff is shipped?"

"I'll let you know."

"How could you?"

Jeff looked surprised. "Didn't I tell you?" he said blandly. "Murdo Sayles has given me a job at the Happy Day."

III
GUN-TRAP ANSWER

Jeff stayed in town three days, and most of his time was spent at the Rain Peaks Saloon until word came down from the hills that the road to the Happy Day was passable. He left town with the certain knowledge that Murray Lowden was the man directly responsible for the lawlessness here. Before Morehead was elected sheriff he had been Lowden's contact man between the hill hideouts and the Lowden headquarters.

Now that was no longer necessary. Lowden had daily conferences with Sheriff Morehead, and the hardcases didn't bother to keep to the hills any more. Cobalt was in all respects an outlaw town, although it didn't realize it, since Lowden decreed that a modicum of order should be kept.

The trail to the Happy Day was deep with snow, and Jeff's horse labored hard that day. But he labored no harder than Jeff's brain. For, any way Jeff looked at it, the possibility of his convincing Linnet Sayles and her father was remote. Jeff arrived at that conclusion at noon.

At four, he rode into the Happy Day camp. In daylight, it was a much larger place than he had imagined. Down the slope past the big bunkhouse the bulky shaft house of the Happy Day Mine rose among the trees. There was a sizable muck dump below the grade and mules were traveling constantly back and forth as they dumped full cars and hauled back empty ones into the shaft house.

Murdo Sayles was the first to see Jeff. He had returned to the house for a new lantern globe and was on his way back to the shaft house when Jeff emerged into

360

the clearing.

He stood still until Jeff reached him. "You're back, huh?" he asked without much friendliness. "Sort of like to ride at nights, don't you?"

"I learned somethin' you might want to hear, down in Cobalt," Jeff said.

"If it's that Murray Lowden is crooked, I don't want to hear it," Murdo said bluntly. "That it?"

"I got proof, too," Jeff said, nodding.

"The devil you have! A man can prove anything he sets out to prove. That don't prove he's right though. I'm busy." Without another word Murdo tramped off. Jeff watched him go, his anger stirred by the old man's stubbornness. Linnet had told him of their conversation, then, and it had only served to increase the old man's stubbornness.

He looked up, sighing—and saw Linnet Sayles in the door. She was wearing a blue dress with a full apron over it, and Jeff thought he had never seen a prettier girl.

"If you want to talk to me, you'll have to hurry," she said coldly. "I'm about to sweep out the men's bunkhouse."

Jeff dismounted and she stepped inside.

He looked at her and wondered how he was going to begin.

She began for him. "I heard what you said to dad. His sentiments are pretty close to mine."

"Even if I know that Murray Lowden is behind all the lawlessness in this county?" Jeff asked.

"That's a lie!"

"Is it? Listen." And he told her, fact for fact, word for word, of his coming to Cobalt, of his reception by the sheriff, of his talk with Murray, and of their plan to rob the fake bullion shipment. Linnet listened, and as he progressed with the story, he noticed her getting paler and paler. When he had finished, he asked quickly, "Anything wrong, miss?"

"Wrong!" Linnet cried. "Oh, you fool! You simple fool!"

Jeff winced.

"I never heard such vicious nonsense in my life!" Linnet blazed.

"You don't believe it?"

Linnet was speechless with anger. She ran out into the yard and called, "Dad! Dad!" Old Murdo was almost at the shaft house, but he turned at the sound of his daughter's voice.

"Come up here," she called, "and bring Doug with you!"

Murdo appeared in a moment with a young bareheaded giant of a man beside him. Linnet marched up to Jeff and said, "Now tell dad what you just told me."

Jeff did. He tried to make them understand, but while he talked he saw that granite stubbornness rise up and wall them away from him. His voice trailed off at the end. He almost believed himself that he had been dreaming all this, to look at them.

"So you've got proof that Murray Lowden is just a penny-ante crook?" Murdo sneered. "What would you say if I told you that over a period of ten years he's loaned me forty thousand dollars at no interest? What would you say if I told you I thought so much of him my daughter is going to marry him?" His eyes narrowed. "What would you say if I told you to get the devil out of here? And now!"

"Why hasn't he been up here with a new deed then?" Jeff countered desperately.

"Because he gave his word!" Murdo roared. "He'll buy this place in his own good time—and in spite of you!"

There wasn't anything Jeff could do. It was like try-

362

ing to push over a wall of stone with words.

"Mister," Murdo said finally, "get out of here!"

But Jeff Bleeker had a stubborn streak in him too. "Hanged if I will!" he exploded. "You've got to listen to me!"

Murdo said, "You're a sick man. We took you in and nursed you. But if you don't get away from us, you'll be a danged sight sicker and you'll need three nurses where you needed one before."

Jeff's eyes smoldered with anger. "And who'll make me sick?"

"I warned you," Murdo said, his voice choked with anger.

"And I'm warnin' you."

Murdo turned to the tow-headed young man beside him. "Doug, throw him out of here. Knock him unconscious if you have to, but try not to hurt him any more than you can help."

Doug nodded and took a step toward Jeff. Jeff slugged out with his left, catching Doug on the side of the head and staggering him.

"Keep away from me, fella," Jeff said in a level, cold voice.

But Doug was a man bred among miners, and liked to fight for the pure joy of it. Strong, untaught, but stout-hearted, this was just another scrap to him. He sailed into Jeff, arms flailing, and Jeff straightened him out with an uppercut that snapped his head back, exposing his throat. A hook followed immediately into Doug's throat. It was a blow that hurt, a blow that would have taken the fight out of an ordinary man. But the youngster doggedly bore in, and Jeff had to give ground. He found that his stiff leg was hindering his movements. Once, when one of Doug's wild slugs landed on his shoulder, it almost paralyzed his arm.

They circled around in the wet snow, Jeff holding his

363

opponent off with long looping blows. But the man seemed unconquerable and Jeff knew that if he was to end this, he would have to end it soon.

He planted himself, dodged two wild swings, then dug in with his feet and started boring in.

Suddenly, his foot hit a strip of ice and he stumbled to one knee. Like a cat, Doug was on him. A savage right to Jeff's head sprawled him his length in the snow. He tried to gather his knees to his chest to protect himself from Doug's certain leap, but the bandage on his right leg held it rigid.

And then Doug landed on him with a drive that knocked all the breath from him. He tried to cover his face, and felt his guard beaten down. Then he tried to wrestle the bigger man off, but it was useless. Savage, slogging blows, timed like the ticks of a clock, rained on his face. And slowly, slowly, a kind of paralysis seized his arms. It was put to an end finally by a crushing blow on his jaw that made huge spinning pinwheels of stars bright against the darkness engulfing him.

When he came to, he was lying against a tree far down the trail. Whoever had brought him there had been thoughtful enough to cover him with a blanket, build a fire and tie his horse to a nearby tree.

He sat up, gingerly rubbing his jaw, the memory of the fight returning. He smiled ruefully at the thought of that strip of ice which had meant his downfall. Murdo Sayles had made his threat good—he had thrown him out. Still, there was no rancor in Jeff's heart against the old man, only a kind of stubborn pity. But how could you save people who wouldn't be saved? If they persisted in not believing anything bad about Murray Lowden, they were doomed.

He dragged himself to his feet and started back to town. As soon as he was clear of the tall timber, he started to examine the country. An hour later, he found what he wanted—a road that sloped off to the east toward the railroad. He settled down to straight riding, and by afternoon he had come to a way station on the railroad. A sun-blistered board on the side of the tiny shack announced that it was Pinon Wells.

He had everything he needed now, and he put his horse toward Cobalt, following the tracks.

Murray Lowden was in his office when Jeff came in.

"I thought you went to the Happy Day," Lowden said.

"I did. Can you shag ten of your men together tonight?"

Murray's eyes widened. "Is it tonight they're shipping?"

Jeff nodded. "I came down to get a buckboard for 'em. When you didn't come up today and Murdo saw that the road was passable, he got scared. They're shipping tonight. He even made me go over the road to Pinon Wells to see that it was open."

"Will the train stop?"

"I gave the agent a gold eagle to flag it down." He smiled knowingly at Lowden. "Well, there's your chance, mister. Just like I said."

Murray smiled with satisfaction. "Who's takin' the stuff down?"

"I am. Doug is guardin'. Just the two of us."

Murray nodded and frowned thoughtfully. "Let's see. Don't that road angle sharp where it narrows to dive into Meeker Canyon?"

"I dunno what canyon it's called, but it sure narrows there in one place."

"That's the place we'll stick you up, then. That all right?"

"Yeah. But be sure those rannies of yours know it's me on the buckboard. I don't want any blind shootin'."

Murray Lowden's eyes veiled over with some inner amusement, but his face was impassive. "Of course. There'll be no shooting. Know how much will be in the shipment?"

"They didn't say," Jeff replied.

Afterwards, he went downstairs and crossed over to the livery stable. The memory of Lowden's eyes when he promised there would be no shooting fed a slow anger in Jeff that was hard to control. Lowden's orders to his men would be to cut down on both Jeff and Doug, for in that way the two shares that were to go to Jeff would be saved. It was murder, but Lowden wouldn't stop at that. That was the law of the dark trails, dog eat dog. But as long as Lowden thought Jeff was simple enough to propose such a proposition, it suited Jeff.

He dickered for a buckboard with the hostler, and once that was settled he bought two mules and rented an extra saddle horse. The saddle horse was tied to the endgate of the buckboard. Then, as soon as the mules were hitched up, Jeff began to trip back to Happy Day.

If he could once prove to Linnet Sayles that Murray Lowden was the crook Jeff knew him for, then things would be easier. And tonight, hell or high water, he was going to prove it.

He reached the Happy Day about ten o'clock and on foot. His team and saddle horse he had left down the road out of sight. A brief survey of the camp disclosed that the men were in bed, since there was no light in the bunkhouse. But there was a lamp lighted in Murdo's place, indicating that they were still up.

Jeff stood out there in the cold night and figured. If he broke in and tried to drag Linnet out at the point of a gun, Murdo would fight. The hullabaloo would attract the attention of the miners, and once they were aroused, their handling of him would be considerably less gentle than Doug's. No, that was out. There must be some other way.

And then he remembered that supper Linnet had given him. It was fried eggs he had eaten that night. Maybe those eggs came from town and maybe they didn't. He'd see. He made a slow circle toward the barns and there, just on the other side of the woodshed, he found the chicken coop. That would serve his purpose.

He found a stick, unlatched the door and threw the stick inside. Immediately there arose a startled squawking. Jeff looked over at the shack window and saw Linnet's head framed in it. He opened the chicken house door again and threw another stick. Linnet's head disappeared at the sound of the renewed squawking and presently the door to the shack opened and she came out with a lantern, a sheepskin coat thrown over her shoulders.

Jeff ducked behind the chicken house and heard her approach and open the door. Softly, then, he tiptoed around the corner. She was standing there in the doorway, scolding the chickens.

When Jeff was almost to her, he stepped on a fragment of ice and it crunched loudly under his foot. Linnet wheeled, and Jeff leaped toward her. One mittened hand circled her waist, while his other clapped over her mouth. There was a fierce struggle for a moment, then Jeff said swiftly, "You're all right! It's me, Jeff! Only don't make a sound!"

She stopped struggling at that. His hand still over her mouth, Jeff picked her up and carried her around the barns and down the road.

When they reached the buckboard, he set her down in the snow. For a moment, all she could do was gasp.

"Is this a kidnapping?" she asked angrily, at last.

"Sort of." Jeff grinned. "You and your dad are so

stubborn I reckon I had to do it.''

"Dad will kill you for this!''

"I reckon he would if he caught me. But he won't. That's why you better climb in.''

"I'll yell!''

"Go ahead. We're too far away to be heard anyway.''

Linnet subsided at that. She was a small erect figure in the dark, and so lonely-looking that it almost made Jeff sorry he had done this.

"Where are we going?'' she asked in a faint voice.

"Lady,'' Jeff said, "if you wasn't so stubborn, you'd know. I got beat up today for suggestin' that Murray Lowden was crooked. Tonight I'm goin' to prove it to you.''

And then Linnet said the last thing Jeff had expected. "Are you hurt?''

"Only my feelin's,'' Jeff growled. "Now get in that buckboard.''

"But I haven't any wraps.''

"You take my coat. There's a robe there. And take my mittens. You'll be warm enough.''

It seemed that Linnet wasn't going to argue, and Jeff was relieved. He had pictured himself driving one-handed, down a twisting road while with his free arm he tried to keep a frantic woman from jumping off into the snow.

As it was, all Linnet said was: "Jeff Bleeker, this doesn't make sense. Why are you doing all this? Can't you leave us in peace?''

To which Jeff replied, "No ma'am.''

Soon Jeff had other things to occupy him. He began to worry for fear he might unknowingly take the turn into Meeker's Canyon, and the thought of what might happen if he did turned him cold. He looked obliquely at Linnet. She was huddled up close to him, her hands folded under the blanket. Jeff looked away quickly, resisting the temptation to take her into his arms.

When the road began to slant downward Jeff peered ahead into the darkness and said, softly, "Here's the place. Get down quiet and untie them two saddle horses." He paused, a suspicion in his glance that Linnet could not see. "You wouldn't run away from me, would you, lady?"

"I would not," Linnet said firmly. "Any man that wants to prove something as bad as you do should be given a hearing."

When the horses were untied Jeff wrapped the reins about the seat spring, then cut them off short. With these as a whip, he started in on the mules. Within a hundred yards, they knew the driver meant business, and broke into a long gallop. Jeff stayed with them a few seconds longer, bringing the reins down with long slashing blows. Then he jumped, landing and rolling over in a bank of snow.

On the road once more, he made his way back to Linnet. She was standing there, holding the horses. He paused beside her to listen.

And then, far down the canyon, a sudden burst of gunfire roared into the night. They could see the pinpoint gun flashes winking out on each side of the road. Distant yells reached their ears, and Linnet recognized the strident voice of Murray Lowden.

Jeff looked down at the girl. "Well?"

"Let's ride," Linnet said in a low voice.

They went back up the road, Linnet silent. She no longer sat erect, and to Jeff it almost seemed as if the night had crushed her. He began to wonder if she really did love Murray Lowden. Well, it was out of his hands now. If they persisted in selling the mine to Lowden, then it was because they went into it with their eyes open, willing to take the chance.

369

Linnet said suddenly, "Thanks, Jeff."

Jeff murmured something. Suddenly he was aware that Linnet was crying. He pulled up and said, "What's the matter, girl?"

"N-nothing," Linnet stammered. "Only, Murray planned to kill you!"

IV
SHOW-DOWN TALK

The camp was in an uproar when, just at daylight, Jeff and Linnet rode in. Linnet had to use a sharp tongue to keep Doug and the others from beating Jeff up. Murdo was away scouring the hills, almost frantic with the fear that Linnet had been kidnapped.

Linnet asked Jeff in and she went immediately to the kitchen to get breakfast. A messenger was sent to find Murdo and tell him Linnet had returned.

But if Jeff thought Linnet was going to talk about the happenings of the night, he was mistaken. She was pale and quiet, and Jeff was just as silent. He wanted to leave now, immediately, but he wanted even more to see Murdo and talk to him. What was the Happy Day going to do to protect itself, now that Murray Lowden was unmasked? He had to talk to Murdo and warn him to prepare.

He wandered down toward the shaft house, his impatience eating at him. If he didn't clear out of here and clear out soon, Murray Lowden's gunnies would be after him.

It was midmorning by the time he emerged from the shaft house and started back for the shack. Almost to its door, a sound attracted him and he wheeled.

There, already in the clearing, was Sheriff Tim Morehead, ten of his gunnies and Murray Lowden.

Linnet appeared at the door, her face pale and tense. She gave a startled cry at the sight of the visitors, then fell silent as Lowden rode up.

He was smiling as he doffed his hat. "Mornin', Linnet." He gestured to Morehead. "The sheriff and I found we were traveling to the same place this mornin', so we came together." He dismounted and stepped aside. "Get your business over first, sheriff," he said. "I can wait."

Morehead dismounted now and came over to Jeff. "My business won't take long," he said gruffly. "Mister, you're wanted for murder."

"Haven't I heard that before?"

"Likely," Morehead sneered. He reached in his pocket and brought out a slip of paper. "This came in on this mornin's train." He unfolded it and handed it to Jeff. It was a reward dodger offering five thousand dollars for the capture, dead or alive, of Jeff Bleeker. The dodger had been issued from Cheyenne. The description was accurate, and they had only missed his weight by two pounds.

Morehead said, "You'll notice it's even got scars mentioned there. Says you got a deep one low down on the back of your neck, another on your left elbow." He stepped forward. "Let me look."

Jeff's face was dark with fury. It was suicide to argue with Morehead and these men, however, so he let Morehead pull down the collar of his shirt.

"It's there," Morehead said grimly. "See, miss?"

"I see," Linnet said coldly.

"Now your elbow," Morehead said.

Jeff pulled up his sleeve, showing the marks. Of course, that day when Morehead had burst into his room while he was shaving was the clue to all this. With his sleeves rolled up and his shirt collar turned down, the scars had been visible to anybody who cared to look. It clinched the reward dodger, gave it an appearance of authenticity that a man couldn't deny.

"Didn't mention my grizzly bear marks, did it?" Jeff drawled. "You could easy have got them in when you had the dodger printed this mornin'."

His glance shuttled to Lowden, who looked faintly amused.

"Funny, ain't it?" Jeff asked him.

Lowden shrugged. "My good man, don't blame me because your crimes have caught up with you. Personally, I think Sheriff Morehead has done a good piece of work."

"Who has?" Jeff asked.

"Morehead."

"You have, you mean," Jeff said, angrily. Lowden only looked blankly at him.

Linnet said suddenly, "What do you want, Murray?"

"I've come up here with the new deed," Lowden said.

"Dad isn't here and won't be today. I think you're wasting your time," Linnet added. "Now and forever."

Lowden scowled. "You mean your dad isn't going to sell?"

"Not to you. But you might ask him."

Murray shrugged. "I'll come back when you're in a better humor, my dear."

Linnet ignored him. "What are you going to do with Jeff?" she asked Morehead.

"Ship him back to Cheyenne."

"Let's see that dodger."

Morehead gave it to her. Linnet read it, then rubbed her thumb over the printing. The ink smeared because it was still fresh.

Jeff thought he saw a fleeting change in her expres-

372

sion, but she only said, "Good-day," and shut the door in their faces.

Jeff made an attempt to follow her, but Morehead whipped a gun into his stomach and growled, "None of that, hombre. Come along."

Lowden smiled faintly, but said nothing as he headed for his horse. Jeff tramped through these silent men, his thoughts bitter. He had risked his life for her, and now she walked out on him, without so much as a good-by! This girl—this girl he loved had done that! For he did love her. He wasn't going to fool himself any longer. She was the reason for his staying here, for taking beatings, for lying, for all of it. Linnet Sayles! And she'd walked out on him!

He climbed into the saddle of the horse Morehead had provided for him.

"These stirrups are short," he complained.

Lowden said, from beside him, "Don't worry. You won't ride far enough to have it trouble you."

Jeff whipped his glance to Lowden. "What do you aim to do with me?"

"When we're out of gunshot of the house, you'll see," Lowden said quietly.

So Linnet had let him walk into a beefing, hadn't even protested, hadn't fought to save the life of a man who had risked his own for her. He hung his head as they rode out of the clearing, too bewildered and hurt to think of escape.

Lowden's voice roused him. "You're a clever devil, Bleeker, but you don't know what you're buckin'. What was the idea of that empty buckboard last night? What did it get you?"

Jeff said jeeringly, "It proved to Linnet Sayles and her father that you're as crooked as a corkscrew, Lowden."

Lowden laughed. "Is that why she was so haughty?"

"Yeah. That's why."

Lowden laughed. "Well, I was foolish to try it this way to begin with, I'll just take the mine, now."

They turned a sharp bend in the road where it arced above a deep canyon. Before him and behind him, as well as on both sides of him, there were men. Desperately, he cast about for a way to escape, any way.

It was hopeless. He couldn't snatch a gun from them, for they'd cut down on him in a second. He couldn't make a run for it because the way was blocked.

This was it, then, death by bushwhack.

And then, from the steep sheer of the bank to the right of them, a voice called down in stentorian tones, "Stop where you are and throw down those guns!"

Every man in the sheriff's crowd looked up at the bank. There, in a long line, were a dozen rifles slanting down at them. Suddenly it came to Jeff what had happened. Linnet had run for the shaft house, roused out the crew, armed them and ordered them to cut over the hill and fort up on the road where it cut deeply back to avoid the canyon.

For one tense second no one spoke, and then Lowden yelled, "Fight!"

On the heel of his order, Jeff exploded out of the saddle, the short stirrups giving him leverage. He lunged into Lowden, who was on the side bordering the canyon. The impact of his thrust carried the outlaw leader out of the saddle, and they landed on their sides, just on the edge of the cliff.

A clatter of gunfire burst from above. With one desperate shove, Jeff pushed Lowden and himself over the edge. He held tightly to his man as they started to roll. The slope was of loose shale, smooth as glass, and there was nothing to stop their slide.

A quarter of the way down Lowden fought free and started to slug. He tried to gain his knees, but Jeff dove

374

into him again. Over and over they went, picking up momentum, until Jeff became dizzy. But he hung on grimly, clawing under Lowden's coat in an effort to get his gun.

And then their pace slackened and Jeff started to slug. Lowden, on his back, made a grab for his gun, at the same time pushing Jeff away from him.

He staggered to his knees, but Jeff sprang at him again and began chopping at his face with short, savage blows.

He landed one uppercut that lifted Lowden backward and sent him spinning down to the flat. Jeff went after him, and leaped on him just as Lowden's gun cleared its holster. They fought to their feet, Lowden trying to drag his gun up, Jeff fighting to keep it down.

Jeff's hand worked downward till it gripped the barrel of the gun. He put his whole weight on the weapon, slowly forcing Lowden to his knees.

And then Lowden, his strength conquered, resorted to trickery. He shifted his weight, throwing Jeff backward over his knee. Jeff felt himself going and gave one last vicious wrench to the gun. It came free as he sprawled on his back.

Lowden lunged at him in a long dive. Jeff raised both legs, met the impact of the heavy body and held it off that split second necessary to get the gun in his fist. And then, as Lowden fell on him, Jeff shot.

Lowden was so close to him that the gun flash set fire to his shirt. Jeff heard a grunt, and saw an expression of surprise flick over the man's face.

And then Lowden crumpled.

Jeff crawled out from under him and heaved himself to his feet, panting. He turned at a sound, and saw Linnet running toward him.

Automatically, he opened his arms, and she was in them, sobbing.

"Darling!" she cried in a choked voice. "Are you all right?"

Jeff stammered something as he hugged her.

"Did you think I deserted you, Jeff?" Linnet murmured. "I had to!"

"Sure, honey," Jeff murmured.

Suddenly, Linnet pulled away from him and stooped down to pick up something. It was the shield of a deputy United States marshal.

"Is this—is—" She looked at him.

"Mine," Jeff said, flushing a little. "Anybody could bluff with a shield, honey. I had to put up the goods or get run out, and I was out to clean this country."

Linnet only smiled and came into his arms again. The firing up on the road had ceased, and Murdo, standing on the brim of the canyon wall, called down to them that Morehead was dead.

Linnet snuggled deeper into Jeff's arms.

"Dad got back to the mine just in time to come with us," she explained. "He thinks you're fine, Jeff, and was wondering if—"

"And what do you think?" Jeff interrupted.

"I think you're wonderful," she whispered, adding suddenly, "Do you love me, Jeff?" Then, before he could answer, she said, "Of course you do! I've known it all along."

"You waited long enough to tell me," Jeff answered. But he was smiling as he bent down to kiss her.

ROUGH SHOD

When a soft knock came on the street door up front, Cole Preftake paused in his work; for a long moment, he looked down absently at the stick of type he held in his hand; then he lifted his tired gaze, peering beyond the tight circle of light from the overhead lamp through the gloom of the shop to the front door. This couldn't be it, he was thinking. He laid the stick on the edge of the type-case, his glance seeking the sack under the make-up table. Beneath it was his gun. Rubbing his hands on his soiled apron, he made his way past a clutter of printing gear to the partition rail, passed his desk and unbolted the door, easing it wide. When the woman stepped through, he only said, "Oh," and then bowed a little.

"I have only one light. Will you come back?" he asked.

She nodded. He bolted the door again and led the way back to the light; and while he cleared off the rough bench for her to sit on, he decided he would not pretend ignorance of why she was here.

Before she sat down, she looked around her at this mass of black machinery, and then looked at him and said: "The smell—what is it? I've smelled it before."

"Ink. When you get your *Advocate* each week."

"Of course."

The bench was directly under the working-light, so that when she sat down, the light beat pitilessly on her. And he was surprised that this light, which made pouches under his own weary eyes, and gave his square face an unpleasant pallor, should not change her face any. The shadows it made were small, as if her clean and modeled features held not the smallest distortion. The light did not pale her face, which was wind-flushed and held a sprinkle of tiny freckles across the bridge of her nose.

Looking at him, she said slowly: "Are you well? You have no color."

He stepped back out of the light, and leaned against the make-up slab, folding his arms.

"I've missed some sleep lately," he said briefly, and waited.

"You know who I am, don't you?"

He nodded, a kind of patient courtesy in his somber face.

"I think so. I have seen that same sort of hair on Dave Younghusband." She was wearing it in a braided coronet, and it was thick and as pale as moonlight, with a bright strange sheen.

"Martha Younghusband," she said, and did not smile. "I rode in this afternoon."

"Yes."

"My father didn't send me," she volunteered. "You've got to believe that."

"I do. That is not Dave Younghusband's way of fighting."

"Ah," she said quickly. "Then you think he will fight—we will fight," she corrected herself.

Preftake nodded; and she asked:

"Has it occurred to you that by fighting us, you are destroying this country?"

"Yes. The part I want destroyed."

"Haven't we got a right to live?" she asked swiftly, quietly. "Is it just for the excitement of it that you are doing this? We hire riders, pay taxes, and keep a law in this country, don't we?"

"So did the feudal barons."

She said: "They told me you would be reasonable, that you would talk without getting angry. They said that you would listen to other people. Will you?"

"Yes."

"And you will listen to me?"

"Yes." He took the pipe from his mouth and leaned forward a little. "On one condition: that you will listen to me, too. I've tried to talk to Dave and Jeff Younghusband, but they're above that. There is a time that comes with success when a man thinks he doesn't have to explain any more—that he can ride rough-shod over other people. I would like to talk to one of you Younghusbands."

While he was speaking, she picked up the wry and humorously bitter flavor of his way of talking, but she had been warned of this too, so that it did not anger her. She put her elbows on her knees now, like a man, and crossed her legs, and she looked at him level-eyed.

She said: "All right. Our part of it is very simple. Dad and Uncle Jeff and Myron Sammons came in this country thirty years ago. They starved and sacrificed and went thirsty. They lost their wives and their children, and there were Indians and drought and floods and raids, but they didn't run. They fought, and they planned, and they were stubborn; and each year saw a little increase in their herds." She paused, and he nodded attentively. "Don't you think that deserves a reward? They fought the country and broke it for other men. Now you are trying to break them, aren't you?"

* * *

"Before I answer that, let me tell it," he replied quietly, and began: "Some thirty years ago Dave and Jeff Younghusband and Myron Sammons came into this country together. In all the fifty-mile length of this basin, they found only a band of Indians. As you say, they did starve and fight and sacrifice, and they held all they could. That was thirty years ago, wasn't it?"

"Yes."

"Then there were three men and their families here. Today there is a town of two hundred people, and a hundred more on ranches. But the Basin still measures fifty miles. Where three men lived and prospered thirty years ago, three hundred are trying to, today—and can't."

"But must you take away from Dad to give to them?" she asked passionately.

He waited until the echo of her words had died in the still shop, letting the sharpness of them rebuke her, and then he said: "No man is taking away what they have." And now his voice took on an undertone of savage protest. "But is there no end to a man's greed?"

"Greed!" she replied swiftly. "We have herds! They must have range! If you take the range from us, then you take the herds from us! Unless we lease these Indian lands you are trying to keep from us, we are ruined!"

"Then cut your herds down," he said curtly. "Unless these small ranchers get the Indian lands, they are ruined too. And they haven't a hundred thousand other acres to fall back on, like Dave Younghusband."

"But isn't that taking away what we already own, what Dad has slaved and fought for?"

"It is not," he said bluntly. "Cattle have never been more important than men." He said more gently: "Tell your father that a man cannot be God on this earth—not if he climbs to his heaven on the necks of a hundred other men.''

She rose now, holding her gloves loosely in her hand, and he could see that her convictions were unchanged.

''The paper comes out tomorrow, doesn't it?''

''Yes.''

''And will it carry what people say it will?''

He said: ''Yes. A call to all those poor devils to bring in everything they own, all the money and goods they can gather, so that on Monday we can stand before the government agent and bid one cent more an acre than Dave Younghusband for these Indian lands.''

''And if you can't match his bid?'' she asked.

''We didn't go into this blindly. I know how much your father and uncle and Myron Sammons can afford to bid. We only want one of the three blocks open.'' He smiled crookedly now, and it was almost apologetic, as if to excuse what he was about to say. ''We will bid them up on two blocks so high they cannot afford to take the third.''

''But that is spiteful and vicious.''

''Yes. It's blackmailing too. You can tell your father about it, so he'll be forewarned.''

She nodded, still-faced, her eyes curious now, and searching. Then she said slowly: ''You believe in yourself, don't you?''

''Yes. In a man's right to live, too.''

She added dryly: ''And in any man's right to own a printing-press and raise a rabble according to his whim.''

''Rabbles don't rise unless they are goaded and have a leader.'' He said calmly and without anger: ''Sometimes I think that is the finest use of a press—to bring justice to strange corners.''

''And to bring—''

A racketing, imperative knock on the front door cut into her speech and silenced her. Lips parted a little in surprise, she looked at him and saw that he had not moved, had not even seemed to hear.

"Who is that?" she asked softly.

"Your father, I would guess," he told her, watching her.

"But he mustn't find me here," she said quickly, looking about her. "Is there a back door?"

"It is locked, and my printer has the key." He motioned to the shadowed back corner of the shop where a huge closet reached from floor to ceiling. "You can hide in there."

He waited without moving until she had made her way back through the tangle of machinery to the closet, and then he lounged erect, looking again at the towsack which covered the gun. This, then, was what he had known would come, and he wondered for an instant if she had known it too, and had tried to stop it before it bred the violence that was inevitable. Walking again to the door, he straightened against the weariness that was drowning him, telling himself that after this night it was done.

Even as the second door-shaking knock came, he unbolted the door and swung it wide, while the first of the three men, Dave Younghusband, entered. Preftake gestured back toward the light, saying nothing.

In Dave Younghusband's walk as he made his way back through the shop there was no haste. He was a giant of a man in a shapeless black suit, with a shock of pale hair that contrasted strangely with the deep mahogany of his seamed face. He moved with the deliberation of a man upon whom events and other men wait. Jeffrey Younghusband, his brother, was a foot shorter, eight pounds lighter, a bantam of a man with an angular, close-knit face and with an air of unconscious truculence about him. Sammons, the last through the door, was only a shrewd storekeeper whose fortunes had risen with the Younghusbands because of proximity, a sallow, spare man with a counting-desk pallor.

Preftake followed them into the circle of light and said: "I'd ask you to sit down, but this won't take long, I suppose."

Under the flare of the light which his head almost touched, Dave Younghusband looked around the shop with an air of regal and mild curiosity. His hands were on his hips, so that his coat was parted, showing the shell-belt hanging slantwise to his hip, and the gun that sagged there.

He said without looking at Preftake: "No. Not much." Then he settled his gaze on Preftake. "I hear you are organizing the basin squatters to bid for the Indian lands."

"That's right," Preftake said.

"Why?" Younghusband's voice was patient, curious; but in his eyes was a quiet mocking contempt that was good-naturedly ruthless.

Preftake said: "Because they need range, and that is the only way they can get it, by banding and outbidding you for a block of it."

"Is that all?" Younghusband persisted mildly.

"Not all. Because you've hogged and bought up all the grass in the country. These men must live."

But big Dave Younghusband had lost interest. He was looking over the equipment; and without turning his head he said: "You don't look like a man that could be bought."

"I can't."

Sammons said: "What do you make off an issue of the *Advocate*, Preftake?"

"Enough to pay a printer, meet the installment on

383

my press, and eat fairly well five days out of the week.''

Sammons smiled now, almost laughed. "Not a thousand dollars, then.''

"Nowhere near it.''

"Would it be worth fifteen hundred for you to skip this next issue?''

Preftake smiled too, and said: "Not fifteen thousand.''

Jeff Younghusband looked at Dave, but Dave ignored him. He said: "You could get this around by word of mouth. Why don't you?''

"You've already guessed that,'' Preftake said. "People believe what they see in print. Don't ask me why. Besides, it would take three weeks of riding to see them all.'' This was sparring, he knew—a prelude to what they had come to say; and when it came, he knew it would come from big Dave.

He was not surprised then to see Dave walk out of the circle of lamplight and look at the job press as he passed it. He stopped before the tool-box against the wall, then reached down and brought out a heavy pipe-wrench, which he hefted, almost absently. They watched him in silence as he walked back into the light, the wrench hanging easily from his hand.

"I'll take a man's word,'' he said mildly. "I want yours that you'll drop this business now.''

Preftake only shook his head.

Dave looked at him long, then said: "This country got on twenty years without a newspaper. It can again.'' He turned to look at the flat-bed press. "Is that what you print the *Advocate* on?''

Sammons said: "That's it, Dave.''

"This will likely cost me a fine,'' Dave said. "They'll make me pay for the repairs, too.'' He hefted the wrench and said: "Can I break it anywhere that won't cost much to fix?''

384

"Wreck it," Jeff Younghusband said curtly.

Preftake, who had been leaning against the make-up slab, straightened up; and immediately he felt Sammons jab something into his side. He looked down and saw it was a gun.

"Easy," Sammons said.

Dave Younghusband walked over and regarded the press, the wrench hanging from his hand.

"Wait," Preftake said quietly, and he smiled a little. When big Dave looked up, he went on: "If you want to stop publication, why don't you take my type?" He pointed to the type-case, a huge hinged flat box with innumerable small pigeonholes mounted on a slanting wood frame. He sensed the absurdity of this, his discussing with them the best way to cripple him; but underneath his mocking and helpless calm was a knowledge that this brief and desperate minute held his life for him. So he said nothing more, but only drew the pipe from his apron pocket again and lighted the heel of it, not looking at big Dave. When he flicked out the match, Dave said: "I could do that, yes."

"That press is the only one between Dodge and Salt Lake. It cost a fortune to get here, and will take eight months to fix." He pointed with his pipe to the type-case. "All that type will go into two sacks. Take it with you. After you've robbed the country again, bring it back."

"For you to howl to heaven with," Jeff Younghusband said dryly.

Preftake nodded. "Yes. I'll do that. But it will be too late."

For a moment no one spoke, and then Sammons said: "You can print handbills."

"On the job press only. Wreck that if you want. Wreck it and take my type, and you'll have me hamstrung.''

"Wreck them both," Jeff Younghusband said.

Big Dave walked slowly back to the lamplight, and he said: Dump that type in a tow-sack.''

"Are you going to leave that press whole?" Jeff Younghusband asked hotly. "He'll have the whole country on the prod in a week!"

Preftake watched big Dave turn his head slowly and look at his brother. "This country has been fighting the Younghusbands for fifteen years, but never with a newspaper. We've fixed that. Another fight don't matter much. It will be too late to do anything." He looked at Preftake. "Son, I don't want to wreck this place. If we took the type for that other press too, could you run it?"

"No; but the type's pretty heavy."

"Where is it?"

Preftake told him. While Jeff Younghusband emptied the contents of the type-case on the floor and swept it into two tow-sacks, big Dave ransacked the wall-case containing the big printing blocks and type. The biggest alphabet, carved in wooden blocks six inches high, he left in their place, knowing a single alphabet would be useless. Then he walked over to the galley on the slab and scooped the type from it into the sack. When he saw that the sack would be too heavy to carry with ease, he looked around for another, and saw the one beneath the make-up slab.

He reached down and picked it up and saw the gun lying beneath it. He said nothing, merely plugged out the shells in it, and laid it on the bench, and put the shells in his pocket.

Jeff and Sammons were waiting for him when he finished. He gave Sammons one of the lightest sacks and said: "Put up the gun."

"This is a mistake, Dave," Jeff said.

Big Dave ignored him, and turned to Preftake. "I wouldn't look for this stuff until Tuesday, anyway."

Without saying more, he turned and started for the door, Jeff and Sammons following. Preftake rubbed a half-clenched fist over his burning eyes; and when he heard the door shut, he did not move. Only when he heard the click of the girl's riding-boots on the floor approach and cease, did he look up.

"This is what I was trying to save you," she said simply. "You are a stubborn man."

"More stubborn than you know," he said quietly; and she could make nothing from his faint and weary smile.

"You can't fight them," she said impersonally. "I have seen men try, and I have seen them broken. They were gentle with you."

"Too gentle," he said quietly.

As he finished speaking, the front door swung open, and Riley, the printer, hurried in. He began talking as soon as the door was closed, and he had not spoken before Preftake knew he had not seen the girl.

Riley called: "It worked, Cole! I saw them go out with it! Did they get the hidden——"

Preftake half turned and said: "Watch your talk!" sharply, loudly. Riley, a bald and spare-framed Irishman with a great sad face, stopped short at the rail. He could see the girl now half-turned to him, and he recognized her as Dave Younghusband's girl. He walked slowly into the light, his eyes wary and cautious.

Martha turned to Preftake, and there was a light of understanding in her eyes; and Preftake was glad she had not tried to conceal that she understood. "Hidden?" she asked quietly. "You have hidden some type. You can still print it!"

Riley said dolefully: "May the good God strike me

dead if I saw her, Cole, and may He strike me dumb anyway!''

"It's no matter," Preftake said slowly to her. "I'm sorry you had to hear. I'm even sorrier you have to watch us go through with it."

He had suddenly come alive, it seemed; and he moved with a sure and vital alertness. He pulled the bench over closer to the type-case and said curtly: "Sit here, please."

Martha sat down. She realized she was a prisoner until they were finished; and now she glimpsed the hard and ruthless determination that was driving this man. She said: "I'm not to go?"

"Not until we are finished," he said calmly, and added to Riley: "It's on the top shelf where you left it."

Riley went to the cupboard and returned with two sticks of type wrapped in an oily rag. Preftake took it and set it on the make-up slab within the form. Then he said: "Find sticks, blocks, metal, anything to wedge that lead in the middle of the page. And get me the saw."

She watched Riley go about his business, while Preftake went over to the rack holding the single remaining alphabet of poster type. He reached down four letters, suddenly laid them on the floor and went up and bolted the front door again. Riley was waiting for his return and handed him the saw.

And now Preftake brought the four blocks over to the bench, and Martha said: "Do you want me to move?"

"No. Stay where you are."

She watched him saw each block in two, cutting parallel with the face and about an inch behind it. He worked with a quiet fury while Riley dug out a lantern and lighted it and hung it from the wire over the press. When Preftake had finished his job, he took the letters over to the form, and there ensued fifteen minutes of whittling and measuring and careful tapping with a heavy wooden mallet, as the galley was slowly locked up in the form.

It was taken to the press, and she watched them work there until she could stand her curiosity no longer. She got up and went near it to see them work. Some of their wordless excitement caught her too, and she found herself looking on with stilled breath.

The form, lying on its flat bed, looked meaningless to her. Inside its rectangle, she saw a much smaller rectangle which seemed only a cluster of black orderly smudges, but which she knew was the type. On three sides of it, and deeper in the form, were bits of metal and wood wedged in a crazy pattern so as to hold the type firm. On the fourth side, she saw the four letters from the poster blocks, but she could not read them.

When the galley was locked in, Riley said tersely: "It'll be the very devil to ink."

And then they began to work the press, Riley levering the gears that swung the big jaw down onto the paper which Preftake fed onto the galley. He was scowling; and after each impression he would signal to Riley, who stilled the lever, while Preftake tapped on the letter blocks with a mallet and inked it afresh. Fifteen times they did this, and each time Preftake would scan the page and drop it face down on the floor.

When he was satisfied, they swung into the rhythm of the work, Preftake feeding the paper in and out, and inking, while Riley worked the press.

Martha watched them until the monotony of it almost hypnotized her; then she walked slowly up to the growing stack of finished sheets.

She took one, and Riley stopped the press at a signal from Preftake. The paper she held was a long rectangular sheet which was not yet folded in half. Of the four pages, only one was printed.

Across the top of the page, in bold, black thunder six inches high were four letters which spelled—

GRAB

Below it, she read the summons. In simple, blunt sentences, each one driven home with sledge-hammer English, she first read the legend that her father, her uncle and Myron Sammons had this night sought to smother the right of free speech.

She looked up at Preftake. "You knew they planned coming here?"

"I guessed it," he said.

She read on. The second paragraph told why the attempt had been made. And then it swung into the plea for the ranchers of Whitewater Basin to unite, so that on Monday next, their meager resources would be pooled in a last and desperate effort to lease one block of fity thousand acres of Indian lands in order that their cattle might live. She saw that whoever had written it had avoided dramatics and fine phrases, and had written only facts—and these facts were more eloquent than eloquence. It was the work of a bitter man so sure of his cause that he let it plead for itself. There was no whining, no sentimentality, nothing but the marshaled facts, each in its separate line of type, without exclamation marks. And it slugged home its story with the raw and unlovely truth. At the end, it asked that the *Advocate* office be considered the headquarters, and that books would be kept and range dealt out in proportion to contributions.

She laid it down and looked at it a long moment, and then raised her eyes to find Preftake watching her.

"You will win," she said.

"Yes."

"Will you get this out tonight?"

When he nodded, she said: "And how long will it take you?"

"Two hours."

"You have not told me that if I give my word to keep this secret, I may go. Don't you trust me?" she asked.

"I thought you would rather not give it," Preftake answered. "I trust you, yes."

"And if I give my word, I can leave?"

"Yes."

"Cole," Riley said gently. When Preftake looked at him, he said: "She's a Younghusband. Are you going to risk the welfare of a hundred men for the word of the likes of her?"

Preftake said: "Her father was willing to take my word. I am willing to take hers if she offers it."

Riley looked long at him; and Preftake saw the pity in his wise and cynical old face. Riley shrugged, said nothing.

"You have my word, I will not tell," Martha said. "May I go?"

Preftake nodded. She left by the rear door, which Riley bolted after her.

When he came back into the light, Preftake watched him, waiting for him to damn him bitterly for a fool. Riley only avoided looking at him and said: "The boys are coming at midnight. We'd best get to work."

They worked for an hour in wordless rhythm. For a while Preftake was not sure whether or not it was his weariness that made the pace of their labor seem so exhausting. But later he knew it was Riley who was stepping up the tempo until they were working with a blind and reckless speed. Finally, when he could bear it no longer, Preftake stopped.

He said quietly, a touch of scorn in his voice: "Scared, Tom?"

It was not in Riley's nature to hide what he thought and he did not now. "Aye," he said deliberately.

"Of the girl?"

"And why not?" Riley blurted out. "She's a Younghusband, and the breed is all alike. They'll ride over us in their rough-shod way, and be damned to us."

It was on Preftake's tongue to tell him this was none of his business, and that he was hired to print, not advise, but when he looked at Riley, he saw the worry and kindliness there. He sighed and rubbed a hand over his face.

"We've got three hundred here. Want to get them out?"

Riley picked up his coat before Preftake's last word had been spoken and he turned to the back door. "I'll do that. I'll get Frank and Loosh."

While he was gone, Preftake took the heap of printed sheets over to the paperknife and sheared off the blank half, so that the *Advocate* of this week looked more like a handbill than a newspaper. When Riley returned, he had two boys with him. They split the sheets equally between them, and listened to Preftake's admonition.

"You ride south, Frank; you north, Loosh. You know the families these should reach. When you can, leave four or five at one place, and ask them to ride to the neighbors with them. Forget the subscribers. Take them where they'll do the most good. Leave a dozen in the right stores at Sun Cliff, and another dozen at the Faro Crossing stage station." He pulled some money from his pocket and gave it to the boys. "Stay out till there's none left, if it takes till Sunday. And remember, if anyone stops you, don't pull a gun—run. Right's on our side. We've no need for shooting. Now go on."

After they had gone, Riley's face relaxed, and Preftake wondered if these sleepless nights had so frayed his own nerves that he wanted to curse Riley for a cynical, suspicious and distrustful fool.

They went back to work, this time to turn out the copies which would be distributed around town, and all the time Preftake was fighting off the numbing drowsiness which was drowning him. He thought of the three days and nights he had been in the saddle, hunting out those men he thought would back him, talking, arguing their despair away and in its place leaving a kind of blind courage and hope. Somewhere along the line, he had known, the word of their organization was bound to leak out, and last night he had written his editorial, put it in type and hidden it. For once, he had matched Dave Younghusband's cunning with its own brand.

Martha Younghusband had said he would win. He knew now that he would, but he had been glad to hear her say it and admit defeat. Strangely, he felt no dislike, no distrust of her, in spite of Riley. He thought of her clean, frank face, and her blunt and honest way of speech. And behind it he had recognized that here was a woman who held to a man's code of fighting, a man's honor, and would go down to a man's defeat. And that was well, he thought, for in the next few days the Younghusbands would taste defeat.

Riley stopped the press, and Preftake looked up at him dully.

"You'll fold up in a minute, Cole," Riley said in kindly reproof.

"I'll stick it out. There's not much more."

"Be careful, then; it would be easy to smash a hand."

They were lost again in the monotony of their work when a knock that was a deep and thunderous hammer sounded on the front door. They looked at each other a long moment, and then Riley said bitterly, softly: "Her word is good, is it?"

The door crashed open then, and they both turned. Preftake said softly: "If you've got a gun, don't use it."

The vast bulk of Dave Younghusband loomed in the front of the shop, and when he walked into the circle of lanternlight, it was not with his usual and majestic unhaste. Behind him was Jeff Younghusband.

Big Dave walked straight to the pile of finished sheets and glanced at one of them.

"Have any like these gone out?" he asked, his voice thick with anger.

"Two hours ago," Preftake replied calmly. "Enough to reach every family in the basin."

"You're licked, Dave," Riley said bluntly. "Don't be a fool twice over."

Big Dave glared at him, clenching and unclenching his hands.

Jeff Younghusband said furiously: "There's been a newspaper in this town long enough. An editor, too."

Dave looked now at Preftake. "I've lived twenty years in this Basin without a newspaper. I let one come in on the condition that it didn't bother me." There was no arrogance in his voice, and Preftake with quiet astonishment saw that he meant it, and that it was the truth.

"That was Barkley, who owned the *Advocate* before me?" he asked quietly.

Big Dave nodded. "He could live here because I let him. You can't. I've never let a whelp with a patent-medicine advertiser dictate to me yet. And I won't now. I'll wreck your shop and keep on wrecking it."

"You aren't the first man that thought he could gag the press, Dave," Preftake said. "You can't now. You haven't yet. You won't."

"And if it hadn't been for that girl of yours, you

394

wouldn't even think you could," Riley said bluntly.

"Riley!" Preftake said sharply.

"Aye," Riley said bitterly. "That's the word of a Younghusband!"

And in that moment of Riley's galling speech, Preftake felt that it was the truth—it must be the girl who had betrayed them. He saw big Dave's hand brush back the skirt of the coat, and in that second all the weariness in him was washed away by excitement. He leaped for the big man, caught the hand where it was clenched on the walnut gun-butt, and then he knew that big Dave Younghusband was now gone berserk. He held onto the wrist and was whirled off his feet, slammed down on the edge of the press, and a great driving blow in his chest seemed to crush it. He rolled against it close to big Dave's body, and found that he could reach the gun while Dave's arms were wringing the very life out of him. He flipped out the gun in a small arc, heard it hit the press, and then clink and clatter down into the bowels of the machinery.

Then he stiffened his back, brought a knee up, and shoved with all his strength in his thick shoulders, and his back was gouged against the press as he went free of big Dave. He heard the deep thud, the scrape of a boot as Dave was brought up against the wall.

"I have broken a whelp before," big Dave said, coming toward him. Cole lashed out twice swiftly, and heard the tearing thud of bone on gristle and flesh, and he felt the raw grate on his knuckles of Dave's shelving chin. And then the big arms were around him, and he was slogging at a big and hard body. They fell now, and he felt all the solid weight on him as a fist smashed into his face. The wet salt taste of blood welled in his mouth, and the smashing thud of those fists on his face held his thought tight by the thread of agony. Then he felt his

395

body free of the weight again, and he sprang to his feet. Dave Younghusband was just rising, his face bloody and dogged and ugly with rage.

And then the shot came, and he felt a sharp slam in his side that threw him back against the press just as the second shot crashed. It was the noise that shuttled his gaze to Jeff, and he saw him clutching his throat with both hands, and gag and retch and finally stagger. There was the feeling that this was seen through gauze, and he shook his head. Abruptly something took the breath from him, and he opened his eyes and could seek the crack in the floor big and wide and full of grease and ink and dust, before the soft curtain of black drifted in from the side of his field of vision—with it a thousand sand pinwheels of fire that lulled him to unconsciousness. . . .

In the eternity of fever and nightmare that followed, there was only one break. Like a slow and ponderous wave, the pain receded and he found himself staring at a ceiling he did not recognize. Looking around him, he smelled the medicine, saw the lamp burning low on a table. He moved slowly, and something in his side shot a knife of pain into his very bowels.

He thought of what had brought him here, and of the fever that was just dying, and a sudden panic gripped him. What day was it, what night? Had he lain here for days possessed of this fever while the Government sale took place?

He tightened his belly muscles to yell, but the contraction was like a hot wire around his waist. Sweating, cursing, he threw the covers from him and stood up. It was the agony of his side that washed away the vertigo. He held his breath, waiting for it to subside, and it would not. He made five staggering steps toward the door before it opened, and he saw Martha Younghusband there, a look of terror twisting her face. And then he fell, and somebody was sobbing over him before he fainted again.

The next time he wakened, there were bright shafts of sunlight in the room. He looked around him carefully, but before his head was fully turned, he heard her voice, low, husky, half-choked:

"Oh, thank God, thank God!"

She was on her knees beside him.

He stared at her long, and the sudden recollection of her broken word welled into his consciousness. He looked away and said, "What day is it?"

"Tuesday."

He remembered it was Wednesday night that he had seen her in the shop. He said, "The sale is over, then?"

"Yes."

He did not want to ask the outcome: he already knew. He turned away, and when she spoke, he hardly heard.

"Your men got it, Cole. Don't you want to hear?"

Slowly he turned to her, a wordless question in his eyes.

"It was the shooting that did it, that and the *Advocate* piece. They answered your call by the dozens and they brought their cattle and furniture and money and horses to contribute. There was twice the money needed."

"Did your dad and Jeff bid?"

"Riley killed Jeff. Don't you remember? Dad and Sammons were whipped. They bid, but their bids were forced so high on two of the blocks that they could not bid for the third."

He smiled briefly at the ceiling—until he thought of that night, and how she had betrayed him. Strangely, he felt no anger. He turned to her and asked curiously:

397

"Why did you betray me? I had a duty to do. Couldn't you see?"

"But, Cole, I didn't tell Dad!" she said quickly, earnestly. "Riley came to me Thursday morning, and he said that if you died, he would kill me himself, law or no law, gentleman or no gentleman, hell-fire or no hell-fire. He cursed me, till I got a chance to tell him."

"Tell him what?"

"That Dad and Jeff stayed in town until late, and that on their way home they saw a light in Michael's place at Roan Creek. They knew his wife was sick, and stopped to see if they could help. Your messenger had already left a paper at Michael's and Dad saw it. That is what brought him back."

He felt a great congestion in his throat, and he turned his face to the wall.

"Do you believe me, Cole?" she asked swiftly.

He only nodded and reached for her hand and there was a long silence before he realized she was crying—her body was shaking with sobs.

Gently, he put his hand on her hair, and at his touch, she looked up.

"Does it matter much whether I believe you, Martha?"

"More than anything in the world," she said huskily.

"Strange," he murmured; "strange that I should greet the only woman I ever wanted to marry by calling and thinking her a liar."

She was still now under his hand, her face averted, and he went on: "Do you suppose it's possible for a man to make up for that by loving a woman all his life the way I love you now—the way I have since I first saw you?"

And now she looked up and she was smiling too.

"I think it is," she said simply.

TOP HAND

Gus Irby was out on the boardwalk in front of the Elite giving his swamper hell for staving in an empty beer barrel when the kid passed on his way to the feed stable. His horse was a good one and it was tired, Gus saw, and the kid had a little hump in his back from the cold of a mountain October morning. In spite of the ample layer of flesh that Gus wore carefully like an uncomfortable shroud, he shivered in his shirt sleeves and turned into the saloon, thinking without much interest, *Another fiddle-footed dry country kid that's been paid off after round-up*.

Later, while he was taking out the cash for the day and opening up some fresh cigars, Gus saw the kid go into the Pride café for breakfast, and afterward come out, toothpick in mouth, and cruise both sides of Wagon Mound's main street in aimless curiosity.

After that, Gus wasn't surprised when he looked around at the sound of the door opening, and saw the kid coming toward the bar. He was in a clean and faded shirt and looked as if he'd been cold for a good many hours. Gus said good morning and took down his best whiskey and a glass and put them in front of the kid.

"First customer in the morning gets a drink on the house," Gus announced.

"Now I know why I rode all night," the kid said, and he grinned at Gus. He was a pleasant-faced kid with pale eyes that weren't shy nor sullen nor bold, and maybe because of this, he didn't fit readily into any of Gus' handy character pigeonholes. Gus had seen them young and fiddle-footed before, but they were the tough kids, and for a man with no truculence in him, like Gus, talking with them was like trying to pet a tiger.

Gus leaned against the back bar and watched the kid take his whiskey and wipe his mouth on his sleeve, and Gus found himself getting curious. Half a lifetime of asking skillful questions that didn't seem like questions at all, prompted Gus to observe now, "If you're goin' on through you better pick up a coat. This high country's cold now."

"I figure this is far enough," the kid said.

"Oh, well, if somebody sent for you, that's different." Gus reached around lazily for a cigar.

The kid pulled out a silver dollar from his pocket and put it on the bar top, and then poured himself another whiskey, which Gus was sure he didn't want, but which courtesy dictated he should buy. "Nobody sent for me, either," the kid observed. "I ain't got any money."

Gus picked up the dollar and got change from the cash drawer and put it in front of the kid, afterward lighting his cigar. This was when the announcement came.

"I'm a top hand," the kid said quietly, looking levelly at Gus. "Who's lookin' for one?"

Gus was glad he was still lighting his cigar, else he might have smiled. If there had been a third man here, Gus would have winked at him surreptitiously, but since there wasn't Gus kept his face expressionless, drew on his cigar a moment, and then observed gently, "You look pretty young for a top hand."

"The best cow pony I ever saw was four years old," the kid answered pointedly.

Gus smiled faintly and shook his head. "You picked a bad time. Round-up's over."

The kid nodded, and drank down his second whiskey quickly, waited for his breath to come normally. Then he said, "Much obliged. I'll see you again," and turned toward the door.

A mild cussedness stirred within Gus, and after a moment's hesitation he called out, "Wait a minute."

The kid hauled up and came back to the bar. He moved with an easy grace that suggested quickness and work-hardened muscle, and for a moment Gus, a careful man, was undecided. But the kid's face, so young and without caution, reassured him, and he folded his heavy arms on the bar top and pulled his nose thoughtfully.

"You figure to hit all the outfits, one by one, don't you?"

The kid nodded, and Gus frowned and was silent a moment, and then he murmured, almost to himself, "I had a notion—oh, hell, I don't know."

"Go ahead," the kid said, and then his swift grin came again. "I'll try anything once."

"Look," Gus said, as if his mind were made up. "We got a newspaper here—the Wickford County *Free Press*. Comes out every Thursday, that's today." He looked soberly at the kid. "Whyn't you put a piece in there and say 'Top hand wants a job at forty dollars a month'? Tell 'em what you can do and tell 'em to come see you here if they want a hand. They'll all get it in a couple days. That way you'll save yourself a hundred miles of ridin'. Won't cost much either."

The kid regarded him thoughtfully a long moment, and then said, "I never heard of anybody gettin' a ridin' job that way."

"Neither did I, but I thought you'd try anything once," Gus said.

The kid thought a while longer and then asked, without smiling, "Where's this newspaper at?"

Gus told him and the kid went out. Gus put the bottle away and doused the glass in water, and he was smiling slyly at his thoughts. A green kid. Putting a piece in the newspaper asking folks to come see him if they had a riding job open—a riding job as top hand. Wait till the boys read that in the *Free Press*. They were going to have some fun with that kid, Gus reflected.

Johnny McSorley stepped out into the chill thin sunshine, and the snap in the air was rather pleasant against the fire set by his two drinks. Turning upstreet, he saw four riders pulling into the tie rail in front of a store up ahead. The lone silver dollar in his pants pocket was a solid weight against his leg, and he was aware that he'd probably spend it in the next few minutes on the newspaper piece. He wondered about that, and figured shrewdly that it had an off chance of working.

The four riders ahead dismounted and came up to the boardwalk and paused a moment, talking. Johnny looked them over with an incurious eye and picked out their leader, a tall, heavy man in his middle thirties who was wearing a mackinaw unbuttoned, and whose bold and scowling face suggested authority and worries. As Johnny approached, the men stopped talking and looked at him, and since the situation seemed made for it, Johnny stopped and said, "You know anybody lookin' for a top hand?" and grinned pleasantly at the big man.

He, in turn, worked Johnny over briefly with his unblinking gaze and for a second Johnny thought he was going to smile. He didn't think he'd have liked the smile, once he saw it, but the man's face settled into the scowl again. "I never saw a top hand that couldn't vote," he said.

Johnny looked at him carefully, not smiling, and said, "Look at one now, then," and went on, and by the time he'd taken two steps he thought, *Voted, huh? A man must grow pretty slow in this high country,* and he began to whistle now as he searched the opposite side of the street for the newspaper office.

He saw it and ducked under the tie rail and when he came into this shady side of the street he shivered a little, and he thought behind thought, *No job, no clothes,* but he was still whistling.

The window where he paused said across its face in white letters edged in black painted on the glass *Wickford County Free Press. Job Printing. D. Melaven, Ed. and Prop.* The light was so reflected from the buildings in the sunlight across the street that the glass was opaque. Johnny pressed his face against the glass and shaded his eyes with his hands and looked inside. It was a dark hole, Johnny saw, lighted by an overhead lamp in the rear. And then, as his eyes came into complete focus, he saw a girl, her face perhaps two feet from his, seated at a desk against the window. She was staring uninterestedly at him, tapping a pencil absently against her teeth.

Johnny backed off, more surprised than embarrassed, and looked around for the door, which was up-strect. He went inside, then, and looked immediately toward the cluttered desk. The girl was there, still staring at the street, still tapping the pencil against her teeth. Johnny tramped over to her, noting the strange smell in this place, noting also, because he couldn't help it, the infernal racket made by one of two men at a small press under the lamp behind the railed-off office space.

Johnny said, "Hello," and the girl turned tiredly and said, "Hello, Bub." She had on a plain blue dress with a high bodice and a narrow lace collar, and she was a very pretty girl, but tired, Johnny noticed. Her long yellow hair was worn in braids that crossed almost atop her head, and she looked, Johnny thought, like a small kid who has pinned her hair up out of the way for her Saturday night bath. He thought all this and then remembered her greeting, and he reflected without rancor, *Damn, that's twice,* and he said, "I got a piece for the paper, Sis."

"Don't call me Sis," the girl said. "Anybody's name I don't know, I call him Bub. No offense. I got that from Pa, I guess."

That's likely, Johnny thought, and he said amiably, "Any girl's name I don't know, I call her Sis. I got that from Ma."

The cheerful effrontery of the remark widened the girl's eyes. They were very handsome eyes, Johnny thought—a kind of off gray-green that held a hint of temper which was canceled by the full friendly mouth. She could have been seventeen, he decided, a year younger than himself. She held out her hand now and said with dignity, "Give it to me. I'll see it gets in next week."

"That's too late," Johnny said. "I got to get it in this week."

"Why?"

"I ain't got money enough to hang around another week."

The girl stared carefully at him. "What is it?"

"I want to put a piece in about myself. I'm a top hand, and I'm lookin' for work. The fella over there at the saloon says why don't I put a piece in the paper about wantin' work, and anybody that needs a hand can come and get me over at the Elite. That's instead of

404

ridin' out lookin' for work."

The girl was silent a full five seconds and then said, "You don't look that simple. Gus was having fun with you."

"I figured that," Johnny agreed. "Still, it might work. If you're caught short-handed, you take anything."

The girl shook her head. "It's too late. The paper's made up."

Johnny regarded her patiently, and said, "I can pay for it."

"I'll take your word for that, but it's too late." The girl's voice was meant to hold a note of finality, but Johnny regarded her curiously, with a maddening placidity.

"You D. Melaven?" he asked presently.

"No. That's Pa."

"Where's he?"

"Back there. Busy."

Johnny saw the gate in the rail that separated the office from the shop and he headed toward it. He heard the girl's chair scrape on the floor and her urgent command. "Don't go back there. It's not allowed."

Johnny looked over his shoulder and grinned and said, "I'll try anything once," and went on through the gate, hearing the girl's swift steps behind him. He glanced briefly at a stooped and dirty old man who was turning out leaflets on a small press, and then saw the other man. He had his back to Johnny, and he wasn't tall, but square built and solid with a thatch of stiff hair more gray than black. It was a stubborn back, Johnny decided, and he halted alongside the man and said, "You D. Melaven?"

"Dan Melaven, Bub. What can I do for you?"

That's three times, Johnny thought, and he regarded Melaven's square face without anger. He liked the face; it was homely and stubborn and intelligent, and the eyes were both sharp and kindly. Hearing the girl stop beside him, Johnny said, "I got a piece for the paper today."

The girl put in quickly, "I told him it was too late, Pa, that everything was locked up. Now you tell him, and maybe he'll get out."

"Cassie," Melaven said in surprised protest.

"I don't care. We can't unlock the forms for every out-at-the-pants puncher that asks us. Besides, I think he's one of Alec Barr's bunch." She spoke vehemently, angrily, and Johnny listened to her with growing amazement, and when she finished he saw that the eyes had won over the mouth; she was mad.

"Alex who?" he asked.

"I saw you talking to him, and then you came straight over here from him," Cassie said hotly.

"I hit him for work."

"I don't believe it."

"Cassie," Melaven said grimly. "Come back here a minute." He took her by the arm and led her toward the back of the shop, where they halted and engaged in quiet, earnest conversation. Johnny shook his head in bewilderment, and then looked around him. The biggest press, he observed, was idle. And on a stone topped table where Melaven had been working was a metal form almost filled with lines of type and gray metal shapes of assorted sizes and shapes. Now, Johnny McSorley did not know any more than the average person about the workings of a newspaper, but his common sense told him that Cassie had lied to him when she said it was too late to accept his advertisement. Why, there was space and to spare in that form for the few lines of type his message would need. Turning this over in his mind, he wondered what was behind her refusal. Cassie and her father were now engaged in a quiet but vehement argument, he saw, and he looked over at the printer, who was watching them, too, and said, "He's got him a handful there."

"Don't think she ain't, too," the printer observed.

Presently, the argument settled, Melaven and Cassie came back to him, and Johnny observed that Cassie, while chastened, was still mad.

"All right, what do you want printed, Bub?" Melaven asked.

Johnny told him and Melaven nodded when he was finished, said, "Pay her," and went over to the type case.

Cassie went back to the desk and Johnny followed her, and, when she was seated, he said, "What do I owe you?"

"I'll tell you later."

"You'll tell me now," Johnny corrected, his voice not very friendly.

Cassie looked speculatively at him, her face still flushed with anger. "How much money have you got?"

"A dollar."

"It'll be a dollar and a half," Cassie said.

Johnny pulled out his lone silver dollar and put it on the desk. "You print it just the same, I'll be back with the rest later."

Cassie said with open malice, "You'd have it now, Bub, if you hadn't been drinking before ten o'clock."

Johnny didn't do anything for a moment, and then he put both hands on the desk and leaned close to her. "How old are you?" he asked quietly.

"Seventeen."

"I'm older'n you," Johnny murmured. "So the next time you call me 'Bub,' I'm goin' to take down your pigtails and pull 'em. I'll try anything once."

He straightened up and then walked out into the chill

morning. Once he was in the sunlight crossing toward the Elite, he felt better. When he'd reached the boardwalk he even smiled, and it was partly at himself but mostly at Cassie. She was a real spitfire, kind of pretty and kind of nice, and he wished he knew what her father said to her that made her so mad, and why she'd been mad in the first place.

Gus was breaking out a new case of whiskey and stacking bottles against the back mirror as Johnny came in and went up to the bar. Neither of them spoke while Gus finished, and Johnny gazed absently at the poker game going on at one of the tables and now yawned sleepily.

Gus said finally, "You get it in all right?"

Johnny nodded thoughtfully and said, "She mad like that at everybody?"

"Who? Cassie?"

"First she didn't want to take the piece, but her old man made her. Then she charges me more for it than I got in my pocket. Then she combs me over like I got my head stuck in the cookie crock for drinkin' in the morning. She calls me 'Bub' to boot."

"She calls everybody 'Bub.' "

"Not me no more," Johnny said firmly, and yawned again.

Gus grinned and sauntered over to the cash box. When he came back he put ten silver dollars on the bartop and said, "Pay me back when you get your job. And I got rooms upstairs if you want to sleep."

Johnny grinned. "Sleep, hunh? I'll try anything once." He took the money, said "much obliged" and started away from the bar and then paused. "Say, who's this Alec Barr?"

Johnny saw Gus' eyes shift swiftly to the poker game and then shuttle back to him. Gus didn't say anything.

"See you later," Johnny said. He climbed the stairs

whose entrance was at the end of the bar, wondering why Gus was so careful about Alec Barr. Cassie didn't like him, and neither did Dan Melaven, he guessed. The silver dollars were heavy in his pocket now, and he was mildly grateful to Gus for wanting to keep him around, even if Gus did it so he could have some fun with him.

He tried the door to the first room and looked inside and saw it was empty. The tightly closed windows, with the sun streaming in, made the room warm and inviting, and as he pulled off his boots and lay down on the bed he was warm for the first time in days. He slept immediately.

A gunshot somewhere out in the street woke him. The sun was gone from the room, so it must be afternoon, he thought. He pulled on his boots, slopped some water into the washbowl and washed up, pulled hand across his cheek and decided he should shave, and went downstairs. There wasn't anybody in the saloon, not even behind the bar. On the tables and on the bartop, however, were several newspapers, all fresh. He was reminded at once that he was in debt to the Wickford County *Free Press* for the sum of half a dollar. He pulled one of the newspapers toward him and turned to the inside page where all the advertisements were. There were a bunch of brand notices and advertisements on the third page, but his was not among them. Neither was it on the fourth. He began again, this time carefully, to scan the entire newspaper. The first page he passed up, since it was all news items about people he didn't know.

When, after some minutes, he finished, he saw that his advertisement was not there. A slow wrath grew in him as he thought of the girl and her father taking his money, and when it had come to full flower, he went out of the Elite and cut across toward the newspaper office. He saw, without really noticing it, the group of men clustered in front of the store across from the newspaper office. He swung under the tie rail and reached the opposite boardwalk just this side of the newspaper office and a man was lounging against the building. He was a puncher and when he saw Johnny heading up the walk he said, "Don't go across there, Jack."

Johnny said grimly, "You stop me," and went on, and he heard the puncher say, "All right, getcher damn head blown off."

His boots crunched broken glass in front of the office and he came to a gingerly halt, looking down at his feet. His glance raised to the window, and he saw where there was a big jag of glass out of the window, neatly wiping out the Wickford except for the W on the sign and ribboning cracks to all four corners of the frame. His surprise held him motionless for a moment, and then he heard a voice calling from across the street, "Clear out of there, son."

That makes four times, Johnny thought resignedly, and he glanced across the street and saw Alec Barr, several men clotted around him, looking his way.

Johnny went on and turned into the newspaper office and it was like walking into a dark cave. The lamp was extinguished.

And then he saw the dim forms of Cassie Melaven and her father back of the railing beside the job press, and the reason for his errand came back to him with a rush. Walking through the gate, he began firmly, "I got a dollar owed—" and ceased talking and halted abruptly. There was a six-shooter in Dan Melaven's hand hanging at his side. Johnny looked at it, and then raised his glance to Melaven's face and found the man watching him with a bitter amusement in his eyes. His glance shuttled to Cassie, and she was looking at him as if she didn't see him, and her face seemed very pale in

410

that gloom. He half gestured toward the gun and said, "What's that for?"

"A little trouble, Bub," Melaven said mildly. "Come back for your money?"

"Yeah," Johnny said slowly. Suddenly, it came to him and he wheeled and looked out through the broken window and saw Alec Barr across the street in conversation with two men, his own hands, Johnny supposed. That explained the shot that wakened him. A little trouble.

He looked back at Melaven now in time to hear him say to Cassie, "Give him his money." Cassie came past him to the desk and pulled open a drawer and opened the cash box. While she was doing it, Johnny strolled soberly over to the desk. She gave him the dollar and he took it, and their glances met. *She's been crying,* he thought, with a strange distress.

"That's what I tried to tell you," Cassie said. "We didn't want to take your money, but you wouldn't have it. That's why I was so mean."

"What's it all about?" Johnny asked soberly.

"Didn't you read the paper?"

Johnny shook his head in negation, and Cassie said dully, "It's right there on page one. There's a big chunk of government land out on Artillery Creek coming up for sale. Alec Barr wanted it, but he didn't want anybody bidding against him. He knew Pa would have to publish a notice of sale. He tried to get Pa to hold off publication of the date of sale until it would be too late for other bidders to make it. Pa was to get a piece of the land in return for the favor, or money. I guess we needed it all right, but Pa told him no."

Johnny looked over at Melaven, who had come up to the rail now and was listening. Melaven said, "I knew Barr'd be in today with his bunch, and they'd want a look at a pull sheet before the press got busy, just to make sure the notice wasn't there. Well, Cassie and Dad Hopper worked with me all last night to turn out the real paper, with the notice of sale and a front page editorial about Barr's proposition to me to boot."

"We got it printed and hit it out in the shed early this morning," Cassie explained.

Melaven grinned faintly at Cassie, and there was a kind of open admiration for the job in the way he smiled. He said to Johnny now, "So what you saw in the forms this mornin' was a fake, Bub. That's why Cassie didn't want your money. The paper was already printed." He smiled again, that rather proud smile. "After you'd gone, Barr came in. He wanted a pull sheet and we gave it to him, and he had a man out front watching us most of the morning. But he pulled him off later. We got the real paper out of the shed onto the Willow Valley stage, and we got it delivered all over town before Barr saw it."

Johnny was silent a moment, thinking this over. Then he nodded toward the window. "Barr do that?"

"I did," Melaven said quietly. "I reckon I can keep him out until someone in this town gets the guts to run him off."

Johnny looked down at the dollar in his hand and stared at it a moment, and put it in his pocket. When he looked up at Cassie, he surprised her watching him, and she smiled a little, as if to ask forgiveness.

Johnny said, "Want any help?" to Melaven, and the man looked at him thoughtfully and then nodded. "Yes. You can take Cassie home."

"Oh no," Cassie said. She backed away from the desk and put her back against the wall, looking from one to the other. "I don't go. As long as I'm here, he'll stay there."

"Sooner or later, he'll come in," Melaven said grimly, "I don't want you hurt."

"Let him come," Cassié said stubbornly. "I can swing a wrench better than some of his crew can shoot."

"Please go with him."

Cassie shook her head. "No, Pa. There's some men left in this town. They'll turn up."

Melaven said, "Hell," quietly, angrily, and went back into the shop. Johnny and the girl looked at each other for a long moment, and Johnny saw the fear in her eyes. She was fighting it, but she didn't have it licked, and he couldn't blame her. He said, "If I'd had a gun on me, I don't reckon they'd of let me in here, would they?"

"Don't try it again," Cassie said. "Don't try the back either. They're out there."

Johnny said, "Sure you won't come with me?"

"I'm sure."

"Good," Johnny said quietly. He stepped outside and turned upstreet, glancing over at Barr and the three men with him, who were watching him wordlessly. The man leaning against the building straightened up and asked, "She comin' out?"

"She's thinkin' it over," Johnny said.

The man called across the street to Barr, "She's thinkin' it over," and Johnny headed obliquely across the wide street toward the Elite. *What kind of a town is this, where they'd let this happen?* he thought angrily, and then he caught sight of Gus Irby standing under the wooden awning in front of the Elite watching the show. Everybody else was doing the same thing. A man behind Johnny yelled, "Send her out, Melaven," and Johnny vaulted up onto the boardwalk and halted in front of Gus.

"What do you aim to do?" he asked Gus.

"Mind my own damn business, same as you," Gus growled, but he couldn't hold Johnny's gaze. There was shame in his face, and when Johnny saw it his mind was made up. He shouldered past him and went into the Elite and saw it was empty. He stepped behind the bar now and, bent over so he could look under it, slowly traveled down it. Right beside the beer taps he found what he was looking for. It was a sawed-off shotgun and he lifted it up and broke it and saw that both barrels were loaded. Standing motionless, he thought about this now, and presently he moved on toward the back and went out the rear door. It opened onto an alley, and he turned left and went up it, thinking, *It was brick, and the one next to it was painted brown, at least in front.* And then he saw it up ahead, a low brick store with a big loading platform running across its rear.

He went up to it, and looked down the narrow passageway he'd remembered was between this building and the brown one beside it. There was a small areaway here, this end cluttered with weeds and bottles and tin cans. Looking through it he could see a man's elbow and segment of leg at the boardwalk, and he stepped as noiselessly as he could over the trash and worked forward to the boardwalk.

At the end of the areaway, he hauled up and looked out and saw Alec Barr some ten feet to his right and teetering on the edge of the high boardwalk, gun in hand. He was engaged in low conversation with three other men on either side of him. There was a supreme insolence in the way he exposed himself, as if he knew Melaven would not shoot at him and could not hit him if he did.

Johnny raised the shotgun hip high and stepped out and said quietly, "Barr, you goin' to throw away that gun and get on your horse, or am I goin' to burn you down?"

The four men turned slowly, not moving anything except their heads. It was Barr Johnny watched, and he saw the man's bold baleful eyes gauge his chances and decline the risk, and Johnny smiled. The other three men were watching Barr for a clue to their moves.

Johnny said, "Now," and on the heel of it he heard the faint clatter of a kicked tin can in the areaway behind him. He lunged out of the areaway just as a pistol shot erupted with a savage roar between the two buildings.

Barr half turned now with the swiftness with which he lifted his gun across his front, and Johnny, watching him, didn't even raise the shotgun in his haste; he let go from the hip. He saw Barr rammed off the high boardwalk into the tie rail, and heard it crack and splinter and break with the big man's weight, and then Barr fell in the street out of sight.

The other three men scattered into the street, running blindly for the opposite sidewalk. And at the same time, the men who had been standing in front of the buildings watching this now ran toward Barr, and Gus Irby was in the van. Johnny poked the shotgun into the areaway and without even taking sight he pulled the trigger and listened to the bellow of the explosion and the rattling raking of the buckshot as it caromed between the two buildings. Afterward, he turned downstreet and let Gus and the others run past him, and he went into the Elite.

It was empty, and he put the shotgun on the bar and got himself a glass of water behind the bar and stood there drinking it, thinking, *I feel some different, but not much.*

He was still drinking water when Gus came in later. Gus looked at him long and hard, as he poured himself a stout glass of whiskey and downed it. Finally, Gus said, "There ain't a right thing about it, but they won't pay you a bounty for him. They should."

Johnny didn't say anything, only rinsed out his

glass.

"Melaven wants to see you," Gus said then.

"All right," Johnny walked past him and Gus let him get past him ten feet, and then said, "Kid. Look."

Johnny halted and turned around and Gus, looking sheepish, said, "About that there newspaper piece. That was meant to be a rawhide, but damned if it didn't backfire on me."

Johnny just waited, and Gus went on. "You remember the man that was standing this side of Barr? He works for me, runs some cows for me. Did, I mean, because he stood there all afternoon siccin' Barr on Melaven. You want his job? Forty a month, top hand."

"Sure," Johnny said promptly.

Gus smiled expansively and said, "Let's have a drink on it."

"Tomorrow," Johnny said. "I don't aim to get a reputation for drinkin' all day long."

Gus looked puzzled, and then laughed. "Reputation? Who with? Who knows—" His talk faded off, and then he said quietly, "Oh."

Johnny waited long enough to see if Gus would smile, and when Gus didn't, he went out. Gus didn't smile after he'd gone, either.